ALSO BY LÁSZLÓ KRASZNAHORKAI
FROM NEW DIRECTIONS

LÁSZLÓ KRASZNAHORKAI

Herscht 07769
Florian Herscht's Bach Novel

Translated from the Hungarian
by Ottilie Mulzet

A NEW DIRECTIONS
PAPERBOOK ORIGINAL

Originally published in 2021 as *Herscht 07769: Florian Herscht Bach-regénye:
elbeszélés* by Magvető Kiadó, Budapest.

The translator would like to thank the Hungarian Translators' House
in Balatonfüred, Hungary, for their kind support through their Home Office program.

Manufactured in the United States of America
First published as New Directions Paperbook 1608 in 2024

Library of Congress Control Number: 2024031971

2 4 6 8 10 9 7 5 3 1

New Directions Books are published for James Laughlin
by New Directions Publishing Corporation
80 Eighth Avenue, New York 10011

Hope is a mistake.

RAINBOW STRANDS

Angela Merkel, Chancellor of the Federal Republic of Germany, Willy-Brandt-Straße 1, 10557 Berlin—that was the address he wrote down; then, in the upper left-hand corner, he wrote only Herscht 07769 and nothing else, signaling, as it were, the confidential nature of this matter; no point, he thought, in wasting words by adding any more precise indicators of his own self, as the post office would send the reply back to Kana based on the postcode, and here, in Kana, the post office could get the letter to him based on his name; most essentially, everything was contained on the piece of paper which he had just now folded twice, nicely and accurately, slipping it into the envelope, everything formulated in his own words that began by noting that the Chancellor, a learned natural scientist, would clearly and immediately understand what was on his mind here in Kana, Thuringia, in wishing to call her attention to the need for such a personage as herself, who, in addition to tending to the everyday troubles and cares of the Bundesrepublik, must also attend to seemingly distant troubles and cares, especially when all of these troubles and cares were besieging everyday life with such destructive force, and now he was obliged to speak of a siege, a staggering presence, in his view, threatening the existence of the country, indeed all of humanity, as well as societal order, a siege looming from ever more directions, but among which he must emphasize only the most important: the seemingly unanswerable distress signal emitted by natural philosophy in the course of the vacuum experiments, concealed within methodological descriptions—although it had come to light a long time ago, he himself had realized only now that in a completely empty *space*, demotically understood, *events* were occurring; and this in and of itself was enough reason for the leader of the country, as well as one of the most influential people in the entire world, to prioritize this and exactly this matter and convene the UN Security Council—it was the very least she could do—because at stake here was not merely a political matter, but one of immediate existential import, and he sketched out the details briefly, and that was it: he was of the opinion that it would be best to be succinct, as he knew the addressee would have very little time to read his letter, no point in being verbose when writing to an expert, he signed the letter, folded it twice, slipped it into the envelope, and addressed it, but no, he shook his head, it wasn't good, he took the letter out of the envelope, crumpled it up and threw the paper to the ground, as he said to himself (as he usually did): I must start from the assumption that the Chancellor is a trained physicist; this meant that he did not have to explain everything in detail but could hit the ground running so the Chancellor could at once grasp the importance of this matter and act immediately, at a minimum, convene the Security Council, and he leaned with his elbows on the table, resting his chin in his hands clasped together, he picked up the piece of paper, smoothed out the wrinkles, read through what he had written, and since he had a pen that could write either with blue, green, or red ink, he took the pen and, clicking on the red ink cartridge, strongly underlined the words "Security Council" several times, then the expression "at a minimum"; he nodded to himself as if signaling his approval despite his earlier misgivings, folded the paper twice again as before, nice and neatly, following the earlier fold lines, put the letter back in the envelope, and already he was on his way to the post office, where altogether there were two people waiting in front of him, the first person was done quickly, but the second one, holding a small package, was trying to find out something with dreadful thoroughness, wanting to know how much it would be to send a package by regular mail, how much by DHL ExpressEasy registered, how much by DHL ExpressEasy unregistered, or how much by registered mail alone, she really didn't want to finish, she kept dragging it out, asking more and more questions, then she just hemmed and hawed like someone who was having a very hard time making up her mind, although the person standing right behind her didn't have too much time even with his extended lunch break, because the Boss hardly ever let him out, the Boss was suspicious of Florian, clearly he considered his supposed toothache an unacceptable pretext, a German doesn't get a toothache, he thundered, but still he had no choice other than to let Florian start his lunch break one half hour early so he could get to the Collier Dental Clinic, but only to see Dr. Katrin, and in no way Dr. Henneberg, because he was afraid of him, and, well, to tell the truth, it wasn't too convincing when Florian started bringing up this toothache again, although he had no other choice, as he didn't have the courage to tell the Boss the truth, moreover, as far as that went, already, in the beginning of the beginning, he hadn't had the courage to tell the Boss the truth because he knew him well, he knew the Boss, to initiate him into this matter would have meant allowing a glimpse into his self, more precisely into that one single hidden compartment of his own self where the Boss hadn't yet reached, only Frau Ringer had reached there, and not the Boss, because Florian did not want to hand over his one single secret, no, not this single secret, because otherwise Florian told the Boss a good many things, or, in other words, the Boss was always able to get nearly everything out of him, he was an open book as far as the Boss was concerned, I know everything about you, the Boss used to repeat, even what you don't know about yourself, you are my responsibility and so you always must tell me everything, because if you don't tell me everything I'll sense it, and then you know what will happen, and Florian knew, because ever since the Boss had prevented him from becoming a baker and taken him into his own business, Florian had become a wall cleaner and was on the receiving end of the Boss's countless blows for everything, because everything he did was bad: not like this, don't put that over there, don't do that now, do it later, don't do that later, do it now, don't use this, use that, not so much, not too little, nothing Florian did was ever good enough for the Boss even though he'd been working with him for five years now, in a word, no, he had to be quiet about this matter, and Florian was quiet, truly from the beginning of the beginning, namely from that point on when, for the first time, he felt as if he were struck by lightning as he was walking home from Herr Köhler's house, and he was thinking about what he'd heard, because truthfully put, he didn't understand, for a long, a very long time he hadn't understood what Herr Köhler was trying to say, only then, as he was headed home, it was truly as if he'd been struck by lightning because he suddenly realized what Herr Köhler was trying to say, and he was very frightened because this meant that the entire universe rested upon the inexplicable fact that in a closed vacuum, in addition to every one billion particles of matter, one billion antiparticles also arise, and when matter and antimatter meet they extinguish each other, but then suddenly they don't, because after that one billion and *first* particle, the one billion and first *anti*particle doesn't arise, and so this one material particle remains in existence, or directly it brings existence into life: as abundance, as surplus, as excess, *as a mistake*, and the entire universe exists because of this, only because of this, namely without it, the universe never would have existed—this thought frightened Florian so much that he had to stop, he had to lean against the wall when he got to the end of Oststraße, and turned left on Fabrikstraße, going toward the Shopping Center, his body was flooded with fever, his brain was buzzing, his legs trembling, he couldn't bear to go on, namely according to Herr Köhler, science had not yet been able to explain this, and as he spoke, Florian was still thinking about how earlier, he'd said that something could arise from nothing; Herr Köhler had explained that the process within a closed vacuum begins in such a way that within nothing and out of nothing suddenly there will be something, or rather: this event begins, which is fully impossible, nonetheless it begins with the simultaneous birth of those one billion particles of matter and those one billion antiparticles which immediately extinguish each other such that a photon is released—Florian was still thinking about this part of Herr Köhler's explanation, trying to grasp it; he could still hear Herr Köhler's voice as he explained the conclusion to this process which, in his view, was even more startling, although the gist of Herr Köhler's explanation only became fully clear to Florian as he passed by the abandoned train station and its lance-holding saint bolted onto an iron arch; he staggered alongside the boarded-up windows, he staggered along the empty street, then somehow he got home,

within nothing out of nothing

and he staggered on farther, dragging himself up the staircase like someone who'd been beaten, it was too late to go over to Frau Ringer so what else could he do but go home, but it was so hard for him to get the key into the lock, and so hard for him to open the door, and he found the kitchen filled with some kind of murky fog as if some kind of evil force were preventing him from reaching his usual spot in his own kitchen to finally plunk himself down, he was broken, he just sat there, holding his head in his hands so it wouldn't explode from the throbbing, and only his thoughts were dragging themselves on, so that it was no surprise that the next day as he got into the Boss's car at the corner of Christian-Eckardt-Straße and Ernst-Thälmann-Straße, the Boss immediately noticed that something was amiss, he asked him, too, goddammit, what the fuck is your problem now, and after Florian only shook his head, staring fixedly in front of himself, the Boss only added: well now, fuck it, today's getting off to a good start, and it looks as if you didn't even shave!! by which he meant that Florian had a screw loose again, but no, he only felt burdened, very burdened by everything that Herr Köhler had told him yesterday, and it wasn't so easy, because first he had to understand Herr Köhler, to try to understand what Herr Köhler was saying and what it meant, this in and of itself was already difficult, partially because his knowledge of physics was confined to whatever he had managed to read ever since childhood and whatever he'd been able to comprehend in the course entitled Modern Paths of Physics given at the Adult Education School located in the Lichtenberg Secondary School building: Florian only had a secondary school certificate, afterward graduating from baking industry vocational school: every Tuesday evening he would sit there among the other students, for two years now, he'd walk up the hill along Schulstraße, and he listened and he paid attention and he took notes and he finished up the year industriously, then he registered once again for the following year so he could attend the same course again as the first time around he had not understood many things properly, and it was good to hear the instructor, Herr Köhler, once again as he explained *the wonderful world of elementary particles*, as he termed it, and then one day Herr Köhler suggested to Florian that if he helped him cut down a large, dried-out spruce tree in his yard on Oststraße he would explain to him everything that he hadn't understood about *the wonderful world of elementary particles*; it was only at the end of the second year that Florian had been able to pluck up his courage and gone over to Herr Köhler on the last night of the course in the basement of the Lichtenberg Secondary School where Herr Köhler held his adult education classes, to tell him that, regrettably, a few things were still not completely clear from the lectures he had been attending for two years, no problem, Herr Köhler replied, Florian was welcome to come over if he would assist him in cutting down the tree, but of course Florian wouldn't let Herr Köhler assist him in this task, and the very next weekend he chopped down Herr Köhler's tree all by himself, neatly trimming away the branches, bringing them out to the garden gate, then, as Herr Köhler watched him dumbfounded, Florian grabbed the trunk of the tree, and,

6

just as it was, took it outside in one go as if it were just a little twig, and he piled it on top of the branches to be hauled away, it wasn't a such big deal, but the result was that not only did Herr Köhler explain everything to him again, but that from that point onward, Florian could pay a visit to Herr Köhler every Thursday at seven in the evening, it was in fact Herr Köhler himself who suggested this, at first it was just the following Thursday, then it was the Thursday after that, then it became a regular occurrence, and now here he was in the post office with this woman in front of him who would not finish up with her package, and he only had twenty minutes left in his lunch break, what was he going to say to the Boss if he was late, he couldn't lie anymore about so many people waiting at the dental clinic, because the Boss knew it wasn't so busy there at this time of day, they hardly saw any patients after twelve noon so he couldn't use that excuse, the best thing would be to finish up everything quickly, he watched Jessica behind the glass as she answered the old woman's questions nicely and patiently, but when it was finally his turn, things didn't go so speedily, because now it was Jessica who started dragging things out, saying, ha, what is this supposed to be, Florian? Angela Merkel?! ha, what are you thinking, that you can just write her a letter and she's going to read it, eh? and Florian didn't know what to say to this, because Jessica was not well known for demonstrating comprehension in matters outside of the scope of daily life at the post office; Jessica and her husband, after they had moved away from Bachstraße, both always assumed that everything was uniform and transparent, moreover Jessica's husband, Herr Volkenant, even trumped Jessica at such times, he'd say, no need for all that nonsense, everything was just as simple as a punch in the face, and that was it, although Florian's view of these matters was quite different, as it was in this instance, too, as Herr Volkenant called out from the parcel storage room behind Jessica's back: she's not going to read it, and if you want to send this letter for eighty cents, Florian, then you might as well just take your eighty cents and throw them out the window, do you understand? and he said again: it's as simple as a punch in the face, and because this "punch in the face" reminded Florian of what was clearly waiting for him once he got back to the Boss, he urged Jessica on, and counted out the eighty cents on the counter, not replying to either of them, they didn't force the matter but only looked at each other, obviously they couldn't care less, Jessica shrugged her shoulders, and, with a grimace, stamped the envelope forcefully, while the expression on her face said that as far as *she* was concerned, Florian could toss his coins out the window; and the Boss didn't say anything either, he just smacked him once, he didn't rebuke him with either this or that, just smacked him as usual, Florian pulled in his neck and provided no explanation, like someone who knew that there was no point, it was 12:47 and he was seventeen minutes late, so what should he say, that there had been a lot of people waiting at Dr. Katrin's office? there was no point, the Boss realized anyway Florian hadn't gone to any dental clinic, but he didn't resign himself to Florian keeping it a secret: you may have no secrets from me! he yelled at him in the car as they turned off at the intersection on the B88 on the way to Bibra, but Florian held out, he didn't answer, only stared fixedly in front of himself, and for the time being that was enough, because the Boss didn't say anything to him until they got to Bad Berka, but there he only said "get a move on already," and "take out the goddamned Kärcher"; after treating the pavement with chemicals, they were still mutely scrubbing where "some miserable idiot" had spilled paint that wasn't easy to remove, they had been called because they were known throughout all of East Thuringia, the Boss's prices were good, his work always carried out thoroughly, accurately, to everyone's satisfaction, and he didn't care what had been spilled or what kind of graffiti had to be removed, their spectrum was broad, they dealt with everything: cleaning, protection, sandblasting, scratched glass, even removing chewing gum; almost everything fit into the *spectrum*, as the Boss called it, and the *spectrum* had to be broad so as to contain almost everything, do you understand, Florian, not only graffiti, but everything, because that's how we make our living, do you understand, of course you don't understand, such a giaaant, but he never understands anything, because that's what the Boss called him if he was in a good mood—it happened rarely, but sometimes the Boss was in a good mood—then he would come out with this giaaant, saying, well, such a fucking huge giaaant made of pure muscle, but he understands nothing, because for him there's only the universe, of cooourse, the universe, then the Boss would hit the steering wheel and glance over at him—and now, with much less conviviality, he almost spat out the words: Florian should leave the universe for the Jews to figure out, the Boss said, and pay more attention to practical things, as, for example, every single line of the national anthem, did he know the entire national anthem, because he should know it, and a German should always begin from the beginning, did he understand?! and not with the third stanza, what kind of lib criminal gang is forcing this crap on us, telling us we can't sing our own national anthem from the beginning to the end, no one can take it away from us, those mother-fuckers, because for us, this is the beginning of everything: by then, the Boss was yelling at the top of his lungs; in his fervent excitement, as he thought about the entire national anthem, he pressed down hard on the gas, nearly standing on the pedal when emphasizing this or that word, making the Opel's engine roar, and now he started yelling even louder to be heard over the noise of the engine, he hollered: sing, Florian, sing—those goddamned motherfuckers—sing, let that wonderful first stanza ring out, then the second stanza, no one here is going to tell us what OUR NATIONAL ANTHEM is, and Florian had to start singing immediately:

Deutschland, Deutschland über alles,
Über alles in der Welt,
Wenn es stets zu Schutz und Trutze
Brüderlich zusammenhält . . .

the engine roared, they were going 135 or 140 kilometers an hour, that was usually the maximum the Boss dared to go with the Opel as they raced along to the next job and the one after that, and Florian couldn't not join in, because whenever they were driving somewhere in the Opel the Boss made him sing as well—your voice is so fucking insipid, Florian, are you some Jew or what? the Boss thundered at him on every occasion, then he bawled: well, fuck it, you won't be appearing at the Semperoper anytime soon, that's for sure, and he took his foot off the gas a bit, as it were expressing his contempt for Florian and everyone else who sang so falsely; a German has a clear, beautiful ear for music, he kept saying, so that Florian had to renounce his Saturday morning strolls with Frau Ringer; instead, he had to wash his overalls on Friday so they could more or less dry out on the radiator by the next day, and every Saturday morning at eleven a.m. he had to be present at rehearsals to train his musical hearing, but his musical hearing didn't improve, his voice remained insipid during the repeated singing of the national anthem in the Opel which the Boss had purchased off the books, secondhand, the car was four and a half years old, and of course it needed tinkering with, this or that part was always breaking, that's how it is with an old car, the Boss muttered, and he didn't curse the car but praised it, because at least it's German, he explained irritably, and an Opel will always be an Opel, no? it's just that you have to tinker with it now and then, because those Yanks messed it up, they really ruined this masterpiece, so that the Boss was always tinkering with it, he was happy to do so, and exclusively by himself, meaning that when he was doing so Florian didn't have to be at the Boss's place, he wasn't even allowed to set foot in the Boss's yard, which he never liked to do anyway because of the dog, sometimes, though, the Boss would discuss this or that with the neighbor, Wagner, but only with him, and they just chatted, and only he, the Boss, was allowed to touch the Opel, do you even know who Adam Opel was? the Boss turned to Florian sometimes in the car, and Florian was already replying that he was the father of Wilhelm and Carl, at which—like a joke they both enjoyed repeating—the Boss corrected him: Wilhelm *von* Opel and Carl *von* Opel, he said, only that Florian wasn't really so happy to repeat it, because for him it wasn't so funny or interesting, to tell the truth he was a little bored by it, all this is boring to you, eh? the Boss sensed, as he made him answer the question again, oh, of course not, Florian shook his head unconvincingly, but of cooourse, you're bored by this whole thing, I can tell! the Boss would yell over the engine, for a while they drove along in silence, then Florian got a whack on the neck, as the Boss jokingly called it, just like that, unexpectedly, one whack and that was it, and the discussion was closed: Florian took the Boss closing a discussion of this or that topic with a whack as perfectly natural, and, as one accepting of his fate, he merely pulled his neck in at such times because the Boss was his fate and that could not be changed, he accepted it and waited for an answer to his letter from Berlin, but then, when the answer was clearly delayed, he began showing up at the post office whenever he could get there during their open hours as Herr Volkenant closed up at six p.m.; sometimes, coming back in the Opel, they got back late, and then Florian ran over to the Altstadt to no avail, because the post office wasn't open so he couldn't make any inquiries, but sometimes he did manage to get there in time; Florian always asked the letter carrier too because he knew he'd be at the IKS pub every evening drinking until it closed; he asked, but nothing, both Jessica and the letter carrier just shook their heads, although as far as that was concerned, the letter carrier now shook his head without even being asked, continuously, and chiefly around closing time—no, nothing, and the Boss too started asking after a while: why the fuck do you keep going over to Jessica in the post office, tell me nicely already—what was Florian supposed to say to that—you like her, eh? well that's very nice, going after a married woman, I'm about to piss myself, the

Boss smirked and slapped his knee, and that was just the beginning, because then he started laughing in his own way: his mouth gaped open but no sound came out, he just shook his head with this gaping, opened mouth, then he leaned into the other's face, and he thought it was hilarious; the Boss always laughed as he was laughing now, then he smacked Florian on his back once, then once again, which Florian should have perceived as a kind of recognition although Florian did not perceive anything of the sort, he only turned completely red, his smile constrained as if conceding what the Boss suspected him of, in the end though he slunk away to get out of the Boss's sight, because for as long as they were together he had to be horrifically on his guard, he could never know what the Boss was going to come up with, although the Boss suspecting him of carrying on with Jessica was actually the best outcome, because everything became much harder when the Boss informed him that the homeland needed everyone, and so it was high time for him, Florian, to quit putting things off—time for him get into line and ask to be taken into the unit, because that's what the Boss called his pals, the unit, and—although it wasn't entirely clear what this meant—Florian knew he had no desire to be a part of them, he was afraid of them, all of Kana knew about them: Nazis, people repeated in lowered tones, which made the Boss's ever more belligerently expressed wish even more threatening, because if Florian signed up with the unit, then he would have to struggle, day by day, not only alongside the Boss (with full devotion), but among these Nazis, too (of course with no devotion), as he could be certain—he knew them well enough—that they wouldn't leave him alone, he'd be under pressure to get tattooed, and he was more afraid of this tattoo than of the dental clinic, he had no wish to be tattooed, no Iron Cross, no red-tongued German federal eagle which the Boss had been recommending vehemently, Florian got goose bumps on his arm just thinking about the needle and the tattoo machine with its frightening whirring sound which he himself had heard on occasion when accompanying the Boss, after rehearsals, to Archie's studio as another newer or older member lay down beneath the machine while the others waited outside, he felt like running away, insensate, in the opposite direction from where this needle and this tattoo machine were operating—no, no to this, and inasmuch as he felt able, he even pronounced it decisively aloud, no, he was never going to have himself tattooed, that wasn't his style, he added softly, at which, of course, the Boss's face turned crimson in rage: what, you don't belong with us?! you do belong with us!! wherever I belong is where you belong, because how many times do I have to tell you that you are my responsibility, how many times do I have to keep repeating into those deaf ears of yours: think it over, and make up your mind, either an Iron Cross or a red-tongued German federal eagle, because next week you're coming with me, and you're going to lie down underneath Archie's hand, fuck it, even if you come out of there bawling; but thank God, Florian had managed to get out of it so far, and he had not yet lain down beneath Archie's hand, although he still regularly had to admire the Boss's chest made of pure muscle upon which there bloomed the Iron Cross, because I earned it, the Boss said, and you too have to earn it, and he said nothing else, he pulled his shirt down again and by way of explanation only said to the others: Florian doesn't have his tattoo yet, he's just like a kid peeing in bed, the only problem is that he's so, but I'm telling you, so strong, that even five of us wouldn't be able to hold him down under the needle, do you get it, not even five of us, he's strong as a bull, boys, that's what he's like, one time the road construction made us go sliding off the B88, it was muddy, and we couldn't get the right side of the car out of the mud, and this here Florian got out and he lifted the entire Opel out of the ditch with me inside, get it? with me inside, and he lifted the car back onto the road, so all of you will have to persuade Florian that he wants this tattoo, to which the others said not a word, they only looked at the Boss, who wasn't too pleased with this wordless gaze, he quickly ordered beers, distributed them to the unit, and he said: to the Fourth Reich, and they clinked their glasses in the old way, just like real Germans used to do, meaning that as they clinked their glasses a few drops of beer spilled into the other's glass or onto his hand; discussion of this question was put aside for now and Florian could hope for a bit of breathing room: there wasn't usually talk of the tattoo during weekdays but toward the end of the week, most often on Fridays when clearly the Boss had the upcoming weekend meetings on his mind, if there were no problems with the Opel, because there were always problems with the Opel, either the propeller shaft or water pump or radiator, always this or that, some indicator or other was always flashing, which meant that on Saturdays, the repairs had to be taken care of first, they went for spare parts either to Adelmeyer's or Eckardt's, but in no way to Opitz's, because their noses were stuck in the air, those Renault people, they didn't know shit about Opels, the Boss instructed Florian, and so they went to Adelmeyer's or to Eckardt's; after which Florian wasn't allowed to set foot in the yard, the Boss went in and Florian closed the gate quickly after him as the dog barked, pulling on its chain, and Florian only said: well then, I'll be off now, and he left, if it was raining, then he went to the Herbstcafé or to see Frau Ring in her library, and if it wasn't raining he went to his favorite spot on the banks of the Saale, where there were two benches beneath two chestnut trees in front of the sports fields, situated almost directly on the riverbank near a small bridge; Florian really liked this spot, and if the Boss was working on the car and it wasn't raining, then hours stretched before him, hours in which he could sit here alone on the shorter bench of the two and continue to think over what he had heard from Herr Köhler in order to digest, here on the bench, the developments as he sat idly; the handball field was relatively far away, the yelling from there was barely audible, and he was thinking about what he should do, what could have happened in Berlin, because no reply had come; yesterday, he had been over to ask Herr Volkenant and he'd asked the letter carrier as well, but they both just shook their heads, although not sarcastically like at the beginning, but rather regretfully, so that Florian had things to think about, namely what should he do, or should he do anything at all, this is what he racked his brains over as he sat beneath one of the chestnut trees by the little bridge, because his excessive impatience was also a factor here: he surely could not expect the Chancellor of Germany to immediately read his letter, understand it, and already be writing him *back*, so perhaps it would be best if I try to be patient a bit longer, he decided, while sitting on the shorter bench beneath one of the two chestnut trees near the small bridge, and then he listened to the sound of the Saale's small rapids as the brisk waves of the shallow water broke over the river stones polished smooth in their path, he listened to the peaceful, tinkling, sweet gurgling of the water, and he thought about how difficult, but how horrendously difficult it was to connect this sweet gurgling together with that spatial vacuum in which from nothing there will be something; in reference to this, Herr Köhler had also said this was exactly why he'd ceased his own inquiries into quantum physics, resolving to speak on this topic only at his evening classes, and only for as long as he still had students signing up; he turned away from quantum physics precisely because it could not be reconciled with common sense, and therefore he sought something else that would require, only and exclusively, common sense—of course he didn't discuss these matters at the Adult Education School where he confined himself to *the wonderful world of elementary particles* as opposed to the horrific world of elementary particles—Herr Köhler had sought and found that something, and that is why for years now his primary occupation had been meteorology, he even ran his own little amateur meteorological station, as well as a Private Weather Station listed with the state radio broadcaster Mitteldeutscher Rundfunk and the *Ostthüringer Zeitung*, he had built it up by himself through the work of long years, and now he had everything he needed for such a Private Weather

Station: he could measure temperatures, wind speed, air humidity and pressure, at the beginning he could do that much, then as his reputation grew and he could draw upon both Norwegian and MDR meteorological data, the desire within him to expand the number of tools at his disposal, as he termed it, grew ever stronger, he wished to construct his own chemical actinometer—because all he had was a Michelson-Martin actinometer purchased on the sly, a commercial chemical actinometer was out of reach pricewise, but still—he asked himself—what kind of an amateur meteorologist would he be if he didn't prepare his own measuring instruments; and Herr Köhler took the plunge into homemade implementation, and the attempt proved so brilliantly successful that his neighbors, who understood absolutely nothing about this, came over right away to see the miracle, but people from the MDR and the *Ostthüringer Zeitung* came by as well, marking the starting point of a fruitful collaboration, Adrian Köhler—Herr Köhler raised his voice a bit—had at his disposal a recognized weather forecasting station, although the professionals didn't really like this kind of thing, they usually just smiled at the amateurs, just as they smiled at him at the beginning, and quite right too, he added, but eventually they accepted him, thanks to his implementation, if he could put it that way, of the homemade chemical actinometer; he hoped and believed that the German and Norwegian meteorological services as well as the MDR sometimes took a peek at his data, maybe, he tilted his head a bit to the side, who knows, in any event, he was able to provide fairly reliable weather forecasts to Kana and the surrounding area, and he was satisfied with that, he had no desire to compete with anyone, how could he even do so, he'd simply fallen in love with meteorology; this was nothing like quantum theory where acceptance of the absurd was a basic requirement, in meteorological forecasting—although of course it entailed relativity and uncertainty—one dealt in probabilities, but only until it began to snow or until the temperature climbed above 28 Celsius, if he predicted snow, he was happy, and if he predicted temperatures above 28 Celsius, he was happy too, because Kana was enough for him, and it was enough if people—or at least a few of them here—recognized that it was worthwhile to follow his weather forecasts, as many felt that Herr Köhler made his predictions just for them: don't drive too early on the L1062 heading toward Seitenroda because early morning mist is probable, and better to avoid that forest road for a bit, or to take an umbrella because rain is likely, a thirty-five percent chance of rain between two and six p.m. was high enough to warrant tucking an umbrella into one's bag, and as for me, said Herr Köhler, smiling, that is enough, in a word, I'll admit to you, Florian, that I'm doing all of this just for my own amusement, some people like to grow roses, others repaint their houses every year, but as for myself, I would simply like to know if there will be fog on the B88 in the early morning for the next three days, meaning that the residents of Kana should set off in their cars a little later, and that is all, he said, and as a matter of fact, Florian, you should also find some kind of simple science that you would enjoy, why not stick with what you studied? why not become a baker? but Florian just shook his lowered head, as if to say: unfortunately, this has not been given to me, this is not something I may choose for myself, I must be preoccupied with the essence of what you, Herr Köhler, have shown me, and I am very worried—come now, Herr Köhler made a gesture, you have nothing to worry about, my dear son, because one day the quantum physicists will figure things out, only we won't live to see that day; well, that's the thing, Florian said, looking at him sadly with his two large light-blue eyes, that's what I'm afraid of, that I won't live to see it; but there's nothing to be afraid of, Herr Köhler shook his head, and he adjusted his glasses: look at the sky, look at those clouds, these rays of sun coming in, these are tangible things, you don't need to get so wrapped up in this whole vacuum question because you could end up sinking into it for good, especially since what weighs on you so heavily is not the bankruptcy of quantum physics, but the bankruptcy of the limited human mind—that's what Herr Köhler said, but in vain, because Florian was so deeply immersed in that one single thought that had grabbed hold of him from everything that Herr Köhler had been explaining to him every Tuesday for two years now in the basement of the Lichtenberg Secondary School, explaining to him accurately and with truly illuminating, nearly incendiary, force, so much so that Florian had to come to a standstill, and he did come to a standstill, and then he sank, and he sank into it definitively, and he felt—he confessed at times to Herr Köhler—that he would never again be the same as he was before, because he never could have thought that the world, under the danger of a redoubtable fact, would be laid open to a destruction that could occur at any moment, and not only destruction; already, the beginning of the beginning horrified him, and he said: if, in fact, everything teeters on this knife-edge of destruction, then it must have been this way when we came into being as well, and therefore I can no longer be happy, Herr Köhler, when I look up at the sky, because I am fully seized by dread, I sense how unprotected, so unprotected the entire universe is, and because his mentor was seriously alarmed at how Florian always broke down in tears at this point, he tried to console him: look here, my son, it's all just physics, science; and science isn't finding the answer to these questions right now, that is certain, not yet, my son, not yet, for the time being, and it has ever been thus, science is always posing questions for which it has no answers, and yet: despite all the difficulties, the answer will come to pass, and the answer to this seemingly unsolvable question will come to pass as well, you can be completely sure of that—and after one of these conversations, as Florian left, Herr Köhler sat slumped in his armchair, accusing himself and asking himself why he had spoken about the unsolvable problems of physics to Florian; in certain respects, he was still a child; although surprisingly clever and

18

susceptible, he didn't really understand anything but merely transformed it into his own peculiar system; in other respects, his poorly interpreted knowledge only kept his overly sensitive soul, inclined to melancholic ecstasy, in a state of unnecessary excitement; how many times had Herr Köhler wanted to stop talking about *the wonderful world of elementary particles*, because the world of elementary particles was precisely not wonderful but horrific; Herr Köhler himself didn't take the whole thing so much to heart, but here was this kid grown to giant size, this child to whom it was only pointless to keep repeating, to try to persuade by argumentation (it was too late for that now anyway) that science would, one day, solve this problem, because it was not clear that science would solve it—disheartened, Herr Köhler watched a tiny beetle on the floor as it struggled onward in a thin crack from somewhere to somewhere, of course there were some questions for which physics needed to give answers, meaning that physics did not know the answers to the *most essential and fundamental questions*, moreover, physics continually put itself in the position of posing unsolvable questions, forever colliding with itself then leaving people in despair, leaving them to wonder just what was coming next, what exactly was going to come from all this, which of course did not mean that Florian was correct in thinking that the experimental proof of both Dirac's prediction and Lamb's shift had opened Pandora's box; in the sacred conviction of Herr Köhler the future was not at all as frightening as that; Florian was overexaggerating, and yet Florian himself did not think that he was exaggerating anything, so that when it occurred to him, as it did after a while, that perhaps his letter never even reached the Chancellor, that it might have gotten stuck in some kind of bureaucratic labyrinth, he did not choose patience this time but instead determined he would sit down in his first free hour to draft a new letter with the intention of explaining the *grave import of the consequences*, but then, when he had that free hour, Florian began by calling the

Chancellor's attention to the problem: beginning with the subatomic state and progressing toward dimensions perceivable by us, we are witness today to a process of sustained deceleration down below in the atomic and, respectively, the subatomic chaos—regardless of the fact that nothing like "velocity" exists down there—an event-series of horrific velocity, or, how shall I put it, even quicker than horrific velocity, it is hard to formulate this with words as I write to you, Mrs. Chancellor, a *perpetually lightning-quick* series of events is taking place and even this, this "lightning-quick," only approximately, moreover misleadingly, expresses what happens, unfortunately, as we proceed toward the larger units to an increasingly decelerating *conceptual* field; inside, as seen from the deep world of quarks, where accordingly there is no time for time, if we proceed from here, employing this method, we approach the macroscopic dimensions, then, within this very, very, very decelerated state, we must hypothesize that Something which we perceive as the world, and it is only in this state of extraordinary deceleration that it makes sense to speak of time and space within this crazy infinity of coming into being and cessation, because generally speaking there is no time or space in the depths, and well, here is precisely the problem, because with regard to the deep structure of reality, the question of coming into being or ceasing to exist is EXACTLY not the point: in that annihilating world of matter and antimatter, nothing comes into being and nothing passes out of being, because by the time something comes into being it already *doesn't exist*, because the photon which is liberated in that moment is light, and light is *nothingness* itself, the velocity of time and space *does not exist*, and there also *does not exist* any kind of Something, unfortunately, and an even bigger problem is that, consequently, down there below in the depths *nothing at all exists*, for that Something we would need to raise ourselves toward a different point of view, we would need other circumstances, and the essence of these circumstances—I repeat!!!—is that we must decelerate our perception horrifically, so that there may appear to us, as space, as time, as the locale and duration of events, the Something; but shit—here, the words stopped functioning and the pen stopped in his hand, because Florian knew all too well that one may not speak in such a manner, especially to a Chancellor, Angela Merkel did not appreciate curse words, in particular vulgarities, and she would consider this a vulgarity, Florian wrinkled his forehead, the face of Angela Merkel appeared before him, then the entire Angela Merkel, her movements, her posture, her gait, and that attractive face, that fine beauty which he must take into consideration, it wasn't as if he were expressing himself in a particularly uncommon way, no, not at all, here in Kana even old ladies frequently used the word "shit," but in this case, in a letter written to the Chancellor, this clearly could not be permitted, he read the letter over again, and the word really popped out, he was ashamed at how it had slipped out of him at the end of the letter, and yet he couldn't cross it out either, because how would that look, how would a letter to the Chancellor look in which there was a crossed-out or hatched-out "shit," no, he had to start over, he decided, so he set to it and recopied everything he had written onto a blank piece of A4 paper, but now without the word "shit," and he continued on calmly, indicating that he was writing all this down as he thought it worthwhile to expand upon the threatening situation sketched out in his previous letter, namely he was of the opinion that his earlier description of the hair-raising state of the world provided more than adequate demonstration of the grave import of the situation—of the world in which we live, in which our days are numbered, only that we don't know how many days are left, perhaps hardly any—and that was why Florian had taken upon himself the courage to address the Chancellor, and he hoped his letter would meet with her understanding as he eagerly awaited her reply here in Kana, he was Herscht, he wrote, full name Florian Herscht, eagerly awaiting her reply, and he sealed a new envelope and was already headed to the post office, and although he had plenty of time he hurried along Bahnstraße, then along Jenaische Straße, to Roßstraße, to get at last into line in front of Jessica; Herr Volkenant called out when he saw Florian: well, what can we do? nothing came for you today either, at which Florian motioned to him: oh, it's not about that, and he pointed at the new envelope, oh my goodness, Jessica shook her head when he handed her the envelope and she saw the addressee, this again?! Florian, can't you understand that high-up people like that never read these kinds of letters? we can't get to them, you know, they're up there, and she pointed at the ceiling, then she pointed to the ground, and added: we're down here below, do you understand? but Florian only smiled and counted out his eighty euro cents, he took it as a matter of certainty that things weren't like that and Angela Merkel wasn't like that, Angela Merkel listened to the voices of ordinary citizens, moreover in the past few days he'd been feeling calmer about his first letter as he also took it as certain that his first letter would make its way to its addressee sooner or later, bureaucratic labyrinth or no, only that the Chancellor had to consider, amid her thousands of tasks, what was to be done, for this matter was very important, more important than anything else: if the Chancellor understood this—and Florian was doing everything in his power to make sure she did—then it was entirely clear that she would hesitate not a moment longer and convene the Security Council, for naturally she, Angela Merkel, could not handle this matter all by herself, *unfortunately*, all the heads of state were needed, or at least the most important ones, the top decision-makers, and with lightning speed, for this could brook no delay; relieved, Florian strolled uphill along Roßstraße, because he wanted to go down the hill in the other direction to the Porcelain Factory near the Hochhaus where he had been living on the highest floor from the beginning of the beginning, ever since he'd been discharged from the Institute and the Boss took him under his wing, because that is how he had to describe what the Boss had done, truly everything was thanks to him, his being able to get an apartment in this Hochhaus, not having to remain unemployed in this great unemployment—as the Boss reminded him, his training in the baking industry was getting him nowhere—he had no personal belongings, only a backpack that he kept clutching, whereas the Boss got him a pair of gray overalls and a Fidel Castro cap and instructed him in the art of surface cleaning, namely, he was providing him with a genuine trade, the Boss explained to him, weekly pay in his pocket, Hartz IV benefits with the rent subsidy and everything—Florian's life was on a secure footing now, and for this he had the Boss to thank, the Boss who had neither child nor wife, so that it was as if Florian were his son, you are a child who has been entrusted to me, Florian, and that's why you will do what I say, you will do it when I tell you to do it and you will keep on doing it for as long as I tell you to, and the Boss had to explain everything in crystal clear detail and repeat it continually, because, well, the Boss explained to his cronies, even though he seems like someone who might have gone to university, I wouldn't even put a cell phone in his hands, because on the one hand he's a genius, but on the other, this child is off his rocker, somehow he isn't aware of his own self, you know what a giant he is, but if you yell at him he runs away, it never even occurs to him to stand his ground and fight back, although if he wanted to he could finish us off with his bare hands, that's what I'm telling you, to which the others said nothing at all, although they didn't tend to talk very much anyway, that's the kind of unit this was, few words and many deeds, that was the spirit that guided them when, on a Friday or Saturday evening, or if there was a holiday, they gathered and made their plans, expressed in few words, if it became necessary to show force, extend protection, or if they had to demonstrate resistance, simply put: if they had to be present somewhere; and they gathered together, of course, on *real* holidays, because those were plentiful, the past is rich, we shall never exhaust it,

Fritz noted, no one can take that away from us; among them, no one was named as chief, commander, unit leader, no one was designated as such; they regarded the Boss merely as a kind of thought leader, because here among them there was democracy, *this*, comrades, one or the other would pronounce, is a real democracy, and our unit here is based upon words and deeds that are open, direct, and sincere, because what we protect is a value, a single value which still existed at one time, although its survival now depends only on us, that's how it is, comrades, it's all on us now, they said to each other in the house at Burgstraße 19, because it belonged to them and so they called it the Burg, "the Castle," and as for this Burg, those filthy cops couldn't mess with them here; it symbolized perfectly everything that united them, their pledge of protecting the homeland, that and nothing more, and this was not such a small task, this was everything, surrounded as they were by a hostile environment, because of course, for the most part, the town and the entire precious Thuringia were populated by scum, cowards, and opportunists, and not only Thuringia but the entire country had been sold out to antinationalist powers via the machinations of mendacious and—as Fritz put it—international fiscal authorities, it's gone, they said, everything here that once spoke of the glorious past, the sacrifices of fathers and grandfathers, self-sacrifice, fidelity, German ideals, and the proud protection of race—gone, so that they, the few, must stand in readiness, they knew this: no one had called upon them, everyone had come together of his own accord and found the others, they did not have to be organized, the unit simply assembled at one point and waited for that time when they could step into action, as they named that moment which would indicate the start of the battle for the Fourth Reich, at one point Day X would arrive, they had been waiting now for years, for that day and that hour when they would say: this far and no farther, and they would arise from their stools at Burgstraße 19; they would take their weapons from their hiding places and set to their task, and there would be no mercy—they drank to this every Friday or Saturday evening at Burgstraße 19 or at the conclusion of a genuine holiday when they went back to the Burg, they didn't frequent any pub or anything as did so many other similar groups in Thuringia or Saxony, not them, because they had no interest in making a show of themselves, there were groups like that in Thuringia and Saxony, and elsewhere too, they knew about them, of course they knew about them, those other ones for whom it was enough to have an internet connection, they put on their brown uniforms and waved their shrewd little flags around here and there as during the May Day march in Plauen, but in the unit's view this was just a circus, and they did not want a circus, they wanted war, and it's not the migrants we have to be afraid of, the Boss said, we're not like those other groups bawling day after day about the migrants this and the migrants that, how they're letting in the tablecloth-heads and the wrap-heads, the veiled and the pipe-smokers who are going to take Germany away from us, goddammit, he raised his voice, it's not the migrants we have to focus on, but the Jews, because they have *already* taken what is ours, and no and no, we have no reason to create an alliance with any other group because we don't want to be big, we want Germany to be big again, this is our mission, at which the others nodded, day by day this message inspired them, this was how they inspired each other in the Burg, not with pompous speeches, they despised pomposity, this was a unit and they were soldiers, comrades struggling in the weighty, fateful situation in which Germany found itself, the Boss frequently spoke of this to Florian so he could understand clearly this huge fucking situation, but his words scarcely reached Florian, are you even listening?! he thundered at him and whacked his neck, at which of course Florian nodded: he was listening, of course he was listening, but he wasn't listening, because all he could think about was whether he had been able to express himself clearly enough in the two letters he'd sent, between which there had now passed more than two months, and if there had been any point in mentioning, in his second letter, that the relativity of time and space and so-called events would sooner or later lead to the inevitable disappearance of reality, and whether or not it was correct to have raised this topic without expounding further upon what the exact focus of attention should be in Berlin, but he could not answer the questions he posed to himself with any reassurance, so that on the next working day, after he'd sent the second letter, he regretted having mentioned time and the desperate ungroundedness of all fundamental concepts associated with it; I have only managed to confuse the Chancellor, he thought ever more irritably, because this is not the essence, I must speak to her of the essence, and not of my own consternation, that is my own problem, while the essence pertains to the German Chancellor Angela Merkel, she is the one who must act because only she can be trusted, as long as I formulate things clearly and distinctly, Angela Merkel will understand—but it would come to nothing, namely, his clear and distinct formulations would come to naught, because that evening, when, after work, he went home to the seventh floor of the Hochhaus and sat down to draft a newer warning to Berlin—a correction to his previous missive—Florian was no longer capable of succinct formulation, and the thought that he might not be able to seize the essence of what he had to say made him feel so irritated that he couldn't get down a single word even though the next day he didn't have to go to work but straight into combat, that's what the Boss yelled at him when early next morning, much earlier than their usual meeting time—it was in fact the middle of the night—he rang the buzzer to his seventh-floor apartment, and as Florian sleepily leaned out the window, the Boss yelled, red alert! Florian! red alert! no need to shave because we're going into combat, I just got a call from Eisenach, he explained in the Opel, leaning over the steering wheel and stepping on the gas, the Bachhaus has been desecrated, I wanted to bring my submachine gun, but for now let's have a look and see what's there,

26

and they looked and saw what was there, the Bachhaus in Eisenach, which functioned as a museum, was not Bach's birthplace as previously thought, the Boss explained as they approached the scene, the house where Bach was born was located on Ritterstraße, but birthplace or not, it was the Bachhaus building in Eisenach that had become the center for the cultivation of Bach's heritage, and we accept that, that's fine by us, and the Boss's explanation came to a halt because they had arrived, they parked the car and approached the building, and the Boss only emitted an inarticulate scream as they faced two large graffiti apparently sprayed with acrylic paint on either side of the entrance gate the previous night: it wasn't there in the evening, the museum guard, who always closed up at six p.m., stated, everything proceeded as usual, I locked the entrance, that's what he told the police officers, then I looked back, like this, and he demonstrated how he looked back, because I always do that, everything was just as usual, it must have happened late at night, because in the evening there are still a few people around here, mainly youths and homeless drinking beer, but I'm positive it wasn't them, these kids and homeless from Eisenach are bad, they're bad, but they're not capable of something like this, it was some migrant, I swear it was some migrant, and the museum guard held his two hands apart, and then in the same way, using the same words, he told the story again and again to the interested and the horrified, who, seeing the commotion and the police car with its flashing lights, quickly gathered after the museum opened and Florian and the Boss got to work; the Boss examined the paint thoroughly as at least fifty or sixty locals stood there gaping at him, taking a sample and slowly crumbling it between his fingers, all the while looking up at the sky, his eyes closed as if he were not only examining but vigorously scrutinizing that material with his fingers, murmuring "hmm," then he took another sample, placed a speck of the paint in his mouth with his fingertip and spat it out forcefully; he struck the wall in rage, slamming the muzzle of the paint-sprayed animal face on the left side of the

27

entrance with his fist, which made the crowd pull back a bit, and finally the Boss told Florian to bring a certain kind of solvent and a certain kind of brush, this spray gun and that sandpaper, Florian brought everything, clearly frightened, not of the people standing around but of the Boss's unusual behavior, he didn't understand what was going on and he was a little confused, he knew that if the Boss was acting like this, there was a big problem—because what did that scumbag want?! the Boss raged in the car going back, his face beet red, what was he trying to prove by spraying the word WE and that WOLF HEAD, can you explain that to me?! you can't, because there's no explanation for a scumbag like that, and now fucking tell me why that droopy-mouthed piece of scum, saliva running down his face and mucus dripping from his hooked nose, would desecrate and revile a place like this, a National Symbol! this is the BACHHAUS!! this is EISENACH!!! motherfucker, Florian, I'll kill him, fuck it, I'm going to find him and strangle him with my two bare hands, slowly, just as slowly as I can, I'll watch his eyes as they pop out, I'll watch that bastard's tongue hanging out because he is going to pay *for this*, we are going to make him pay *for this*, and the Boss hit the steering wheel and kept stepping on the gas or braking, not even once glancing into the rearview mirror, every time they braked Florian was afraid they were going to be hit from behind, I'm going to slice off his cock! the Boss yelled, I'm going to shove it into his drooling mouth, then I'm going to take a spray gun and I'm going to shove it UP HIS ASS, do you get it?! Florian?! are you paying attention?! Florian nodded, afraid, but he felt so tense that his head trembled as he stared fixedly at the B88 and at the B90 on the way home because he dared not say a thing, dared not ask anything although he wouldn't have had anything to ask about, for just like the Boss, he couldn't understand the meaning of this incomprehensible graffiti sprayed on the entrance to the Bachhaus, ever since he had begun working with the Boss nothing like this had ever happened, usually they were hired to clean graffiti off concrete walls, out-of-the-way houses, under bridges, alongside railway tracks, off of trains, suburban fire walls, all these and similar kinds of places, but a museum—this was completely unprecedented and outrageous to Florian as well: the Boss explained that supposedly the unwritten law of these sprayers besmirching the world was, thank God, never to attack statues, fountains, palaces, churches, or museums—until last night, of course—and just look at the Bachhaus, that fact alone would have shocked Florian if he hadn't been even more shocked by the Boss's state of mind, he had never seen him like this, although Florian knew well what Johann Sebastian Bach meant to the Boss: not merely one composer among many, but an empyrean presence sent from heaven, a prophet, a saint who, as he frequently mentioned to Florian when they were having a better day, *inscribed* into every single note the essence of the German Spirit, the connection of Germans with the Highest Ideals; it was not Hitler or Müller or Dönitz or Model or Dietrich or even Dienel whom the Boss wanted to festoon on the unit's banner (as did the others) but BACH, although he was shouted down, and the others said: better Hitler or Müller or Dönitz or Model or even Dienel: they couldn't reach an agreement, so for now the question of who would end up on the unit's flag was unresolved, the most important thing was for the flag to be guarded in the most secret place, not in the Burg where the cops could pounce on them again—because some scumbag had reported them after the first big brawls and a SWAT team showed up and arrested Fritz, under whose name the house was rented, and those cops didn't get them because they don't even know their own laws, although they could show up again—so they had distributed the most important items to different hideouts in undisclosed locations, but enough about that, said the Boss to Florian, when he himself started talking about the flag upon which I—he said, pointing at himself with his right hand, while he steered with his left—can only and exclusively imagine

BACH, which is why I founded the Kana Symphony, and that is why you must immerse yourself in what you hear on Saturdays at rehearsals, because in order to understand Bach you need a good ear for music: you have the soul for it, but not the ear, and this was followed by another smack, Florian pulled in his neck and gazed listlessly at the road through the windshield, and the Boss started up again: you're always so interested in the universe, but why are you interested in that, why aren't you more interested in Bach, Bach lived here, all the Bachs lived here if you don't happen to know, and as a matter of fact this is a National Bach Region, a real Thuringian German gets involved with Bach and not with the universe, because for us the universe starts in Wechmar and ends in Leipzig, understand?! got it?!—Florian nodded, but he didn't get it, and life began to return to its usual routine, it never occurred to them that what happened in Eisenach might occur again, the barbaric attack seemed a one-time event, and after a while even the Boss stopped mentioning it, the months went by, it was summer and then the beginning of fall, then the weather turned cold, but Florian hardly had to turn on the heat, the central heating in the Hochhaus was always turned up so high that he had to open the window, because on the milder days it was still so warm at night that he couldn't sleep, only next to the open window, then real winter came, then one day the radio announced that winter was over because spring had arrived, then once again everything went almost rushing into summer, then that day arrived, the deadline which Florian had given for a response to arrive from the Bundeskanzleramt, but no response arrived, so that from this point on, Florian was of the opinion that some official creating an obstacle in the Bundeskanzleramt could be the only reason for him not having received a reply, a year had passed since he'd sent his letter but now it was already August 31st, and so Florian went one last time to the post office, and, having discerned that no letter had arrived, he hurried down the hill and sat down at the buffet run by Ilona next to the Baumarkt for a Bockwurst and a Jim Him raspberry soda, and on this occasion he did not take part in the conversation with the other customers, namely he wasn't listening to them talk about how outrageously long the repairs on the B88 Autobahn were taking, or how the Hartz IV benefits were one day late again, nothing was being done, no apologies even, Florian didn't listen to them because he had to decide what to do, and he decided, he ate his Bockwurst, he drank up the Jim Him raspberry soda, and he went up to his seventh-floor apartment in the Hochhaus, took out a piece of A4 paper, folded it in half, at the fold mark he tore off the bottom half, and on the top half he wrote: Angela Merkel, Chancellor of the Federal Republic of Germany, then he wrote: *Sehr geehrte Madame Chancellor, I will arrive on September 6th at noon, Herscht,* and he put it into an envelope, he addressed it in the usual manner, he gave it to the Volkenants, then he hurried on to Herr Köhler's house, who greeted him precisely on this day by saying it was good Florian had come over because he had something very important to discuss with him, Herr Köhler sat Florian down, and after he himself paced up and down the room for a good while, silently, he stood in front of Florian, adjusted his eyeglasses on the bridge of his nose with two fingers, and spoke: look, my son, there is something I have to tell you, first and foremost that you are mixing up two things, at least two things; from everything that I have explained to you, you somehow think that something arises from nothing, therefore that something will also end up in nothing, and you never took in how I always treated this subject with reservations, you weren't paying attention, therefore pay good attention now: the consequences ensue from very sensitive premises, it is not possible to deduct reckless inferences, I am, by my original training, a mathematics and physics teacher, but only a teacher, and not a highly trained scientific mind, and perhaps that is why I did not speak of these matters clearly enough and why I haven't been able to give a credible picture vis-à-vis the questions you have been asking

31

me; now, however, I can no longer stand by as you get ever more wrapped up in your own interpretations, because I've heard from the Volkenants that you're sending letters to Angela Merkel, do not do this, my son, Angela Merkel is never going to read your letters, they wouldn't even give them to her, but what's worse is that even if they did, then what would Angela Merkel think of us here in Kana? that everyone here is crazy?! because I know, or to be more precise, I suspect what you're scribbling to Angela Merkel, I know what you're afraid of— that's what you wrote to her about, is that not so? yes, it is so, Herr Köhler answered his own question, because Florian was silent, but, my dear son—he now sat down across from Florian—

from somewhere to somewhere

I've said it a few good times already, but in vain, because you never pay attention, you're mixing up two things: the events that presumably took place in the first one-hundredth of a second after the Big Bang and the process taking place ever since then and in our presence, you mix them up and you think that this "arising from nothing" is occurring now, but it isn't, my son, pay attention to me, you are torturing yourself unnecessarily in connection with the Big Bang, because that is only a theoretical ratio, it was never proven experimentally, which I explain in the following manner: the emergence of the material world occurred in the synchronicity of one billion particles of matter alongside one billion particles of antimatter, then at a certain point or immediately in that first one-hundredth of a second after the emergence of the universe—there is no way for us to know—after this one billion particles of matter plus one particle of matter, there does not arise, after the one billion particles of antimatter, one more particle of antimatter, meaning that this plus one particle of matter emerges as a surplus, as the starting point of matter from which there will be something—the material world, reality—but all of this happened during the time of the

Big Bang, Florian, and not today, which means that today, after one
billion particles of matter plus one particle of matter arise, there AL-
WAYS arise one billion plus one antiparticles, and this annihilation is
continuous and perfect, namely, they destroy each other, and from this
conflict, one billion photons are released, you understand, these are
two different things, my son: on the one hand there is that one single
event that occurred, or rather that might have occurred, during the
time of the Big Bang, and on the other hand there is what occurred
afterward, during our own present time, and what will be occurring in
the future for all of infinity, and you keep mixing up these two things,
and you mistakenly draw the conclusion that inasmuch as the world
arose from this one single error, therefore this single error is going to
occur again but in reverse, and I don't know how you picture this happening, perhaps you think that at one point in the future an event will
occur that will annihilate the entirety of the presently existing material
world? this is nonsense, my son, nothing like that is going to happen,
understand this already, I'm asking you, do not let this lead you to despair, believe me, you are getting worked up over nothing, and so you
are repeatedly sending these letters to the Chancellor for no reason at
all, I don't want to hurt your feelings but those letters make you look a
little ridiculous, but not only you, myself as well, and our entire town,
Kana is a proud place, no matter what anyone says, and our citizens will
be indignant if you end up casting our Kana in a bad light—only that
Florian had closed his ears at the beginning of Herr Köhler's speech
because in his view this explanation only proved that Herr Köhler was
trying to lighten the horrific burden that lay upon all of them, but, well,
this burden did not need to be lightened—it wasn't even possible to
lighten it—but instead, something had to be done, the worst of out-
comes prevented, which, because it could happen, would happen,
there was no question as far as Florian was concerned, and it would
happen without explanation just as at the time of the Big Bang; Florian
could not be consoled, he understood things much too well for that,

he recognized the danger, the catastrophe would occur, he said, sorrowfully, slowly raising his two light-blue eyes to Herr Köhler, but not so that Herr Köhler would again utter some consoling phrase, but because he wanted to make it clear: he could not be consoled, because there was no more room for consolation, the situation was what it was, their one hope lay in the Chancellor and the UN Security Council and the responsible people there who could call upon the world's greatest experts in these momentous questions; Herr Köhler just shook his head, took off his glasses, massaged the bridge of his nose, then he didn't put his glasses back on again, they remained in his now powerless hands, he just sat there and didn't return Florian's goodbye when he left the room, in part because he had started thinking about something which he spoke about over the telephone later on to his friend from Eisenberg, Jacob-Friedrich, he said: inasmuch as we do not approach the question in this way, but instead by presuming that in the ten-to-the-minus-forty-third second after the Big Bang there were material particles and antimatter particles, and if we leave aside this whole annihilation theory and concentrate only on there being matter and antimatter, we can therefore state that matter does exist, can we not, but then what happened to antimatter? it is not to be found in reality, we cannot find it anywhere or show it from anything, in other words: WHERE IS IT?! well, this was partially why Herr Köhler had been immersed in his thoughts when Florian left, the other reason was that he perceived his own powerlessness: he'd done what he could under the circumstances, meaning that no one could fault him for the eventual consequences of Florian's irresponsible despair—because, he thought bitterly, something was going to happen, and it did happen, only not in the way that Herr Köhler was expecting; instead, on the next Sunday early in the morning, the Boss's telephone rang, he slept so well that the ringing hardly woke him up, those motherfuckers, can't they leave me in peace even on a Sunday? then he ran to the Opel and

was about to drive off, but then he looked at the clock on the dashboard indicating the time: 4:10 a.m., much too early to show up because at this hour there'd be no one in Wechmar apart from the custodian, the Boss went back inside but couldn't fall back asleep, he didn't
even dare to because the entire thing sounded so unbelievable, I can't
believe it, he kept saying to himself in the car, repeatedly hitting the
steering wheel as usual while Florian clutched at the bottom of his passenger seat, *I can't believe it*, the Boss shook his head incredulously, that
bastard mangy scumbag again, and lacking the words, not knowing
what to say, he kept hitting the steering wheel because the custodian
of the Bach Mill in Wechmar had told him: the same hand—the one
that attacked the Bachhaus—spray-painted WE and the WOLF HEAD
on the Bach Mill last night; the custodian, being a poor sleeper, always
stepped outside the building a few times to get some fresh air; he noticed the graffiti and in his stupefaction immediately called the police,
then he called the Boss to come right away, if at all possible right away,
because what kind of uproar will there be if the locals see this, better
for the Boss to get here at once, the custodian's voice trembled on the
telephone shortly after four a.m., but the Boss looked at the clock on
the Opel dashboard, had a moment of lucidity, and only left—rousing
Florian, too, of course—when, by his calculations, the police would be
getting there from Erfurt, which is what happened: the Boss, with Florian, and the police arrived almost simultaneously at the Bach Mill, the
first *settled residence* of the Bach family, as the Boss termed it in the car,
because the Boss knew everything about Bach, and Florian really ad-
mired this in the Boss, he knew everything, he knew when Veit Bach
had arrived in Wechmar from Hungary and really the smallest details
of everything that occurred afterward, he recited all of the Bach memorial sites by heart, I can rattle them off even if woken up from a dead
sleep, he affirmed on a Friday or Saturday evening as he related over
and over again to the others what happened with the Bachs in

Thuringia, first and foremost what happened with Johann Sebastian, but there was no point in telling them because nobody was interested in Bach, they were interested in Hitler and Müller and Dönitz and Model and even Dienel; Bach didn't grab their attention, they acknowledged him as a true Thuringian, but that was all, they weren't into music, so that well, only the musicians in the Kana Symphony were interested, they were happy to listen because as long as the Boss was preaching about how, in the Bach Mill, Veit Bach, then his son Hans, took out the zither brought from Hungary, and as the wheat was turned into flour, Hans played such beautiful music on that zither, so beautiful that the memory of it has remained, because otherwise how could I—the Boss pointed at himself, meaning at the Iron Cross on his chest—how could I have ever known about it, the musicians were happy to listen, and the Boss never realized that it was not because they wanted to hear his stories about Bach, but because the rehearsal was paused as he told the stories, because—to confess the truth—the Kana Symphony was comprised of amateur musicians who all demonstrated a certain degree of competence on their instruments but not to the extent demanded by the music of Johann Sebastian Bach, they were prepared for such classics as "Let the Sunshine In" from *Hair*, the Beatles, or "Dragonstone" or "Blood of My Blood" from *Game of Thrones*, pieces like that—Bach was difficult for them, to put it mildly, and the Boss got fairly angry, because in his view there were too few rehearsals, once weekly wasn't enough and that was why nothing was working, why the Fifth Brandenburg Concerto or the orchestral sections from the *Matthäus-Passion* kept falling apart over and over, so that when during this or that rehearsal the Boss couldn't take it any longer, he smashed his fist down on the timpani so hard that everyone immediately put down their instruments and listened in shame to the diatribes he rained down upon them; they liked it better when he was telling them about Bach and there was a pause in the rehearsal, and in the clarinet player's opinion there was no point in trying to force it, but the Boss shouted him down: nothing would ever come of the whole Kana Symphony if they didn't set big goals for themselves, and Johann Sebastian was a big goal; well, said the clarinet player, I agree with that, but he said nothing else because none of the musicians wanted to get into any serious conflict with the Boss who had founded the orchestra and all that; most of them meekly picked up their instruments and kept trying, and that's how it went: Florian sat there in the Lichtenberg Secondary School gymnasium every Saturday to improve his ear for music, but in vain, as it didn't improve, and the Boss simply didn't understand: I don't understand, he shook his head when among his comrades, ever since we've been rehearsing I told Florian he has to sit there, and he does sit there, but his ear for music is just as much of a catastrophe as it was in the beginning, nothing sticks for this Florian, absolutely nothing, but I'm not giving up, the Boss concluded his remarks, and the others reacted indifferently, saying: yes, don't give up, Boss, something will come of it, because they addressed him as "Boss," he demanded this of everyone, no one could have said when they began calling him this and why, very few knew his real name, and sometimes he remarked that even he hardly knew his real name, only if someone kicked him in the ass, then something might dimly occur to him, they drank to this, they knocked their beer bottles together and the beer went down, but Florian didn't drink, everyone knew that, only nonalcoholic beverages, and only when they were gathered somewhere together outside of the Burg, because he never went to the Burg, I only drink alcohol-free beverages, Florian would raise his hand as they placed their order, and of course no one wanted to bring shame upon themselves so Florian had to fetch his own drink, and because this was uncomfortable for the others, Florian had gotten away with being around them only rarely, and even then they didn't gibe him too much, they accepted that he only drank nonalcoholic beverages, although no

37

one knew why, only the Boss knew why, but he didn't tell anyone that alcohol caused a reddish rash to break out over Florian's entire body, on your ass too? the Boss asked smirking the first time when Florian admitted it to him, yes, there too, Florian lowered his head, everywhere, well, fine, then don't drink any beer, drink wine, I can't drink wine either, Florian answered, it doesn't matter what kind, if it contains alcohol I get these red blotches, it's your liver, the Boss nodded, your liver is weak, well, there's still Bach, just be there every Saturday at eleven a.m., and then both your liver and your ear for music will improve, because how does it look when one of my own workers doesn't drink beer and has no ear for music, that's not okay, fuck it, be there at eleven; and ever since then Florian was always there at eleven, he was never late: the Boss wouldn't have tolerated it, just as he never tolerated any kind of lateness, if, for example, one of the violinists, flutists, bassists or cellists were late by even one minute, the Boss immediately upbraided them, speaking to them of homeland and duty, and he never forgot it, which is to say he never forgave anyone who was late, lateness is the sign of a weak character, he said, standing next to the chair meant to symbolize the conductor's podium, which, because of democracy, no one could step up to until the occasion of their first performance still looming in the distant future; whoever is late deserves no kind of music, and especially not Bach, and everyone knew that the Boss wasn't joking, namely, the Boss never joked, and if he did no one ever would get it, or rather no one realized that what he had said was supposed to be a joke, the Boss had an intimidating appearance which commanded the respect of his colleagues in the Burg because they weren't muscular, broad-shouldered, and thick-necked like him, but instead—as the Boss used to say at the beginning, perhaps intending to joke, but no one laughed—with those pale mugs of yours and those limp limbs, you all look like TB patients about to croak, but then he stopped repeating it, even as a joke, because somehow he might have

sensed, from his comrades, that they didn't take it as a joke, he saw
something in their eyes he didn't like, so he backed off, he stopped in
the middle of what he was saying or doing and began picking his nose
or rubbing his shaven head from the back to the front then from the
front to the back, he scratched the Iron Cross on his chest, and by the
time he was done everyone had forgotten about it, after that the Boss
only dared to draw their attention from time to time to the benefits of
physical exercise; pure Germans like you, he said, are in need of two
kinds of strength: bodily strength, but strength of character as well, and
the Boss truly led by example, because whenever he had time after
work, he was in the Balance Fitness Club behind the railway crossing,
lifting weights, running on the treadmill, rowing on the rowing machine, doing one hundred sit-ups, so that at the age of fifty-three he was
still in excellent condition, as he said to Florian, but you, fuck it, you
don't have to do anything, you Lucky Hans, every night I'm lifting at
home or in the Balance, and you don't do anything, just that universe
of yours, and you can lift one hundred and fifty kilos like it was a
feather, without wobbling; once, he lifted one hundred and fifty kilos—the Boss told the others during a Friday evening meeting—just
lifted it, then when I told him—get this, but only *when I told him!!!*—
he put the weights back like it was nothing, he didn't even realize he'd
just fucking lifted one hundred fifty kilos, the guy is sheer muscle, but
whether you believe it or not, he himself doesn't know, he has no
ideeea that he's cut from such fucking hard wood, well, enough about
that, and the Boss raised his beer stein, and he yelled out: to Strength;
but today he didn't feel like joining the others in the Burg, even though
it was Sunday and he had worked the entire day at the Bach Mill, more
precisely the wall cleaning had been finished in less than an hour after
they'd been forced to wait a good half day to begin, because the Erfurt
police kept dawdling as if they were doing something important, although they weren't, the Boss said to Florian, these cops just take a

look, walk around, snap some pics, and that's it, what's the fucking point of dragging things out, why make all these phone calls, or let them make their phone calls, but let us finish our work, because when it was getting on to noon the Boss couldn't stand it anymore, Florian tried to calm him down but couldn't, the Boss kept approaching this or that policeman asking when they could start cleaning already, they'd been here since dawn, but the policeman only waved them off, calm down, they would be told when to start, and then nothing happened for a good long while, the cops were making calls on their cell phones, strolling around here and there, chatting with each other and drinking coffee, in a word they just kept on dawdling, and that was why the Boss and Florian got permission to start working with the paint remover only a few minutes before two p.m., but the Boss was foaming at the mouth so much, as he put it, that he sent Florian while he himself stayed in the Opel and smoked cigarettes, well, this was his one passion which, unfortunately, he could not renounce; when he was asked: what's the point of all those workouts for a smoker, he admitted, grudgingly, that it was a passion, he himself didn't really understand why, but he didn't betray the real reason, that smoking was the only way for him to calm the continual tension within him, because this tension, located in his chest precisely behind that Iron Cross, tortured him, he couldn't free himself, and cigarettes were the only thing that helped him, especially now with this sickening outrage in Thuringia, he didn't even know if he should direct his rage at the police or indulge his own murderous impulses churning up from that continual inner tension, the impotent outrage he felt at the "unknown perpetrator or perpetrators," because that's what the cops called them, "unknown," and "perpetrators," although the "perpetrator" was a tattered, drooling moron, a nail-chewer, a weakling fag, and they'll never get him, the Boss remarked heading back in the car, these Erfurt cops are fucking useless, they couldn't even nab a pickpocket on an Erfurt tram let alone this sneaky lizard, and then Erfurt, they're so proud of Erfurt, the Boss raged, Erfurt, what a crap town, agreed? he asked Florian, who had little choice but to agree, so he agreed with the Boss about Erfurt, and they drove along the A4 to Susla at one hundred and thirty kilometers per hour, then homeward on the B88 at ninety kilometers an hour because these were the legal speed limits, and now the Boss was keeping to them, not only that but quite a few times he even slowed down at this or that turn, he was somehow more cautious driving back than driving to Erfurt, that so-called unknown perpetrator was really on the Boss's mind, Florian suspected, and he cast a sideways glance to try to ascertain if it were true, but he couldn't tell because the Boss's face only betrayed deep immersion in his own thoughts, he was chewing on the corner of his mouth and brooding on something, but he did not initiate Florian into what he was thinking, he was saving that for the unit, although not that day, because on that day, Sunday, he had to think over things further, at home, alone, think things over, he kept repeating within himself as he sat in his room with his back to the TV, leaning with his two elbows onto the table, burying his bald head in his hands, then he took an ice-cold shower, because to think, and to think, to think calmly, that's what he needed now, a cold head for thinking, and this wasn't so self-evident, he had to exclude everything else and concentrate on one topic and that topic only, because he had to perceive what was going on here and the best strategy, for which not only concentration was required but time as well: the Boss racked his brains for an entire week, and then that week was enough, everything came together, so that on the following Friday when the unit gathered in the Burg, the Boss told them what was going on, the words sprang out of him as if each and every syllable he pronounced were already a command, the comrades—the ones who'd shown up—listened to him, and then there was nothing else to discuss, the plan came together within minutes, the unit dispersed in many directions, their movements coordinated, but in different directions, namely: you don't shoot a faun in the spot where it's running, but in the spot where it's running to, am I right?! the Boss said, but he didn't have to explain, even Jürgen understood, and the others understood as well, only: no excitement, no doubts, we're going to catch that motherfucker; they looked deeply into each other's eyes and everyone agreed, they were going to catch him, the Boss filled them in on the details, and as if he had taken the words right out of their mouths, they grasped his intent immediately, and now they put the Boss's precise knowledge of the Bach locales in Thuringia and Saxony to good use, for the time being, they concurred, they would concentrate on Thuringia, and the maneuver began that evening, everyone stationed after midnight: Karin in Ohrdruf, Jürgen in Arnstadt, Fritz in Mühlhausen, the Boss himself in Erfurt; the others joined up with Karin, Jürgen, Fritz, or the Boss, everyone, within a matter of minutes, found suitable hideouts for surveilling the assumed locales of the next attack, contacting each other via cell phone—but nothing, they reported on the hour every hour, then it was the next day and already growing light, and they returned to Kana, we registered no movement, because well, yes, that fucker is damned smart, he's waiting it out, just like up till now, the Boss nodded, murmuring, whereas I— Andreas spoke—I kept changing my observation post, I did too, Fritz joined in, then Gerhard and Karin and all the others, but nothing, Jürgen concluded, then, as was his habit, he pressed the tip of his tongue into the gap where his eyetooth was missing, which distorted his face slightly, licking the gap as if signaling his readiness to nab that piece of scum, and although he had plenty of ideas of what to do with him once he was caught, he did not have any idea of how to anticipate what that piece of scum was up to now and what he was planning to violate next, and this word "violate" was in fact Karin's, Karin who always seemed so indifferent, as if this were a discussion about who would collect the empty beer bottles, she only did what she had to do, she had gotten

42

into her own battered little CJ7 and driven off to Ohrdruf with the other three, and they had hurtled over there into the small-town muteness of Ohrdruf at such a late hour, they arrived at about midnight, and it was already so deserted, no one around, no lights on in any houses, Karin drove to the Johann Christoph House located between the Lyceum and the Michaeliskirche, then parked on Wilhelm-Boss-Straße, signaled to her three companions to take up their positions, and stationed herself a few meters away from the church, because according to the Boss—he'd made precise drawings showing all the locations of the possible surfaces of attack—the church in Ohrdruf was the most vulnerable point, that was where they expected something to happen, because that goddamned cocksucker is certainly not going to be satisfied with defacing a museum, but search for ever more outrageous targets, Karin nodded, and with her usual calm, she turned on her heels, double-checking her bayonet as she approached the car, but only out of habit as she always kept it in the right leg pocket of her fatigues, then she got into the car with the other three comrades, they closed the doors, and they were already driving through the Altstadt, doing what they had to do, Karin was the type of person even her companions were somewhat afraid of, perhaps because she had a glass eye where her left eye should have been, and that made her look frightening, or because nothing ever made her lose her calm, she always remained perfectly disciplined, always the same in every situation, that's Karin, they would say, and it gave them the impression of a great inner force, the kind of force that naturally compensated for the fact that she weighed less than fifty-three kilos and was only one hundred and sixty centimeters tall; she, Fritz noted, commending her when she was taken into the unit, will never show any kind of emotion, and she was the same even now with her own unswerving gaze and indicating to the unit members, with only a quick nod of her head, the best observation points on Kirchstraße, she positioned Gerhard and the other two, and she herself

43

lay down on one of the benches in the park that encircled the church, turned on her side with her back to the church, covering her body entirely with a long coat she'd brought along, pretending to be a homeless person simply trying to survive the night on this bench, and that's exactly what the others did as well, one troop stationed in Arnstadt, another in Mühlhausen, and the third in Erfurt, they all got there before midnight, and in these perfectly deserted towns they waited for him to appear, but he did not appear, the next morning at eight a.m., everyone went back to Kana and recapitulated the events of the previous night, which meant that they sat down in the Aral gas station and ordered coffee from Nadír, whom they were unable to hate despite her origins, moreover this was the most neutral meeting place, they were quiet for a while, then the Boss said that he had to go, and they would continue the maneuver tonight, and that was it, everyone dispersed, the Boss picked up Florian at the corner of Eckardt and Thälmann, and Saturday or not, they were already sweeping into Jena to remove graffiti in a few different locales, the Boss had downloaded the list with the exact house numbers at home, and Florian held on to it while they were working, and following the list, they went from one address to the next, the orders had come in yesterday, but because of what had happened, or rather because the Boss needed an extra day to see what would happen, they had delayed the cleaning by one day, Jena, the Boss muttered through clenched teeth as they stopped at the first address, what a bunch of fags, do you hear me, Florian, it's one big fag party here, got it? got it, Florian answered, and he took three AGS graffiti removers of varying strengths out of the trunk and did a trial spray with a 270, but already got a smack for it because, don't you remember what we used in Eisenach, you idiot child? this is exactly the same kind of acrylic, don't you see? but for this we need the 60, and the Boss pointed at the sprayer with 60-strength fluid; Florian quickly put the two unnecessary sprayers in his overalls' side pocket and was already spraying the area to be cleaned, the Boss spread his hands apart, looked up at the sky, and kept on muttering: it boggles my mind, how could anyone be such an idiot, he remembers nothing, I have to explain everything again and again, then he lowered his gaze to see if Florian was doing something idiotic again, the sky was covered with heavy, dark clouds, in the past few days there had been more and more signs and now definitively that autumn was coming, then there would follow the icy rains and the morning fog, once again it would be impossible to drive along the L1062, although recently they had been getting most of their orders from the towns that lay in that direction, Neustadt, Berg, and Münchberg, as opposed to the regions served by the B88, they had more than enough work, nothing to complain about on that score, and that also explained the enormous explosion in the Boss's brain when Florian asked for a day off on Thursday, only one day, he said to the Boss, who, at first, looked at him uncomprehendingly, as if he were deaf, then merely repeated the words back to him, just one day, Florian insisted, I'll leave in the morning and be back by night, but I can't go on the weekend because it's something official, and it's not enough for me to go into the Employment Center in Jena, they sent a letter that said I have to go to Berlin, to the Arbeitsamt in person, Florian lied, because he had decided that if necessary he would lie, just so long as he could go, although, in the first moments, it did not seem as if he had succeeded, because the Boss, when he realized what Florian was asking for, of course began raging at him: and now Berlin!!! have you lost your mind?! you want to leave now when there's so much work?! no, no, no—Florian said in self-defense, it's only a day, and I would never leave you here Boss, ever, and in any event Florian really did believe that he would never leave the Boss, it never occurred to him, although sometimes Frau Ringer in the library, or one or two of the older ladies from the Hochhaus who didn't like how the Boss treated Florian, occasionally mentioned to him that he should quit and look for some kind of

45

respectable job at the Czech Bakery and Confectioner's or the Porcelain Factory, but Florian didn't understand what they were getting at, he viewed the Boss as someone who had always been there and would always be there; in Florian's eyes, life was unchanging, everything always proceeding in the same way: the mornings, the evenings, the seasons, the years, everything, always the same, he couldn't imagine that one day he might wake up and there would be no Hochhaus, no Boss or Kana, not even the Federal Republic of Germany, this was unimaginable to him, just as he couldn't understand those clearly well-intended recommendations to get yet another off-the-books job to supplement his Hartz IV benefits, how could he do anything like that?! he replied to these suggestions, the Boss was not only his employer, but he was his father in place of his father as well, so that the old ladies waved their hands in resignation, then, grimacing, left him there, while Florian, smiling, called after them: thank you for the advice, but well, no; and no, said the Boss: you're not going anywhere, I'm the one who always handles the Employment Center and I'll handle it this time too, show me the paper you got from them, oh, the paper, Florian continued to lie, the piece of paper, it's somewhere at home, I don't know exactly where, but I have to go in person, that's what it said, please understand, he repeated persistently, and he looked at the Boss with such a pleading gaze, and kept repeating that *he had to go*, the Boss was genuinely surprised by his persistence, and after his rage had run its course he didn't even say anything but only made a gesture that said: go if you want to, at least he's getting more independent, he thought, and Florian stood there Thursday morning next to the double-rail track that indicated the Kana station, because the station building itself was no longer in operation, it was only because of the long-distance bus stop that a bas-relief located across the street from the main facade had been restored, and, now resplendent in brilliant colors, it enjoyed the status of a public monument, depicting a woman holding a lance, the locals derisively referred to this bas-relief as "Saint George's wife slaying the dragon," and otherwise everything had gone to ruin both inside the building and without, doors, windows, but it hadn't been demolished, only the roof had been repaired, although the fate of the train station building was clearly sealed, no one needed it, so that rail passengers, if there were any at all, simply waited on one or the other side of the tracks, as did Florian too, but he had begun waiting there more than an hour before the arrival of the earliest possible train from Orlamünde; he'd been afraid he would fall asleep and miss the train and so hadn't slept a wink the night before, and moreover he kept thinking of the great task that lay before him as he tossed and turned, throwing himself from one side of the bed to the other while he tried to formulate the message he would convey personally to Frau Merkel— briefly! only briefly!—and so he would begin: one could dispute, and rightly so, the extent of his knowledge of quantum physics, but no one could dispute the sufficiency of the knowledge he had gained from Herr Köhler to warn the German state, and its embodiment, Frau Kanzlerin Angela Merkel, as to what awaited them if they did not move quickly, namely that something must be constructed against the contingent, which, in his view, could no longer be termed the contingent as it could ensue at any moment, because it could ensue, moreover—as he planned to inform Mrs. Merkel—it could ensue even in the next moment, he could not see into this subatomic world, how could he, but this world had nonetheless revealed itself to the mind and it had betrayed that inasmuch as it is true that something arises from nothing, it can also occur that after the emergence from nothing of one billion antiparticles along with one billion particles, the one surplus material particle does not appear as it presumably occurred during the Big Bang, as stated by Herr Köhler, but that instead, due to a diabolical breaking of symmetry in the usually balanced emergence of particles and antiparticles, there could suddenly arise, in one horrific moment, one surplus *antiparticle*, and while the one billion particles and one billion antiparticles are busy annihilating each other, and the well-known one billion photons are floating away, the remaining single surplus antiparticle could be creating a new reality, an anti-universe, the lethal mirror image of reality, and of course this numeral, this one billion, only indicates a ratio that occurred during the emergence of these particles—this is how Florian would explain what he had come to understand: namely, after the emergence of *every* one billion particles and one billion antiparticles, there always arises one surplus material particle and one surplus antiparticle, but what could also occur—as a horrific contingency—is a diabolic surplus, the emergence of one surplus antiparticle, and so forth, this is, of course, only an example, expressing a ratio, a measurement to better help us understand, but the essence, he would explain—if uninterrupted by Mrs. Merkel—was that inasmuch as that one surplus material particle inexplicably emerged during the Big Bang, we cannot exclude the possibility of the emergence— just as inexplicable, caused by the same breaking of symmetry, after one billion antiparticles and one billion particles—of one surplus antiparticle; it could occur, just as incomprehensibly, resulting in the birth of a reality comprised of antimatter, and what this means for us is (Florian had decided to say this much and nothing more the previous night when he'd had enough of tossing and turning and left for the train tracks one hour early)—what this means for us here is catastrophe, not merely on this Earth, not merely in our own galaxy, but in the entire universe, because if the universe of matter collides with this universe of antimatter, then—in Florian's estimation—both would be immediately annihilated, meaning that the Something would disappear, and that which bears the opposing sign would not remain, or, as Herr Köhler might phrase it, the Anti-Something with its opposite charge would not remain, meaning the supervention of Nothing for us: everything in the universe would return to where we started out, to that

Deathly Light which, for us, is identical with Nothing, in vain is the existence of this Nothing disputed, the very first geniuses of civilization trembled from the mere thought of this Nothing, but we do not have to tremble, we must face facts, face the Great Dialogue between Something and Nothing, something must be done—Florian had at least filtered out this much from Herr Köhler's lectures in Kana, and this was how Florian would conclude his report to Mrs. Merkel in the Kanzleramt, and he waited for the train, and the train was late arriving from Orlamünde, there was no place to sit down, there was only the asphalt-covered walkway next to the tracks, whoever emerged from the concrete tunnel onto the tracks going toward Jena could stand there and wait for the train, there were no benches, just standing and waiting, that's all there was to this train station, and Florian was standing and waiting, and he was seriously worried he would end up missing his connection at Jena-Göschwitz or in Halle, but then the train arrived albeit twelve minutes late, and Florian spent the journey worrying about making his connection, he had never traveled so far by train in his entire life, he had never even traveled anywhere outside of Jena by train, he was always being driven somewhere by the Boss in the Opel, he had no experience with these trains, as the Deputy from the Hochhaus also noted when Florian asked him for help using the ticket machine to buy the tickets for the long trip: listen here, Florian, he said, don't be nervous about making your connections going there or coming back, these days the trains are always late, but if you have to change trains, the connecting train waits at the station, so there's nothing to worry about if your train is a bit late, or if the other train leaves a bit early, you'll get there, don't worry, that's how things are, the Reichsbahn isn't what it used to be, nothing is, in today's world there's no precision, no schedules, nobody cares anymore, said the Deputy, then he motioned to Florian to take the ticket from the lower tray of the ticket machine, it's ready, he said, Florian took the ticket and thanked the Deputy, you don't have to thank me, you know that at my age a person is happy if someone like you asks for a favor, people of my age aren't worth anything anymore, the Deputy was sad and didn't even notice when Florian said goodbye in front of the former train station building as he had something to do in the Altstadt, he just waved mutely, and he felt so sad from his own words that he slowly trudged away, because he couldn't really say these sad words to anyone anymore, he had no one to say them to, in the Hochhaus most of the other residents were unknown to him, not even saying hello, not even knowing who the Deputy was, he himself didn't speak much, why would he; the Deputy trudged slowly home toward the Hochhaus while Florian was thinking, the ticket in his pocket, that he must unconditionally tell Frau Ringer that he was going to Berlin, he must tell her unconditionally, as she was the only person whom he held in deepest confidence, even from when he began visiting the library to look for a book about physics, but the library didn't even have one single book about physics, only Frau Ringer, but she listened to him, moreover, she was happy to listen to Florian, so that ever since then he gladly went to see her to tell her this or that confidential matter and to seek her advice; Frau Ringer was almost like a mother to him, although she was hardly older than forty, but this did not disturb Florian in seeing her as a kind of mother, which did not mean that he divulged everything, but absolutely everything to her, he couldn't, because there were things he dared not admit to her, for example, that he was afraid of women, or that he really wasn't afraid of them but he felt that physical love was of no concern to him, and he could never talk about this with Frau Ringer even though she too had been a young woman once, he wouldn't even talk about this with his real mother if she were to turn up, this is something, thought Florian, that a person wouldn't even talk about to himself, in this matter everyone is alone, so that Frau Ringer didn't try to force the subject when a number of her acquaintances suggested she try to help Florian, because certainly the problem was with him being well over the age of twenty or who even knew how old he was and still unmarried, but no one even knew if Florian had ever had any kind of relationship with a woman; although Frau Ringer refrained from mentioning any sexual matters, she understood and respected that Florian had no desire to speak of these things, but the Boss, that beast, Frau Ringer thought to herself, if he's there already with Florian why doesn't he talk to Florian about this, and what a mouth he has on him, he has such a filthy nature that it would be no skin off his back, but the Boss always was content to slap Florian once or twice on the back and yell: well, so I hear you're getting married on Saturday, why didn't you tell me, and he needled Florian whose face turned flaming red, this wasn't even the Boss's favorite topic, though, because why—as he explained to the others in the Burg—what good would it do me if he got married? or if some rapacious slut turns his head? it wouldn't be any good, because he's too susceptible and he would leave me, so the Boss dropped the subject and, generally, he didn't push it very much, he enjoyed watching Florian turn red, but the kicker wasn't really in that, the Boss preferred to change the topic, before it occurred to him that he too had a cock between his legs, as he put it, and with that the discussion was closed, of course, Florian was relieved that the others weren't goading him anymore, although he had been afraid at the beginning that this topic—women—would always be the main subject, but when he saw it wasn't the case he calmed down, because the general fact was that women weren't like Frau Ringer or the old ladies from the Hochhaus, Ilona from the Grill, or the Chancellor, but—and he was well aware of this, no need to think he was an idiot—were either lovers or whores or even worse, they had breasts and peed differently, wore skirts and all that—all of this bothered Florian greatly, he did not know what to do with women and sexuality, he knew it wasn't right to think about women in this way, but he couldn't bear to think of them in any other way, and moreover there was Frau Ringer and the old ladies from the Hochhaus and Ilona from the Grill and of course Frau Kanzlerin, you could always cling to them because they weren't women like the other women that he didn't know and he didn't even want to know *like that*—and it wasn't as if she didn't want to listen to him, Frau Ringer defended herself if her husband asked her why she wasn't doing something, when clearly Florian couldn't get away from the Boss, she would listen to him, she protested, the devil she would, but as far as Florian was concerned, if there was anyone, then it was she who knew how uninterested Florian was in sexuality, his seeming embarrassment whenever the topic came up was only that, an appearance, because in reality this question bored him; this was Frau Ringer's deep conviction, she had never met someone quite like this before, but she was quite certain that Florian viewed sexuality as something of no concern to him, if he turns red, well, then he turns red, said Frau Ringer, in her view this was because he was discomfited by people asking him these questions, it was they, and not sexuality itself, that made him confused, because he didn't dare state that for him sexuality was shameful, that it was subjugation, a lack of transcendence with regard to nature from which everyone must try to liberate themselves—from sexuality and everything that tied a person to nature—and, in her opinion, that was what was behind those blushes of his that were so mocked, Frau Ringer concluded her remarks; only that if Florian had known her opinion, most likely he would have distanced himself from it, because deep down inside he didn't consider that a person needed to keep himself distant from nature, how could one even do that if he was a part of nature, and in every one of his molecules, in every atom and every subatomic reality the ruler was nature itself, only we do not know who this nature is or what it is exactly that we call "nature," we have no idea who nature is, Florian often thought about this sitting on the shorter bench beneath the taller tree, that is, before Herr Köhler had opened his eyes as to which direction, when immersed in thinking and unalloyed contemplation, he should adhere to; the basis must be found for everything, this was the realization that he had gained from Herr Köhler over the past two years, as he, Herr Köhler, had given his lectures—to Florian, among others—on the subject of *the wonderful world of quanta* once weekly in the basement of the Lichtenberg Secondary School as there was no space anywhere else, only down there in the basement: in the beginning, Herr Köhler's pride was somewhat injured at only being able to negotiate this basement classroom from the school principal and the regional directors of the Adult Education School, but he resigned himself and he took it, and the public was enthusiastic, there were not very many students, but in the eyes of the ones regularly attending his lectures there glimmered that light which, in Herr Köhler's opinion, made what he was doing worthwhile, and he did not stop, he taught his classes, relating everything as if to children, every Tuesday evening from six to seven thirty p.m. he tried to initiate his students into the enigmatic depths of the science of physics as if speaking to children, that was his feeling, and it was not without basis, because the depths of the mysterious science of physics into which he ushered his audience were indeed profound, and his students were not in the least prepared for this level of comprehension, Herr Köhler knew that, he could tell from the last ten minutes of class when his audience posed questions sorely lacking in any fundamental knowledge of mathematics and physics which would have made it possible for them to grasp what he was trying to open up and to introduce to them, so he had no way of managing all or any of the conclusions they might come up with after one of his lectures, or what would happen, in those unprepared heads, to everything he had recounted with words, illustrations, short films, and sometimes, although only rarely, experiments conducted by himself, although in the end it didn't bother him so very much, chiefly it didn't weigh on him, and most of all, he felt no responsibility for

where his audience was being led by his lectures until this child Florian
came up to him to share his so-called worries about the universe and
ask him for advice, well, then he began to feel that he was in trouble,
and that he could not recklessly do or say whatever he pleased, it was
because of Florian that he felt, for the first time—and he was feeling it
now too, he admitted to his good friend, the psychiatrist Jacob-Friedrich—somewhat remorseful; Jacob-Friedrich lived in a neighboring
town a little distance away, and he was the only person whom Herr
Köhler had known since his youth and whom he liked, shortly after
he'd finished his university studies, he'd returned to the vicinity of the
village of his birth and ever since then had not left, everyone else whom
Herr Köhler counted as a friend had either died or moved far away, so
that only he remained, this Jacob-Friedrich to whom Herr Köhler
spoke of his recently awakened pangs of conscience, and who at first
brushed off the matter with a joke, because he was glad that Adrian had
allowed this young man to get closer to him, so he did not demonstrate
a more specific understanding, mainly he did not permit his friend to
sink into remorseful conscience, he said to him: if you're feeling pangs
of conscience, then don't lie to yourself that you didn't cause it, but
instead face the situation and try to help yourself by helping him,
namely persuade this Florian to give you time to think over your arguments, in the meantime ask him if he could assist you with some of the
work around your Weather Station, then nicely and gradually, in a sensitive way, lure him into the wonderful—for you—world of meteorology, believe me, he'll forget about the whole thing, he'll be freed of his
worries, which means that you will be freed from your worries, because
as I see it, with this theory of his, it's as if this Florian is having more of
an effect on you than vice versa and that's what's making you so nervous; that's what Jacob-Friedrich, his old friend from Eisenberg, said,
and Adrian, while chasing away the thought that Florian might be having an influence on him—no, not that—he still listened and nonethe-

less considered that there was some wisdom in Jacob-Friedrich's advice, and he even figured out a way of implementing it, but unfortunately, Florian did not show up on the following Thursday evening, so that Herr Köhler himself went, on Saturday, to the Hochhaus to see if there was any problem, but it seemed as if his young disciple, as Florian's neighbors called him, wasn't at home, or at least he did not respond to the intercom, it was almost noon and Herr Köhler could have justifiably thought he'd find Florian at home, and in fact Florian was at home, he heard the buzz of the intercom but just at that moment he was in the middle of the fourth letter, and he suspected it was the Deputy, as he rang his intercom frequently, usually not at that time but at around seven p.m., when, chiefly in the autumn, the evenings felt oppressive to him and so he invited Florian over for a little exchange of ideas, only that now Florian was rather uncertain and did not respond to the buzzer, he said to himself, but only to himself—because he only dared to call the Deputy Friedrich when talking to himself—fine, old uncle Friedrich, I understand, just be a little patient until I finish, then I'll head downstairs of my own accord, it never occurred to Florian that it could be someone else, and especially not Herr Köhler, how could it have been Herr Köhler, he was much too important to come looking for him here in this building, the Hochhaus was a kind of blemish in Kana: it had been built as a part of the Porcelain Factory when it still employed several thousand workers, and it was considered a blemish for many reasons, partially because it had been built for the so-called fraternal nation of the Vietnamese people, which made sense in that the Porcelain Factory's workbenches were filled for the most part with Vietnamese guest workers, although of course it was not only Vietnamese who lived there, but numerous other sons and daughters of similarly "fraternal" nations hailing from Africa and other continents; but it was also a blemish because of how life here had always gone in a certain way, and for that reason it was all too easy to imagine how things would go in this Hochhaus, the residents of Kana said to each other at the beginning when construction began, all these men and three times as many women together in one building, that'll be nice, well, but not a single local resident could predict what would end up happening in reality, a morass, as the Deputy summed it up—this was right around the time he was appointed as the building's Deputy; the position of superintendent remained vacant, since there was no one to fill it—compared to this, Sodom and Gomorrah is nothing, nada, the Deputy burst out to the neighbors on Ernst-Thälmann-Straße one year after the Vietnamese had moved in, we need the police here, said the Deputy, real police officers, and he made a report, but in vain, nobody came, it seems that this is what they devised for the Porcelain Factory, they planned it exactly this way, it's in the Five-Year Plan, comrades, the locals—who'd all been let go by the Porcelain Factory—guffawed in the IKS pub, mainly Hoffmann, who was a jokester in the IKS, but also in the Grillhäusel, the men are running away, he related to his foolish audience, just imagine, I heard it from the Deputy, the men there—whether Vietnamese, black, yellow or bright blue, they don't go home after work, but instead they *sneak* back home, that's how hungry those dames are for them, and of course it ended up with a lot of teasing, and not only in the IKS pub; but then it came to an end, and as it had begun, the topic of the Hochhaus itself began to fade away, after a while no one was interested in what was going on at the Hochhaus, nothing of any particular interest was going on there anyway, but its seedy reputation remained, especially after the Porcelain Factory declared bankruptcy, and beginning in the early 1990s, when it ended up in the hands of a private firm in Munich and could only employ a few hundred people, the Vietnamese went home and for the most part the apartments in the Hochhaus remained empty, and the ones that were not empty were primarily occupied by students attending university in Jena and a few older people living alone, and of course Florian, living at one end of the seventh floor, he was hardly able to grasp it, so happy was he when the Boss moved him in: his very first apartment of his own, he was filled with a feeling of unspeakable gratification when, after the bed, table, and a few chairs had been moved in, he could stay there by himself, he put on his worker's overalls and his Fidel Castro cap and clutching his backpack to himself, head slightly bowed, because the ceilings were low in relation to how tall he was, he began walking back and forth between the main room and the kitchen, he ran the tap in the bathroom several times to see for himself: even after the second or third or fourth time water still flowed out, he was happy, he looked out the window from where he could see the beautiful landscape, the mountains surrounding Kana, of course not all of them, but he could still see the Dohlenstein from here, from the seventh floor; before, his only possession had been this backpack, and now he had a table, a bed, and three chairs, and it was all his, all for him who had never been able to possess almost anything at all, because in the Institute personal property was not permitted, only a backpack that had been given to him when he got there, so he didn't really have too much of an idea of what it was like for someone to have something, for example that someone such as himself would now have an apartment of his own, his joy lasted for weeks, for months, and in fact it never really passed, it only became mixed up with the gratitude he felt toward the Boss, and after a while he no longer distinguished between the two, he looked at the slopes of the Dohlenstein, at the snowy forests in the winter, at the fresh green foliage in the summer, and he thought of the Boss, some- times when he got up from the table he even caressed its edge, just like that, unconsciously, he caressed the edge of the table, and at times like that he always thought about the Boss, how he was to thank for all of this, this apartment, this table, everything, and so nothing much changed in the apartment after he moved in, sometimes the Boss wanted to give him a cupboard or a proper bathroom mirror, but Flo- rian said no, he only accepted a reading lamp and a kind of wooden bench that had once been used in a guesthouse that the Boss had found somewhere, but he accepted these only with difficulty because he wanted to preserve the original state of the apartment, wanting it to always remain as it had been when he first moved in, sometimes the Boss asked him: well now, but why don't you get some curtains, fuck it, or something like that, but Florian always brushed this away with some kind of joking remark, for example apropos of the curtains, he said: why, Boss, who's going to be looking in my window on the seventh floor? in other words no, he regularly saved money from his weekly pay, but he didn't buy anything, and it was a good three years on from his having started working with the Boss when he stated to him that he had saved up three hundred and seventy euros, and he asked the Boss to help him buy a cell phone, he'd always dreamed of owning one, and maybe even a laptop, because a cell phone for work and a laptop for his studies would, he felt, be useful, at first the Boss was completely negative, reacting to the idea of a laptop with rage, but it was the cell phone that made him really tear into Florian: what do you need a cell phone for?! what?! I'm the only one you should be talking to, fuck it, and you don't need a cell phone for that, but at least a laptop, Florian entreated the Boss, upon which the Boss stepped back a bit like someone who wished to thoroughly examine the ulterior motives of the one standing before him, then he bawled at him: it's because you want to research that goddamned universe, right?! you should be studying Bach, goddammit, look at me, when I listen to Bach the hair immediately stands up on my back, because listen here, I have a heart, because otherwise how would I be able to have so much admiration for Bach every time I listen to him, it's the end of me, the strength goes out of my arms, sometimes I can't even play with these weakened arms, because for the drums, strength is needed, a strong will, that's why I play the drums, that's why I chose the drum when we were deciding who would play what, I don't say that I always have to keep drumming, but sometimes you have to give that drum a good bang, I look at the score and bang! 4/4 time?! 3/4 time?! it's all in my little finger, and listen, because when we start playing whatever it may be, the umpteenth opus of this or that in D Major, then I'm in the universe, get it?! because *this* is the universe, fuck it, because you were born, or at least you were dropped on your head, here, in this exceptional place, where we are not born as half-wits, and I'm going to beat that imbecility out of your head and I'm going to beat Bach into it, but Florian knew all too well these invectives of the Boss's—he engaged in them more out of habit, he wasn't really angry, so that although the Boss seethed that a cell phone was out of the question, and what the fuck do you need a laptop for, there isn't even any internet in the Hochhaus, and there's never going to be anything like that, goddammit, and don't ever count on coming to my place, because don't think you're going to sit there banging on that keyboard for hours, fucking goddammit, but Florian persisted, and he simply persuaded and persuaded him, arguing that it was true that there would never be internet in the Hochhaus, but there was internet in the Herbstcafé, and Frau Uta wouldn't mind if he sat there, he had asked and she said yes, and then, when the Boss finally gave in, and got him an HP laptop off the books, installed the basics, then showed him the first steps, in a strange way it was as if Florian understood everything immediately, as if he already knew how to use a laptop, although he denied it, but still it was immediately clear to him what it meant to search for something on Google, or how to save or delete or drag something onto the desktop using the touchpad, and truly it was as if he understood the basics right away: the desktop, the programs, charging the battery, and everything else, so that the Boss didn't have to explain much to him but let him become immersed in his laptop, but afterward Florian, on that first day, didn't really dare touch it, he simply placed the device on the kitchen table in his apartment, and he looked at it, entranced, he walked around the table and then he hardly slept, because he kept having to go out to see if it was really still there, and from the second day onward nothing else existed for him, only this HP, his very own HP, he opened it, closed it, opened it again, turned it on and pressed a key on the keyboard, he was completely immersed, and this lasted for days while he tried everything, and then he took the laptop with him into the Herbstcafé, and he began to search out the things that were important to him, and of course for him this meant materials related to physics, everything he'd first heard about from Herr Köhler, only that he didn't really understand the essence of these matters; he read through the articles and studies he had access to slowly, many times over, but to no avail, he sought out simplified descriptive interpretations and explanations, but in vain, and in the end he closed the laptop one day in the Herbstcafé, and after two years he gathered up his courage, he went down to Oststraße, and that is when the shared history of Florian and Herr Köhler began, which of course was immediately evident to everyone, Kana was a small town, and everyone here knew everything about everyone — or at least they wanted to — so that at first the neighbors at Oststraße jokingly asked Herr Köhler what Florian was doing there, had he hired a frog to help him predict the weather because his meteorological instruments were no longer working? then one day Frau Ringer asked Herr Köhler about Florian when she ran into him in Lidl, and expressed her joy that the boy, as she called him, finally had a genuine figure of support in his life, and Herr Köhler was not so happy to hear this as he did not want to be Florian's figure of support, he simply was fond of the boy who, with his own enormous physical strength and goodwill, could help him out too, whether it was fixing the roof or positioning a new instrument at the top of his Weather Station, which was difficult for him, something was always coming up and Florian was happy to help, and Herr Köhler, too, in the beginning, enjoyed these little Thursday talks, he liked to lecture, perhaps that is why he had chosen the path of physics teacher and not that of theoretical physicist or computer-science researcher for which he also had a good instinct, and he had the requisite knowledge, too, but no, he liked it when people were standing or sitting in front of him and he could talk to them about things he was knowledgeable about, he liked to win them over, to see that glimmer in their eyes which he considered the greatest of recognitions because it meant that someone—a little sixth-grade scamp, a pensioner from the tuition-free Adult Education School, or even, more recently, Florian himself— suddenly appeared to understand something; this had, for decades, filled him with the greatest of pride and satisfaction, what more could I want, he explained to Jacob-Friedrich when they met up every two or three weeks at his house in the Oststraße or at Jacob-Friedrich's house in Eisenberg, you yourself know this is everything I could ever want, and well, it was exactly that sudden glimmer of understanding which he now had to place under a microscope because of Florian, and the results were—again because of Florian—more than appalling, this signified, at once, the bankruptcy of his entire pedagogical career, as well as his own definitive disillusionment with science; for it could have been largely around this time that Herr Köhler first observed the dangerous signs of obsession in Florian, realizing that the boy had not really understood anything, and that the glimmer in those light-blue eyes only meant—something which also applied to his entire career—that the person in question had found a route which was completely misguided, the person in question had arrived at a solution that was completely misguided, that the person in question had drawn conclusions which were completely misguided, conclusions that could lead his students—especially Florian—to any outcome at all; Herr Köhler no longer had any influence over Florian, he could no longer persuade him that his interpretations of what he'd heard were incorrect, that he was sabotaging correct analysis, because Florian was working himself into a frenzy over a misunderstanding, incorrectly interpreted information, an oversimplified reading from which even the good Lord himself would not be able to extricate him, because Florian had already dug himself into this world-explanation built upon misunderstandings, Florian, who understood nothing at all about how the vacuum is not identical with philosophical emptiness, who did not comprehend that the Nothing does not even exist; Florian, who had not grasped the analysis of microwave background radiation and not even a single element of relativistic quantum field theory, and who had not in the least perceived that if he was going to get bogged down in theoretical conclusions, then it was not these abstruse theories of potentially apocalyptic occurrences that he should be getting lost in but instead that lightning-like flash in the human brain when it realized what occurred during the mutual annihilation of the particles and the antiparticles, namely electromagnetic radiation, which itself broke down into matter and antimatter until the universe cooled to an approximate temperature of 3,000 Kelvin, thus creating the circumstances through which, in the domain visible to us, light could be born, because light—and everyone, including Florian, should take note—could only come into being within a certain time period of this electric magnetic radiation, as beneath a certain Kelvin number it could not exist, so that afterward, we don't know exactly when, but with the birth of the sun and the stars, light once again dawned from these new sources, and Florian! my goodness! this light shines even today—but it didn't matter anymore, because Herr Köhler was in no way, but truly in no way capable of influencing Florian's train of thought, and there will be problems from this, Herr Köhler thought, and he didn't even know that Florian had gone to Berlin and returned, because Florian said not a word about this when he showed up again at Herr Köhler's house after one week's absence, he didn't say he'd gone to Berlin or that he'd been anywhere at all; it was only two days later, on Saturday, that Herr Köhler heard from Frau Ringer, once again in Lidl, this time by the vegetable counter—Herr Köhler wanted to get some tomatoes on the vine at half price—

that he heard about Florian's trip to Berlin, but perhaps it hadn't gone well, said Frau Ringer, because Florian hadn't told her about it directly: did Herr Köhler know anything about this by any chance? well, not only do I not know anything about this trip, Herr Köhler replied with a drawn face, but I know nothing about this entire affair at all—what the devil could he have been doing in Berlin, he fretted later on at home when he sat down for dinner, he liked tomatoes on the vine, mainly he liked the fragrance of the greenery, he ate sliced salami with a bit of cheese and tomatoes on the side, that was his dinner, usually he ate little in the evenings, only if he could get some of these tomatoes on the vine which he couldn't resist, he sniffed them and tasted them slowly in his mouth, there's nothing better than tomatoes on the vine, he said to Jacob-Friedrich, for this it is worthwhile to survive the winter, and unfortunately he had already eaten an entire package, well, there it was, everyone has their weakness, and this is mine, he explained, laughing a little shamefacedly to Jacob-Friedrich, tomatoes on the vine are my weakness, to which his friend only replied: still much better than if your weakness were Ferraris, and they both laughed, it was always like this, Jacob-Friedrich always knew how to cheer him up, he was very good at that, and so Herr Köhler was grateful to fate for granting him such a friend, and he tried to signal his gratitude, for example by remembering his friend's birthday, as well as the birthday of his wife, their child, and their anniversary too; he never neglected to show up with some small gift before the more important holidays because he didn't spend holidays with them, Herr Köhler respected that, holidays were for families, and Jacob-Friedrich appreciated this as well, he never openly thanked his friend for his attentiveness but he did make his gratitude clear, so that they were very good together, neither one of them would have been able or would have ever wanted to imagine that one day this might come to an end, although it was necessary to think about that, for surely both of them were already of an age when

... but no, Herr Köhler thought it best not to even bother with this question, better to enjoy each other's friendship while they could, and that was all, and so the matter was closed, the Weather Station continued to function, it collected data while Herr Köhler also observed data from the DWD, the MDR, or the Norwegians, he maintained his own website, updating it, and was happy when sometimes people on the street addressed him as "Herr Weatherman," he lived in peace, alone, but in peace and tranquility, and this, he decided, could never be disturbed by anything, not even this matter with Florian, and so he began to preoccupy himself with how he might bring his connection with Florian to an end, he even asked Frau Ringer, the next time he saw her in Lidl, for her advice, but Frau Ringer turned pale, and she said: no, no, don't do this, don't even let it enter your mind, Herr Professor, Florian worships you, he will become ill if you don't let him come see you, better to speak to him about his problems, if you could turn him into such an ardent admirer of yours, then I'm certain you can get him out of this, you are a great pedagogue, Professor, everyone knows that, a truly wise person, I am convinced—she stepped a little closer to Herr Köhler—that you will be able to awaken Florian to the error of his ways, to show him a clear goal which will no longer burden your relation, because I know, Frau Ringer continued, that you are capable of miracles, you have done good for so many here in Kana, this town is filled with your grateful students who, thanks to your magnificent tenure in the Secondary School, became acquainted with physics and science in general, and so I'm asking you—Frau Ringer grabbed Herr Köhler's hand with her two hands—do not let Florian go, do not leave him by himself, Florian is an extraordinary person, he's just a little sensitive, please listen to me, and because by now she seemed a little desperate, Herr Köhler pulled his hand away from hers and said goodbye, Frau Ringer stood motionless for a while next to the meat counter where they'd bumped into each other this time; Herr Köhler wanting

64

to free himself from Florian sounded a bit threatening, moreover, almost fatal, and in her great consternation, she hadn't even told Herr Köhler how much Florian was *truly* enamored of him; she herself recognized that this adoration was justified, the entire town felt this way toward the former physics and mathematics teacher, and that was precisely why he could not—and definitively not now—leave Florian on his own, she related this later on at home to her husband as she roasted pork chops with a special brown sauce on the side, she herself was not so crazy about this gravy, moreover, if she were to be sincere, she betrayed to one of her loyal readers in the library, auntie Ingrid, she was bored of brown sauce, but her husband liked it, and he always liked it in a certain way, so there it was with the pork chops, and she and auntie Ingrid laughed, and auntie Ingrid confessed that she was the same, ever since she'd been a child there was always just brown sauce and boiled potatoes with pork chops, it's a tradition with us and that's that, said the old lady, holding a few romance novels in her hand, clutching them to herself because she'd already checked them out, and once again they laughed at the whole thing, yes, brown sauce, that goes best with roasted pork chops, only she—Frau Ringer pointed at herself— to put it frankly, she was a little tired of it, she would reaaallly like to make something else to go with pork chops, but her husband ... well, yes, auntie Ingrid nodded, and she said goodbye, she stepped out of the library, Frau Ringer thought that still she might try to sneak in something different for weekend lunch, just so it wouldn't always be those same old pork chops with brown sauce, it was a good and cheap meal and everything, but still, for once they could try something else—while Herr Köhler was ruminating, on the way home from Lidl, about what was going on again, why had Florian gone to Berlin, and did this have anything to do with what had happened between them? he couldn't make up his mind quickly, but recalling Florian's letters he suspected the worst, Florian's letters which, ridiculously, he had sent to ... the Chancellor, wasn't it ... according to the Volkenants; in any event, Herr Köhler decided to get to the bottom of the matter, feeling ashamed he'd waited so long as he was not the kind of person who chewed for weeks on a problem, he always thought it was best to resolve these stressful matters as quickly as possible, so that even before he got home he turned around, but then he remembered that he was carrying the discounted chicken meat, an entire week's supply, in a plastic shopping bag, along with a thin slice of veal and some porkchop slices, which had to be placed in the refrigerator, so he went back to his house, wrapped the chicken, pork slices, and the thin slice of veal in plastic-wrap layers, then placed them nicely next to each other in the refrigerator, and he was on his way, and already he was ringing the bell at Florian's apartment, who, on this occasion—because someone had also rung the bell of his apartment one week ago, but he hadn't been able to find out who it was, and this time it couldn't be old uncle Friedrich, even if it clearly had been him before, because he usually rang Florian's buzzer in the evenings and now it was almost twelve noon, it's just like one week ago, thought Florian—he stopped what he was doing at the kitchen table and opened the window, he leaned out and nearly fell out of the window in surprise, because down there, by the front door, he saw Herr Köhler himself, I'll be right down! I'll open the door!! he called out, and he ran down the steps because, as usual, the elevator was out of order, unfortunately the elevator is out of order, Herr Köhler, he said to him, barely comprehensibly as he was out of breath, that's no problem, Herr Köhler answered seriously, he wasn't his usual self, Florian perceived immediately, there must be some weighty reason if Herr Köhler was coming to see him in his own apartment, what should he do, Florian mused, as he jumped in front of his guest to apologize for the mess that awaited him in the apartment above, then doubling back behind Herr Köhler because he didn't want to be rude, in the end they somehow made their way upstairs, and Florian could not apologize enough for the elevator being out of order, we've reported it so many times, but our Deputy is useless, he always just spreads his arms apart and tells us he reported it to the relevant firm, but then they don't come and they don't come, and we've already gotten used to it, Florian explained cheerfully while the tempo of their progress up the stairs, dictated by his guest, grew ever more incremental, and for many good long minutes that guest was speechless until they got to the apartment and Herr Köhler was able to sit down in the kitchen, so out of breath that he could only pant, he took off his glasses, sat in the kitchen chair completely hunched over, still hardly catching his breath, I can hardly catch my breath, he said, panting, then he asked for a glass of water, Florian ran to the tap and brought it immediately, he sat down facing him, and he cast a happy and proud glance at his visitor, largely because—with the exception of the Deputy, who, if the elevator was working, sometimes came up to see him—he never had any guests, the Boss never came up to his apartment, I'm supposed to go up to your place on the seventh floor? I'm not some idiot, fuck it, he brushed off the idea in his own way when Florian suggested that he come up for a cup of coffee, and what's more, your coffee is shit, Florian, you need to change it, but nothing changed, because Florian had no idea what he was supposed to change about the coffee, so that now, he apologized when Herr Köhler spoke to him, answering his queries as to if he wanted a bit more water? or perhaps coffee? or another glass of water? yes, fine, he would take a coffee, and of course Florian's coffee wasn't so good as in town, but he would do everything he could to please Herr Köhler, who of course did not understand what Florian meant by this, what could make a coffee more pleasing to anyone, coffee was the same everywhere, it should be not too strong, kept at a warm temperature, and that was it, otherwise Herr Köhler was thinking about how to begin and what to say, but then he grew angry at himself for hesitating, so that when he had more or less caught his

67

breath, he began by saying: Florian, listen to me, I came here because things can't go on as they have been until now, I could say that I'm already old, which is true, and that I can no longer be at your service on a weekly basis, but that's not what I want to say, what I want to say is that it seems that you have created an image in your head of a potential cataclysm and referred it back to me, but this picture is mistaken, and it is most certainly wrong for you to make any kind of reference to me, what I'm telling you now, what I told you for two whole years in the Night School, is not at all the same thing as what you have gleaned from this, look, this world picture of yours has nothing to do with me, it is completely of your own making, and before it causes you some greater problem, I must warn you that you are drawing false, incorrect, and completely unacceptable conclusions from everything you heard from me, conclusions for which I will be held responsible, already people are talking about it in town, and I'm not too happy about this at all, I … although it is possible that I will supplement my own research— and, I acknowledge, partially because of you—by means of participation in a new project concerned with calculating the massive black holes into which I suspect antimatter of having disappeared, we don't know where it has gone—but this is just a hobby, because my main preoccupation is the Weather Station and not quantum field theory, and your main preoccupation is ensuring that ALLES WIRD REIN, ALL WILL BE CLEAN, as it says on your firm's cars, and that's how it should remain, this is just a friendly piece of advice, you will either accept it or not, but if you are listening to me, you will accept it and there will be no problems, Herr Köhler drank his coffee, but just a sip, because it was undrinkable, probably because of the water, he thought, either there was too little coffee or the coffee had been sitting in the machine for a few days already, who knew, he pushed the cup away from himself, setting it down on the kitchen table, he thanked Florian, stood up, and in parting only said, or you can see things this way: I'll take over from here, and you just look after yourself, my son, and on the following Thursday Herr Köhler did not respond to the doorbell, Florian kept pressing on it, he kept trying, he pressed harder and harder, he pressed the bell three times, one after the other, quickly, then he tried pressing only the edge of the doorbell, although Florian could hear the doorbell in every case, you could hear it from here outside, but nothing, Herr Köhler did not come to open the door as he usually did, but where could he be, Florian wondered, Herr Köhler was always at home on Thursdays after six p.m., was there some problem? and he looked in through the windows, but the blinds were pulled down so he couldn't tell what was going on inside, he couldn't see into the yard from the front gate, maybe he's outside with his instruments, he thought, and he called out: I'm here, it's me, Florian's here, but nothing, so he slipped away; a few neighbors, especially the two who spent nearly the entirety of the second half of their lives peeking out the window to see if anything was going on out there, were decidedly glad this time: well now, look at this, he's not letting Florian in, that's nice, and even though they didn't know what it meant, they were happy, because they were happy about everything, but especially when something unusual happened here on Oststraße, and that was a rare occurrence, Frau Burgmüller even opened her window to look across at Frau Schneider who had not yet recovered from her surprise, so that they only discussed the matter later on when they both had come out before their respective houses, and then Frau Schneider said: well, what do you think about this, and Frau Burgmüller answered: he's at home; at home? certainly not, Frau Schneider contradicted her, while Florian, head bent, walked along Bahnhofstraße, then along Bachstraße, then he turned to the right and headed back because it was too late to go to the library, the Herbstcafé was closed so he couldn't go there, although he would have really liked to have spoken with someone about how Herr Köhler wasn't at home, and exactly him, Herr

Köhler, the image of punctuality, but when, after walking around for an hour, Florian came back to Oststraße and rang the bell again, Herr Köhler still wasn't at home, so that he rang the bell at the house across the street, Frau Schneider opened the window immediately, but when Florian asked if she knew where her neighbor had gone, she just shook her head and betrayed nothing, it wasn't for her to get involved in other people's affairs or to comment, so Florian once again trudged off while he kept looking backward to see if possibly Herr Köhler might suddenly appear from the other direction, but he didn't appear, Florian went home, he shaved, sometimes he had to shave twice a day as his facial hair grew in so quickly, and when he was done, he drank a large glass of water and decided he would not try again today but would leave it for tomorrow, he sat down at the kitchen table, he opened his laptop, then he closed it, he pulled the new draft he'd begun after his trip to Berlin to the edge of the table, but now he wasn't satisfied with how the influence upon him of the trip to Berlin was perceptible in every line, this wasn't what he wanted, this had nothing to do with anything, he rebuked himself rereading the draft—because now he was reading it over for perhaps the fourth time—he discovered, in the draft, this or that revealing word or phrase which made it all too clear, despite his firm intention, that what had happened there still weighed on him; I must begin with a blank sheet of paper, he decided, and he began writing on a new piece of paper, and he wrote that the time had come to reveal something about himself, because this too pertained to the entire truth, although to be more precise it did not really concern his own self but a certain Herr Köhler who had led him to elementary particle physics and his own subsequent conclusions—described by him three times previously—although if Herr Köhler knew that he, Florian, now wished to reveal to Madame Chancellor just what a great role Herr Köhler had played in his, Florian Herscht's, decision to disclose his identity to the Chancellor, he would be very angry, for a mere week or so ago Herr Köhler had been at his place, strongly pressing upon him that he would find it extremely worrying if Florian were to somehow get him, Herr Köhler, mixed up in this affair, therefore Florian wished to unconditionally clear Herr Köhler's name from any possible accusation or suspicion, and thus he was reporting again because the Chancellor should know that every conclusion he had drawn, the results of which he had conveyed in writing three times previously to Berlin, had absolutely nothing, but nothing at all to do with Herr Köhler, on the contrary, Herr Köhler had, several times, and ever more vehemently, tried to dissuade him, Florian, from conveying his conclusions to the Kanzleramt, briefly put, he was only writing now in order to fully exonerate Herr Köhler, should the question ever emerge of his role in this affair, Herr Köhler was the best, most honorable, and the wisest person he had ever met, he would have been very happy to bring him to Berlin, but well, this, due to the well-known resistance of Herr Köhler, was possible only in imagination, and so that was how he traveled with him to Berlin, and he couldn't find a seat on the train, even though he had a reservation, the crowd was enormous, at least from Halle onward, everywhere there were people standing or lying down, they sat on the floor, they sat on their suitcases, in addition there were people continually coming and going, never leaving this chaotic crowd in peace for a moment, he found a place next to one of the toilets, if you could call it a place, he had said this as well to Frau Ringer, the one person to whom he had related his journey, apart from the Deputy, although he didn't tell Frau Ringer everything; Florian never could have imagined that such a crowded train like that could even exist, well, I too could tell you stories, replied Frau Ringer scratching her arm because her relatives, as Florian knew, did not live in Kana but in Zwickau, and in past years she had traveled there at least four times a year, and the ones who say that things like that happen only on the Intercity trains have never traveled by train there, because you don't even want to know, she said to Florian, what we went through at times, especially on the weekends, but never mind, because now I only go there once a year with my husband, sometimes even by myself, either at Easter or Christmas, so I know what you went through, well, that's what it's like if you get on a train, because no longer can you sit there comfortably gazing out the window, watching the landscape gliding by, because to sit there comfortably gazing out the window on a train, especially these days, is impossible, in addition you never get to where you're supposed to be going on time, this whole Reichsbahn, or what do they call it now? I don't even know, the entire railway is one big catastrophe, but do you think it's any better in a car?! not at all! there are so many cars on the road that you just end up in one traffic jam after another making things even more unpredictable, and moreover people today don't even know how to drive like they used to, no one follows the rules, I — Frau Ringer pointed at herself; usually if she pronounced the word "I" while speaking, she would do so emphasizing the decisiveness of her words, a gesture which had similarly become a habit — she wasn't one of those crazy Brandenburg drivers, but that's how it was, the roads today were simply horrific, either by car or by train, people really had to think twice before setting foot outside of their own home, and the Ringers never really left Kana very much, only traveling around the vicinity, the mountains surrounding the town offered many joyful moments, as Frau Ringer expressed it, you should come with us one time, she said to Florian, there are such beautiful mountains here in Kana, just think, for example, of the Dohlenstein, there's the Lookout and the view of the Saale Valley, and of course there's also Leuchtenburg, marvelous places, and she said as well to her husband later on at home, placing the warmed-up supper in front of him: we really should take Florian with us one day, what do you say, well, I'm really not too thrilled by that idea, my dear, Herr Ringer shook his head very cautiously, because he knew his wife's sensitive point was this half-witted orphan child, so he tried to remind her that their outings were rare occasions when they could be alone together, just the two of them, of course, in the kitchen and in the bed it was also just the two of them, but they were really together only in the mountains, so that this matter went no further, although Frau Ringer didn't give up, and she was certain that if she pestered her husband enough, the next time he would agree with her, because Florian never went on any outings, Frau Ringer knew exactly where and how he lived his life, this poor child is imprisoned in the life of that beast, she complained to her husband, because that's what she always called the Boss—that *beast*—never forgetting that when she herself had been seventeen years old, that same man, about eight years her senior, had tried to rape her behind the Rosengarten, only he did not succeed because, thank God, she was made of sterner stuff than that, and before anything could happen she kicked him where it counted, she had never forgotten this, she didn't want to, nor could she forgive him, and when the Boss brought Florian to Kana and set him up in the Hochhaus, and Frau Ringer got to know Florian in the library, even then she had threatened the Boss, telling him that if he harmed this child in any way, she would report him to the police, and Frau Ringer always held this threat over the Boss who did not appear to be very threatened, but because of Frau Ringer's strong character and her even stronger loathing of him, he still had to keep an eye on her, well, he wasn't afraid of being reported to the police, he wasn't afraid of anything, but he preferred not to get into any conflict with Herr Ringer, who—while in all probability not knowing anything about the whole dalliance with his wife, apart from the fact that he always looked at him as if he were a nobody when they bumped into each other at the Shopping Center—was clearly much stronger than him—broad shoulders! sculpted chest! strong bone structure! sturdy arm and back and leg and abdominal muscles!—and this was despite the fact that Ringer did not frequent the gym by the railway crossing,

Ringer had been born that way, the Boss kept chewing it over, of course, he didn't have the same kind of muscles and bone structure as Florian, because there was only one like that in the world, but that piece of scum Ringer would still be able to take him down, in addition his own mind and his schooling could not be compared to Ringer's, the Boss had attended middle school in Jena and hadn't even finished because he had to start working, well, and that Ringer was a Jew, meaning he was part of the conspiracy; the Boss never missed an opportunity to curse them wildly, even though he knew only a few Jews personally, including Ringer, and his connection to him was tenuous, at least looking at it from his point of view, so he opted instead to hold his tongue, I hold my tongue, he said to the others if Ringer's name happened to come up on a Friday or Saturday evening, I hold my tongue because that muscleman scumbag has only brought trouble to Kana, remember how the Thuringia Heimatschutz came to an end, what happened in Leuchtenburg and the Timo Brandt case, what happened to the Hate-brothers, or Wolfleben or Madley, behind all of this was that goddamned Ringer, believe me, he is our biggest enemy, but for the time being I'm holding my tongue, and I suggest that you all do the same if his name comes up, because one day we're going to blow up his repair shop, let there be no doubt about that, but for now we have to wait for the right time, timing, comrades, our strength is in timing, so that today—the Boss looked the others up and down—today we will drink to Timing, and he yelled out ACHTUNDACHTZIG, at which the others also yelled out: ACHTUNDACHTZIG, then they bumped their beer mugs together, and the beer did them good, beer always did them good, in the Burg they always drank Köstritzer, of course at other times Ur-Saalfelder went down their throats, and Altenburger and Apoldaer and everything that was Thuringian, for example, Jürgen once explained to a Hungarian comrade at a gathering in Hungary, just imagine, fuck it, in our own Thuringia, fuck it, there are altogether 409

74

different kinds of beer, well, how fucking amazing is that, fuck it?! and as the Hungarian knew a bit of German, he understood what Jürgen was saying, and he nodded in recognition and said: *das ist gut*, fuck it, *shpater buzuche ich dich doch da*, because really, as Jürgen sometimes noted when they were together and they didn't have anything to talk about, well, who else can say that there are 409 different kinds of beer in his native land, and that's only the beer, came the Boss's riposte, because we also have Johann Sebastian Bach here, isn't that so? yes, yes, the others conceded, they were bored with how the Boss was always bringing up this Bach, they recognized that Bach was Bach, but when you have to listen every single week about Bach this and Bach that, then it starts getting on your nerves, no? Fritz explained his position to Karin, fiiine, we have our Bach, but we also have Zeiss and Brehm, because what about the children? Fritz looked at Karin, don't they count? fuck me they don't! every kid around here knows who Brehm is, but who knows Bach? just a few like the Boss and a couple of know-it-all highbrows, well, I'm not saying that Bach doesn't count, he does count, I'm only saying that it's not just Bach, we have so many famous people that we can't even count them all, we should make a big book and put in everyone who lived and did something in Thuringia, no? and he looked at Karin, seeking her approval, but Karin just stared straight ahead, puffing on her cigarette, this was her usual state, hence at such times—meaning almost all the time—it wasn't a good idea to bother her for too long; Fritz left her and started chatting with another comrade, because Fritz was a talkative kind of person, always chattering on about something, and Karin was the exact opposite, meaning they didn't get on too well, sometimes Karin told Fritz to leave her the fuck alone and let her smoke in peace, well, and as far as that was concerned, Jürgen and Andreas really couldn't stand each other too much either, one of them was a fanatic Chemie Kana fan, the other an ardent supporter of BSG Wismut Gera because he was from Gera and not from Kana, so they never agreed on who was the better player, for example Marcel Keißling or Maxi Enkelmann—the others, in whom there was a healthy interest in soccer, but who were not blood fanatics like Jürgen or Andreas, faithfully went out either to Kana or to Gera if one or the other team had a match there, but they saw both of the teams as their own and were all too happy to brawl with the fans of the visiting team, howling out the other teams' anthems together; but there was only one problem, when the two great teams of Ostthüringen were competing against each other either in Kana or in Gera, well, then they were silent in the standing-room section, agreeing with either Jürgen or Andreas's remarks that things could not go on like this, the defending midfielder had to be sent off and the referee ground to a pulp on the field because of how he let that foul pass, although it didn't matter anyway because they were going to punch out his eyes after the match, briefly put, they got involved in everything, but never forgetting their true mission, and especially not the Boss, because, while he said, okay, everything for sport, it brings the community together, but everyone should feel that way even more so when it comes to Thuringia, so that when, on a Monday in the middle of November, everyone's cell phones rang, and the Boss said: people!! at the ready!! then they were all in the Burg by eight p.m. listening to the Boss's latest strategy to position guard posts after midnight, but this time only in one place, Mühlhausen, because that motherfucker douchebag has showed up again, the Boss hissed, I can see his hooked nose, his thin, greasy hair hanging down into his eyes, I see, the Boss continued, his thin bones beneath his T-shirt, and even though he's wearing a hoodie I can see that scumbag's face, he's right here before me, look, and he raised his hands as if about to grab him—this is dean Schwarz calling from Mühlhausen, a voice had said to the Boss early that morning, the entrance to our church has been defaced, might you be able to send someone to clean it up as soon as possible? to which the Boss answered that the firm, of course, could always send someone, but if this was the Divi Blasii, then he himself would immediately get into his car and set things straight in Mühlhausen, and the Boss rattled out this last word "Mühlhausen" so harshly that the pastor didn't understand what he was saying; it only became clear to him when the head of the cleaning company arrived and he found himself greeting an ancient Thuringian in the person of the Boss, I am an ancient Thuringian, the Boss grumbled through his teeth, and he said no more, although he usually explained the background to this statement; now, though, he turned away from dean Schwarz and headed toward the church entrance, he then stopped, and, unbelieving, his face entirely red, he could only spit out the words: I'll kill him, and he clenched his teeth while he started applying the AGS 60 to remove the two marks of graffiti, he hadn't brought Florian as he didn't need him this time, he was the one who was needed here, in general they were all needed, all of you are needed, as he told them that evening, pointing at the comrades in the Burg before they set off for Mühlhausen, all of you together, because that lame rat didn't finish the wolf's head this time, clearly he was interrupted, but I'm going to get him, and the others, without thinking things over too thoroughly, felt the same way—aggrieved and vengeful—as they headed back toward Mühlhausen: vengeful, because in the past few months they had waited in vain at those holy Bach shrines where, they conjectured, a fresh attack would occur, they could never anticipate or figure out this scumbag's thinking as to where he was going to strike next, and now it had happened in Mühlhausen, I've had enough of this little dried-out cunt, the Boss grimaced as he paused for a minute, in the Burg, assigning positions around the church to the comrades, this rat has conspired against Thuringia, against the German past, he has conspired against us, the Boss started up the Opel and they set off for Mühlhausen, and everyone was stationed before midnight and they waited in the silent, empty town, stationed around the large church, and when they returned to Kana at dawn, no one dared ask the Boss, whose face was crimson from rage, no one dared ask what the fuck they had been looking for in Mühlhausen, because the probability of that sprayer, after he had defaced the temple entrance, returning at midnight to finish the WOLF HEAD and risk being caught was approximately zero, they needed to be much more coolheaded about this, the comrades looked at each other, sitting on the benches of the Aral gas station, steaming cups of coffee in their hands, but no one said this, they only puffed away at their cigarettes; Nadír allowed them, and only them, to smoke if there were no other customers, or rather, they were the only ones to whom she didn't dare say no when they lit up here inside, but only them, they puffed on their cigarettes and blew the smoke out, and there was silence, then they dispersed, the Boss went to pick up Florian, do you have the list? he asked in the car, because he knew that today they had to go to Jena: ever since Florian got a laptop it was his job to compile the list of addresses with the streets and house numbers, and the list was in order, they downloaded it in the Herbst-café from the Jena City Administration website, so there was nothing for the Boss to find fault with, of course beyond the fact that why couldn't Florian already, at his age, learn how to shave properly, because the Boss always noticed the faintest of stubble as he did now as well, and he pointed at the problematic spot, and he didn't fail to give him a slap, Florian pulled in his neck and stared ahead into the dense traffic, what a fucking fag town this Jena is, the Boss snarled, did you know, Florian, that this Jena is a gathering of motherfucking faggots, Florian nodded although he didn't completely understand why the Boss had a problem with Jena, but he had gotten used to not understanding, the Boss cannot be understood, he explained to Frau Ringer, defending him: deep down inside he lives a very, but a very impulsive life, and his words don't reveal what is going on with him at a given moment, but Frau Ringer just made a face as she always did when Florian began talking about the Boss, then she asked him: how do you know a word like that, "impulsive"? and that was the end of the discussion, Florian didn't continue, he knew that Frau Ringer didn't like the Boss, he never understood why, but he accepted it, and now he was telling her what happened in Berlin, but Frau Ringer was listening with a somewhat abstracted expression on her face, Florian didn't think she wasn't paying attention, she was certainly paying attention, it was just as if something were weighing on her, which she either could not or did not want to conceal, so that Florian asked: is there some problem? to which Frau Ringer only replied: oh, it's nothing, namely she had no wish to speak, only at the end before she was about to say goodbye to Florian from behind the checkout desk at the library, and she asked him: Florian, you don't happen to know where Herr Köhler could be? and Florian looked at her, amazed, so surprised was he at the question, then he confusedly blurted out that he didn't know either, and he found this to be very odd, because imagine, Frau Ringer, he said, that when he, Florian, rang the doorbell at his house as usual on Thursday evening at six p.m., Herr Köhler did not answer the door, and he asked the neighbors, but they didn't know anything, nothing like this had ever happened before, because Herr Köhler was the image of punctuality itself, Florian didn't want to disturb him on Friday or on the weekend or even at the beginning of the next week, but he could hardly wait for Thursday to come around again, and truly he could hardly wait, on the other hand, in the meantime, he'd made his trip to Berlin, so that it was only the following Thursday when he pressed the doorbell again, and nothing, Herr Köhler did not come out to open the door, he pressed it a few more times, he could tell it was functioning because he heard the ringing inside, but still nothing, the neighbor from across the way called out: Herr Köhler isn't at home, we haven't seen him in ages, that was Frau Schneider, who was immediately corrected by Frau Burgmüller hanging out of her window as well: ah, don't listen to that old lady, she doesn't know anything about this, because I tell you, young man, there has been no sign of life from Herr Köhler for exactly thirteen days, well, that's enough already, Frau Schneider contradicted her, what do you mean thirteen days, it's been at least three weeks, dear neighbor, and they argued about this for a while, in any event, Florian did not stick around to see what decision they reached, slowly, his head bent, he slipped away from Oststraße to wherever his feet might take him, sadly, because the suspicion had arisen in him that there might be some connection between the visit Herr Köhler had paid to his apartment and Herr Köhler not being at home, and from here it was not difficult, sitting on his bench on the banks of the Saale where he had fled, to reach the conclusion that the whole thing was because of him: Herr Köhler no longer wished to see him, that was the only explanation, and of course the neighbors hadn't seen him, because Herr Köhler himself had good reason not to come outside, because not only was he not opening the door, but he must be reproaching himself for having misled Florian, which was not true, absolutely it wasn't true, Florian shook his head bitterly beneath the larger of the two chestnut trees, and he watched the light breaking on the foam of the rapids of the Saale, no one had misled him, Florian shook his head again, he had merely filtered out the lesson from everything that he had learned from Herr Köhler, and he had filtered it out by himself, and now he was responsible for everything: for how Herr Köhler wasn't updating his website, how he wasn't opening his door to Florian, and therefore presumably not to anyone, it pained Florian to know that all of this was happening because of him, but now there was nothing he could do, this is how it was, Herr Köhler had tried, futilely, to hold him back, but Florian did not have to be held back, namely it wasn't Florian who had to be held back but the catastrophe which was just as likely to ensue as not, and that is what drove a person crazy, and he was certain that it was this completely extraordinary peril and his own awakening to it that had

led Herr Köhler to sever his connection with the world, because apart
from the fact that he was not updating his website, Herr Köhler did not
come out of his house either the next day or the day after that; and now
Florian, once the workday was finished and he was back in Kana, always hurried over to Herr Köhler's house and pressed the doorbell,
and the doorbell was still working, but nothing, and the two female
neighbors diagonally across the street no longer said even a word to
him, they just looked at each other, shaking their heads, knowingly
silent, continuing to stare at Florian like two people who sympathized
with how he wasn't being let in, but they didn't call out to him that
Herr Köhler wasn't at home, they didn't say anything, because what
would be the point, they only nodded their heads slightly, then after
Florian left, they came out in front of their respective houses, and Frau
Schneider shook her head: impossible for Herr Köhler to leave the
house without their knowledge, that could not happen, Frau Burgmüller, however, was of the opinion that one had to speak of a disappearance here, absolutely not, her neighbor retorted angrily, she had been
living in this town long enough to know everything about everyone,
and our dear neighbor has not and has not left his house, and Florian,
although he took no part in this debate, would have sided with Frau
Burgmüller, because he kept thinking: what if Herr Köhler was put
under so much strain by this whole thing that he decided to abandon
his Private Weather Station and simply left, meaning that Florian
would no longer be able to ask him questions, because clearly this too
was oppressing him, if it hadn't always been oppressing him, and the
tension had increased to such a point where a person might justifiably
consider that with a departure, a change of circumstances, making a
move away from something, he could beat the whole thing out of his
head, only that how could you beat something out of your head in this
way, how could anyone forget, even for a moment, what might happen:
the world could disappear at any moment, Florian was so certain that

he saw things correctly that, when he caught the Intercity in Halle, and, after an agonizing journey, arrived at the Hauptbahnhof and studied a map of Berlin to figure out how to get to the Reichstag, until that point, every word he was planning to utter was in its place, he had sought out these words and practiced them so as to not feel ashamed in front of the Chancellor, although perhaps, standing in front of the map at the Hauptbahnhof, he should have seemed anxious or uncertain, or at least somewhat hesitant, but he was neither anxious nor uncertain, and especially not hesitant, he knew exactly what he wanted, whom he wished to convey his realizations to and where, and that is why he did not adequately consider that in this capital city with its horrific tumult, he might lose his way, although he did not lose his way, in addition the map clearly told him that he was very close to the Reichstag, he could even go there on foot, so he went there on foot, setting off along the banks of the Spree, hurrying across the Kronprinzenbrücke and he continued walking along on the other bank of the Spree, very soon he arrived at the Reichstag, he gaped at the enormous cupola on the roof of the building and the tiny people strolling about here and there on the various levels, he got mixed up in various Asian and non-Asian tourist groups, then he extricated himself, this was frightening, so many people at once, even though, he reflected with appreciation, there's nothing like that in our town, nor in Jena, moreover, not even in Dresden, this is Berlin of course, and he was proud to see all of this, but he only allowed himself this pride for a moment—for the duration of that moment he forgot his reason for having come here—and after this momentary forgetfulness, he could only think that very soon he would be tasked with personally recounting everything that he hadn't been able to fully convey in his letters, he saw that clearly now, as he stood here facing the Reichstag, he saw this much more clearly than he had at home when he had decided to come here and the reason for this sudden clarity was the Reichstag itself, he saw the Reichstag and immediately realized that his letters he sent were not worth even a farthing, his letters had not delineated his aims clearly enough, he even mentioned this to the security guard as he entered the building having waited at the end of a long line, he asked the security guard to tell him where he could find Chancellor Merkel, and seeing the look of surprise on his face, he asked him to please reassure the Chancellor: this time he would explain everything he had said in his letters to her clearly; the security guard looked at him thoughtfully for a moment, wrinkled his eyebrows, and finally he turned away from him to order back a throng of schoolchildren who were going in the wrong direction, then once again he turned to Florian and he noted that today there was an open house in the Reichstag, yes, an open house, but not that open, although Florian did not allow the conversation to stray from the subject, he grabbed the security guard's arm, pulled him toward himself, and in a confidential voice, he told him that he was Herscht 07769, the Chancellor was expecting his arrival, he had written to her that he was coming at twelve noon, and now it was twelve noon, he pointed at his watch, and indeed the watch showed that it was nearly twelve noon, the security guard adjusted the ID card hanging from his neck, which moved just a hair's breadth as Florian grabbed his arm, then he said to Florian politely that the Chancellor wasn't here, she's not here? Florian asked, well, where is she? well, he didn't know, answered the security guard, therefore Florian would have to confer with someone else about how

the world was disappearing

but the security guard had no information about that, at which Florian, sensing from the congeniality in the security guard's voice and his eyes that here was a person sympathetic to himself and his cause, told him that when he'd identified himself as Herscht 07769, he'd wanted to convey that he came from Kana, Thuringia, but this was merely a determination of locale, because looking at it from another point of view, he had arrived from the world of particle physics, directly from there, he nodded at the security guard, and this was a serious affair, and swift action was called for, which was why he had traveled to Berlin by train with the earliest possible connection, at which the security guard motioned to Florian that he should follow him, and he led Florian as far as the steps, he pointed to the left, and he asked: do you see those stands at the edge of the park? well, yes, I see them, Florian answered uncertainly, you get something cold to drink there, and while you're at it, I'll try to find out where the Chancellor is, okay? do they have Jim Him raspberry soda? Florian inquired, maybe, the guard answered, alright then, Florian looked into his eyes with gratitude, and the encounter reminded him very much of when the Boss came to the Ranis Kinderheim for the first time and that had also been the very first time that someone had looked at him that way, because when the Boss was introduced to him—someone pointed out, yes, that's Florian—he immediately looked at him *that way*, and he wouldn't say, he would never say, that most of the carers at the Children's Home weren't well-meaning, for the most part they were well-meaning, but the way the Boss looked at him was different, the Boss looked at him the way a father looks at his son or an uncle looks at his nephew, no one else has that look in their eyes, Florian immediately sensed he was in good hands, we will clean walls, the Boss looked the boy up and down—Florian was a good two heads taller than he was with his enormous bone structure—as they set off from Jena to Kana, we will clean walls and everything else that your motherfucking peers are busy scrawling, graffiti aaaartists, well, of cooourse, the Boss dragged out the words sarcastically, and although Florian was shocked at the ugliness of the Boss's speech, he thought he would get used to it, and he did get used to it, after one month the words "fuck it" and "motherfucker" and "cock" and "shit" meant nothing, he didn't even hear them, it was as if he were hearing the words "and" and "well," they became words that he didn't even notice, who would grimace or even notice the words "and" or "well," no one, and of course Florian would hardly claim that everything in the Ranis Kinderheim was somehow bad or strange, not everything had been bad or strange, well, but when the Boss took him up to the seventh floor of the Hochhaus, and said to him: well, Florian, fuck it, this is your apartment, Florian nearly jumped around his neck, and the Boss could hardly protect himself from a show of gratefulness that nearly toppled him over to the floor, but he managed to peel off Florian's powerful arms, and said: but you have to work with me, work? Florian answered, his face beaming, I will work hard! and he did work hard, but in vain, because nothing was ever good enough for the Boss, even though Florian knew that he merely wished to raise him to learn that one can never do one's work well enough, it's a process, the Boss explained sometimes, you have to get better and better, because that's the tradition with us Germans, everything always better and better, so that Florian understood everything from the Boss as part of a training process where everything was always getting better and better, and he tried, the Boss was strict, but Florian mastered the trade pretty quickly, he could already tell from afar which graffiti had been sprayed with acrylics, oil paint, or felt-tip markers, he learned the ropes in a month or two, and he did what he had to, he always stood there in his workers' overalls, his Fidel Castro cap on his head, at the appointed time at the corner of Christian-Eckardt-Straße and Ernst-Thälmann-Straße to be picked up, as happened today as well, the Boss came for him exactly at seven thirty a.m., Florian got in the car, but then the Boss did not tell Florian: out with that fucking list already, instead he said that today we're going to Gotha, oh, said Florian, that's really far away, but the Boss didn't say anything, he just blew the cigarette smoke out of the half-opened window and he drove, he never let Florian drive, even though Florian had a driver's license, and that too was thanks to the Boss, he had signed him up for driving school in the first year, and he himself taught Florian how to do a three-point turn, how to park looking only in the rearview mirror, how to brake on winter roads, and things like that, but he never let him drive the Opel, you should get a car too one day, the Boss had mentioned only once, then we could go work in two different directions, but then he never mentioned it again, he didn't trust Florian to take care of even the simplest things by himself, although he should have, Florian had even told the Boss, when he helped him buy the laptop, that from now on he was saving his money for a car, then we can take on more work, he said, no we can't, said the Boss, because you are never going to drive me anywhere, you'd be the terror of the roads, you'd start daydreaming about the universe, and that would be it, already in the ditch, so that nothing ever came of the car nor of the Boss and Florian taking different routes, I have enough on my hands with this idiot child than to let him out by himself, the Boss said to the unit, of course, they'd end up coming for me, it would be all my fault, I know this, that's why I'm never going to let him drive even once in his goddamned motherfucking life, and that was the end of the story with the car, and to tell the truth, Florian wasn't so troubled by this because he was afraid even when sitting in the Opel passenger seat, although he never admitted it, he was afraid of how the Boss tailgated the cars in front of them, how he suddenly braked, he was convinced that one day they were going to crash into someone or another car would slam into them from behind, just as he feared that now too, because that's how the Boss was driving again, everyone getting in his way, it was clear he'd be very happy to run over every single vehicle in front of them on the road heading to Gotha, but the Boss didn't say why they were going to Gotha, and Florian himself couldn't figure out why when they arrived and parked by the Schloß and the Boss didn't even comment on the impudence of such a high rate for one hour of parking or anything although he usually grumbled whenever they had to put money into the parking meter, the Boss walked over to the Schloßkirche but didn't go inside, instead he circled the building, slowly, continually looking around, always turning around to double-check on Florian trotting along behind him; Florian tried to get the Boss's attention in case the Boss might reveal what they were doing here if it wasn't for a cleaning job, but the Boss continued to say nothing and explain nothing, he just kept puffing away on his cigarette, sometimes he sniffed, took some photos with his cell phone from one angle, then from another angle, then he motioned for Florian to get back to the car, Florian got in, the Boss went over to the parking meter, and as there was still some time left, he pressed a button to try to get some change back, but of course nothing came out, so there was nothing left for him to do but to slam that parking meter once, good and hard, already they were back on the A4, and the Boss was still not too talkative, just pressing on the gas like a madman, braking like a crazy man, yelling out the window: goddamned motherfucker, have you got fucking eyes?! and that was it, he wouldn't say anything else, although he could have said something, at least Florian was waiting, in every moment, for the situation to be cleared up, but nothing was cleared up, because once again the Boss shared his thoughts only with the comrades, although in this case he was unusually tight lipped, because he suspected that the next attack would be in Gotha; and he was wrong, because for the next two nights the unit stood guard in Gotha but in vain, the Boss's hunches are misleading him, Jürgen noted as they headed back to Kana, not bothering to conceal the scorn in his voice, of course he didn't dare mock the Boss in his presence but only before they all sat down together in their usual spot at the Aral gas station to have a smoke and a cup of coffee, the coffee was hot and on this occasion was especially tasty; Nadír always said to her husband: the customers don't pay attention to price, but if the coffee beans are well roasted then they will come, and she was right, there were many who didn't even tank up here but only came for the coffee, news began to get around that the coffee at Nadír's was good, so that they even had a neon sign made, ordering it with the permission of Aral, and it blinked: COFFEE ONLY AT NADÍR'S, sometimes they asked Nadír—mainly

Jürgen, his tongue poking at the gap where the eyetooth used to be—what is the secret of your coffee, it's so good, but her husband, Rosario, was immediately standing right next to her, because he knew it wasn't the coffee that was being praised, but that they were flirting with Nadír, and he, Rosario, was not going to let that happen, he was known to be jealous, which only increased the prestige of his wife, people in both trucks and cars came from the east and the west and the north and the south, and they all tried their luck with Nadír, but Rosario was sharp, he had a sixth sense, as he called it, always sensing the seducer in someone, always sensing the danger, the comrades agreed, huddling together, and they laughed behind Rosario's back if, on the weekends, he got together with them to play foosball in the Rosengarten, the constant jealousy could have gotten on a person's nerves, but it didn't get on Nadír's nerves; if her girlfriends asked, in the Herbstcafé, how she could stand Rosario, she just shrugged her shoulders and replied: I really don't mind, you know, because at least I know I still mean something to men from two different directions, at which laughter broke out, and always, if they were talking about this, her girlfriends looked at her appreciatively as someone who held her own while they suspected that her situation couldn't be so rosy, because out of all of their husbands, this Rosario was the most enervating, not to mention his small rounded beer belly hanging down inertly into his lap, not even disguised by the T-shirts or the untucked long-sleeved shirts he always wore hanging out, nothing covered it up although he was visibly ashamed, while Nadír was radiant in every moment, possessing a kind of animallike, irresistible sensuality, she was radiant when she brought the coffee to a table in the small garden buffet next to the gas station, and she made Florian, who frequently came to help out in the buffet, decisively embarrassed, and Nadír enjoyed this a little bit because she had thought this Goliath of Kana, as she and her husband sometimes called Florian, would be so utterly distant from thinking about her *in that way*, Florian spoke only with her husband, Rosario, whenever he got a message in his postbox and he came over to the gas station to do some work, loading or painting or chopping down a tree, usually he worked with Rosario as the latter mainly needed his strength as a helper, and he himself had no time for small talk while working, but afterward, Rosario always sat Florian down and gave him whatever he wanted to eat and drink, well, my friend, he would say to him at such times, here you can eat and drink whatever you want, and as a tasty sandwich or a special syrup materialized in front of Florian, Rosario was already telling an interesting story, and he kept telling it and telling it, he liked to tell stories and he was a good storyteller, stories either about his family or Brazil, and Florian listened as if Rosario were really telling him a fairy tale, namely he loved Rosario, Rosario living on the perimeter of local society, just as he did, clearly might have played a role in this, so that the strong sense of togetherness existing between them came easily, a sense of togetherness which neither one felt toward their other Kana connections, in addition to which Rosario greatly appreciated not only Florian's oxlike strength, but how he didn't shy away from hard work, he was persistent and thorough, Rosario greatly praised this, and he never let Florian leave without paying him something, Florian made excuses in vain, saying that all the tasty food he'd been offered was more than enough payment, still, depending on the nature of the work, Rosario stuffed either a ten- or even a twenty-euro note into Florian's overalls pocket, and after a while Nadír sensed that her beauty made Florian embarrassed, so that when he was working at the gas station, she tended to leave him alone with her husband, but when she placed a sandwich or a soft drink in front of him, she couldn't stop herself from smiling, and although this smile was merely a sign of her gentleness, Florian immediately began staring at the floor, and he thanked her, still staring at the floor, because Nadír was beautiful, and her smile made her even more beautiful, no one could escape the influence of that smile, Jürgen was the first one in the unit to fall for her, although he didn't talk about this: because of Karin, sex was a prohibited theme in the unit, but it was very clear that he had fallen for Nadír if only from how he ran his tongue along the place of the missing eyetooth whenever she appeared with the coffee, or when it was cold outside, and inside at the counter, she smiled at Jürgen and asked: what can I get you? and Jürgen could hardly stammer out a word; Nadír and Rosario had been living in Kana since the old times, although most immigrants, after the Porcelain Factory had been forced to close, had left the town, and not only the town—they left Germany as well, *the Vietnamese are leaving*, that phrase was heard on the streets of Kana at the time of the changes, and although in the old days the word *Vietnamese* carried a negative connotation, when they left, the residents of Kana repeated this phrase with sincere regret, because at the time of the changes everything became different all at once, everything was emptied out, abandoned, sometimes one had the feeling there were only old and sick people tottering around on the streets, because not only had the Vietnamese left, any and every self-respecting local youth wishing to make something of themselves had taken off as well, and the only ones left behind were those who had nowhere else to go, and yet, what a pretty little town we have here in East Thuringia, people said sadly, and the situation didn't change when the houses began to be restored, and the Altstadt became more beautiful perhaps than it had ever been, after a while, beginning in May every year, tourist guides began showing up with this or that group, but they only took the visitors around to see the old buildings, in the best of cases they ate lunch at the Hopfs' restaurant, then they were gone, the tourist group was dragged onward to Jena or Erfurt or most often to Weimar; in winter, the Hopfs' restaurant was completely shut down, we're closing, Frau Hopf told this or that hotel guest in the Garni, we only open at the beginning of the season, partially so that we'll have something to keep us busy in our old age, partially because our pensions aren't so much, we need this little bit of extra income, and the guests just nodded in agreement, what could they have done, they understood the Hopfs, for the most part they came to spend one or at the most two evenings on the weekends to visit their adult children who were studying in Jena but living here in Kana, in the vicinity of Jena, that is to say nineteen kilometers from Jena, as it's much cheaper here, they told Frau Hopf, much cheaper, even if the poor child had to go in to Jena to university every day and come back again, of course Frau Hopf understood, how wouldn't she know what these expenses meant? she nodded, serving tea or coffee to her guests, depending on what they wanted for breakfast, with a lovely smile, Florian knew the Hopfs very well, because in the peak season they often asked him to help with unloading supplies on delivery days, and of course he was happy to help them, he particularly was fond of Frau Hopf, because Frau Hopf was always sympathetic, her husband was as well, but he was quieter, perhaps because he was ill, and therefore he did not converse too much either with the guests or with Florian, only if, for example, some delivery came in, and he marveled again and again, saying: Florian, you, how can you carry all of the boxes and crates *all at once?!* and Florian didn't understand what all this amazement was about, because these few boxes and crates *all at once* were hardly a drop in the bucket for him, he stacked them quite nicely one atop the other and brought them in, Frau Hopf always gave Florian lunch or breakfast, whether he was hungry or not he had to have lunch or breakfast, such a big strapping young man as yourself has to eat, otherwise you'll go to rack and ruin, said Frau Hopf, and she smiled, Florian liked that smile, and he liked it when Frau Hopf burst out laughing, and Frau Hopf liked to laugh, and Florian told her what was going on in Thuringia, that someone was disfiguring buildings connected to the great composer Johann Sebastian Bach, with hideous graffiti, at which Frau Hopf lowered her voice, indicating, with a movement of her head toward somewhere outside, and only said, looking into Florian's blue eyes: Nazis, and Florian understood what that meant, namely that Frau Hopf was indicating the residents of Burg-straße 19, the Burg, where the Boss went every weekend, and of course Florian made no reply, he regretted having said anything at all, and he no longer mentioned, to Frau Hopf or anyone else, anything about what was going on in Thuringia with the great composer, although he would have had things to talk about because now it was December, with snow falling in the mountains on this or that morning, when Flo-rian understood from the Boss's behavior that the sprayer had struck again, the Boss once again was acting different than usual, because he wasn't banging on the steering wheel but instead blowing out the ciga-rette smoke through the window wordlessly, and although he made Florian sing the national anthem, he stared fixedly at the road, and his facial muscles made it seem as if he were continually and rhythmically chewing on something although there was nothing in his mouth, the Boss never chewed gum, he hated chewing gum, and only Florian knew why, it was because he had dentures where his upper row of teeth should have been: when he was young, the Boss had once revealed to Florian, when he was still a boxer, his upper teeth were knocked out; the protector had fallen out, so he lost all his most important teeth, and that's why he never chewed gum so that the gum wouldn't inadver-tently pull down this upper prosthesis, but the Boss never told anyone else about this, only Florian, the unit had no idea, they only knew that the Boss didn't like chewing gum, and that was all, Florian finished singing the national anthem, then he squinted at the Boss, but the Boss was motionless, not speaking a word, until he told the unit: it seems like the little Vaseline King came back to Eisenach, but what we don't know is what he wanted, he must have been interrupted; and the in-dignation was general, let's go, said Karin, we're going, said Andreas and Jürgen and Gerhard and everyone—where?! the Boss looked at them in rage, where are we going?! and now he was yelling, are you really all such idiots?! I already told you that we must get *ahead of him*, not *behind him*!! he explained, and he gestured in resignation like someone who was thinking how he had to repeat this to them yet again although to no avail; they weren't getting anywhere because they couldn't figure out what this scumbag was thinking, the problem is that we can't figure out how he thinks, said the Boss, rubbing his face with his open palms as if trying to wake himself up, to somehow wake up to the solution of this problem, because this was the problem: we don't understand why he's doing this, the Boss continued, until now we only wanted to get him, and we weren't thinking, and now we have to start thinking, got it?! and everyone nodded, but they didn't look too much as if they were thinking, or as if a solution were about to spring out of their heads, it did not spring out, and the Boss saw, as he looked them over, that he wasn't going to get anywhere with these ones, he needed more people, he wrapped up the discussion for that day, knocked back his beer, and left the others without a word, sat down in the Opel, and went home, he locked the gate, let the dog off the chain, went into the house, sat down in front of his laptop, lit up a cigarette, and then blew out the smoke, slowly, he watched the smoke drifting upward, then, supporting his bald head in his two hands, he thought; but the day had been long, because then he suddenly started awake, his head was resting on the laptop, the cigarette had gone out, still there between his two fingers, he stubbed it out, staggered over to the bed, and flung himself down still fully clothed, and on that day he thought no more but slept deeply until morning, he had not slept so well for a long time, he himself found it odd, but later on he attributed it to having posed the correct question, namely: why? and this was the key to the whole thing, this is what he thought, and he repeated it to himself that evening: the key to the whole thing—and, in view of the extraordinary situation, they no longer met up only on the usual days, but every single blessed day after finishing work, that is for the ones who were still employed, because Karin and Andreas were living off their Hartz IV benefits, and Jürgen worked as a cleaner but for starvation wages; if we can find an answer as to the why, the Boss continued, we'll get him right away, only one thing is certain, he continued to himself on the way home, these graffiti all connect up with Bach, therefore Bach not only signifies to him the need to defile the holiest of holies, but he is directly a Bach hater!! this drooling, pimple-faced, hoodie-wearing psychopath, and the Boss tried to find something—anything—in the lifework of Bach that could be connected to wolves, because he was not bothering with this WE, at least for now, only with those WOLF HEADS sprayed identically onto walls by that grimy-souled, shifty vermin, because not only did these WOLF HEADS all resemble each other, but they were all in fact exactly the same, as if he were using a stencil, sometimes these douchebags do use stencils, the Boss had seen that before, but before, it was always small-time crooks, inexperienced beginners, not real sprayers, but this one was the real deal, the Boss established, and in his torment, he scratched the steering wheel as he drove down Jenaische Straße to Bahnhofstraße, we're dealing with a professional here, that's for sure, he concluded, he's not even using a stencil but he's practiced this WOLF HEAD so many times that he can spray it over and over again, and clearly this was his plan in Eisenach, to respray what we cleaned off, he uses yellow and green and brown acrylics, that we know, the Boss enumerated to himself what they knew, he works in the pre-dawn hours, but the Boss stopped there, he braked in front of his house, but he didn't open the gate in order to drive in because he was sunk in thought, wondering how the sprayer could feel so safe, because even after the first desecration in Eisenach, it was as if this fingernail dirt was "working" in complete and total security, how was that possible? the Boss asked himself, sitting in the Opel in front of the gate, well, goddammit, it dawned upon him, because he isn't acting alone, he's not alone! not alone, that's it! and he unlocked the gate, he adjusted the sign hanging there that read: *Mein Haus, mein Hof, meine Tür, meine Regeln,* and he drove in, he locked the Opel, let the dog off the chain for the night, went into the house and sat down, then, circling around, swinging his fist into the air as he repeated: he's not alone, this is a well-organized criminal gang, and he repeated this the next evening in the Burg as well, when it turned out that he was the only one who had arrived at a conclusion via the act of thinking while the others had arrived at nothing, because this is a gang, he told them, and he jumped up, waving his cigarette in the air, we need more people, because he clearly has some kind of security backup, get it, he's a professional, and everyone agreed, a little relieved too, because at first this seemed to absolve them and explain their lack of success, it was all because he was so hard to catch, and so, said the Boss, his face turning red, we don't have to coordinate things from here, but locate our comrades on-site, understood?! yes, that's right, the others nodded, and there was no need for any further discussions, everyone understood what the Boss wanted, Florian too sensed the change, it was as if the Boss had become a completely different person, which made Florian even more curious, and he asked him about it, but only got this response: calm down already, fuck it, you'll find out in good time what concerns you, until then keep your trap shut, and Florian kept it shut, who could he even tell what he had no idea of, because he couldn't even be completely certain that the Boss was thinking of the sprayer, that there had been some progress in the matter, so he asked no more questions, and anyway he had his own problems, his own personal crisis to deal with, as he had gotten thoroughly entangled in what had happened with Herr Köhler, namely he wasn't there, he's not here, Frau Ringer greeted Florian with these words every time she saw him in the library, and with an ever more uneasy gaze, as she looked at Florian almost accusingly, and Florian himself did not find this to be unwarranted, so that once back at home he pulled out yet another piece of paper to write a new letter to Angela Merkel in Berlin in which once again he would, of course, urge the full exoneration of Herr Köhler: please understand, Mrs. Chancellor, if, recognizing the grave import of this matter, you have decided to entrust it to the National Security Agency—evidently, this has occurred—therefore, Florian wrote, he now appealed to her to instruct the National Security Agency to leave Herr Köhler completely out of the matter, namely he, and only he himself, Herscht 07769, was responsible for those waves stirred up by his own missives; only he himself, and not Herr Köhler, and he could only repeat that Herr Köhler was responsible for nothing, because he, Herscht 07769, had arrived at his conclusions entirely on his own, and moreover, he reiterated, in the explicit absence of Herr Köhler's approval, namely Herr Köhler had directly repudiated the correctness of his, Florian's, conclusions, wishing only to protect him, only that no one could be protected from the consequences, consequences which could be confronted only by the means of a decision planetary in its scope, because this was the issue now, about facing up to it, facing the fact that the world arose by sheer contingency, and that sheer contingency could just as easily take it back, this was something that science was obviously not clever enough to comprehend, because here it was necessary to approach the starting point of a frighteningly unknown process, which was impossible, its inconceivably horrifying content only designated and labeled by the term Big Bang Theory, but that conveyed nothing about it, neither mathematics nor physics, and especially not cosmology, could do so, science is troubled, jittery, and—most horrendously of all: it is either mute or merely continues to natter away, but if we do not understand this, if we do not take some action in reference to the entire Earth to counter this fact, then we have lost, then we can simply wait for the end of the world, the universe, the whole, the Something, and we shall perish, but there is no need to wait for apocalypse, for we must understand—Florian wrote to Chancellor Angela Merkel in Berlin—that apocalypse is the *natural* state of life, the world, the universe, and of the Something, the apocalypse is now, Mrs. Chancellor, this is what we have been living in for billions of years and in comparison to the Beginning it is nothing, and with that Florian concluded his letter, certain of the fact that he would not have to wait long for Mrs. Chancellor's reply, but until that point, Florian wrote, he implored Mrs. Merkel to *implement the necessary measures* for the release of Herr Köhler, but Herr Köhler was not released, just as no reply from Mrs. Merkel arrived, Jessica took no heed now of Florian as he posted this most recent letter, then when he kept stopping by to see if there was an answer, they got used to him in the post office on Roßstraße: there was morning, there was evening, there was airmail, there was registered mail, and there was Florian with his question as to whether any mail had come bearing the name of Herscht, and Frau Schneider also mentioned to Frau Burgmüller that this Herscht child no longer came to visit their lovely neighbor, as they called Herr Köhler when talking among themselves, and not at all like the others who called him "Herr Weatherman" and suchlike, how very disrespectful, Frau Schneider stated, and Frau Burgmüller exceptionally agreed with her, because if anyone knew how decent a man Herr Köhler was, it was they who did, both considered him an excellent neighbor, namely a good neighbor is a true blessing, and in particular such a gentleman as Herr Köhler, for him they could only speak words of praise: how he always greeted them, and how, on International Women's Day, he never failed to call out a few pleasant words to them in the window, and how—only once, but still—he allowed them into his courtyard so they could admire one of his new instruments, the news of which had also somehow reached them—a true gentleman, well, Frau Schneider adjusted a former lock of hair on her forehead, but only a former lock as in accordance with the demands of the modern age she had long ago had her hair cut short; and clearly an educated person, Frau Burgmüller did her one better, and they left it at that, then they tried to figure out where

Herr Köhler might have gone, and here Frau Burgmüller's opinion triumphed, in this subject there was no longer any point of contention between them: the dear neighbor is not in his home, impossible for him to have stayed inside for so long, he must have left at night while they were sleeping, for example, there's the 23:46 to Jena, Frau Burgmüller suggested, he could have taken that to visit one of his relatives, at midnight? the other woman retorted, I very much doubt it, and they gossiped about the matter for a while yet, but did not agree on which train or bus Herr Köhler might have left on, only upon the fact that he had left and that there was no one in the house, and they were not too happy about that, just as they were not too happy that Florian no longer came by, not on Thursdays or any other day, clearly he knew something about this, the two neighbors agreed, although Florian knew nothing about this, he knew nothing, he only saw in the Herbstcafé that Herr Köhler's website wasn't being updated, so that from one day to the next he was becoming ever more worried, tortured by ghastly images in which he saw Herr Köhler sitting in a cell or in an examining room where light was being shone into his eyes, and these torturous images began to appear even more frequently after one Tuesday when he saw two men in civilian clothes waiting for him in the park in front of the Hochhaus, two men chatting with the Deputy, then when the Deputy saw Florian, he gestured to the two men, that's him over there, and one of the men came over and stood in front of Florian: we have some questions, could you spare us a bit of time? and they said they had come from Erfurt, of course, said Florian, suspecting the worst, then he took them up to the seventh floor, gave them each a glass of water, waited for their wheezing to calm down, and then he posed the first question: is this about Herr Köhler?!—look, one of the men answered, no, we're interested in you, yes, yes, but how is Herr Köhler? who is this Herr Köhler? they asked, well, never mind, they said, brushing Florian's questions aside, and it turned out that they wanted to know if he had been alone when he had sought out Mrs. Merkel in the Reichstag, if he had written his letters alone, and what he wanted from Mrs. Merkel, and Florian reassured them, and they ended up talking for a long time, the two men asked questions and Florian answered, and that was it, they knew nothing about Herr Köhler, or at least they claimed to know nothing, namely Florian was interested in nothing else, so that they left and he was none the wiser as to where Herr Köhler was, where he was being held, or anything at all, Florian felt very despondent, he didn't even go down to Ilona's to have dinner as he usually did if Ilona's buffet was open, although it wouldn't have hurt, because now, when he was facing such difficult times, those part-time asphalt workers, pensioners, and people on Hartz IV benefits, all of whom he had known for years, all regular customers who turned up at Ilona's every day for a beer, would have distracted him; Ilona, with her husband, had converted a mobile home into a buffet in such a way that you could even sit down inside: there was a counter, a shelf, three benches and three chairs, with a funny sign hanging on the inside of the door that read *Militärgebiet-Lebensgefahr*, and on the roof of the trailer was a sign, GRILLHÄUSEL, it wasn't much, but for the regular customers the friendly atmosphere was more than enough, and the buffet stood in front of the Baumarkt, diagonally across from the Hochhaus, Florian need only to take just a few steps and he could have found himself in company where there was always someone to cheer up the mood, that's why it was good at Ilona's, especially with that Hoffmann who worked a four-hour warehouse shift in the Porcelain Factory, he was regarded as the chief joke master on duty, he only had two jokes, but they always met with success, exactly because the regulars already knew them so well, and Hoffmann was always particularly glad to tell one of them when someone strayed into Ilona's for a Bockwurst, and Hoffmann, seeing a new customer, began with great enthusiasm: listen here—he jumped into the middle of the room and pointed at the floor—this is London, got it? and this is the Thames, got it, yes? on the left bank there is a tree, and Hoffmann pointed at where the tree was, and on the right bank there is a tree, and he pointed at the second tree, and here is my question: what's in the middle? and of course the stranger had no idea, to the greatest joy of the regulars, at which point Hoffmann gestured to him: well, it's not so difficult, just pay attention, I'll tell you one more time: this here is London, and he pointed at the floor again, and this here's the Thames, and on the left bank there's a tree, on the right bank there's a tree, what's in the middle? and of course by now the stranger was completely flummoxed, the regulars laughed loudly, relishing Hoffmann with his red-splotched face and how he always tried to bamboozle someone with the same gusto, and he always succeeded, which visibly made him, Hoffmann, very happy, the mood at Ilona's was at its highest point, another round of beers was ordered, and of course Florian was always able to forget about whatever was weighing on him or holding his thoughts captive at that moment, and that was precisely why he didn't go down to Ilona's right now, because he did not want to not be weighed down, to not be held prisoner by how the two men in civilian clothes hadn't been willing to betray anything about Herr Köhler, although Florian suspected that they knew everything, it never occurred to him that they didn't, he was certain Herr Köhler had been taken away, just as he was certain that Herr Köhler had been taken away because of him, he had no idea of how to remedy what he had done, he didn't know how to get Herr Köhler released; surely, more than anyone else, it was he who knew that Herr Köhler was completely innocent, and that they—whoever they were—must release him, because the one who should not be released was he, Florian, and it wouldn't even be a problem, because then Herr Köhler himself could finally return, and Florian himself would be closer to those individuals who could act in this matter of great interest to him, if they had not done so already; Florian was unsure on this point, his interpretation of having received no replies to his letters depended, for the most part, on the kind of day he was having, although in any event something was certainly going on up there, they'd taken notice of him and what he had to say, and it was also possible—Florian entertained this thought sometimes—that the silence in Berlin indicated precisely that he, namely Florian, had accomplished his mission, and now others were in charge, yes, yes, that was highly possible, and at such times he saw, in his mind's eye, with almost complete clarity, that enormous conference table at the UN Security Council; on the table there lay an equally enormous dossier, and it was HIS DOSSIER, because he was convinced that Angela Merkel, the Chancellor of the Federal Republic of Germany, the most powerful woman in the world, had immediately understood what he'd been trying to convey to her, Mrs. Merkel was very intelligent, and if someone had, at one point, studied physics the way that Mrs. Merkel had, he was completely certain, if she had studied it, then there could be no doubt that she'd immediately understood and had immediately taken action, in addition to which there was her husband who was also a scientist, this was even printed in the *Ostthüringer Zeitung*, and the picture appeared before him as Mrs. Merkel and her husband discussed the matter at home, well, what do you say, Mrs. Merkel was asking, well, I'm not sure, her husband answered, then, after brief reflection he added: it is certain that this matter must be dealt with, because we must not underestimate the danger; Florian pictured the entire scene as taking place more or less like this, but Berlin was silent, and he was standing there in front of the Boss who told him after work—they had finished very early that day—that no, we're not going home yet, you're coming with me, and he sat next to the Boss in the Opel, and they parked by the Aral gas station, because they were going to leave from there later on, Florian kept seeking out Rosario's gaze, because hitherto he'd always come by himself to the Aral gas station, and now he had arrived here with the entire unit as if he were one of them, but no, he was only there because of the Boss, he tried to somehow convey this to Rosario through his facial expression but he couldn't because Rosario was avoiding his gaze, namely Florian didn't care that no one had told him where they were going and why, the unit members were now conversing among themselves in their jargon, smoking cigarettes and drinking coffee, the Boss paid for Florian's coffee, and when Florian wanted to thank him, the Boss waved his hand, irritated, for him to leave it, no point in niceties, and he gestured urgently for Florian to drink up because they had to go already, and so they left, heading first on the B88 to Weimar, then on the A4, then at Gelmeroda, they turned at the road leading into the city, the Boss making turns here and there, finally parking in front of a house, he motioned silently to Florian to follow, the Boss rang the bell at the house, an older man wearing a dressing gown came out, his head covered with tattoos, but everywhere, his chin, his forehead, the crown of his head and both ears, Florian could not look at anything else, only at the tattoos on this chin, this forehead, the crown of his head and those ears, the Boss kept on talking about something for a long time, the man listened in silence, stock still, only nodding at the end and as they were leaving, and he accompanied them to the gate of the house, he shook each of their hands once, indicating that he understood, his handshake was strong but his hand was very sweaty, Florian kept wiping his hand off on his overalls until they got into the car, and by the time he was about to ask something, they were already standing in front of another building, and this too was a Hochhaus, only it had more stories than the one Florian lived in, they rang the bell, somebody asked who it was, the Boss answered, I'll be right there, came the reply, and this time it was a young guy standing in the doorway, let's go over there to the park, it's better there, he said quietly to the Boss, okay, answered the Boss, and they took a few steps in silence, they sat down on a bench at the end of the park in front of the apartment building, the only other person was a homeless man sleeping on another bench three benches away, Florian had the sense that the homeless man was about to fall off the bench, he's really lying on the edge, he pointed out to the Boss, and he indicated the homeless man with a movement of his head, shut up, the Boss said to him out of the corner of his mouth, whereupon of course Florian shut up, he too saw that there were more important things going on here, it was only that he was fairly anxious for the homeless man not to fall off the bench: if somehow he turned over onto his other side it was obvious he would fall, so that the entire time Florian was waiting tensely for when the man would try to turn over, and Florian decided he would jump over to the other bench and try to catch him, but the homeless man didn't move, he lay on the bench like someone who was never going to get up from there ever again, even in the car Florian couldn't get it out of his head, because he was certain that sooner or later the homeless man was going to turn over on his other side, and there would be nobody to catch him, this thought kept running through his head, and he didn't ask anything, although perhaps it would have been better if he had done so as it was obvious that a conversation about a very important and secret matter had been taking place—it has nothing to do with me, thought Florian, but in that he was mistaken, because not too long after that, when they turned out onto the Autobahn 4 leading out of Weimar, the Boss broke his silence, and he said: I hope you understood that you were my cover just now?! and that now you're part of a very significant deployment, deployment? Florian asked in wonderment, yes, fuck it, deployment, the Boss snarled at him, we can't wait any longer now, consider yourself initiated, we need every German patriot on our side, and you're a patriot, right?! and what could Florian say except for yes, he was a patriot, fine then, the Boss concluded, then Florian had to sing the national anthem, the Boss once again fell silent, clearly immersed in his own thoughts, and on the B88 they rear-ended an old Škoda, Florian didn't really see what had happened, it was so quick, only that both he and the Boss were thrust forward, both of their heads knocking violently against the windshield, while the quickly released airbags pressed them back into their seats and the seat belts tightened across their chests, well, fuck it, that's all we needed, the Boss scrambled out of the car, he walked over to the driver who was examining the back of his Škoda, and he knocked him down with one blow, then gave a good kick to the face of the person lying on the ground, then as if nothing particular had happened, he strolled back to the Opel, sat down, switched on the ignition, and already they were on their way, you think I'm waiting for the cops or what?! he snarled to himself, and really he seemed like someone who didn't give a fuck about the whole thing, I don't give a fuck, the Boss noted later on when Florian asked if that man might have gotten hurt? and so of course Florian shut his mouth again as he had no desire to get hit himself—he was hit, but it was only a slap on his neck for not paying attention, because of course the incident had shaken him up and he hadn't realized that the Boss, for a while now, had been talking to him, what's the point of me talking to you if you keep zoning out, but, but, but I'm paying attention, Florian nodded, and really from that point on he did pay attention, and he learned from the Boss that drivers like that should all be lined up in a row and shot in the head, because they don't watch the road, they brake and don't even give a fuck that I'm right behind them, those cheeky goddamned motherfuckers should croak exactly where they are, why does anyone like that even get into a car?! well?! why?! and since Florian didn't reply, the Boss supplied the answer: well, fuck it, it's so that I can rear-end that motherfucker, but that numbskull got what was coming to him, he'll never brake in front of me on a right-hand turn ever again, people like that deserve the stake, and a Škoda to boot, do you know what a Škoda is, do you Florian?! it's one big pile of shit, *that's* what a Škoda is, fuck it, they stole our German VW, and now they flash along here

104

with their one hundred and fifty kmh, let them flash, but then it'll be the end, a knockout, because that asshole deserved it, all those assholes deserve it, because what am I going to do now with the front bumper, that piece of scum nearly smashed up my radiator with his rear hatch, you know how much a radiator like that costs?—Florian didn't know, and once again his attention strayed, he let the Boss keep on talking, as he knew from experience that if the Boss somehow made a mistake— because now he had made a mistake—he would just smear it all on the Škoda driver, this was clear, and Florian was precisely aware that the Boss was also precisely aware of this, and that's why he was so angry, but never mind, at times like this Florian could disconnect, because the Boss would just keep on talking and talking and talking until he finally calmed down, at the most he would get a slap and that was it, they turned onto Ernst-Thälmann-Straße, stopped in front of the house, Florian got out, he opened the gate, the Opel rolled in, Florian closed the gate, then he stood there for a bit in case the Boss needed him for anything else, but the Boss switched on a pocket flashlight as dusk had already started to fall, and he was examining the front of the car and sizing up the damage to the radiator, the dog was barking, pulling on its chain, well, I'll be off now, Florian called in through the gate, and as he received no answer, he quietly slunk home, because it turned out, when he opened up his postbox, that he had more than enough to deal with, as firstly, Frau Ringer had left him a message saying that she wanted to speak with him immediately, and secondly, there was also a message from Frau Hopf saying she needed his help, and thirdly the Deputy had also tossed a slip of paper into the mailbox instructing Florian to come find him right away because it was IMPORTANT!! no matter what time!!! that was written on the piece of paper, and so now what should Florian do first? his watch showed five p.m. and eleven minutes, I'll go down to old Friedrich, and he rang his bell, well, at last you've come, the Deputy greeted him, come in and sit down, oh, I can't, Florian tried to find an excuse, so they stood in the doorway, as, leaning in very close, the Deputy said: you better watch out for yourself, because those ones—you know whom I'm talking about—well, the matter is fairly serious, and I'm an experienced person, and you know that I wish you no harm, so you best pay good attention to what I'm about to say, because I'm saying that you better watch out, because those men from Erfurt aren't joking around, I know them from the old times, and they're the same as they ever were, I'm an experienced person, in a word, better for you to take my advice, and my advice is this, whatever it is that you've got yourself mixed up in, get yourself out of it right away, because those men aren't joking around, they'll throw the book at you, then you can see for yourself, they'll destroy you for a lifetime if they want to, I'm speaking frankly, fine, I understand, Florian nodded, and slowly he began to edge toward the exit, raising both his hands to show that yes, he took this seriously, and he would follow the Deputy's advice if necessary, but he had to go now, and for the most part this is also what he heard from Frau Ringer when he reached her in the library, oh, I've been waiting for you, she said, and she sighed, and for a while she simply looked at Florian until it became uncomfortable that she was looking at him for so long without speaking, listen here, Florian, I know you as someone who always has spoken very honestly with me, tell me, do you really not know anything about Herr Köhler? no, no, no, he said, but Frau Ringer raised both her hands for him not to answer immediately, sit down here, and think well before you answer, and Florian sat down on a small bench in front of the checkout counter, and he thought, and then he said that he didn't know what Frau Ringer could have in mind, have in mind, have in mind, she replied in irritation, you know very well what I have in mind, but it still wasn't clear to Florian what she could possibly want from him, although once he understood, he stated that he had no direct involvement with the fact that Herr Köhler was nowhere to be found, but he was almost too late, because Frau Ringer interrupted him curtly: you were thinking for too long, you're not being fully sincere with me, isn't that so? and Florian didn't know what to say, because, well, of course I'm being sincere, he said, only I don't know what it is you need from me, and I don't know what to say, so please, whatever it is you need to know, you can calmly ask me, but Frau Ringer was not in the least capable of asking calmly, because she posed the question: were you not at Herr Köhler's even before you stated he was not at home, based upon the fact that he didn't answer the door? when was I there? I don't understand, Florian shook his head, I asked you—Frau Ringer looked at him more sternly than ever before—if you were at Herr Köhler's before you stated to me that he did not answer the door to you? well, of course I was there, I went there every Thursday, and the last Thursday as well, and after that Herr Köhler came to my place, to your place? when? Frau Ringer asked, astonished, yes, Florian continued, Herr Köhler came to my place, he had never been in my apartment before, and I was really happy, only that he got really out of breath climbing up the stairs, because for a while now the elevator hasn't been working, and our Deputy, too, several times ... stop! Frau Ringer stopped him, don't get off topic, Herr Köhler came to see you in the Hochhaus? why, for the love of god? well, it was to convince me not to think about what I was thinking about, what are you thinking of? well, that the world is going to come to an end,

the silence in Berlin

and are you sure that Herr Köhler didn't say to you at that time that he was going somewhere? no, he didn't say anything like that, only that I shouldn't get him mixed up in my affairs, but you did get him properly mixed up, Frau Ringer bowed her head sadly as if it were already the end of everything, although it wasn't the end yet, because the Boss told him: Florian, now our time has come, he said this a few days later after finishing work, once again much earlier than usual, when they had wrapped things up in Ilmenau, they didn't head back to Kana but instead drove toward Dornheim on the A71, the Boss drove straight to the Traukirche, he rang the bell at the Pfarramt, then spoke for a long time with the pastor, Florian waited a few steps behind them, but still, he heard precisely what they were speaking about, that namely for the protection of Thuringian values, in the following weeks, and perhaps in the following months, certain individuals would be patrolling the church at night, so that if the pastor experienced any unusual activity around the church, if he saw any unknown youths, he should immediately contact the Boss, day or night, here was his number, then they said goodbye to the pastor who, visibly distraught, withdrew into the Pfarramt, and they walked around the church, the Boss employing the same procedure as on previous occasions, looking around everywhere, taking photographs of the entrance from various distances and from the vantage point of various streets, from Am Angertor, Neue Straße, and Kirchgasse, but then they didn't leave Dornheim, but rang the bell of a certain Möller at an address by the Wolfsbach, a certain Möller, the Boss noted before he rang the bell, and he looked at Florian significantly, but this time Florian didn't hear what they were speaking about, because as soon as this certain Möller appeared, the Boss sent him to see what was on the menu at Poppitz's, but the Boss had misremembered in thinking that Poppitz's served lunch, because it was only a bakery, not a restaurant, but by the time Florian was able to tell him that the very most they could get was some bread or Apfelstrudel at Poppitz's, he and the Boss were already on Hauptstraße with the Opel, no problem, he shrugged his shoulders, and they turned onto the A71, we'll have lunch at home later, and this is what happened, they ate lunch at home just as they usually did, separately, the Boss went back to his place and had a cold lunch, which for the most part did not actually mean a cold meal but preserves warmed up in a can, whereas Florian went to Ilona's for a good Bockwurst and for the atmosphere which would do him some good before going out to his bench on the banks of the Saale, because he really had to do some serious thinking there about what on earth those strange questions of Frau Ringer's could have meant, and what could have been on her mind; somehow he felt as if an accusation were hanging over his head, a fully unfounded accusation instead of what he really could have been accused of, but all the same what he really had to consider right now was a plan of action to find Herr Köhler, because already on his way over there, walking along the little narrow street which passed alongside the Kleingarten-anlage on the way to the Saale and the sports fields, he had already decided that he was not going to stand idly by and observe passively, he himself was going to find him, and immediately he thought of Herr Köhler's friend, if anyone knew the whereabouts of Herr Köhler, then it would certainly be him, everyone who was close to Herr Köhler knew he was his best friend, and moreover since childhood, Dr. Tietz in Eisenberg, I'm going there, Florian decided, he looked at his watch, but it was already too late today, alright, then tomorrow, and that's what he did, that night he looked at the schedules in the Herbstcafé to see when the buses and trains were departing for Eisenberg and returning, then the next day after work he quickly shaved, because once again it was necessary, then he just managed to catch the 3:30 JES train to Jena Paradies, there he transferred to a bus, and exactly twenty stops later he arrived, and although he had never been in Eisenberg before, it was very easy to find Dr. Tietz because the first person who got off the bus with him immediately pointed at the building where Dr. Tietz had his practice, only that Dr. Tietz had left for the day already, that was the problem, but Florian wasn't going to give up so easily if he had already come this far, and he was lucky because Dr. Tietz resided where his practice was, so that Florian plucked up his courage and he rang the doorbell at the house, for a while nothing happened, and it was only after he had rung the doorbell for the third or fourth time that a little boy of six or seven years of age appeared and said that his papa wasn't home, when is he coming home, asked Florian, I don't know, the little boy answered cheerfully, making a buzzing sound perhaps imitating a motor, and then clumsily ran back inside, Florian could ponder what in the world he should do now, but there was no question that he would wait, if he got back late, that would be no problem, the last regional bus going back to Kana left Jena Paradies at 9:16, only he didn't know where to wait, there was nothing near the doctor's house on Richard-Wagner-Straße, if he went back to the bus station he wouldn't know if Dr. Tietz had returned home; but as Florian didn't have too much of a choice, he went back to the bus station where there wasn't anything much besides a vending machine, luckily he found enough change in his pocket to get a coffee and a sandwich in a cellophane packet, he sat down on one of the metal bars that served as a bench, and he waited; he decided that he would go back every half hour, but he couldn't wait that long, he kept going back earlier, and the little boy, ever more cheerful, always came out, and told him without even being asked that his papa wasn't home and that he didn't know when he was coming back, then once again he ran back clumsily into the house making those buzzing sounds, and it went on like this until at one point, at some point after nine p.m., a light in the yard was turned on from inside, and now a man came out, this was Dr. Tietz himself, bespectacled and with a kind expression on his face, roughly about the same age as Herr Köhler, and then, his expression already less kind, but instead like someone who had been interrupted while doing something, he blinked and asked, who are you looking for? at which Florian answered that he was looking for Herr Köhler, Herr Köhler? he's not here, well, that's exactly why he'd come to see the doctor, Florian said humbly, because the situation was such that not only was Herr Köhler not here, but he

110

wasn't anywhere, no one in Kana knew anything about his whereabouts, and already many people were very worried about him, and
especially he, Florian, and Florian introduced himself, to which the
doctor said: well, I'm very sorry to hear this, but I can't help you, how
long has it been since you last saw Herr Köhler? it's been several weeks
already, Florian bowed his head, but wait a minute, the doctor said,
looking the visitor up and down, aren't you the young man who was
studying physics with him? and his face brightened a bit when Florian
answered yes, it was he, Florian Herscht, and he was so worried about
Herr Köhler that he'd traveled from Kana to see if the doctor might
know something, and you yourself have no idea? Dr. Tietz asked Florian, no, nothing, he had no idea at all of where Herr Köhler might have
gone, I was hoping, Florian pointed at Dr. Tietz, that perhaps you
might have some idea, because in Kana, we can only imagine that he
has somehow left, but the doctor standing in the doorway just shook
his head, left? and he just kept shaking his head, Adrian? without en-
trusting his Weather Station to someone? no, no, in addition, if he had
traveled somewhere, I would certainly have heard, he always tells me
about things like that, if nothing else he would have left me a message,
well, thank you very much, Florian suddenly took his leave, the doctor
held out his hand, but Florian didn't notice in time, and it was too late
for him to turn back when he did notice, so that he only waved once
uncertainly, and then he was already at the bus station, he sat down on
the nearest metal bar, and he leaned forward with his two elbows on
his knees, then he became so immersed in the sight of the cigarette
butts strewn all around the garbage pail next to the perch he was sitting
on that he only noticed the bus pulling into the station at the very last
moment, he jumped up, and if he'd had to recount what happened to
him on the way back, he wouldn't have been able to, because nothing
happened to him on the way back, that's all he might have said, a thick
fog settling upon his brain, he could not think, he felt deathly tired as

he dragged himself home back to the Hochhaus across the completely deserted town; at night, Kana did not give the impression of a place where people were sleeping nicely and peacefully, but of a place from where everyone had already moved away, and so, to a stranger, it could have offered a ghostly sight, although of course in Kana there were no strangers, and especially no one sticking around at night if at all possible, not even one single night, as if it had been written with invisible letters, but still very legibly, on the foreheads of the tourist-group pensioners who came visiting here: NO; the nights in Kana were particularly miserable once the bad weather set in with rain pelting and ice-cold winds blowing, and when, to top it off, snow fell, although Frau Hopf liked that the best, I like it here the best when the snow falls, well that, my dear sir, is priceless, a picturesque sight, she would encourage those few guests in the Garni next to the breakfast table, if she got to chatting with them, trying to get them to stay one more night, she said: if I were in your place, I would stay one more night, and then I would come back again and again, but I would especially come back here during the winter, you know, the mountains, the trees, those delightful strolls on the snowy mountain slopes, and in vain, the people she was addressing looked at her somewhat indignantly, because what are you speaking about, my dear lady, Kana, even now, whether in spring or summer, creates such an impression that I fail to understand why you do not flee from here, but to no avail did the guests at the Garni look at her this way, Frau Hopf would not have understood, for her, despite everything, Kana was home, I was born here, you know, she would turn to this or that smaller family breakfasting with their adult children so as to spend every minute together, because the children would be remaining in this desolate place, whereas they, the parents, would be traveling back home, you know, Frau Hopf smiled, for me, Kana is home, I was born here, I will be laid to rest here with my husband and my children, and I don't see it as so many others do, as this nest of Nazis or anything like that, I only see a little pearl nestled, for centuries, in between the mountains, this is a small place, I admit, she tilted her head to one side, but it is ours, as people say, and here I know every corner, every street, every house, and no one could ever chase me away from here, although in reality she wasn't so sure of that, perhaps she kept saying this because she was afraid of the Nazis, and she held one of the greatest blows of fate to be how the Garni and its restaurant precisely faced the side wall of Burg 19, that notorious nest where there were so many unsavory types turning up, and now too so many evil-looking characters were living there, that if she had to pass in front of that door on Burgstraße, frequently left open in daytime, she dared not even look inside, that's how afraid she was, she quickened her steps, and would even deny that she'd set foot there, that she'd even passed by, just so as not to have to know who her neighbors were, if you could even call those people neighbors, grimy with piercings in their ears and mouths and noses, all covered in tattoos, it's a horror show, Frau Hopf looked at her husband, as if supplicating, but at the very least seeking his consent, he who, however, could not be of help, he could only agree, because he was already of an age when he wanted nothing else but tranquility, and if it were up to him, he would have already closed those few rooms in the Garni for good, because altogether he only wished for his grandchildren to come visit now and then from Dresden and to doze off in front of the TV every afternoon, that's what he liked the best, in the afternoons, after lunch, to take his place in the rocking chair, and his wife would gently cover him with a plaid blanket and leave him to himself because she had something to do in the kitchen or behind the counter in the Garni, and he could sink into idleness, and he rocked, he rocked a little bit in the rocking chair, and he dozed off on this afternoon, and in that he was not alone, because Florian, at one time, had also really liked those minutes or even those hours on the weekends when, either in the Herbstcafé, sitting on his bench by the

Saale, attending a rehearsal of the Kana Symphony, or sometimes at home at his own kitchen table, he would just sit and not do anything, not think of anything, but he could only do so during the day and never at night when, amidst frightening dreams, terrifying images rattled him and startled him awake, only during the day and in exceptional circumstances, and only before he had begun to run the gauntlet of trying to understanding what could not be understood, because it was occurring frequently now, not only at night, but during the day as well, he continually felt tortured by worries at the forefront of which naturally there stood Herr Köhler, what should he do, what, go to Berlin again? go to Eisenberg again? neither option looked too promising, so that on the following weekend, after the rehearsal of the Kana Symphony, when the Boss let him go, he set off by train to Erfurt, of course he hadn't told anyone, he knew how to buy the ticket by himself now, the Deputy would have tried only to talk him out of it, so that no one knew that he went to Erfurt, where, after lengthy inquiries, he rang the bell at the entrance of the enormous police station building at Andreasstraße 38 to tell them what he wanted, what do you want? the guard asked him; he'd emerged after a lengthy delay, and opened the gate, but then when Florian began to tell him why he was there, the guard didn't even so much as inform Florian that he wasn't in the right place, but only closed the gate with an expressionless gaze, and Florian had no luck in Hohenwindenstraße either, where he'd gone on another person's advice, because a policeman told him: if I had your problem, I would go to the Helios Clinic this weekend, and he laughed at him so strangely that Florian thought it better not to force the matter, what is this Helios Clinic, it seems, he thought to himself, that Herr Köhler is under close supervision, and he took the train back, crushed, broken, and he no longer had any interest in any deployments he had to take part in, no longer had any interest in what was galvanizing the Boss so much, he wasn't even interested in the Boss, keep your Weltschmerz to yourself, the Boss snarled at him in the Opel, but Florian wasn't even listening, he sat next to the Boss in the passenger seat, he did what the Boss told him to do, then he went home, he sat at the kitchen table, holding his head in his hands, and he should have been racking this head for newer and newer ideas, only that unfortunately, he had no more ideas, his letters remained unanswered, his attempts in Eisenberg and Erfurt had ended in failure, and so the winter passed and nothing happened, they walked along slushy streets, they cleaned walls, and sometimes the Boss stationed him for the night in various small cities and villages, but he himself had no idea what he was doing there, and he wasn't even interested in finding out who or what it was they were defending the Reich against, and it was only the Bach rehearsals, held every Saturday, that became ever more important; earlier, for years, Florian had hardly even paid attention, using the hours spent there to brood upon his worries, withdrawn deeply into his own self, excluding the Kana Symphony from his consciousness, now, however, something was prompting him to pay attention to this or that detail of the music being rehearsed, he didn't care if this or that musician fell out of rhythm, or if the bassists were incapable of keeping the tempo, he was no longer interested in the Boss's continual rages because the horn players had yet again completely jumbled up their parts, he still felt touched, at times, by a certain beauty in the harmony, which he hadn't been able to hear before, but now he did, and perhaps it was because he had lost Herr Köhler, and something in his soul had cracked open, and through this fissure, any kind of solace could easily slip in, and some of the motifs, when the instruments succeeded in harmonizing, were truly comforting, there would be a certain section that uplifted him by its simple, painful melody, he understood it now, I understand now, he thought, and he began to pay attention to what was happening in the gymnasium, and now he noticed many things, many things that were of secondary importance, but which he'd never noticed before,

for example, when the music was playing, and the Boss was sitting behind the timpani, not doing anything, and then Herr Feldmann became the real conductor of the Kana Symphony, Herr Feldmann, the
retired German and Latin teacher who played first violin, and who
conducted the orchestra not only with his bow, but with his entire
body, and then the Boss only returned to the spot designating the conductor's podium when it was time to stop, or when they were discuss-
ing what to practice next and who would make copies of the score,
prepared by precisely this Herr Feldmann—as he always did—for the
simplified arrangement of the Bach piece they were working on, because this is how it always was with the Kana Symphony, they would
start with the First Brandenburg, but after a while they would stop
working on it, because it wasn't going so well, then they started on the
Second Brandenburg, but that wasn't going too well either, and so now,
for months, they had been working on the Andante from the Fourth
Brandenburg, but that too somehow didn't want to come together, the
Boss flung down the mallets behind the timpani, and made them start
over again, I can't make it any better for you, so he came to the front,
and he stood in front of the orchestra, play your flutes, you swine, and
he pointed at the two flutists who immediately hung their heads, but
the others didn't get off so easily either, in the end the entire orchestra
looked as if they'd been told: enough already, the end, might as well
pack up your instruments and go home if such a simple task is too
much for you, and from the string section to the two bassists, everyone
felt that the Boss was justified in his anger, they themselves knew it
wasn't working, so that it was a kind of redemption when the Boss began to talk about the kind of connection they should have with Johann
Sebastian Bach, because then they already knew that from this point
on—if they were lucky—the topic of discussion would be Bach, and
they were lucky, and always they breathed a sigh of relief, then they
started up again and played the piece from the beginning, and only
now did the scale of the battle taking place between the Boss and Herr

Feldmann became apparent to Florian: a battle in which the Boss lost his authority while the orchestra was playing, and no longer having any kind of role, always immediately reclaimed it, over and over again, for he was the one in charge of the artistic direction of the Kana Symphony, because the artistic direction is the most important thing, he yelled at the orchestra, and our artistic direction is good, but more effort is required, don't you want that?! he kept on yelling, don't you want to surpass yourselves?! and it was written all over their faces: well, no, not really, while the Boss was swept away by his own passion for Bach, that's how the rehearsals went, and so now it mainly appeared to Florian how they always got mired in this pattern, for the most part it was the Boss who trained the members of the orchestra—who had been preparing, their entire lives, for performances of "Let the Sunshine In" and "Dragonstone" and "Blood of My Blood," and not Bach; although after a few melodies had nested themselves within his soul, Florian began to understand, ever more clearly, the source of the Boss's great passion for Bach, and he began, in the Herbstcafé—very softly at the beginning, so as not to disturb anyone, but then later, when he got a set of earphones, at full volume—to listen to Bach, and not only the Brandenburg Concertos, but other pieces as well, for example the great Passions, he was immediately entranced, and he himself didn't understand why, at the beginning of the beginning, he hadn't listened to the Boss when he said that every secret of life is in Johann Sebastian, although he didn't know what to make of it either when the Boss added, tugging at his arm, "and it is deciphered!" Florian had heard this one hundred times, one thousand times, but he never took it seriously, he never took the effort upon himself to understand what these words meant, although now that Bach had gripped him too, he as well began to think, listening to the *Matthäus-Passion* in the Herbstcafé, that yes, Bach was the secret of life, only he never got anywhere with the statement that "and it is deciphered!" in vain did he keep pondering, the riddle was never solved, he even asked the Boss once in the Opel, after they had finished their usual national anthem singing practice, he asked the Boss if he would reveal to him what it was that was deciphered, well, I see you're beginning to grow up, the Boss turned to him in surprise, but he did not betray what was deciphered: this is something that everyone must find for himself, he added with an enigmatic expression, not wishing to say anything more; for the time being, listen to as much Bach as you possibly can, because on that path upon which you must walk, quantity is also important, quantity? Florian asked, yes, quantity, fuck it, he smacked Florian on the neck, and with that the discussion was closed, and Florian began with the cantatas, but there were very many cantatas on the internet, he felt he would never get to the end, but then he didn't even want to get to the end, he merely wanted to immerse himself in the cantatas, although he only dared to listen to Bach very softly with earphones because there was always someone in the Herbstcafé, yet he felt that even so the messages were getting through to him, that's what he called them—messages—the sounds and the ensemble of the sounds, although he didn't want to decipher them, moreover, his immediate impression was that these messages had no meaning, they were beautiful in and of themselves, they were wondrous in and of themselves, they merely *were*, he did not wish to translate them, and there was no need, because they were not transmitting something, they only were what they were, he could not imagine what the Boss had been thinking of when he spoke of deciphering them, he, Florian, only got this far, and he was content, and so the following spring arrived, and there was still no sign of Herr Köhler anywhere, namely there continued to be no updated information on the website, no one came to the door when he rang the bell when he tried again a few more times at the house on Oststraße, although he tried to think about Herr Köhler as little as he could, partially because he wanted to free himself of the obligation to go there every single day and ring the doorbell, partially because he kept hearing, in his head ever more frequently, the melodies that remained there, and they alleviated, to a certain degree, the grave fact that there was still no response from Berlin, and so he thought that perhaps he should try his luck again, because when he'd gone there the first time he was still very inexperienced in locating someone, especially someone so important, because he'd simply gone up to the gate of the Reichstag, then he'd followed the guard's advice and walked over to the refreshment stand and drunk a Club Cola, because of course they didn't have Jim Him there, but the guard hadn't come for him as Florian remembered him promising to do, and when he went back to the entrance of the Reichstag it wasn't him standing there, but a different guard, who simply chased him away when it turned out that he did not wish to take advantage of the open house and visit the Reichstag, and so Florian had stood there perplexed for a while, he got a sandwich from the same refreshment stand where he'd gotten the Club Cola, and he sat down on the steps of the Reichstag to eat the sandwich, but then someone else in a uniform chased him away, so that he ended up eating the sandwich in the Tiergarten on a nearby bench, and then when he tried to make inquiries again, someone, a Turkish woman in a headscarf, suggested that he not look for the Chancellor in the Reichstag at all, but in the Kanzleramt, I thought, Florian said to her, that the Kanzleramt is in the Reichstag, ah, no, said the woman, the Kanzleramt is that way, and she pointed in the direction Florian only had to follow, and he arrived at an extremely modern building, but at first he had no idea where the entrance was, because the building was closed off from the outside world either by a fence or the Spree or people in uniform among whom only one spoke to him through the fence when he told him what he was doing there, but then the guard asked him strange questions, and Florian in vain kept pointing at his watch with his index finger, showing that it was already well past noon, the time of his scheduled meeting with Mrs. Merkel, the guard kept asking where he'd come from, where was his train ticket, and who sent him here, Florian told him, to no avail, that this was of no importance, because the only thing that was of importance was the time, and in every sense of the word, but this had no effect on the person in uniform, instead Florian had to precisely describe the appearance of the Turkish woman with the headscarf in the Tiergarten, until at the end he realized that he wasn't getting anywhere with this uniformed person, who, moreover, wasn't as friendly as the first guard he'd spoken to at the Reichstag, this one even grabbed him through the gaps in the fence, making sure to take down his name, place of residence, phone number, Hartz IV identification, and everything like that, as if trying to delay him, and not only did he not tell Florian where the entrance was but he sent him away, brooking no dissent, so Florian left while he kept turning around to look back at the Kanzleramt, wondering what might come of all this, but he didn't know what would come of all this, and he didn't know what he himself should do, he felt dreadful, because he was certain that back there, somewhere in that building, Mrs. Merkel was waiting for him, who was outside, unable to enter the building, a horrendous situation, and particularly in its ramifications, he thought, but he was powerless, he could hardly besiege the Kanzleramt, so that hours followed in which he merely circled the building with one question in his head: what what what should he do now, it was getting dark, he felt very despondent about having made the trip here in vain, but there was nothing left to do but to go back to the Hauptbahnhof as his train was about to depart for Halle, and then he just stared out the window, and he couldn't even feel happy he'd gotten a seat as he could only feel the weight of his failure, he'd come here in vain, everything was in vain, the world was rushing toward its demise just as the train rushed toward Halle, and it kept going through his head how when he was standing at the gate of the Reichstag or outside of the Kanzleramt, he felt himself to be very far away from Angela Merkel, but as he grew distant from these buildings, and especially here on the train as he approached Halle, he felt ever more close to her, how was that possible? why did he feel this way, perhaps Angela Merkel wasn't even back there in Berlin? but on her way toward ... Thuringia? or maybe? ... exactly ... on her way to Kana? no matter how aware he was of the enormous degree of absurdity in this hypothesis, it still got him thinking, because absurd, absurd, but ... not impossible, he thought, and from that point on, for a while, every weekend and during weekdays in the late afternoons he walked over to the station, he made a sign with the words ANGELA MERKEL on it, and when a train arrived from Jena, he raised the sign, and he held it up in the air until the last passenger had gotten off, but Angela Merkel did not arrive, in addition, quite soon, it wasn't just the Boss who was mocking him for going to the train station, but everyone he met, because of course the news of whom Florian was waiting for at the train station spread quickly in Kana, because this one thinks that Merkel is coming here by train, and so on, and the punch lines rained down one after the other, which of course led Florian to the conclusion that perhaps he should stop going to the train station, and perhaps it was best to avoid Bahnhofstraße as well, and generally speaking he found it most advisable to simply hide away somewhere during those hours when things were busy in the town, he didn't dare go to either Rosario or to Frau Ringer, but still, Frau Ringer nabbed him one day in the Netto Marken-Discount in front of the canned goods section, I don't understand you anymore, she said, looking burdened with worry, what are you doing at the train station, Florian?! and he hung his head, and he tried to explain that he had to be there in case the Chancellor arrived, because otherwise how would she recognize him? if who arrives?! Frau Ringer raised her voice in anger, you're not seriously thinking that your Angela Merkel is going to come here, do you?! but I do think so, seriously, Florian answered, and he hung his head, because he also felt a little ashamed for believing this; Frau

Ringer, he said to her then by the exit, and by now he had raised his head, nothing else remains to me, only that I believe in this, and it isn't completely impossible, Florian, may God bless you! Frau Ringer cried out in a high, sharp voice, and she repeated it as she threw down her shopping bag, and she grabbed him, and she started shaking his arms, may God bless you! may God bless you! until Florian could gently free himself, and it was very bad, very bad, to leave Frau Ringer there like that, but what could he have done, clearly if she couldn't, then no one else would be able to realize that of course the Chancellor could arrive, if Mrs. Merkel had understood everything he'd written in his letters, why was that so crazy? he fretted, and on the way home he tried to avoid anyone he might know, but of course there was Hoffmann heading from Ilona's buffet, coming from the opposite direction, the large crimson blotches shining even more brightly than usual on his face, you, my little Florian, stop running around so much, and he grabbed him by the arm when Florian tried to say that he was in a hurry and had to be somewhere, you, listen, Hoffmann leaned in very close to him, could you spare one euro? I only have a fiver, Florian answered, no problem, that's fine, said Hoffmann, and he'd already snatched it out of his hand and was happily on his way, Florian ran up to the seventh floor, locked the door twice, and there was no question of him not putting an end to these little trips to the train station, he put an end to them, and not because he didn't believe that they made sense, but because he felt crushed by the many mocking comments, and then primarily by how even Frau Ringer didn't understand, what was the point?! Florian struck himself on the forehead, if the Chancellor arrives, fine, if she doesn't arrive, that's also fine, either the world will be saved or it won't, from this point on it was no longer up to him—Florian would write no more letters to Berlin and he would no longer go out to the train station, he wanted only one thing, for Herr Köhler to be released, and he abandoned the idea of going to Berlin again, instead he turned to the Boss, and he told him the entire story at one of the rest stops on the A4 where they had stopped to eat their sandwiches, the Boss didn't interrupt him, and when he finished, he didn't start mocking him, which felt good to Florian, in contrast to when Florian was still going to the train station to meet Mrs. Merkel, moreover, for a while the Boss was just quiet, not even taking a puff on his cigarette for a bit, he pursed his lips like someone who was thinking, fine, okay, he understood, and now the question was what to do, and that's exactly what he said to Florian: okay, I understand, and now the question is, what should we do, Florian's eyes were shining, because he realized he could count on the Boss, once again he could count on him, and he would have been more than happy to fling himself around his neck, but he knew he couldn't do that, so he only listened as the Boss said what they should do now, because this Weatherman Köhler, I never had any problems with him, the Boss noted, even though he's a Jew, but between us, there are certain exceptions, and this Weatherman Köhler is an exception, I recognize that, a decent character, I used to look at his forecasts myself, and I too noticed that the data has been frozen for a good long while now, so that it's really a shame he's a Jew, well, whatever, in a word you're telling me that he's been gone for months, yes, Florian answered enthusiastically, yes, gone, for months, hmm, said the Boss, I heard something about this, I heard something, but now that you're telling me, well, this is really pretty strange, fuck it, he never let a day go by, not even one single day, without updating his website, and they turned onto the A4, they drove back to Kana, and the Boss smoothly pushed in the gate on Oststraße, then he slightly raised the gate that opened onto the yard, and went inside the house, Florian didn't follow him, he waited outside, there's no one in the house, the Boss said, everything all neat and tidy, but covered in dust, dust? Florian raised his head, but there was never any dust in Herr Köhler's house, well there is now, and this proves you're right, he traveled somewhere or was taken away, the Boss pursed his lips again, yes, said Florian, I thought of that, but I wasn't able to get anywhere in Erfurt, they didn't give him back, they'll give him back if we ask nicely, the Boss winked at him, and for the Boss's part the matter was settled for that day, because as he was going home, as he parked the car and went into his house, still this whole thing was fairly prob-le-ma-tic, namely in his view the question was this: what was the reason for this Weatherman Köhler vanishing into thin air? nothing, there was no reason for it at all, and then these letters from Florian to Angela Merkel?! that bloated, hypocritical clergyman's daughter? no importance at all, although this Weatherman Köhler might have some pretty strange connections, that whole Weather Station and everything, doesn't that point to ... hmm?! then the Boss opened a beer, Jürgen could say that there were 409 kinds of beer in Thuringia, although in reality there was only one which was truly brewed to the Boss's taste, he tossed away the bottle cap and raised the bottle to his lips: Köstritzer and that was it, he took a sip, he burped out what they called a three-movement belch, and he uttered only one word: Köstritzer, and so that day too came to an end, because while he searched for this and that on his laptop, there was yet another Köstritzer, then yet another, until he fell into bed fully dressed as was his habit, while Florian spent his evening very differently, namely, he did not go straight home, but went to Frau Ringer, but without thinking, because he didn't look at his watch, so that he did something he had never done before after finding the library closed, he went down to the Ringers' apartment; nothing like this had ever happened before, the location of his meetings with Frau Ringer had always and exclusively been the library, and that was it, Florian was afraid of Herr Ringer, namely that there was something in Herr Ringer that people respected but at the same time made them afraid, and not only Florian, he knew this because he'd heard it from others; it was very difficult to say what exactly it was, but everyone sensed it, that was certain, so that Florian never dared to go see Frau Ringer in her apartment, not only that, it never occurred to him before that Frau Ringer even lived somewhere, he always went to talk to her in the library, never at their place, to get to the Ringers' he had to go up to Friedrich-Ludwig-Jahn-Straße, not far from the police station which was always closed, for his part Herr Ringer didn't understand this great fear everyone had of him, he who wouldn't hurt a flea, he spent nearly the entire day in his repair shop, why would anyone be afraid of him, in addition, he found it scandalous that in a town like Kana it was exactly him that people were afraid of, because, beginning in the early 1990s, it was the *Nazzis* who were continuously making people alarmed in Thuringia and across the entire republic, one riot after the other, murders and attacks, which, in every single case, had to be put down to the Nazzis, Herr Ringer always pronounced that word in this way, gums bared and teeth flashing, and he said "Nazzi" when he and his friends were talking about this, they should all be afraid of the Nazzis, as he stated, once in the middle of the day at the Rathaus, our town and all of Thuringia must be purged of them, the thought—the Nazzi thought—must be extirpated, so that what cumulated in failure here, occasioning atrocities across the entire world, will never be repeated, Herr Ringer remarked to his sparse audience, and don't think the danger is insignificant, don't think it's just a few deadbeats in that house at Burg 19, because that's always how it starts, with just one or two deadbeats, one or two sad sickos, that's true, but then the moment always comes when they find the "artery within all of us," they find that artery, and once they touch it, everything comes back, Satan comes back, said Herr Ringer, Satan, believe me, but no one believed him, anti-humanist ideas have no place here, they kept saying, and the local representatives didn't think this was pressing, they reassured themselves: they knew exactly who they were, they knew them by name, and so now these few freaks would pose a threat to all of Thuringia?! reeaaally now, I'm asking you, they said to each other, overexaggerating this will only create more problems, because it's enough to paint the devil on the wall, and already it shows up, well, this was not what Herr Ringer thought, as he was convinced that the devil was *already* painted on the wall, and that something had to be done for him not to come to life, and Herr Ringer was not idle, he got to work and he did what he could, even his wife said to him: Mark, my dear, don't do this, don't get mixed up in these things, you have your repair shop, a nice income, you keep the family going, do not tempt fate, because almost everyone here is a Nazi, even the ones who don't realize it yet, you can't do anything about this, you can only personally protect what has to be protected, your family, me, and that is what you must do—no, Herr Ringer vehemently contradicted her, I am responsible for more than just myself and you, well, isn't that wonderful, said Frau Ringer, and now a prophet crawls out of his repair shop, leave me alone!!! and that was the end of the matter that day in the Ringer household, Herr Ringer left the house, agitated, and got into his car, he went where he always went when he needed a change of air—and he often needed a change of air—he didn't stop till he got to Jena, he drank a coffee at the Kaffeebar Ella, near the Planetarium, to calm down a little, then he went over to Café Wagner, where his friends were gathered already, the Wagner was slightly dangerous for them—they were conspicuous there due to their age—but both Ringer and his friends had decided that they weren't going to leave this place to the Nazzis who were thinking the exact same thing: they weren't going to leave this place to those scumbag Jews, in addition it was a beautiful coffeehouse, although the coffee wasn't the best, that's why Ringer, if he had enough time, preferred to have his coffee first at the Kaffeebar Ella, as he had done today, and at Café Wagner he ordered only water and a package of salty peanuts, and they put their heads together, they lowered their voices, they listened to what Ringer was recommending, and they all agreed that not just in Kana, not just in Jena, but in all of Thuringia, what was *decisively* needed was the creation of a democratic milieu, they all agreed on this, and then the conversation turned to

126

how the Nazzis were carrying out these strange attacks on the Johann Sebastian Bach memorial sites, for the time being, Herr Ringer said, he only knew that in Eisenach, Wechmar, and Mühlhausen, the entrances to these memorial sites were defaced with graffiti, he, Ringer pointed at himself, would even dare to affirm that behind all of this was a Kana graffiti cleaner, a well-known Nazzi, of course he had no proof, but there will be proof, therefore he recommended that they establish, here and now, a Bach-protection committee—this was his favorite expression, "here and now"—to catch this illegal gang, because Bach belongs to Thuringia, and they could not sit idly by with these desecrations going on, and precisely Bach, this is outrageous, his friends shook their heads incredulously, and they determined they were ready to protect everything that was Bach and everything that was Thuringia, everyone drank beer except for Ringer, Köstritzer was their favorite, and they drank to their agreement, and Ringer suggested right away that he himself speak with the Office for the Protection of the Constitution in Erfurt, which he did, only Frau Ringer was not at all reassured, in addition she herself knew that the Boss was against the graffiti, or at least she had heard this from Florian, but Herr Ringer just smiled: don't you get it? that's what so underhanded about the whole thing, he sprays at night and cleans it off the next day, that's the kind of rat he is, that's it, Herr Ringer had no desire to debate this topic, but Frau Ringer still had some objections, mainly because of Florian, only that her husband had no interest in hearing them, not in the least, because he wanted to take action, and he was fed up with the Boss anyway, he suspected his wife of having been obscurely involved with the Boss in her youth, he didn't know exactly how, he only suspected that something might have happened, because Frau Ringer always fell silent when the subject of this no-neck primordial Nazzi came up, there was something she wasn't telling him and it was certainly connected to the Boss, so that Ringer assumed the worst, as if what that Nazzi was getting up to with his cronies at Burgstraße 19 wasn't bad enough, everyone knew what had been going on there for more than two decades already, but no one did anything, there'd been one or two police raids, after which there was a brief period of calm, but then they came sneaking back, once again living at Burgstraße 19, where right now there were a lot of comings and goings—and now they were continuously present in the territory, but still not successful, not yet, the Boss emphasized, and he bellowed out the word "perseverance!" so many times that it started getting on their nerves, even Karin said, well, fine, Boss, fuck it, we will persevere, but maybe it's time to try a different tactic? no, fuck it, the Boss reacted vehemently, I don't think so, and he didn't explain why, so that things remained like that, the price of a Köstritzer went up somewhat in the Netto, so that after the Boss's initial resistance, in the Burg they switched over to Ur-Saalfelder, that was a pretty big change, but otherwise things went on as usual, it was spring, the sun shining for hours on end some days, the residents of Kana went to the banks of the Saale, they sat out on the benches on the Bahnhofstraße, things livened up at the Shopping Center, Kana clashed with Gera on the soccer fields, and then it was May Day, still the most important holiday in Kana, already in the morning the older people came to the Rosengarten to get a good seat at the tables, and they sat there with their straight backs, wordlessly, until the light music began on the shell-shaped concrete stage which had to be imagined like this: to one side of the Rosengarten, a lower elevation than the rest of the town, there was a concrete hemispherical structure (dreamed of, then realized) with a pretty wooden roof perched above, behind and above which a train passed by every quarter of an hour or so, completely drowning out, for a few seconds, the music which was performed partially by the locally known musicians of the Kana Symphony, and partially by high school students: in front sat the flutists and the clarinet players, behind them a row of saxophonists, in the third row were the trumpet players, the French horns, and the trombones, and in the very back was the percussionist, a second-year high school student whom the Boss explicitly detested; the more his pals showed up with a tray of beers, the more he hated that boy sitting in the back behind the timpani, but it was hard to decide what he hated more, the boy or what they were playing, because what went down well with this these musicians were the Beatles' "A Hard Day's Night" and "Blood of My Blood" and "Dragonstone" and similar crap, the Boss excoriated those on the concrete stage till intermission, he couldn't help himself, I can't help myself, he shook his head from time to time, and waving his cigarette around he said that this was a conspiracy, a conspiracy of the most devious kind against everything that Thuringia stands for, well, don't you hear it?! yes, yes, of course we hear it, the others nodded, they sipped their beer and everyone was very careful for the Boss not to see them tapping their feet in rhythm beneath the table, they knew that the Boss watched their feet under the table, he watched them continuously, then a train once again passed above the concrete stage shell on its way to Jena, the Boss stood up, tossing out the remark that it was his turn to get the round of beers, and he brought a tray of beers, one for each, and a Bockwurst for each too, he swayed, carrying the two trays back through the crowd from the stands, the crowd somewhat blocking the route between the stands and their table, stop blocking the route, the Boss yelled, balancing the two trays, but he shouldn't have because he stopped paying attention for a moment, the tray with the Wurst in his left hand tilted a little, and half of the Bockwurst already lay on the ground, you goddamned motherfuckers, can't you see that a person is coming here with two goddamn fucking trays?! well, then the crowd parted a bit—it too was waiting for beer and Bockwurst—the Boss lowered both trays onto the ground, picked up the Wurst, and picked up the trays again, and tried to hold them horizontally, and he succeeded, he made his way to their table, well, children, I've had enough, and he collapsed into a chair, I'm not going to last too much longer, and then nothing happened, because the draft beer went down nice and smoothly with the sausage, because of course they didn't need bottled beer if a place was serving draft, the comrades looked around ever happier, daring to glance over at the orchestra playing on the stage only occasionally, which of course the Boss immediately noticed, and he immediately began to disparage Herr Feldmann, who contributed, as a conductor, in creating a cheerful and recreative atmosphere, in addition, Herr Feldmann was clearly greatly enjoying the individual numbers, despite his advanced age, he moved rhythmically with the music, his demeanor—to the audience's minor amusement—was that of a professional big band conductor, namely, supporting himself on one leg, he leaned his body in the other direction, cueing the final quarter notes of the closing bars with his hands, leading to scattered applause from the public, ever more relaxed from the beer, although the atmosphere wasn't good, an older woman noted at one of the tables; there with her son, she had just devoured half of an enormous Bockwurst, and she said to the stranger sitting across from her that May Day was certainly different in the old days, that was *really* May Day, but this here, she pursed her lips, not this! and she took a sip of her beer which she drank from a large stein like the men, her son was drinking Köstritzer in a bottle, and she gave him half of the Bockwurst, because he's hungry, she told the stranger at the table, this child never stops eating, I can hardly keep up, because just imagine that in the morning he eats an entire plate of fried eggs, an entire plate, do you understand? eight eggs every morning, at which the boy, who wasn't too talkative, and was still busy with the Bockwurst, merely smiled with modest pride, indicating yes, that was his breakfast, and lunch, the old woman continued, best not even mention it, meat, meat, meat, meat, meat is everything to him, but here she fell silent, because the person sitting next to her picked up his camera and took a few pictures of the orchestra, only that unfortunately there were a few tables in between the stage and the person taking the pictures, including the table where the Boss and his comrades were sitting, Karin immediately realized someone was taking photographs, and already she was standing next to the picture taker, and she said: you can take photographs, but we do not wish to be in those photographs, so give me your camera, the man was astonished for a moment, then looked at her, a little frightened, and said that he'd only gotten a few shots of the orchestra, but then he complied and handed over the camera, Karin looked for the pictures she wanted gone and erased each one, put the camera on the table, leaned over to the stranger, and never taking her one good eye off the man, pursing her mouth, aiming for the camera's lens, she aimed a sizable gob of spit at it, and that was that, nothing else even happened on May Day, only the usual things at the end when it was already getting dark, the orchestra having come down from the stage quite a while ago and amid great applause and shouts of "bravo!" they sat down at their table; the lanterns were shining in the garden, there was still a lot of grilled meat but no more Bockwurst, in the back part of the Rosengarten a few people began bashing each other's heads in, the moon was shining beautifully, the whoops and yells of youths playing foosball next to one of the buildings could be heard after this or that successful move, the old lady took her son's arm and together they sauntered off, through the underpass beneath the rail tracks back to the town, the Boss and his comrades packed everything up, they bought a crate of beer from the vendors who were also packing up, to have some extra for the Burg, but only Fritz went back to the Burg, everyone else went home, and before they parted, Fritz yelled out TO HELL WITH MAY DAY, which made Frau Hopf pick her head up as she always slept by an open window through which everything could be heard, especially if someone was yelling nearby, for example at Burgstraße 19, well, not this again, she muttered angrily in her bed, and she closed the window, even though she liked to sleep with the window open, as for myself, she revealed to this or that returning guest at breakfast, I always sleep by an open window, you know for me fresh air is everything, I can't even sleep a wink in a room with closed windows because I've grown so accustomed to the fresh air, I'm used to the bedroom being aired out, but still sometimes I do close the window, and she sighed, well, you know—and she wrinkled up her face and motioned with her head in the direction of Burg 19—Nazis, then she explained to the guest all the wonderful places that were worth visiting nearby and how to get there, cleared the table, quickly cleaned up everything, and, if necessary, changed the tablecloth, checked over the breakfast room one last time, and turned off the light, then it was dark everywhere, because she didn't squander electricity in the other rooms, only in this small breakfast nook, the other rooms were always dark, sometimes Florian stumbled, carrying a tower of beer or wine crates, when he had to cross the small room behind the kitchen on his way there, as he almost stumbled now too when, in response to the note that Frau Hopf had left him, he showed up asking how he could be of help, I was expecting you yesterday, said Frau Hopf, but never mind, just the usual, my Florian, my husband can't manage anymore, he wants to but I don't let him lift anything, she explained to Florian, who carried in what had to be carried within a few minutes, he ate the breakfast she gave him, and in the meantime he listened to Frau Hopf: your friends over there, and she motioned with her head in the direction of Burg 19, they were on the rampage again last night, tell me, she leaned in toward him, how can you be friends with people like that, don't you know that they're all Nazis?! and it's even possible that they have a hand in what happened to your Köhler, oh, Frau Hopf, I don't know anything about that, Florian answered, I'm only with them sometimes because of the Boss, you know, they don't do anything bad, but Frau Hopf already didn't hear this, because she simply could not believe that this child could be so blind—how could someone be led by the nose like that? she asked her husband later on, but she did not await a reply, because she continued: he's a good boy, this Florian, but I think that there's something not right here—she pointed at her own temple—something is off, and truly something was off in that head, Florian knew that too as well, as these past few hours were weighing very heavily upon him, he had already listened to the Deputy, he had listened to Frau Ringer, and now he had listened to Frau Hopf, he had taken care of the three slips of paper, but he had ended up only hurting himself, because it was as if precisely those three whom he loved the best—the Deputy, Frau Ringer, and Frau Hopf—had only wanted to see him today in order to impress upon him that the recent disappearance of Herr Köhler also meant the disappearance of Herr Köhler from his life, of course Frau Ringer's words particularly hurt, they really pained him, which of course had not been Frau Ringer's intention in the least, she truly loved Florian just as the entire town loved him, they overlooked his eccentricities, as they termed them, but they did not consider him to be insane, only sometimes when a resident of Kana lost their patience with him, as eventually happened, for example, among the neighbors on Oststraße, with Frau Burgmüller, namely it was her opinion, when the Köhler matter turned into a case, and a squad of detectives turned up from Erfurt, and they asked her if she thought that the key to this mystery lay with a certain young man named Florian Herscht, although she could also say that he was the village idiot, he is an unpredictable character, I'm telling you, and then she grabbed the arm of one of the detectives, and pulled him closer to herself, and said into his ear, as if it were a secret:

the only message was that they were there

that in her personal opinion, this figure was a clear disgrace to Kana, I'm telling you, she said, ever since he came here he's been working for an extremely aggressive individual, no one knows where he came from, no one knows where his family is, supposedly he's an orphan but who knows, and he was brought here from Jena by this extremely aggressive individual, but she—Frau Burgmüller pointed at herself with one hand, and with the other she grasped the detective's arm, for what was in her heart was on her lips—didn't believe this, this whole Herscht person was a mystery, please, the detectives had to get a hold of him, and if they listened to her they would get a hold of him, because that boy was coming here every single week, then when Herr Köhler disappeared, he acted as if he was worried about him, and he kept coming back and roaming around here as if he were looking for him, but she, Frau Burgmüller, was convinced it was all a sham, well, fine, my dear lady, the detective freed his arm, we'll look into this, and he took her information, namely Frau Burgmüller's, who, while she was conveying this data, kept proudly glancing over at Frau Schneider whom the detectives were not questioning, and who was observing these events with a fairly sour expression on her face, hardly able to wait until it was her turn to set straight the falsehoods that Frau Burgmüller was piling up here, but her turn didn't come, nobody wanted to question her, so that Frau Burgmüller went back into her house, head held high, without glancing even once at her neighbor's window, and even so she knew that Frau Schneider was destroyed, that this was the end of Frau Schneider, once back inside she put on her slippers and took up her observation post by the window, not opening it but merely sitting next to it, and in this way she could observe everything pretty well, namely that the detectives spent about an hour in the house of their lovely former neighbor, but then they emerged carrying a large box, and everything outside became quiet, suddenly the street was dead, no one came and no one left, Frau Burgmüller brewed herself a cup of tea, she took two biscuits from the kitchen cabinet, she never ate more than two biscuits with her tea, that was enough, she had determined decades before, and she never veered from this routine, two biscuits and a cup of tea, and that was her afternoon by the window, but today these two biscuits and this tea tasted so good, they hadn't been so tasty for a very long time; she once again sat down by the window, and, sipping her tea, looked outside, she was filled with an unspeakably good feeling, for she knew that a mere few meters away, Frau Schneider was doing the same thing, she too was sitting next to the window, but in what kind of state? Frau Burgmüller put the question to herself, then she tipped the last mouthful of tea into her mouth, and that was it, that was the end of that day, on the next day, however, Dr. Tietz appeared once again at Herr Köhler's gate, so there was something to watch again, because Dr. Tietz had also been questioned by the detectives from Erfurt, he hadn't even finished his morning appointments when they came in, his assistant announced to him, face burning red, that the police were here, but unnecessarily as it turned out, because the detectives were already inside his office, standing at his desk, he excused himself to his patient and asked him to wait a few minutes in the outer room, then he answered the detectives' questions, but he said that he knew nothing, only that something might have happened to his friend, and that he—Dr. Tietz took off his glasses and rubbed the bridge of his nose—had been informed of Herr Köhler's disappearance by a young man who had been looking for him here, but with no result, because nothing, either in their last meeting or even their last phone conversation, indicated that something like this might happen—why? one of the detectives interrupted him, what do you mean, why? the doctor looked at them alarmed, and this alarm made him confused, well, the detective asked: what did you mean by "something like this might happen," what exactly was going to happen? that was the question, and they waited for an answer to this question, and the doctor, if possible, looked at them with even greater alarm and his confusion became even greater, it was as if they were accusing him of withholding important information, but he was withholding nothing because he knew nothing, I really don't know anything, he repeated, and he felt that his shame was obvious, his fright clearly visible, and he himself didn't understand why he felt this way, there was no reason as he really had no idea what could have happened to Adrian, he said to his wife, flustered, when the detectives finally left, and he hurried over to his apartment to have lunch, do you understand this?! they acted as if I knew something, but I don't know anything!!! to which his wife only said: of course you don't know anything, what the devil could you possibly know if he never even said anything to you? sit down and have something to eat, I'm not hungry, the doctor pushed the plate away from himself, listless, even though it was his favorite meal, fried pork liver with potatoes, parsley, and beetroot, he really liked this, although he kept this a secret from his guests, because then the first course was always Zwiebeltiegel or something like that, as the season permitted, then for the main course there would be Tote Oma or Frikadelle, that kind of thing, or, if they were receiving more distinguished guests, such as the pharmacist from Erfurt or the head psychiatrist of the Helios Clinic, then they served oysters, shrimp cocktail, or flounder roasted with vegetables, but never pork liver, only he could get that, and only when it was the two of them alone, and this, too, was infrequent because his wife looked after his health and allowed him to have pork liver once every two weeks, sometimes once every three weeks, but no more than that: there was a meat day, followed by three fish days, then a pasta day, well, and then sometimes his favorite, fried pork liver garnished with a bit of ground pepper, or—his secret favorite—boiled knuckle of pork with a glass of beer, well, this he got really only very infrequently, maybe once every two months, because his wife said: at your age, a person needs to look after their health, and since you're not willing to do so, I'll tell you what to eat and when, because if it were up to you, you'd eat meat every day and more meat, and maybe some liver too, and it doesn't work that way my dear—unfortunately, the doctor added to himself—however, his wife continued, as for what happened today, I suspected something, what? Dr. Tietz asked, well, that Adrian ... what about Adrian? well, that there might have been some reason for him not telling you anything, some reason, of course not, the doctor noted bitterly, there was no reason, the two of us always discuss everything together, and the reason why Adrian said nothing to me was because there was nothing to say, that's the situation, my dear, and then? his wife snapped, and then? what then?! Dr. Tietz pulled the steaming plate closer to himself and despondently sliced a piece of the liver, but he had no appetite, the police interrogation in his office had set his nerves on edge so much, but still liver was liver, and the fragrance of the freshly ground pepper overcame the doctor's resistance while his wife just kept on talking, because she kept on going about Adrian this and Adrian that, and Adrian would show up, and nothing could have happened to him, to Adrian that is, and he, Dr. Tietz, should calm down already, and eat his lunch properly while the doctor gulped down one bite after the other, the meal was tasting better and better, so that at the end he asked for a small second helping, and his wife, in view of the extraordinary circumstances, gave him a second helping, because the food would get cold if he didn't eat it, she had eaten her fill, so she gave him everything left in the pot, and otherwise the Boss too was very fond of pork liver, even if he cooked pork liver very rarely himself, he usually pan-fried it, of course for that you had to get up early, because those louse-ridden hags were already standing there when the shop opened, he growled at Florian sometimes, standing around in front of the Netto even before it opened so they could pounce on the fresh pork liver, because it was cheap, so that he had to talk to someone in deliveries, if pork liver comes in, set aside two packages for me; you just call me, Boss, and you stop by for them anytime, the unloader winked at him, usually this happened on Fridays, because if the Boss cooked, it was only on Saturdays, but not immediately after he came home from the rehearsal, because he always needed at least an hour to calm down, he just sat on his bench in front of the television, he didn't turn it on, he just sat in front of it and he tried to forget what the Kana Symphony had wrought yet again, he simply didn't understand, in the end, they all knew how to play, everyone at his own level, they all could play, so why wasn't it coming together?! the Boss had gotten the use of the gym with the agreement that the Symphony would show its gratitude within a year by performing a full-length concert at the Lichtenberg Secondary School—since then almost three years had gone by—we just need a bit more time, the Boss resolutely warded off the principal's inquiries as to when the concert would be taking place, Johann Sebastian doesn't give himself up so easily, the Boss explained, and both he and the Kana Symphony wished to only offer their very best, and they would not step up before the public until it could not be clearer than day that they had achieved their very best, they were going to produce a performance worthy of Bach, and the name of the Lichtenberg Secondary School would shine throughout all of Thuringia if the principal could just be a little patient, well, of course everything had its limits, the Boss also realized—sitting on his bench as he tried to calm down after this or that rehearsal in the gym—that the whole thing was such a pile of scandalous shit that he simply had no idea of what to do with his musicians, if they were so good at those fucking Beatles and that other crap, then why weren't they making any progress with Bach?! if only he could see a bit of uplift, a little improvement, a tiny step forward, but he was seeing no kind of uplift and no kind of improvement and no step forward, but why not?! he hit the armrest on the bench hard, namely he was not calming down but flying into a rage, but the Boss didn't give up, he started on the pork liver and he decided that on the following Saturday he would beat everything out of them, although on the following Saturday he wasn't able to beat anything out of them, he had already spoken with Feldmann to ask him if he didn't have anything a little easier, something they could manage during their rehearsals in the gym, but Feldmann merely answered haughtily: when it comes to Bach, nothing is easy, forget about it, or just quit the whole thing—this was his perpetual advice to the Boss anyway—but the Boss hung on to his self-control and swallowed back what he wanted to say, because he was at the mercy of Feldmann, because this Feldmann could create orchestral arrangements of the works of Bach they were rehearsing commensurate with their skills, namely their skills *would have been* commensurate, if the Kana Symphony *had been at all* inclined to make an effort in the direction of Bach, only that the Boss knew that this was precisely the problem: the musicians simply had no desire to exert themselves, although—he explained to them as he jumped up from behind the timpani to once again halt, at a given point, the unbearable cacophony—the peak can never be reached without effort, he said, his gaze ranging over the members of the orchestra as they sat silently with heads bowed, because at times like this they sat silently with their heads bowed, until finally, as always, the Boss waved his hand in resignation and sat down once again behind the timpani for them to take it from the beginning, and the only thing that consoled him a bit was that he had noticed the German patriot awakening in Florian; at last his attendance at the rehearsals was bringing about the desired result, namely it was clear that Bach was having an effect on him—you like him, right?! the Boss looked at him during a cigarette break, I like him, Florian answered, smiling, and he really did like Bach, more and more notes were staying in his head; he felt ever deeper comfort in being carried away by the sudden transition of a melody from a major to a minor key, these transitions stupefied him, because how could there be something so wondrous? he enthused in the Opel to the Boss, who nodded in satisfaction: you see, you wayward child, I told you to come

139

to rehearsals, because you would get something there—fuck it—that you won't get anywhere else, and it was true that Florian didn't get what he got at the rehearsals anywhere else, because it was around that time that he began to think about going to Leipzig and listening to a Bach performance in the Thomaskirche, he didn't say anything to the Boss, because he didn't know how he would react to this, although he did tell others about it, first Frau Ringer, who supported him, as she saw, in this proposed trip, the sign that Florian was beginning to heal from his melancholy over the loss of Herr Köhler, then Florian told the Deputy as well, who welcomed this idea in a solemn manner, because the name of Bach, in his mind, was stored away on the appropriate shelf, as he expressed it, even if it was also true that he couldn't bear his music for too long, because I'm a practical man, not some music fanatic, he explained in the IKS pub to the others; he went there as he couldn't stand Heinrich at Ilona's buffet, and that was it, because for me one piece of music, he continued, is just like another, I don't like any of them, with the exception of what the brass band belts out, well, yes indeed, the Deputy raised his bottle of beer and he drank to that, yes, that's what I like, only that unfortunately those lovely old military parades ended a long time ago, and it's so rare to hear a brass band these days at this or that beer festival or anything like that, and even then only in Jena or Leipzig or Erfurt, and who even goes to Jena or Erfurt or Leipzig anymore? *ja*, that is so, the others nodded in the IKS pub, but the regular customers in the Grillhäusel also nodded, those old beautiful days are over, and they downed another beer, Ilona cheerfully placed the fresh bottles on the counter and they collected them from there, because that's how things worked, you had to go get the beer from the counter yourself, unless one of them ordered a Bockwurst, because then Ilona had to go out from where the customers were sitting to the tiny kitchen built into the side of the buffet stand, and there she would heat up or fry or boil the Wurst which she then carried back in and served to the customer at his table, of course she knew everyone here, only regulars came to her place, those who were used to how things worked here, Ilona sometimes also gave some of her regulars a beer or a Wurst on credit, not all of them, but sometimes she would say to one or the other, bring me the money next time, and she wrote it down in a notebook, and this notebook was the magical center of the entire Grillhäusel, as it happened fairly frequently, primarily in the few days before the Hartz IV benefits were paid out, that her customers didn't have any money, but then after they got the Hartz IV, for the most part, they paid her back, sometimes this also occurred with Florian, but Ilona gave him food on credit without even thinking about it, she knew Florian well, and she liked him, as did everyone, and not only because no matter what she asked of him, he did it immediately—bringing a few crates in from the delivery, installing an advertising sign on the roof—no, it was because he was a good-natured boy, he's a good-natured boy, she made excuses to her husband at home when he looked at the takings for the day in the notebook, and shaking his head, he remarked: even this Florian? Florian is a good boy, Ilona brushed him off, and they didn't speak of the matter again until the news spread that detectives had come from Erfurt to investigate Herr Köhler's disappearance, and that Florian was a suspect, well, from that point on, Ilona was forbidden from giving him any credit whatsoever, a prohibition which of course she didn't keep, she unceasingly gave Florian credit for Wurst and soft drinks with the condition that he keep it a secret, you may not tell anyone, either here or elsewhere, that you got credit from me for this or that, Ilona explained, do you understand? Florian didn't really understand, but of course he promised, even if he couldn't bear to keep his promise, no, because he longed to express how much the love of the residents of Kana touched him, and in particular the love of Ilona, so that already on the following day he blurted it out to the Boss—they were on a mission in Gotha again—and described what a good heart that Frau Ilona had, just imagine, he said to the Boss, her husband told her to never give him, Florian, any more

141

credit because of his bad reputation, but Frau Ilona didn't comply, and all Florian had to do was never tell anyone about it, what?! the Boss flared up in the darkened Opel, they were lying low in the car near the Schloss, the Boss lowered the binoculars he was using to scan the front entrance, and he hissed at Florian: because of your bad reputation?! what bad reputation, who is saying this?! Florian didn't reply, because he didn't know what to say; although if it was already the case that he had a bad reputation, he did not feel this to be completely unjustified; namely, his sense of guilt over Herr Köhler had never abated, and so he kept silent while the Boss kept on cursing: these putrid, withered old cunts, I'll give them a good kick in the ass, and you have a bad reputation? you're my Florian, and as long as I'm around, no one is going to trash your reputation, because I'll rip their heads off, understand?! I understand, Florian quickly looked ahead of himself, but he didn't have to worry, because the Boss didn't give him even one slap, and he didn't continue but raised the binoculars to his eyes again, and in a much calmer voice he growled under his nose: these fucking wrinkled old cunts, and that was all, and the next day the news came—they were in the middle of their Saturday rehearsal in the gymnasium—that the Ringers were in the hospital, they'd been attacked by a wolf, or at the very least both of them claimed this, they'd gone up to Leuchtenburg Castle as so often, if the weather was nice, and they had just started lunch, Frau Ringer had gotten some nice fresh rolls from the Czech bakers, they opened relatively early, and Ringer didn't like yesterday's rolls, but freshly baked ones, so that before they left the town, they went to the Czech bakers, and Frau Ringer didn't even have to say anything, the bakers knew what she wanted, already placing six rolls in a bag, they knew that she came every Saturday and she always asked for six rolls, this was the only thing she bought fresh, everything else she'd bought yesterday and all now were in small plastic containers: sliced peppers, pressed ham, and cheese stored separately, she'd once found these food containers with three separate storage compartments on sale in Jena, and ever since then she'd made happy use of them, they're so practical, she told her girlfriends, and we always use them, you know, and that's how it was now too, from the plastic food containers and the fresh bread rolls to the pretty little clearing at the top of Leuchtenburg Castle, everything always the same, already in the morning they longed to be outside, and they were outside, and they went for a long walk in the wondrously beautiful landscape, then a few hours later—they didn't hear the bells tolling from the town, but their wristwatches indicated twelve noon—Frau Ringer laid out a blanket, they sat down in their usual spot with a lovely view of both the castle and the surrounding countryside, and began eating their lunch, and out of nowhere they saw a wolf, Ringer said to the police officer taking the report in the hospital, the policeman couldn't talk to Ringer's wife as she was bitten in the throat and in the ICU after the operation, everything happened so fast, said Ringer, one moment it wasn't there, and the next moment it stood there, we froze completely, we didn't even know what it was, already it was leaping at us, there are no wolves here, the police officer interrupted, I know, answered Ringer and he swallowed once, still in a state of shock, there never used to be wolves here, but now there are, and in rare instances wolves do attack people, as far as I know, wolves are afraid of people, the policeman continued, Ringer nodded, but then he burst out: you're not trying to say that I'm not telling the truth, are you?! no, no, of course not, the policeman reassured him, I have no opinions here, for me only the facts matter, you should just realize that to date, in East Thuringia, there have been no wolves, in Bayern yes, and Brandenburg yes, with their movements closely observed, to the best of our knowledge—I understand, Ringer interrupted, irritated, but look at this, and he showed him his arm, and look at this, and he showed him his leg, and look at my back, he turned slightly toward the policeman and he was practically covered in bandages stained through with blood, would you please look at this, Ringer raised his voice, a wolf did this, I don't even know how many hours ago, and it's still at large, he added, then, his face haggard, he turned his head on the pillow to signal that the conversation was over, and it spread like wildfire throughout all Kana that the wolf was still at large, free, reported Torsten, the school janitor and handyman, who came running over to the members of the Kana Symphony in the gym—on Saturdays there was never anyone else in the building, sports training only began after three p.m.—and Torsten had to unconditionally find someone to whom he could relate the dreadful news after Ringer, for some reason, had called him on his cell phone and had whispered to him to call for help immediately, so first he ran to the orchestra, then he ran out of the building, but no one was outside, so he called his wife who just at that moment was standing in line to buy some discounted vitamin C in the pharmacy, and she was so terrified by this news, that she could only bear to cry out, so that everyone could hear that

when it comes to Bach, nothing is easy

there are wolves at Leuchtenburg, and already someone has been attacked, the people standing in line in the first moments couldn't even conceive what was going on, but they understood when they heard more of what Torsten's wife had to say: her husband only knew that there were two people in the hospital, one of them with a fatal wound, which was not completely true, Frau Ringer was in a critical state due to the loss of blood, but her wounds were not life-threatening, as the physician on duty had put it, a resident from the University of Jena, the first one to make a statement to the journalist from the *Ostthüringer Zeitung* who appeared on the scene with lightning speed, the state of the wounded is satisfactory, he added, and nothing else could be drawn out of him, thank you for your attention, he concluded amid the shocked silence, and he turned away from the journalist who just stood there flabbergasted, because the news had touched him not only as a journalist, but as a human being, or at least that's what he wrote later on, and overall, every single resident of Kana was flabbergasted when they heard about the attack at Leuchtenburg, it was hard to accept that something like this could have happened, there were some who didn't believe the news, but in most people the old fears were quickly resurrected again, because there used to be wolves here in the mountains, that was a fact, and the old people still recalled their own fathers who always used to tell their own stories about the wolves, not even trying to scare the children with them, so deeply embedded in their memories was the dangerous proximity to the wolves that people lived in, and on the following Monday, someone came from the Thuringian branch of the Naturschutzbund to alert the residents that the hearsay about a wolf having attacked someone was completely false, wolves never attack people, and they at NABU knew this precisely, so that any fear was completely superfluous, if something like this had happened at all, it was certainly not because of a wolf, but the team from NABU also quickly went to Leuchtenburg and thoroughly circled the area in their Jeeps looking for wolf tracks and fairly soon they found them, the head of the two-man delegation, Tamás Ramsthaler, suggested to his colleague that for the time being they not speak of this, but that they would convene a dialogue between the Thuringian chapter of the Friends of Wolves and the representatives of Kana in which they would present their opinions and their own assessment of the situation as to how what should not have happened, might have happened, because it should not have happened, said Tamás Ramsthaler from Dornburg-Camburg, something completely incomprehensible has occurred, only that he—he explained at the informational meeting taking place four days later—only that I don't like inexplicable events, because I don't believe in them, there is an explanation for everything, because there

145

must be, a wolf doesn't attack humans, never, I would like us to understand this; moreover, it is completely unnatural for a wolf to attack from an ambush position in broad daylight with no external compulsion, this is nonsense, this word "nonsense" was heard innumerable times from the NABU staff as they explained the true nature of the wolf to the residents of Kana: wolves were shy, bashful, avoidant of risk, and prudent actors, and I will say it again, said Tamás Ramsthaler; bashful, bashful, to hell with bashful, Ringer grunted in his hospital bed, and he nearly ripped the IV out of his arm when they told him what the delegation from NABU had said, I *saw* its eyes, and I *saw* as it bared its gums and showed its teeth, so nobody's going to tell me that this monster is bashful, that motherfucker was anything but bashful when it was trying to sink its teeth into Sybille's throat, and I pulled that bastard off of her, and then it bit me for the first time, and if the Boss hadn't shown up we both would have been dead, although this was a fairly strong exaggeration, except it was true that when the Boss comprehended, from Torsten's stammering words, what happened at Leuchtenburg, he immediately ran out of the rehearsal room, he jumped into the Opel and dashed home, then, with a loaded Mauser M03, he hurtled to Leuchtenburg, and within moments he saw the two people from above, he threw himself onto his stomach and crawled in their direction until he realized the direction the wind was blowing, so he changed directions, and turned toward the wind, crawling farther to a thickly overgrown smaller hillock, and his instincts did not deceive him, because the animal was lying on the ground at the base of a shrub, clearly it had made it this far with the leg Ringer had broken, the Boss raised himself a bit, gun fully loaded, and fired off two bullets just in case, without hesitation he shot right into its head, right between the eyes, well, although he hadn't really saved anyone, the Boss protested when he recounted the incident to the police officers from Jena and the Revierförster when they finally showed up after his emergency call, not really, but if he hadn't been so quick, the Revierförster explained later on to the people gathered in front of the Rathaus, if the Boss hadn't gotten to the scene as quickly as he did, the wounded animal might have collected its last strength and crawled back to the source of danger with its broken leg, and might have attacked again, no matter how strange it may sound, I've seen such things, he said, but what is strange, the Revierförster added in a quieter voice, is that its mate did not appear, and not only that, no other mates from the pack appeared, a wolf, in the greatest majority of cases—if not a young wolf that is about to leave the pack—does not attack alone, only with the other members of the pack, or, as one might put it, they attack as a horde, and once again it spread like wildfire: they attack as a horde, and now even those people in Kana who had doubted the veracity of the wolf attack previously were frightened; Torsten had not been one of them as he had immediately believed what Ringer had told him in his hoarse, faint voice on the phone; that night he couldn't sleep, constantly starting awake, he sat up in bed, at which his wife, lying motionlessly with her back to him, suddenly spoke: you can't sleep either, eh? well, no, Torsten grumbled, and he went out to drink a glass of water, and he decided not to lie down again, why bother, until that picture disappeared from his head of that monster ripping the flesh from Ringer's back, not until then, not until Ringer's voice died down in his ear as it called immediately for help ... we're at our usual spot at the Leuchtenburg ... you know ... help ... because a wolf ... Sybille is bleeding ... which Ringer was not too proud of later on, but then he couldn't bring himself to think as he tore the animal away from Sybille's throat, he seized the wolf and broke one of its legs, then as he caught his breath a bit, he obscurely saw the animal, whimpering, crawling away to one side, he pressed something on his phone, and the last number he had called was Torsten's, because Torsten had been there with his car last Friday in Ringer's repair shop, he didn't have any better ideas, namely it wasn't an idea, only the functioning of his instinct, and this instinct suggested to him that he should call the first person he could with a single press of a button, and this was Torsten, because he had called him yesterday, and he came, and that damned Boss came and saved our lives, our lives, he said very faintly, leaning in toward Frau Ringer's ear, when she was brought from intensive care into a regular hospital ward, and he had to fight to be able to see her, the Boss saved us, but it didn't seem as if Frau Ringer understood, because she still hadn't come back to herself, she was awake, but she didn't know where she was and why, it was only on the third day, when Florian traveled to Jena and visited them in the hospital, that they were both placed in a double room next to each other, and later on, when the whole thing had become only a bad memory, Frau Ringer said to her husband: you know, as I saw you in the hospital room and I realized that we were lying there next to each other and that we were alive, I would have been happy to die then and there, because only with you—and she began crying, they embraced each other, Ringer held her gently to his own body, because he felt the same way toward his wife, he could never imagine life without her, and he decided then, on that day, as they stood there in the kitchen embracing each other for about one minute, that they were going to leave together if it came to that, and these words later on became the headline—in the *Ostthüringer Zeitung*—of the article telling the story of their survival, these words they unfortunately had related to the journalist, and of course he loved it as a headline, but what could they do, the article had already been printed, WE WILL TAKE OUR LEAVE TOGETHER, and the subtitle read: *The Shared Decision of a Middle-Aged Couple Who Survived a Horrific Attack*, and so on, Ringer was ashamed of the whole thing, enraged that he had given himself away like this, he had never thought he'd be capable of publicizing such intimate matters without inhibitions, and in a newspaper even, oh, to hell with that, Frau Ringer brushed the whole thing aside, we're beyond it, and now we just have to forget the whole thing, and Florian understood very well what Frau Ringer was thinking as she related to him, in the library, what they'd gone through and how—while she was in the hospital she couldn't speak, not only that, she wasn't allowed to speak for almost three weeks, the wolf bite had seriously damaged not just one of her neck arteries but also, to some extent, her vocal cords, so that her voice had also changed, at least this was Florian's impression when Frau Ringer had completely recovered and returned to normal life—I was covered in blood, Mark was pressing down hard on the vein with one hand, and with the other he was protecting me, at least that's what he said, because I don't remember anything, I must have been in shock, because I lost quite a lot of blood, can you imagine what that poor Mark must have gone through until your Boss got there, and he gunned down that ... that ... but she didn't continue, and later on as well, no matter whom she was telling this story to, at this point she always had to stop, she was incapable of naming who or what it was the Boss had shot down, saving their lives, as she also accepted the general narrative that transformed the Boss unequivocally into a hero, Florian was very proud that others, too, could finally realize the true nature of his benefactor, a hero, he pronounced to everyone at Ilona's buffet, and everyone's face grew serious, and the old stories were recollected about how this happened and that happened, and in the meantime the Boss's heroic act shone with an ever more brilliant light, and from that point on the residents of Kana always double-checked to make sure that they turned the key in the lock before going to bed, and whoever had shutters on their windows happily closed them and bolted them shut, because from this point on no one in Kana trusted either NABU or the police, if it was up to them the wolf would have eaten the Ringers for lunch, this was the general opinion which was only worsened by the news of a new kind of pandemic spreading in the so-called wider world, but the Boss didn't give a crap about that either, as he put it, because, he growled:

what the fuck should we care about what's going on in the wider world when we have to take care of what's destroying us from within, so that he did not feel any kind of satisfaction—instead, it irritated him— when he heard of his own rising reputation, or when people wanted to slap his back in the Netto, leave me alone, until now I was the bad guy, now I'm the good guy, they can go fuck themselves, the Boss growled to the unit, and especially because, he added: I went over there because of the wolf and not because of the Ringers, I don't give a shit about the Ringers, it's not my habit to go around rescuing Jews, and they all drank to that, beer bottles clanking, the price of Köstritzer had never gone down so they had stayed with Ur-Saalfelder, and this really was a big change, because as you first took a sip, the taste of malt was there, but it wasn't the same as with Köstritzer which had a deeper, more serious, more disciplined taste, noted Jürgen, who had been of the opinion, when they were debating the price increase, that they should stick with Köstritzer, if only for historical reasons, although the Boss was the only one who agreed with him because they were all broke, broke, said Andreas, and he grimaced, because even those few cents mattered to them, he said to Jürgen, forty-nine cents is forty-nine cents, you can't beat that, both Jürgen and the Boss acquiesced, and the large crates, each containing twenty bottles of Ur-Saalfelder were delivered, in the end they got used to the change, the only problem was that this Ur-Saalfelder was much stronger than the old Köstritzer, so they got much more drunk and much more quickly, on Saturdays after about ten or eleven p.m. they couldn't really talk to each other, and this was fairly vexing to the Boss, because it was often right about that time that he had important information to convey, and it was hard for him as he didn't know what to do with these drunkards, and he was somewhat disgusted when they started throwing up, and in addition it happened more than once that some comrade who had to throw up didn't make it out of Jürgen's room in time, Jürgen's room was where the solidarity

150

sessions took place, because that's what they called them, "solidarity sessions," namely they always had to be on permanent standby, the Boss explained, especially now, when—as was generally felt—they were finally closing in on the sprayer, and they kept to this regimen later on as well, it wasn't necessary to explain over and over again, everyone in the Burg knew the score as it had been repeated so many times, but the Boss just kept on telling them the same things over and over, they muttered to each other, everyone was sick of it already, because they didn't need to hear the same things over and over and over again, they knew themselves what was meant by Homeland, what was meant by Readiness and why, and yet the Boss did not consider these repetitions to be superfluous, because in the end, he didn't have too much faith in his comrades, or at the very least, he didn't know how much he could count on them in a crisis, Karin was fine, Fritz was also fine, but as for Jürgen or Andreas or Gerhard and the others, weeellll, I don't know, sometimes he shared his worries with Florian in the Opel, and Florian himself wasn't able to make any such distinctions among the members of the unit, for him

it was a source of deep consolation

they were all the same—he was afraid of all of them, sometimes he was more afraid of Karin, other times he was more afraid of Jürgen, and he had no one to talk to about this, because he could not tell the one single person he might have been able to tell, because he knew exactly how she would react: don't get involved with them, Florian, that would be her response, leave them immediately, don't even think of being with them, you'll see—Frau Ringer would have threatened him, just as she once did actually threaten him—there'll be trouble from this, she had said, and looked into his eyes very seriously, because it's already enough that people have seen you with them, only that it wasn't so easy, Frau Ringer didn't understand, so he didn't even mention the topic, only when it somehow turned up in conversation, Florian got to the library fairly late, usually at around five p.m. or a quarter past five, he told her where he'd been that day with the Boss and what their work had been, what the Deputy or Frau Ilona had said, or how he had to get his laptop repaired, because sometimes the operating system just didn't want to work, he talked about this and that, and of course only very rarely about Herr Köhler, for example, he had dreamed the night before that Herr Köhler had rung his bell again in the Hochhaus, and Florian had looked out the window, and it was Herr Köhler, he stood there downstairs completely life-sized, and he even waved up to him cheerfully, hello, Florian, here I am, I'm still here, and how bitter Florian felt when he woke up, he tore down the stairs two at a time, hardly even getting dressed, he tore down the stairs in his pajamas and opened the front door, but Herr Köhler wasn't there, and he wasn't waving to him, saying hello, Florian, here I am, I'm still here, and at times like this how could Frau Ringer console Florian if not to say: listen here, Florian, I really don't think that somebody can disappear without a trace, that doesn't happen, I don't believe it, and when she saw how Florian hung his head, she added: and that's why I don't believe in things like this, because nothing exists without an explanation, and she didn't even suspect how much she had struck a nerve in Florian by saying this, because he already knew that there were things that had no explanation, moreover, for the deepest, the most important, the most fundamental questions there were no answers and there would never be any answers, Florian would take his leave after such a conversation in the library, and he trudged home sorrowfully, he really missed Herr Köhler, and he no longer thought about how he, Florian, would be held responsible once the whole thing was over, but only that he missed him very much, he missed him every Thursday, it had been so good before, he thought, when he would get out of bed thinking that today it's

Thursday, and this evening at six p.m. he and Herr Köhler would be together again, and he would ask questions and Herr Köhler, in his own calm, balanced way, would answer, and he would explain whatever Florian needed to understand, and Florian could go into the kitchen and brew Herr Köhler a cup of linden tea, Herr Köhler had a sweet tooth so that Florian always had to stir a fair amount of honey into the tea mug, but still he always asked, calling out from the kitchen: how many spoonfuls? to which Herr Köhler sometimes replied: only two today, Florian, only two, because he had to be careful, I have to be careful, Herr Köhler explained, I have to watch my sugar intake, sometimes he said two spoonfuls, sometimes he said three, sometimes he wanted even four spoonfuls, and that is why Florian always had to ask as he was infusing the tea, and he would ask: "how many spoonfuls?" now that he had gotten home and was sitting at his own kitchen table, he thought how good it would have been to be able to ask, and Florian had no more interest in those blank sheets of A4 paper that he used to write his letters on when the thought of Herr Köhler weighed upon him, no interest, because at such times his correspondence with the Chancellor didn't seem so important, it was only the next day, if he was lucky, that he woke up, and it wasn't Herr Köhler standing there downstairs, but Angela Merkel, with her own refined gestures, sometimes he could see her wearing a blue blazer, sometimes a yellow blazer, sometimes an orange-red one, but she always wore trousers, and this was better, it was much better than when Herr Köhler appeared, because that always touched his heart directly, but if it was the Chancellor, then ... well, she ... also touched his heart, but from a distance, not directly, she touched his sober mind, his brain, the part of his brain entrusted with the task of speaking out for the protection of the universe, although it had been a long time since Florian had sent her anything; one day, Frau Hopf asked him to mail a few postcards for her, and Jessica said: you, Florian, we hardly see you around here anymore, and that's how it was, he hardly ever went to the post office anymore, that is to say he didn't go there at all, for months he hadn't stopped by there, because lately he had no idea of what to write, more specifically, he didn't know how to write that not too long ago he had discovered the music of Johann Sebastian Bach, and he felt that contained within this discovery were instructions in the event of a catastrophe, but he only felt this, he didn't know the exact contents of these instructions, every Saturday he sat in on the rehearsals of a local orchestra, the Kana Symphony, giving him a chance of perceiving something about this music, although it would be more precise for him to write feeling something about this music— as he expressed himself to Angela Merkel—and this was the difference, exactly this, the difference between insight and intuition, only he didn't know if he was going to write this down at all, would the Chancellor be able to understand what he was thinking here in Kana, namely that he had come upon something important, but even if he had come upon something important, he didn't know what it was—he sat, during the Saturday rehearsals, in his appointed spot, far away from the orchestra, against the gym's wall bars, most likely the Boss had chosen this spot for him because he didn't want him to be able to lean back, you couldn't really lean back against the wall bars, no, because the Boss didn't want his attention to slacken for even a moment during the two long hours of rehearsal, or he simply did not want anyone, including Florian, to be able to lean back comfortably while the members of the orchestra were playing their hearts out, trying to make the Fourth Brandenburg and the Andante come together, and I know he doesn't understand anything about this, nothing, the Boss yelled in the Burg, if someone mentioned Florian to him, saying, why the fuck are you dragging this idiot child around, I know he doesn't understand anything, but what if, what if! what if!!! his musical ear is improving somewhat, because if he exposes himself to music once a week, if he exposes himself to Bach once a week, there has to be a result, and the Boss was not wrong, only that things worked out very differently than he predicted: he perceived that Florian was completely caught up in it, the Boss noticed immediately, one time when, after rehearsal, they were going home, Florian's face had turned red and his eyes were shining: well?! well?! the Boss asked on the way home, Bach got to you, right?! Bach got to me, said Florian, and he could hardly conceal his pride that Bach had gotten to him, he knew that the Boss was really happy about this, these two years had not been in vain, these two years of him sitting against the wall bars in the gym, well, but why, why did Bach get to you?! the Boss yelled at him, visibly happy that his efforts had paid off, that Florian had been floored by German artistry of the highest rank, so is the national anthem going to be good now too? the Boss, in his enthusiasm, was overdoing it, but Florian couldn't promise that, and rightly so, because when, on the following Monday, the Boss made him sing the national anthem in the Opel, after he finished, there were a few moments of dead silence, the Boss said nothing, only puckering his mouth, he hit the steering wheel once, gave Florian the usual smack, and said through clenched teeth: not bad, my son, not bad, you'll get there too, you'll see, you'll get there, which was pretty unusual for him—this encouragement—for which Florian could not find any explanation, if not that in view of his suddenly resurrected interest in Bach, the Boss might have judged that their connection had grown deeper, perhaps because he didn't know, thought Florian, that their connection couldn't be any deeper than it already was, he loved the Boss, and he was very happy that he could show it in a way that the Boss would understand, which wasn't easy, because somehow feelings never really reached the Boss, or only got there by a circuitous route, or only God knew how, and he could usually only communicate with him in that way, with the exception of the past few weeks when Florian had greatly wished to speak to the Boss about certain matters concerning Bach—to understand, for example, what exactly connected him, the Boss, to Johann Sebastian Bach, because he somehow couldn't accept the idea that the Boss was drawn to Bach only because, as the Boss kept saying, Bach was the German character expressed in music, no, this was hard to believe, namely there was something in the Boss's enthusiasm for Bach which seemed to point at something else, something that couldn't be explained through the concepts of Germanness and spirit and suchlike, everything in the Boss was different than how it seemed on the surface: Florian suspected that the Boss had experienced a grave personal tragedy in his childhood or as a young man, a tragedy he couldn't bear to speak about, and it was as if Bach were the salve for this wound that would never heal which the Boss himself did not understand as he was unaware that he carried this wound; Florian sometimes thought of mentioning this, but then it always turned out that it wasn't the right occasion, nor could he find the right time to discuss these things, the Boss's entire bearing, his coarse words and coarse behavior, were a continual warning to everyone around him that there was a border which could never be crossed, and this was partially true, one couldn't simply come close to the Boss, for he would have despised himself, just as he despised anyone who allowed others to come close, a man was determined by his deeds and only by his deeds, this was the Boss's credo, nothing else of him should be visible, only what he does, his deeds, everything was unequivocal and spoke for itself, no time for malarkey, we're not gossiping women, we don't blab about ourselves, we don't blab about others, we look to see what that person did and what he's doing, and that was it, that was the Boss, and Florian knew this too, so that he was almost completely alone with Bach, namely if he could have realized the true origin of the Boss's passion for Bach, then his own connection to Bach would have been easier to resolve, because this connection was not clear-cut, he didn't understand what was happening to him and how he could fall so much under the influence of music, so much so that this one weekly occasion, when, despite the less than ideal circumstances, he could listen to something from the Fourth Brandenburg, was no longer enough, because he yearned to hear a true Bach concert, and that is how he came up with the idea of going to Leipzig where, as it turned out, the Boss was also planning to go, the Boss could never repeat enough how much he wanted to go to Leipzig, only that the Boss wanted to go there with the Kana Symphony, and Florian wanted to go there alone, so he could hear, for the first time in his life, the Thomanerchor; and a bit later on, when it seemed that Frau Ringer had genuinely recovered, as she'd finally been able to remove the bandages, and he didn't have to keep paying sick visits to her in the library, he went to the Herbstcafé and bought a ticket online with his Hartz IV card for the next concert where the cantata *Man singet mit Freuden vom Sieg* was going to be performed, he even mentioned to the Boss that he wasn't coming next Saturday to the rehearsal; but not only did the Boss not seem to notice, he wasn't even interested when later on someone told him that Florian wasn't there, the Boss's worries were much bigger than this, primarily because a few days after the atmosphere had calmed down somewhat regarding the wolf attack, he had become puzzled by the thought of a possible connection between that rotten little sprayer and that wolf attack—it was a sudden, unexpected idea, it came and it went, but then it occurred to him again, then once again, and already this idea wouldn't leave him in peace, and so he decided he would get to the bottom of it, the Boss stopped in to tell Fritz at the Burg that he wasn't going to be around tomorrow, Thursday; Fritz should go ahead and hold the meeting without him, just don't forget to read the next section from Waldemar Glaser's *Ein Trupp SA: Ein Stück Zeitgeschichte*, Fritz promised to do so, and in any event they would have read the section aloud anyway because they loved Glaser, and—as they mentioned among themselves—much more so than Bach, especially his simple writing style, they always understood Glaser immediately, which was not the case with Bach, and not just not immediately—just as Florian was traveling to Leipzig because he realized he couldn't approach Johann Sebastian with his intellect—although he wasn't going there now to change this, because he didn't believe that he could truly reach Bach with his mind, he only wanted to hear what Bach sounded like when a person went to the original place and heard his music live—and this is what happened: Florian picked out a seat for himself in the back, and as he had no experience of what things were like in a church, when the first voices rang out, when the French horns and the trumpets and the trombones sounded, as the audience grew quiet, he leaned back a little bit in the pew, he put his feet in the gap at the bottom of the row of pews in front of him, he clasped his hands together in his lap, and he closed his eyes, because he was so happy that he was here, that he could be here in the Thomaskirche and hear what *Bach was like in reality*, and because of that it was only after a while that he noticed that somebody was gently nudging his side and showing him not to stick his feet into the gap of the pews in front, because that was not proper, Florian quickly yanked his feet back, pulled them under himself and turned red, he had never been in a church, no one had ever taken him there, not even from the Institute, obviously the Boss had never done so, Florian had no idea of how one was supposed to behave here, so that after he was nudged like this he could only manage to focus his attention on sitting up straight, his legs properly pulled in beneath his body, and he awaited the following nudge: namely he heard the music flowing from above, the choir singing, but with his tensed body he could only wait for that poking hand to once again call his attention to something improper he was doing, something he wasn't allowed to do, or, conversely, something that he should have been doing at this or that point, and even though nobody nudged him again he couldn't pay attention to the music, so that when it was over, and he left the church with the crowd streaming out through the doors, he felt such fatigue in his body as never before, every one of his limbs hurt, every muscle was aching, he thought his head was about to fall off, there, in front of the beautiful church portal on the square, so he left the Thomaskirche, wishing to quickly run into a little side street to be alone and sit down somewhere where nobody would be nudging him, only that the area was full of cafés and McDonald's and restaurants and pubs and monuments and museums precisely about Johann Sebastian, he could find refuge nowhere, so he walked all the way to the park next to Schillerstraße where he could finally sit down on a bench, and he could think about what happened to him in the Thomaskirche, this wasn't for him, he thought, being in direct proximity to Johann Sebastian Bach was not for him, he was never going to get so close to him ever again, because that would be the end, everything was hurting, he was completely exhausted, even his lungs were hurting because at times he hadn't even dared to take a breath in the Thomaskirche, or during moments when he only dared to take very small breaths, especially when the chorus soared triumphantly in the enormous space of the Thomaskirche, he had stealthily glanced to the side and seen the happy devotion on people's faces, and it was clear to him that Johann Sebastian Bach was exactly that genius who did not belong to everyone, or at least not in such direct proximity, and so he returned to Kana with the late train, determined to never get so close to Bach ever again; it would be fine to keep on listening to the cantatas or the Passions quietly in the Herbstcafé, he said the same thing the next morning when the Deputy rang his bell, because the elevator happened to be working that day, somehow it started working again all by itself so that the Deputy took this opportunity to visit, which also meant that he had to sit down with him in the kitchen, in a word he told the Deputy that he had gone to Leipzig, and he had listened to a Bach concert, and although it was wondrous, almost incomprehensible, the whole thing made him utterly exhausted, and he was never going to go to Leipzig again, why didn't you ask me first? the Deputy inquired, suddenly attentive, I could have told you straightaway that there's no point in going to Leipzig, I see you know how to get around, traveling here and there like a commuter, I see that, but if you had asked me I would have talked you out of it, and you would have saved yourself the trouble, because these days the crowds and the noise and the stench there are so unbearable that little people like us from Kana can't stand it, let them breathe in that stench, said the Deputy, let everyone breathe in their own stench, and as he had found what he said to be very wise, he nodded a few times to his own words, and he gazed fixedly into Florian's light-blue eyes; it was the habit of the Deputy, whenever he pronounced something he considered to be important, to lean forward a bit, nearly right into his interlocutor's face, only that now he didn't have to lean forward too much because the kitchen table was so small that if two people sat next to each other, there was really no other way to sit there than to lean into each other's faces, but Florian understood the Deputy, and he agreed with him, he too nodded a couple of times, then asked if he'd like a cup of tea, you always ask me this, Florian, the Deputy shook his head, even though you know that I only drink beer, have you got any beer? well, you're always asking me this, Florian laughed, when you know very well that I don't have beer at home, well, never mind, the Deputy made a resigned gesture, like someone whose day had been ruined, let's go down to the IKS pub, what do you say? well, right now, answered Florian, I'd rather not go, it's still early for me, I'm going to lie down a bit more if you don't mind, because as I said, I got home at midnight, so let's have a cigarette, the Deputy played for time, not bothering with the fact that Florian never smoked, because he didn't really wish to go to the IKS pub by himself, which meant of course that he didn't want to be alone: I'm alone too much, and here his voice took on a tone of complaint, and exactly me, who never could stand to be by myself, with Christine gone I haven't been able to find my place, do you know what it means, Florian, to miss someone? ah, how would you know—never mind, obviously you understand that I miss Christine; upon my word, when she was alive, I really couldn't stand her never-ending nagging, because she nagged me, Florian, that woman, you don't even know how much she nagged me, sometimes I was ready to throw her out the window, but on the one hand, we live on the ground floor, on the other hand, well, you know how these things are, now already I miss her— and he would have continued, but Florian was gradually and politely ushering him out of the apartment, then he went to lie down again, he fell asleep immediately, his trip yesterday had really worn him out, to Leipzig and back in a single day, then what happened in the Thomaskirche, he had to sleep it off, and he slept almost until two p.m., then he got dressed and sat down at his kitchen table, he took out a piece of A4 paper, and despite his earlier resolution, he attempted another letter: it has been almost two years since my first letter to you, and now it is almost one year that Herr Köhler has disappeared because of me, and this time Florian did not rack his brain over every single word, he just wrote everything down as it came to him: he was well aware that the Chancellor adored Wagner, but, well, music was music, and he took it as certain that—Wagner or not—Bach was held in as high regard in Berlin as did Florian here in Kana, and that is why he was now turning to the Chancellor with a recommendation he hadn't touched upon in his previous letters as that realization had not yet occurred, for only recently had he discovered that beauty in the music of Johann Sebastian Bach that made one resonate from within, and here he stopped because he was rather pleased with the phrase "resonate from within," he quickly picked up his three-colored pen, clicked on the red cartridge, and underscored the words "resonate from within" twice, but it wasn't just the beauty, he wrote, but that in Bach, he felt, there might be a recommendation as to what to do in the event of a catastrophe, which—as he had already written to her innumerable times—could ensue at any moment, therefore he felt that Bach must be introduced into this discussion, for months now he had been under the effect of Bach, he could not say anything more precise at this time, as approaching such greatness via mere intellect was impossible for him, but perhaps others—the great ones of the nation, of the world—could perhaps do so, and this was his recommendation, and for the time being this was all he wished to append to his previous statements, and with that he closed the letter, wishing the Chancellor good health from Kana, where, as she must know, she was always awaited with open arms, he himself had even gone out, whenever he could, to the train station to wait for her, but it was clear that her thousands and thousands of responsibilities did not permit her to get away, and so he, Herscht 07769, would continue to wait, the Chancellor could come to Kana whenever she wished, he needed only a sign from her, and once again he would go out to meet her, and with this Florian concluded the letter, folded it twice, slipped it into an envelope and addressed it, and it seemed, from the expression on Jessica's face, when he took the letter to the post office, as if she was happy to see Florian again, because I thought you were never coming back, she said, then she took the envelope, she read the addressee's name and said nothing, and only smiling, she winked at Florian, and it was as if Herr Volkenant had sensed this wink, because in that moment he too called out from the back room: well, Florian? Berlin again? then when the two of them were back home, Herr Volkenant brought up the subject at dinner: Jessica, does it seem to you too that Florian needs to see a doctor? and when Jessica brushed the question aside, he added that in his opinion there was going to be trouble, you'll see, crazy things like this don't stop by themselves, and once again I'm telling you that Florian isn't going to stop here, I see what's going on, I see enough people every day at the post office, when someone starts acting strange like this, it doesn't stop, you'll see, it will be the same with Florian too, but Jessica just laughed off the whole thing, really now, how can you think something like that? Florian is such a lovely boy, he's not crazy or anything like that, he's just a little odd, and well, why—she turned to Volkenant—do you think he's the only one in Kana with a screw loose? well, I admit you're right about that, Volkenant laughed, and that concluded the discussion about Florian, and now they really started seriously in on their dinner, tonight they were celebrating because they had met each other precisely nine years ago today, and they always commemorated this occasion in the same way, Jessica roasted an entire chicken in the oven, crispy brown, first they drank champagne, then after dinner, in the living room, a good bottle of Rhine wine, and this happened today as well, the wine was properly cooled, Volkenant had bought it yesterday and put it in the fridge, it was a wonderful evening, they leaned back on their sofa bed, the chiseled wineglasses in their hands which they only used for celebrations such as tonight, Jessica closed her eyes and she said: you know, Horst, I'm happy, I'm happy with you, I like my work, I like people, our savings are growing in the bank, maybe in two years or so we can exchange the Ford, my dear, I don't wish for anything else—really, nothing else? Volkenant grinned at her, and when they went into the bedroom, Volkenant threw himself on her; the only thing that Jessica didn't like about her husband was that he didn't bother with his socks, even though they were living together as a married couple, he still just threw his socks all over the place, and she couldn't stand these rolled-up socks thrown all over the place, somehow this put her off, sometimes she complained about it as well: you know, this is just so ... so ... well, how can I even put it, it's one of those things that can make a person feel disillusioned, well, but there was no point in talking about this to him, because Volkenant didn't care, for him it was a minor detail undeserving of attention, only that, well, it did matter to Jessica: if he could have done something about those socks, as they were living together as a married couple, her happiness would have been complete, but even so she was happy, although she rebuked him: but for those scattered socks he would be the ideal husband, still, she never dared betray to him that what really bothered her was that these socks always smelled like feet when Volkenant took them off, she tried everything, she bought all different kinds of antiperspirants, but none of them helped, what should I do, she sighed to her mother in Jena during this or that visit when they were alone, nothing helps, Horst is just the type who has sweaty feet, that's how it is, well, my girl, her mother consoled her, you'll never find a man without an imperfection, and I myself have always thought that Horst is one of the best, oh, I think so too, Jessica laughed, and that was it, she resigned herself to there being no solution, and life went on, as she always liked to say, and life did go on, although Florian didn't come to the post office for a while as he was thinking that if a letter came from Berlin then the postal carrier would bring it to him if he wasn't always strolling over to the post office to check, which also meant, of course, that his hopes of receiving a response had somewhat dwindled, Florian realized that world leaders could not address these problems all at once; he had to be more patient, no matter how difficult it was, in addition, he too was well aware that the most important thing was not whether he himself got a reply or not, but rather what the Chancellor would do in this state of high emergency, for a while now he'd also been following the UN Security Council meetings on the internet, and even though he didn't understand English, by using Google Translate he was able to more or less make out what was going on and when, and for the time being he hadn't come across any topics that seemed to indicate that the questions he'd proposed were being tabled, and of course it was possible that the whole thing was taking place behind closed doors, moreover the matter could already be in the early phases of preparation, and this possibility reassured him, moreover one weekend, as he was sitting on his bench by the Saale, a thought came to his head: what if Herr Köhler had disappeared precisely because it was Adrian Köhler they were questioning about this matter in New York instead of him, he jumped up, and suddenly the whole thing seemed so rational, yes! he punched his fist into the air, that's it! and he punched the air again, and a small songbird in the foliage of the chestnut tree, frightened, darted away, Florian jumped up, and suddenly he understood the what and the why, oh, why hadn't he thought of this already?! and he feverishly set off toward the handball field, then he went back, and walked along the narrow lane leading to the small garden plots, how could I have been so stupid?! he shook his head in his joy, and with every single step he was ever more certain that this was the only explanation: Herr Köhler had been found to be more suitable than himself for explaining every- thing to the decision-makers, well of course it was Herr Köhler and not him, because what did he, Florian, know about these things, all he'd done was sense the existence of a problem; of course the real expert was Herr Köhler, and moreover it occurred to Florian that when he'd seen Herr Köhler for the last time, he'd said something like: "from this point on, he would handle things," well, and now everything appeared in a completely different light, his face radiant from relief, from libera- tion, Florian rushed back to the town, and he could only say to the people he knew whose paths he crossed that there was no problem, everything was fine, everyone could calm down now, the matter was in good hands, and so on, which, of course, made no sense to anyone, only if Florian either had finally gone mad, or if he'd finally gotten mar- ried, because these people were, for the most part, of the opinion that Florian's only problem was that he did not have a wife, a man needs a wife, Herr Heinrich analyzed the situation to the others at Ilona's buf- fet, where he was a kind of job allocator: he could occasionally get black-market work for people on Hartz IV with a 25 percent cut, and therefore he was held in fairly high esteem there; a young, strapping man like Florian without a woman isn't even a man, and this will lead to something bad, he said, and he said it now, too, as Florian came running in, and breathless, he stated: everyone could calm down, he realized what was going on, and already he had stormed out, he's been snatched up, Hoffmann interjected and he quickly looked around to see if everyone had gotten the joke, and they had, because the regulars burst into laughter like one, Ilona only smiled behind the counter, usually she hardly took part in the conversation, preferring to listen, at times adding a comment here or there about this or that, but only rarely, it was not her job to keep the customers entertained, as her husband always used to say, but instead to draw the boundary as to how far they could go, because a boundary had to be drawn, because sometimes the beer slid down a little too smoothly, especially on paydays, and it had its effect, the stories got a bit out of control, and Ilona had to cool down the runaway atmosphere with a more sober sentence, but one or two such remarks were always enough, because Ilona was a saint in the eyes of the regulars, as soon as she spoke, her wish was fulfilled, Ilona was the star here, Hoffmann frequently said it good and loud so that the person he was speaking about would also hear him, even if the electricity were shut off, we'd still be able to see in her shining light, at which everyone raised their glasses and they drank to her, they drank to Ilona, they drank to this island of peace which was truly the only light in their lives, and although they referred to Ilona as their queen, who of course did not think that way at all, she was aware her customers loved the Grillhäusel, but it was enough for her to know that her customers were satisfied, that was her goal, the business went on, it didn't bring in a lot, but it was enough to survive in this great unemployment when she had arrived here all the way from Transylvania to get married: the task had been clear, at first they converted her husband's house, located in a small settlement on the outskirts of Kana, into a pension, more precisely the upper floor, and they themselves moved into the ground floor, and lived in one room with an adjacent kitchen and bathroom, and at the beginning it seemed like a good idea, but then the Vietnamese started moving out of the Hochhaus, and no one could believe all the alarming reports about the Porcelain Factory going bankrupt, but that was exactly what happened, and out of many thousands of employees, only a few hundred remained, no one was expecting this, let alone Ilona and her husband, they had been thinking that these enormous changes would bring not bankruptcy, but prosperity, because to tell the truth the Porcelain Factory hadn't been so glittering even in the old days, before the changes, but now at any time a big investor might come from the West, everyone was thinking this, at least for a while, Ilona and her husband thought the same thing, but no one came from the West, not only that, but whoever could left Kana, so that the pension was hardly operational; to stand on their own two legs they needed something else and that's when Ilona got the idea of the Grillhäusel, this would place them on a sure footing, or as she herself expressed it, eight certain concrete columns, because this shack will stand for a while, Ilona and her husband reassured each other at home, and it was true: as soon as one customer stopped frequenting the Grillhäusel due to sudden illness or from having passed away, another, from the immediate neighborhood, would show up, and so the number of customers remained more or less stable, exactly enough to make the Grillhäusel worth the energy they had invested, as Ilona expressed it, so that they could make ends meet, and in the past few years as well tourism had begun to increase, and so now it was worthwhile for them to think about making some improvements to the house so that they could rent rooms not only to workers but tourists as well, of course they needed money for that, and they saved diligently, two more years, said Ilona's husband, and we'll be out of the red, but they didn't get out of the red, because the appearance of the wolves changed everything, because now everyone was talking about not a single wolf but wolves, the news of other attacks also spreading, people cursed Brandenburg, they cursed Bayern and the Poles and the Czechs, they cursed the police, they cursed the state government, but they cursed NABU most of all—they'd learned of the existence of NABU only after the first attack, but then NABU quickly became the chief target of the residents of Kana, well, NABU and the Jews, announced the hero of the Burg when he finally turned up, because nobody had seen any trace of him for two weeks, that's exactly how much time he had needed, exactly that much, he said, but at least now he knew that those ink-slinging hacks and the wolves, they were one and the same, at which the comrades looked at him, uncomprehending, and the Boss's face turned paprika red: what, this again, what the fuck do you not understand about this?! don't you get it?! and he held his arms apart, and: no, the answer was mute silence as they really didn't know what he was talking about after these two weeks; what I'm thinking, comrades, the Boss said in irritation, is that this is a conspiracy, and we're not talking about some hoodie-wearing douchebag hack with who knows how many accomplices randomly spraying these Bach walls, this is an attack here, and do you know against whom and against what?! he looked from one to the other, but from their faces it was only possible to read that they were waiting for the answer from him, the answer, however, did not come, the Boss merely waved his hand at them, downed his beer, and left the Burg without a word, slamming the front door so angrily that it echoed throughout the entire neighborhood, Frau Hopf sat up in bed, frightened, and could not fall asleep again for about a half hour, convinced she'd heard a gunshot, but the Boss was already ahead, the overall situation was clear to him, and well, of course he lost his patience, he explained in the Opel to Florian, still blinking from drowsiness, the Boss had woken him up a bit after five a.m., saying: let's go, there's work to be done, but there was no work, Florian had to stay in the car when the Boss got out in Eisenach in front of the Bachhaus, and he ran his index finger all along the wall on both sides of the entrance, where, despite the cleaning, the graffitied WE could still be made out after all this time, even if faintly, as well as certain details of the WOLF HEAD, the Boss muttered something to himself, then got back in the car, and they set off driving around the town, and as soon as the Boss saw the first homeless person, he slammed on the brakes, jumped out of the Opel, grabbed the man by the collar, he shook him and shook him again, then he pressed the homeless man up against the wall where he had been sleeping, and hissed into his face: I'll kill you, motherfucker, if you don't answer me honestly, at which the homeless man just blinked at him in fear and tried to nod once, indicating that he would answer honestly, the Boss hissed at him: you know anything about the sprayer?! what, me, who?! the homeless man whimpered, so the Boss had to explain: the sprayer who defaced the entrance of the Bachhaus, fuck it—him; him? I don't know anything, the homeless man shook his head, I only heard that... what?! what did you hear?! the Boss immediately squeezed his throat, well, well, well, that Franzi, the Austrian, saw him, the unlucky man said, and tried to catch some breath but without too much success, because he had already gotten the next question: who, fuck it, who saw him? to which he could only answer: well, that, that, that criminal, so where is this Austrian Franzi? the next question came swooping down—over there, by the church, the homeless man forced the words out of himself, and he indicated the direction with his eyes, and the Boss knew what church he was thinking of, he let him go and shoved him aside like a scrap of rag, and within a few minutes he was already squeezing the throat of another one: are you that Franzi?! me, me, what the hell...?! is it true that you saw the sprayer who defaced the entrance of the Bachhaus two years ago?! yes, just let me go already, and the Boss let up on the pressure, but didn't let go completely, he leaned into his face: was it you?! of course not, answered the frightened man, then who was it?! it was a man, a man?! what kind of man, fuck it?! well, like... a man in a jacket, came the response, at which the Boss let him go, tapped him on the face, and said in a calm voice: if you describe to me exactly what he looked like you'll get one euro, and this set off an avalanche, because by the time the homeless man had finished saying that the sprayer had been wearing a green windbreaker, a beret, and brand-new sneakers, and they got back in the car and drove to the next corner, who knew how the news had spread so fast, because the next homeless man had already appeared, and he said to them: ah, that Franzi is always wasted, don't believe a word he says, because the sprayer looked about twenty or twenty-two years old, with a bleached white mohawk, with eyeglasses that wrapped around his ears, and he looked at them through the opened car door and held out his palm, then they questioned him for a while longer, then circled around again, they went back to the church square, but then a fourth figure jumped in front of them with great velocity, this time an older woman, and when she saw that the car was braking and someone leaning out of the rolled-down car window, she took a few steps back so as to pull a nearby shopping cart closer to herself, and she clutched the shopping cart tightly as she said: may lightning strike me if it wasn't a man about thirty-five years old, wearing a mask, mask, well, go on, the Boss rolled down the car window some more, yes, a mask, she continued, a kind of black or dark mask, the kind bank robbers wear, you know, and he was walking so slowly that I hardly heard him as he glided past me, just then I woke up, because I was sleeping down there, I remember exactly, she said, I was sleeping on the little square above the museum, you know, on one of the benches, and suddenly someone glided past me without making any noise, but of course I woke up, I said to myself: fuck it, Rosalind, what the hell was that, so that I watched the whole thing to see what he was doing, because he painted the word GOD really big, then he painted that dog's face, I said to myself: Rosalind, this'll be a big mess, and so it was—well, that's enough for now, Granny, get lost, the Boss

170

interrupted her, you run along now and get yourself some fucking treatment, and he pressed ten cents into her hand, at which the woman pulled a long face, raised the coin as if she couldn't see it well, then she looked at the Boss with rage, but he had already rolled up the window of the Opel and turned off from the square, we're going to lock *them* up in the camps as well, the Boss said through clenched teeth, and he sped up, with one hand, he tapped a cigarette out of the pack, stuck it in his mouth and lit the cigarette up in the corner of his mouth, tilting his head to one side so the smoke wouldn't get in his eyes, but it had already done so, so he started blinking with one eye and he kept on cursing, but only to himself as if Florian weren't even there: I'm not getting anywhere with this, godfuckingdammit, they didn't see anything at all, and he hit the steering wheel, then, in answer to Florian's question of how did they even know? the Boss snapped: they didn't fucking know shit, because these motherfuckers only knew who we were looking for, obviously the cops were already prowling around here asking questions, and the locals as well; that explains how they knew who we were looking for, said Florian, but I still don't understand how the news spread so fast among them, ah, the Boss waved him off, and once again he pulled down the window a hand's breadth to flick the ashes from the end of his cigarette, they don't find out these things from each other but *they sense* when you need something from them, they always sense when there's a chance to milk a loser, the Boss explained, because they still have a life instinct, and that functions only in one direction, in the direction of the smell of money, well, the whole thing goes in that direction, if you get my drift, but I just don't know— the Boss's face clouded over, like someone who was thinking of something else, but still wanted to complete his train of thought—I don't understand why they're not cleared away, the garbage truck comes around every day, no?! ah, whatever, let's leave it, he concluded, and they drove out to the A4, although at the Erfurt junction, they didn't go straight but turned off onto the A71, Florian didn't dare ask why they were going to Erfurt, or if it was even Erfurt they were headed to, but they did go to Erfurt, it was still very early, the Boss looked at his watch, he stopped the car at an Aral gas station and they sat down for coffee, well, this definitely isn't Nadír's coffee, fuck it, the Boss noted after the first sip, and pushed the mug away in disgust, but there was no further conversation, Florian did not wish to disturb him as he saw that the Boss was really thinking about something, they sat for a good long while, Florian ate a sandwich, the Boss didn't want one, he just kept looking at his watch, and he kept wanting to take a cigarette out of the packet and then he kept slipping the pack back into his pocket, finally he stood up, and he told Florian to wait there, he had something to take care of, he didn't want to say what it was, although this time it was something to do with Florian; the Boss got annoyed, having to wait such a fucking long time as he sat next to his cold coffee at the Aral gas station, and it was because of Florian, because the Boss wasn't too pleased with what had happened to that Weatherman Köhler, not because—he explained later on to the comrades that weekend—not because whatever the fuck had happened to him was so important, but because he didn't like it when things like this happened in the town, things they didn't know about, and that was why, once the Boss reached the side entrance of a large building, he called a certain telephone number, and he spoke into the phone, it's me, he said, and after two or three minutes a young man came out, wearing trainers, jeans, a light-blue windbreaker with white stripes, both hands in his pockets, his jacket slightly pulled apart on his chest so that the writing on the T-shirt below could be seen, which read: Albuquerque, and beneath it, in bigger letters, RIO GRANDE; this man and the Boss went to the side of the building where only police cars were parked, and then the Boss asked him: what do you know? and the man looked at him searchingly for a bit, then he answered in a very high and subdued voice: the truth was that they knew nothing, nothing?! the Boss's eyebrows jumped up, for all intents and purposes nothing, the man held his hands apart, and the Boss was filled with rage, and he yelled: I had to wait several weeks for this?! this is why I had to come here at the break of dawn?! why the fuck couldn't you have told me this on the phone?! and he turned on his heels, but he still shouted back at the man: at least you could shoot that fucking Aral gas station attendant, his coffee is so crap that he deserves the gallows, but he didn't wait for a reply, even though the man said something, although perhaps just into the air, the Boss left the parking lot, he went back to the Aral on the corner of Kranichfelder Straße, he motioned to Florian to come out, and already they were sweeping back on the A71, the roads were in decidedly good shape, and not only here around Erfurt, but in almost all of Thuringia, people no longer remembered the catastrophic conditions that earlier prevailed on these asphalt surfaces, they no longer remembered the dangerously wide grilles in the road, the potholes and ditches forming after the frosts, the collapsed roadsides, the troughs and ditches hollowed out in the asphalt in the summer heat by truck wheels, just as no one remembered how they had to drive back then, because the main thing was not to run into one of these potholes or be swept over to the lacerated, crumbling edge of the road, drivers always clutching haphazardly at the steering wheel, suddenly braking or accelerating, making unexpected turns, and of course there were innumerable accidents because it was impossible to pay attention to one hundred things at once, although everything changed quite radically in the new era, this had to be acknowledged, noted the residents of Kana, moreover, even the Boss uttered words of praise, and he knew what he was talking about: I know what I'm talking about, he would say, because it was a death race, fuck it, a death race every time you got in the car, but we accepted it as if it had been ordered by the Supreme Authority of the Comrades, things were better now, even the Boss recognized this, and people got used to the fact that the asphalt was good, and so now people took it for granted, and they were happy to curse the one-way traffic while the repairs dragged on, because the repairs still dragged on, with no start or end date ever announced, just as on the A88 repairs were never announced, this was the road used most by the Boss and his crew, if only even because of its designation, the Boss noted at times, and he winked at Florian, who didn't understand what he was getting at, he recalled that earlier the Opel had had a different license plate which also contained the number 88, then a couple of years ago they had to exchange it, but he hadn't understood then, and he didn't understand now, he tried to ask the Boss about it, but the Boss leaned into his face, grinning mutely, and only said: I'm willing to bet, fuck it, that you don't even know your ABCs, but this didn't help Florian, the Boss seemed to decidedly enjoy that he was such an idiot, this child is such an idiot, comrades, the Boss would tell them, waving his cigarette around, even if only rarely, but when the mood was better: he just can't figure out what this 88 is, motherfuckers, although in a whole bunch of other things his mind is sharp like a razor, physics and the universe and things like that, but now there he is sitting next to me, and he's trying to figure it out, and no and no, he can't figure it out, because this is a giant baby who can't figure out anything that isn't physics or the universe, and the Boss blew out the smoke and concluded the matter with a facial expression that betrayed that not only did Florian's slow comprehension not bother him, but it was as if the whole thing amused him, and yes, in general, it tended to amuse him how this Florian was such a strange character, and there was some pride in how he, the Boss, despite everything and in his own way was fond of this bumbling half-wit, because that's what he is, a bumbling half-wit, I know he is, but I was the one who pulled him out of that fucking Institute, I'm the one raising him, and anyway, he's still developing, and you'll see—the Boss looked around at his comrades—one day he'll be useful to us, because I'm raising him to be a patriot, godfuckingdammit, well, and they drank to that, and Florian kept on wondering, when it came up in conversation, what the devil was meant by this 88, at first, of course, he thought it was a double infinity sign, although he had no idea what this double infinity might be: of course, he mused, if we turn the number eight on one side, then it becomes the sign of infinity, but then why one number eight placed above the other? two infinities, hmmm, that's interesting, he reflected, although he knew that this was not a direction that would most likely lead him to the Boss; he surmised that the Boss wouldn't interpret the two number eights in this manner, but still, what could it be, and why had the Boss mentioned the alphabet? it all seemed so incomprehensible, best to forget the whole thing, Florian thought, it doesn't have any great meaning, he would find out later, eventually the Boss would reveal it, but the Boss didn't reveal it, moreover he got seriously angry at him when they got back from Erfurt, as before Florian got out of the car to open the gate for the Opel, he said: Boss, if you want to do something because of me in Erfurt, don't do it, because there is a solution, and he described it, and as he spoke, his gaze luminous with enthusiasm, the Boss's face grew completely dark, until he burst out: you are really such an idiotic asshole, fuck it, this isn't possible, come down to earth already, because this whole thing is just the invention of your own troubled mind, and the UN Security Council, what Security Council?! are you even fucking normal?! and he began shaking Florian with one hand and Florian clutched the seat belt and hung his head, and he turned bright red, although he would have been more than happy to explain further that yes, he had realized where Herr Köhler was; he no longer dared speak, he only waited until he could finally get out of the car and he went to the gate so as not to get clobbered even more, because you're going to get what's coming to you, fuck it, the Boss leaned out of the car window, if you don't stop this crazy nonsense, you're going to get it, and you know what will happen, and of course Florian knew, he opened the gate, the Boss rolled into the yard, he closed the gate while the dog on the chain barked at him with its foaming mouth, then without saying goodbye or even looking back, Florian sneaked away to the Hochhaus, although the seven floors were enough for him to calm down a bit as on the seventh floor already Florian came to the realization that he clearly had not come forth with his explanation at the best time, and really it wasn't the best time, because the Boss had been very preoccupied with something else—namely, the Boss was very preoccupied with the fact that he had discovered the connection, although to take the next step was not so easy, moreover it was fucking difficult, the Boss acknowledged through gritted teeth, but take the next step he must, because where there was a connection there was also an explanation, only that he could not find it, namely he was only able to do so when on a Wednesday, after they had finished some work in Rudolstadt and were coming back to Kana, they turned off from the A88 toward the town, and the Boss recommended that they not have dinner separately that day, but instead have a good little hot and spicy something in the Panda Restaurant, and as it happened they found Fritz there who motioned for them to sit next to him, then he leaned over to the Boss and whispered into his ear that he'd been looking for him for at least an hour but since he hadn't been able to charge his cell phone, he couldn't call him, and it was important, because he'd gotten hold of some serious information, at which the Boss merely motioned with his head that it would be better for them to talk outside, they both went outside while Florian ordered a sweet-and-sour soup and a long noodle dish called One Hundred Shining Lotuses, Florian could eat, and really liked spicy food, only that of course the Panda's prices were not really tailored for his wallet—not so much that he couldn't come here every now and then, he could, but not regularly, no, that he couldn't do, because the Hartz IV benefits and the ninety euros, the so-called pocket money that the Boss paid him in cash every week, did not permit it, and not only that, but Florian was saving, he was always saving his money for something, now, ever since the Boss had not permitted him a car, he was dreaming of a new laptop, because his HP was often breaking down, and he never knew what the problem was, what he had to do, sometimes he couldn't even restart it, then he would wait for a couple of hours, he tried everything, he pulled out the charging cable and he plugged it back in, he pressed the keys on the keyboard, he tried to do everything differently, and just when he was about to give up, suddenly the machine came back to life and started working again, well, but life with a laptop like this was uncertain, so he needed a new one, well, not a completely new one, but a laptop in good condition for which he was in a pretty good position, because he'd already saved up 210 euros, he still needed to get to about 260 or 280 euros, and then he would speak to the Boss, so that for Florian, life began to show its sunnier side, he regarded the disappearance of Herr Köhler as practically solved, Frau Ringer had completely recovered, only her old voice hadn't come back—he wouldn't say that it had gotten deeper, it had always had a kind of deep tone, instead its timbre had changed, somehow it was sharper, raspier—the Deputy visited him ever more frequently if the elevator was working, or if it wasn't working, he called up for Florian to come down, Frau Hopf seemed ever more visibly fond of him, they were fond of him too at Rosario's, and they also liked him at Ilona's, if he happened to step into the buffet, his heart grew warm from the greetings of those who were sitting there, and now he felt a new laptop to be within imaginable distance, so that he only felt cause for worry if he had to pass by Oststraße, he tried to avoid that area if he could, although still sometimes he had to pass by there and then he felt the pain slashing through him even though he never even looked down the street, he just quickly rushed by and went on his way up to the Altstadt or to Frau Ringer or out to Rosario's at the Aral gas station to see if there might be some work for him, or nowadays he was going ever more frequently over to Frau Hopf's, recently he also had begun looking in there if he had nothing else to do, it was good to be there, and Frau Hopf wasn't surprised, she turned on the light in the breakfast room, sat him down and placed a coffee or tea or soft drink in front of him, whatever Florian asked for, and they chatted—mainly about the wolves—because Frau Hopf, like the other locals, spoke of them in the plural now, and that was the strange thing because that was also Fritz's news as he whispered into the Boss's ear: they're here again, who?! the Boss pulled away as soon as Fritz's decayed, stinking breath struck him, but Fritz once again came close to his ear, and said: well, what else?! what do you think?! and he nodded and held his hands apart, indicating that, well, the Boss must know already, no, goddammit, I have no fucking idea, speak clearly, and what are you even whispering about here?! at which Fritz was slightly offended, and he straightened up: well, the wolves, he said coolly, and he poked the place of his missing eyetooth with his little finger, well, what about them?! they're here again, a whole pack, where?! yelled the Boss, people saw them at Spitzenberg, they even photographed them, supposedly, when they appeared last night, but the Boss didn't wait to hear about what happened last night, because this, he realized, was the explanation: the plan was to wipe out everything that was German with a pandemic, but first the wolves were being let loose on them to instill fear, to drown them in chaos, everything that was Thuringia, Germany, civilization, to fence them in, then force them out, to take their Lebensraum so that they would await the evening, trembling, and to hear, from beneath their blankets, as somewhere nearby, and ever closer, the wolves howling— the components of a never-ending list were clattering around inside the Boss's head by the time he got home, as he kicked the gate open wide and threw himself into the Opel, and even forgetting to throw something to the dog, he drove so quickly out of the gate, onto Christian-Eckardt-Straße that he'd gotten a third of the way to Jena before he realized that he wasn't going in the right direction, he turned around as soon as he could, pressed on the gas, and didn't even look at the speedometer—the Opel could take it—and now he was racing across

Kana in the opposite direction, toward Orlamünde, when he slowed down, the car's brakes squealing, he was almost hit from behind, he pulled down the window and yelled at the person who'd almost rearended him: you idiot bastard, I'll gouge your eyes out!! are you fucking blind?!! and he turned onto the shoulder, his body rocking back and forth behind the steering wheel, and he was blowing out the air and panting, because he knew that the solution was here, he knew this, now he understood, the only thing he didn't know was where the fuck he was going, he thought: the only thing is that I don't know where the fuck I am going on this goddamned road, his heart was pounding so furiously that he could hardly hear the sirens, nor when a police car, lights flashing, stopped next to him, and he didn't care about the cops giving him crap, he blew into the Breathalyzer, he didn't know these ones personally so he paid the fine, and then he was on the road again toward Orlamünde where he had to stop again, then he turned into the first small parking place that he saw, lit a cigarette with trembling hands, and he said to himself loudly: ah, no, they're not coming with drones, and they're not poisoning the wells, ah, of course not! they're sending wolves, for the time being, because for the time being they are only sending these grimacing hordes, but there was a problem with the information he'd gotten, because Fritz had been taken in by the gossip about the wolves, usually people could tell him things and he was always sharp, he never believed it, but today somebody had come with exactly this news, and Fritz made the mistake of believing them, although he shouldn't have, and he only found out after he'd bumped into the Boss and then he went to see for himself, up along the L1062, to talk to the Revierförster in Strößwitz—the information had supposedly come from him, only that it turned out that the information, unfortunately, had not come from him, he knew nothing about this, the Revierförster shook his head, he knew nothing at all about this because he himself wouldn't even be able to say anything about it, as apart from

179

that one single wolf that attacked the married couple, there had been no kind of wolf pack around here ever since ... but he himself never even met up with anyone whom he could have told this to, look, sir, he explained to Fritz, who was visibly nervous, I haven't been down in the town for at least a week, I don't really like to breathe in the same air as all of you ever since the town was sold out to tourists, before there was always the stench of the Porcelain Factory, now there's the stench of tourists, well, the forest ranger gazed fixedly into Fritz's eyes, and he made them flash strangely: to be frank, I don't even know what I hate more, the old stench of the Porcelain Factory, or the stench of the tourists today, but one thing is sure, I hate all of you who made it so hideous, so that, no, he said, he'd been down in the town most recently last Saturday to purchase some needed items, in any event he would describe himself—he kept making his eyes flash at Fritz—as someone whose needs were few: some bread, some beer, he was perfectly fine without any civilization, it's not the wolves you should be frightened of, but the hordes of tourists, that's what I would be frightened of if I cared at all about what was going on down there, but I don't care, as you yourself may suspect, and with that he turned away from Fritz and left him there, he went back into his house; the conversation had taken place in front of the gate, because he had allowed this character only as far as the gate, he knew him well just as he knew the whole gang of thugs, they were all seriously ill characters, the police raided them from time to time, the forest ranger grumbled as he went back into his house, but they just kept growing back like mushrooms, and well, what's so amazing about mushrooms, that's what mushrooms are like, they always grow back, he didn't even understand, he remarked, once inside, to his wife: why is everyone so amazed these Nazis are back again, history repeats itself, didn't Marx say that? they should have been paying better attention to Marx, he sat down at the table and drank the rest of his coffee, because they had just been drinking their coffee when the doorbell rang, you can toss Marx out the window, he leaned back in his chair, apart from a few things he said, because we've grown bitter, and since we've thrown out Marx, we will continue to be bitter, I'm telling you, he told her, then he was silent, his wife did not respond, just as she did not at other times, there was usually not too much in the way of conversation in the Revierförster's household, they only spoke when absolutely necessary, in addition the woman did not agree with her husband concerning Marx, because in her view—which she had expressed only once in their marriage, but she had expressed it once all the same—that in her view the best use of Marx would have been to take both volumes of *Das Kapital*—a deluxe edition with good, hard covers—and to have struck every single one of them, but really, every single member of the leadership of the Sozialistische Einheitspartei Deutschlands, dead with it at the time of the great reunification, because they destroyed us, because they sold us off for one deutsche mark, because they left us in the lurch while they saved their own skins, this was her opinion about Marx, and so much for the great unification, fundamentally nothing had changed, because fundamentally nothing ever changes: they eradicated the forests, slaughtered the animals left and right, they did so back then and they're doing the same thing now, and the bees?! the bees?! there'll be hell to pay, she said; this was her opinion, and she never mentioned it again—Fritz rushed back to Kana, and looked for the Boss in a panic, no one in the Burg knew where he was, not even Florian whom Fritz ran into at Ilona's, and the Boss wasn't even at home, Fritz brooded, although he wasn't the brooding type, but right now he was definitely scared shitless, and that's exactly how he expressed it when he went back to the Burg and told them what was going on: I am definitely scared shitless, the Boss is going to tear my head off, but the Boss didn't tear his head off when he turned up, he just looked at Fritz for a few seconds mutely, his face full of rage, then he kneed him in the balls and stormed off—then the

Boss went home, let the dog off the chain, he turned on his laptop and sat down in front of the TV, but according to his habit he didn't turn the TV on, he looked at the rug on the floor, the patterns on the rug, and how the part of the rug that he walked over regularly was obvious because it had gotten pretty worn out, although he didn't like carpets anyway, he didn't like anything that supposedly made a place more comfortable, that time he had acquired the rug, purchasing the house after having leased it with the furniture, and he had thrown everything out of the other rooms and the kitchen, ripping all the baubles off the walls, as he said to his companions at that time, most of whom were in prison or still sitting there today, or they'd disappeared after the riots, the Boss had no need of baubles in his house, there should only be order, and that was enough, because there was nothing else he wanted from a residence which happened to be his own—no curtains, no little pillows, no carpets, this was his motto, but still at one point he allowed two carpets into his place, he'd found them next to the road at Im Ca- misch, they were still in pretty good shape, they'll be good for the room, he thought, because the floor was cold, especially in that spot where he always sat, by the table on the bench in front of the TV, be- cause he was severe in that regard too, he didn't need any sofas, divans, or fluffy beds, he said, but every item should be made of wood, so he carpentered a bench together himself that became his sofa, then he got some used wooden chairs at a flea market in Hummelshain, he just didn't like anything that was soft, I just don't like it, you understand, he said to his companions in the Burg, because when they—meaning the new troop, the new unit, Fritz and Karin and the others—got hold of the Burg, he said: if I sink into one of those rotten armchairs, I just can't stand it, I get dizzy and lose my balance, and the others under- stood, even though they—although also undemanding—had fur- nished their own apartments somewhat differently, I'm not going to watch TV or a DVD sitting on a bench, Jürgen said, alluding to the Boss's overly rigorous principles, but the Boss strictly kept to them, only these two carpets, one of which had tassels, and in the beginning of the beginning they irritated him, those tassels got on his nerves, if they somehow slipped into his consciousness he determined to cut them off, but then something else more important always came along, so that for a good long while he couldn't get rid of those tassels, now, however, the time had come: he stood up from the bench, because he had realized that this was the moment, he couldn't stand it any longer, just get those goddamned tassels out of here, so he brought in a large pair of scissors, cut them off in the space of one minute, then he swept them up, and he threw the whole thing into the fucking cunt, I threw the whole thing into the fucking cunt, he told Florian in the Opel the next day when they headed off for work, he was very disturbed by what had happened yesterday, but he specifically did not want to talk to Florian about it, at the same time it was eating him up inside, because he was decidedly troubled that the news about the wolves wasn't true, because this news should have been true, so that he was also decidedly relieved when a few days later—it wasn't even seven a.m. yet—someone rang his bell, and it was the Revierförster standing at his door, and he said that he was very sorry about what he'd said the day before yesterday, because the news was true, only that it didn't happen the day before yesterday but today at dawn, Fritz had suggested he tell the Boss, in a word, as soon as he saw them, he took a video of them, which he had also sent to Adrian Köhler, who had put it on his website immediately, the Boss was straining every nerve, and he didn't let the Förster in for a good half minute, he just stood there and looked at him, as if to say: so now it's true? is this some kind of joke?! then he quickly opened the door and ushered his guest in, and from this point on he treated the Förster as he treated every guest, he sat him in his own regular spot, brought in two bottles of beer, cracking them open, he pressed one bottle into the hands of the Förster, then he sat down facing him and had him tell him the whole story from beginning to end: when the Förster had seen the wolves, why he'd gone that way, had he been alone, and how many in the horde; we don't say "horde," we say "pack," the Förster corrected him, we say that they travel in packs, but the Boss wasn't too troubled by this correction, in other situations he probably would have begun yelling that he wasn't here to be lectured at, it was all the same to him whether it was a troop, a horde, or a pack, not now, he drank up the Förster's words, who, moreover, described the situation precisely and in great detail: when he had seen them, why he'd been over there, and once more, how many wolves were in the pack, and so on, briefly put: so they're here after all, the Boss rubbed his palms together, he saw his guest out, and he immediately went down to the Balance Fitness Club by the railway crossing, his mood was so intense that he had to stop lifting the dumbbells when he got to seventy kilos, he couldn't lift any heavier weight than that, I ran out of breath, you understand, he told them later in the Burg, when he had summoned the unit, at seventy kilos I couldn't take another breath, and the reason why was that I couldn't concentrate, because the only thing I could think about was this wolf horde, and now it's begun, and this statement IT'S BEGUN rang in the heads of everyone gathered in the Burg as if a bell had been set clanging, even Karin jumped up, she felt that at last they had arrived at a historical moment, because for her, there was something oppressively monotonous in their weekend meetings—not because of the other unit members, she had no problem with them, apart from them she had no one else, but because what they had been expecting for years never happened—that permanent state of alarm obviating the need for anyone to ever yell out "alarm!": she had been waiting for this, and the others had been waiting for this too, only that in the first hours it still wasn't clear where they would be going, the enemy is invisible, the Boss announced, so the first thing we have to do is ... and Karin interrupted: we must coax the enemy out, to which the Boss said: exactly!!! and he pounded his fist so hard on the table that the beer bottles began to dance, one was knocked over and started to roll away, but no one reached after it, because the entire unit jumped up as one person as soon as Karin did, like people who knew what they had to do, although only the Boss knew exactly what they had to do; when he explained the plan to them, though, every single one of them sensed—as had been the case so many times before—the plan fully formed in their own heads, even before the Boss began explaining it: they went to their hiding places below Leuchtenberg and to Grosspürschütz and Pfaffenberg and Altenberg and Greuda and, of course, to Zwabitz, Karin even went to their cellars in Spitalberg, because you never know, she thought, those hand grenades or handguns might come in handy, so that the end result of their great meeting was an amassing of explosives in such quantities as could wipe Kana, such as it was, off the face of the earth, of course Florian was struck by this, he wasn't really interested in why there was so much activity around the Boss, because although it was customary for the unit to report at the Boss's place as well, it hadn't occurred all that often or almost never; sometimes Florian found the unit members already waiting in front of the gate, and at those times nobody had to say anything to him, he knew what his task was: to scram, because no one had to lead him around by the nose; and it turned out that from this point on he had quite a bit more free time than previously, because he didn't even have to take part in the Saturday rehearsals anymore, although it was a while till he found out why, it was because the Boss had indefinitely suspended the rehearsals, and one day, in the midst of this sudden vista of relative freedom, Florian, sitting in the Herbstcafé, clicked on Herr Köhler's website—he did so occasionally, if only from habit—but what he saw took his breath away, because not only did he see fresh data, but a brand-new video about the wolf horde had been uploaded; Florian didn't even pay for his coffee, he left his laptop open on the table, and he ran out down the hill to Oststraße, panting heavily, and he rang the bell and he rang the bell and he panted, and he rang the bell by the gate which of course didn't close properly ever since he and the Boss had broken in—I hear you, I hear you, a voice came from the yard, but he still didn't see who it was, but the voice was familiar, very familiar, and there appeared Herr Köhler himself, wearing a housecoat, eyeglasses in one hand, he came out from the house upon hearing the bell, Florian just stared at him, turned to stone like someone who'd seen a ghost, what's wrong, my friend, you're looking at me as if you'd seen a ghost, said Herr Köhler, opening the dangling gate and letting Florian in, then he walked in front of Florian into the house, sat him down, and asked if he would like a cup of tea, which had never happened like that, because Florian always made the tea, but now here was Herr Köhler making the tea: well, how are you, Florian, he asked him, when they sat down in their usual places with the tea mugs, have you recovered from those mistaken conclusions of yours while I was away? but Florian could not bear to speak, he looked at Herr Köhler with wide-open eyes, he just kept staring at him, then he put down the mug on the little table next to him, he could hardly bear to hold himself back from jumping up and touching Herr Köhler because he didn't believe it, he simply could not take it in—not that Herr Köhler seemed perfectly fine, not that he seemed virtually unchanged—his clothes were the same, his hair combed in the usual way, he was holding his tea mug in the same way, even blowing on the hot tea in the same way—but that he was here, Florian was incapable of taking this in, Herr Köhler, Herr Köhler, Florian shook his head, well? Herr Köhler looked at him almost roguishly above the tea mug, Herr Köhler, I'm so happy! then, when Herr Köhler said nothing but only kept on smiling, Florian blurted out: where have you been? why, where do you think I was? Florian's host queried, with the same look in his eyes—at the UN? Florian asked, his face brightening, at which Herr Köhler broke out laughing, of course, at the United Nations, that's it my friend, exactly there, at the United Nations, and so as not to spill his tea, he put down the mug on the desk next to his armchair, leaned back, and looked at Florian kindly, and now he asked if there was any news from here at home? but Florian's blindingly blue eyes were burning as never before, and he now believed that he was not dreaming, it was all true: Herr Köhler was sitting here in his armchair next to his desk, his mug of tea was steaming on his desk, but still, for safety's sake, he asked again: Herr Köhler, is it really true? at which Herr Köhler began laughing again, and he answered: well, of course it's true, if you are wondering if it's really me, because it is me, and then he said something a bit odd, namely that: well, yes, I've grown a little unaccustomed to everyday matters, I don't deny that, but it's no problem, don't you worry about that—Florian didn't understand what Herr Köhler was saying, how could he have understood; then they just spoke of the usual things, about the newly updated website, and Herr Köhler asked if Florian felt like helping him repair his Weather Station instruments, as they had gotten somewhat rusty—he did—and certain components were placed too high for him, and lately, Herr Köhler said, and he said "lately" as if Florian knew what he meant, lately he'd been getting a little dizzy if he had to go up the ladder, so it would be good if Florian could look in on him tomorrow when he would have time, not today, because today he was going to bed early as he was a little tired; Herr Köhler saw Florian out, his gaze still incredulous but happy, Herr Köhler closed the gate after him, and before he went back into the house, he waved to Frau Burgmüller who was just then leaning out of her window to see better, because even she didn't believe it, no, she said to herself loudly, and she leaned farther out the window, this can't be true, it's the neighbor! and no one else, well, he's come back, just as I said, she moved back from the window because nothing could be seen anymore across the street, she pulled the lace curtains together and sat down, I was the one who was right, she muttered to herself in satisfaction, and not that crackbrained hag, because there was no problem

187

here, and nothing happened, he's home again and that's all—Florian began running, and came to a dead halt, then again set off running, he didn't know what to do, where he should go first, in this direction or that direction, he suddenly ended up at Ernst-Thälmann-Straße, he stood in front of the Boss's gate, the dog with its manically foaming mouth jumped at him but was yanked back harshly by the chain, he pressed the bell once, he pressed the bell twice, but nothing, the Boss wasn't at home, so that Florian went running into the town where, despite the relatively early hour, a quarter past seven in the evening, he met up with no one, not a single soul in the streets, he wondered, usually at this time there are people about, but not now; since it was too late to go see Frau Hopf, he decided to go to Frau Ringer; the first time he'd shown up at her door, there'd been no problems: Frau Ringer had been a little surprised, but she invited Florian in with no fuss and sat him down in her room, just then Herr Ringer was not at home, and Florian had told her, out of breath, why he was there, it was because he had realized that he had committed a terrible mistake, that he and he alone was responsible for the disappearance of Herr Köhler, it had been a mistake, or he could even say it was a crime, because he hadn't listened to anyone, not the Deputy, nor Frau Ringer, nor—his gravest omission of all—had he listened to Herr Köhler himself, so that it really was a crime, and now he didn't know what to do, he didn't know how to get him back, he'd already tried whatever he could, but with no results, Herr Köhler had disappeared without a trace, even the Boss, with whom he'd recently forced his way into Herr Köhler's house, confirmed this, there had been nothing, only dust, and Herr Köhler never tolerated dust, and although the Boss tried to cheer him up, he too had nothing left up his sleeve, no more ideas, and now Florian really didn't know whom he could turn to, and he told Frau Ringer everything: everything that he had tried and failed at, failed, I failed everywhere, Florian hung his head, while Frau Ringer tried not to show how much

188

this situation was unnerving her; still she consoled and encouraged him, but Florian also sensed that Frau Ringer couldn't help him, and of course he'd seen how this had made her feel sad too; so that now his first order of business was to inform her—if he couldn't reach the Boss, and the library was long since closed—once again Florian headed up toward Am Kantersberg, and of course Frau Ringer was astonished, as might be expected: I don't believe it, she said, her face completely frozen, after they had sat down in the kitchen, and then she just repeated what what what—whaaat on earth?! Florian's eyes filled with tears, while he nodded that yes, this is what happened, and he didn't ask for anything to drink, he didn't ask for anything to eat, right now he wouldn't have been able to take a single sip or bite of anything, because he could hardly even swallow, he just sat and looked at Frau Ringer, responding to her slowly formulated questions, and he was so happy that he could not bear to stay; he said goodbye and rushed off, and he would have looked in at Ilona's as well, but halfway there, it occurred to him that the buffet was already closed, so then he ran off to the Aral gas station, but there was only a light on above the cash register, which meant that in the back, in the apartment, Rosario was awake and watching TV, but already dozing off, as he himself described the "night shift" at the gas station, so that Florian didn't ring the buzzer that rang in the back, because he might wake up Rosario and didn't want to, so he went home and plunked himself down in the chair in the kitchen only to jump up again, and he began pacing around the table, then, in his usual way, his head tilted to one side when he needed to be moving, he paced into the room and out of the room, into the kitchen and out of the kitchen, he stepped even into the bathroom, only there was no room there, so he could only turn around and pace back, and things went on this way through half the night until, completely exhausted, he finally collapsed into bed, and when the alarm clock woke him up the next morning he still couldn't believe it, he would have been more than happy, before waiting for the Boss on the corner, to run over to Oststraße, but there was no time for that, he hadn't thought of this and scolded himself for having not set his alarm earlier, but it didn't matter now, he waited at the usual place, the Opel pulled up before him, punctual as always, and only fifty or sixty meters were required for the Boss to take in the news, he immediately slammed on the brakes, turned back in a sharp curve, and already they were parked in front of Herr Köhler's house, and the Boss only said to the master of the house drowsily emerging from the doorway that he wanted to apologize for having broken the gate and the front door while he was away, but we were pretty worried here, how you just disappeared from one day to the next—ah, that's not important, answered Herr Köhler, I'll have it repaired later on, and I understand, moreover I thank you for being worried about me, but you didn't have to, nothing in particular happened, I was just away for a bit, but now I'm here, so that if there's anything you need, for example, any special data concerning the weather or anything, then I would be more than happy to be at your disposal, said Herr Köhler; there's nothing for the time being, the Boss answered coolly, and he measured Herr Köhler with his gaze, then they said goodbye, Florian beaming with joy, but not the Boss, although he had visibly already gotten over his surprise and already was thinking about other things, but Florian didn't notice, as he never could have imagined that anyone could be thinking of anything else, because not even a hair had been touched on Herr Köhler's head, they'd gotten him back in exactly the same state he'd been in before, because they'd gotten him back, Florian's heart throbbed again and again, and now in his head he was wondering: would everything go back now to the old routine? would there be the Thursday evenings again? and he could brew the tea? and he could ask, above the honey jar, how many spoonfuls? for Herr Köhler got his honey from the Revierförster, who, in addition to his many other activities, kept bees, only that he complained mightily that the bees were dying out, or, as he expressed it more accurately, the bees were *also* dying out, and from one year to the next, millions and millions of enormous bee families were perishing, it's the chemicals, the Revierförster looked accusingly at Herr Köhler, even though he was aware that there was nothing that Herr Köhler could do about this, but still, let's not forget, even in this great joy, that this whole thing looks pretty fucking strange, noted the Boss, and Florian only nodded—because now he could only nod to everything—that of course the whole thing looked strange, but who cared, as long as he was back again? and he said this too, and as a way of reassuring the Boss, he added: later on, Herr Köhler will tell us where he went and what he did, the essential thing has been solved, and in such a wonderful way, yes, such a wonderful way, muttered the Boss, and he flicked the cigarette ashes out the car window, then he continued: still, there's something for me that isn't completely kosher in all of this, but forget it, fuck it, you're right, we've got other things to deal with than to keep chewing on this; you're right, let's not keep chewing on it, answered Florian gaily, and he kept fidgeting from the excitement, in his seat, until the Boss told him to stop fidgeting because you're going to fall out of the car already, and then who is going to represent ALL WILL BE CLEAN? who?! maybe me?! the Boss grinned, and poked Florian in the side who then truly almost fell out of the car, because he was still beside himself, and in his great happiness he was doing utterly incomprehensible things, either brushing the dust off the dashboard, or adjusting the seat cover beneath himself, or fiddling with the door handle again, stop fucking around with that door handle, I'm telling you, the Boss finally yelled at him, if you fall out of here, I'm not going to clean you up, because that's your business, although I doubt you'll be able to handle it if you're pulp on the road, and with that they arrived in Suhl, and the two of them began work on cleaning the walls, Florian enumerated the exact addresses on the piece of paper, and so the entire day they went from one address to the other, until they finally got back to Kana, and Florian immediately ran to Oststraße where the two neighbors were already very much waiting for him, both of them wanted to be the first to say how happy they were that their dear neighbor had come back home, and now Florian was reassured too, and now there were no obstacles for everything to keep on going as it used to, and Frau Burgmüller smiled at him widely, although there was a little shadow in her smile, and Frau Schneider also smiled, her smile, though, had no shadow, it was as if Florian were her little grandchild who was immensely pleased by their words, he understood them, he hurried with them, following Herr Köhler into his house, and the news that Herr Köhler was back signified a kind of undeniable relief to the entire town, because finally something good had happened, people said to each other, because they were really happy that Adrian Köhler was unharmed, he had come back, and once again they could look at the Weather-Kana website to see the weather for tomorrow or the day after tomorrow, the good news occasioned a moment of ease, although of course it could not suppress the overriding disquiet, because even though Herr Köhler had come back, even though the Weather Station once again operated faultlessly, when it began to grow dark, people invariably disappeared from the streets, everyone locked themselves up in their houses, and they waited, they waited to hear as the wolves began howling in the mountains, and no one knew which was worse: to hear the wolves as they howled, or waiting in the silence to see if they would start howling, ever since the appearance of the wolf horde, every night was spent like this, in this state of tension, and in the morning, when people had to venture out, it could be seen that no one had slept the night before, but whoever could bear to get up didn't speak of this but only hunted for newer information, although there was nothing— the Revierförster couldn't keep up with the demand, sales of honey had climbed abruptly within the space of a few days, the supply of blackthorn jelly and the stocks of currant syrup were also snapped up by the residents of Kana within two or three weeks, although to tell the truth they didn't need any honey, blackthorn jelly, or currant syrup; they merely wanted to talk with the Revierförster, every day if possible, so they could be the first ones to hear of any newer, extraordinary incident up there in the mountains, but no, the Revierförster explained: there was nothing frightening in this whole thing, no need to be terrified, it was perfectly natural in its own way for the wolves to be showing up here as well, because it's been years already since they were reintroduced to Bayern and Brandenburg, and one could know precisely that they also appeared in Sachsen, and from Sachsen they trickled over here, Germany is no longer what it was, said the Förster, after one hundred years the wolves are back again, well, and he himself found nothing objectionable in that, he said, in their place he would be much more afraid of certain individuals, consider what's going on with that trial in Chemnitz or in Halle, that hellhole, well, that's terrifying, these criminals among us again, and as if this weren't enough, then you should be afraid and tremble because not only does the old Germany belong to the past, but Europe and the Earth are also not what they used to be, everything has changed, because everything has been ruined, and you are the ones who ruined it, the Förster declaimed energetically, while those—he pointed at himself—who seek to protect an ecological balance never had, do not have, and never will have a say in these matters, because no one listened to them, no one listens to them, and no one ever will listen to them, because it is already too late, yes, the Förster said with prophetic zeal, and they, the residents of Kana, were right to lock themselves in every night, because the old world was done for, and everyone would do much better to stay home and that was all, he sold the last jars of honey and preserves for today, he collected the money, and set off in his Jeep along Im Camisch toward Großpürschütz, the people of Kana withdrew to their houses with the

jars of honey, and eventually those who could also began locking themselves up in their houses during the day, of course Herr Ringer only
saw, in this entire thing, completely superfluous and baseless hysteria,
and he named precisely who was spreading this fear and panic among
people here, and I'm not thinking of that Förster, he said to his friends
in Jena, as his wounds, now healing, allowed him to get into his car, he's
just cashing in on the whole thing so he can sell his honey at who
knows what advantageous price, no, he continued, and he took two
salted peanuts from the small dish that the waiter set down in front of
him, I'm thinking of the Boss, that monster, and from the very beginning I've been convinced that he's the one behind this scandal with the
Bach memorials, namely I have discovered—he leaned in closer to the
others—and this isn't just a mere suspicion as when I first told you,
namely the Boss turns up everywhere wherever these memorials have
been defaced, he was there in Eisenach and he was there in Mühlhausen, he was there in Wechmar and he was there in Ohrdruf, he's always
there a few hours after they find one of these horrible graffiti, moreover, I've realized how clever he is, because every single time, he's the
one they call to fix it, Ringer said, which shows just what a shifty character he is, and once again he proposed that they and every person of
goodwill in Thuringia organize themselves for the protection of Johann Sebastian Bach, we cannot yield our Thuringian home to them,
Ringer's voice grew sharper, and this was enough for the organizing to
truly begin, they decided that first they would hold a demonstration,
and what more suitable day for this than German Unity Day, Octo-
ber 3, and so about 180, or, according to others, even 300 people, gathered on this day and marched through the center of Erfurt, let every
person of goodwill join us, read the posters that Ringer put up in Kana,
and he spread the message by word of mouth as well, but no one from
Kana came, and this made Ringer bitter, he had counted on so many
more, he had counted on so much more courage, as he put it, and Frau

Ringer agreed with him, and she did not forgive the residents of Kana their cowardice, because they're cowards, she said to her husband, that is the great problem, that—now I'm not putting a lock on my mouth—everyone here is scared shitless, lovely people, but if there's a problem not even one of them dares to show their face, and you, where were you? she demanded of Florian after the demonstration, ah, Florian replied with a cheerful expression, first I had breakfast, two rolls and a half liter of milk, in other words the usual, then I looked in at the Boss's to see if he was home, but he wasn't home, then I walked down to the little bridge where I listened to the splashing of the Saale for a long time, then I popped into the Grillhäusel, then I walked up to the Herbstcafé and I clicked on Herr Köhler's website to see his weather forecast for tomorrow, then I ended up sitting on my little bench and I stayed there till about four p.m. ... well, that's enough, Frau Ringer interrupted him, I asked why you didn't come with us to the demonstration in Erfurt? don't these things matter to you? the demonstration? Florian looked at her in wonderment, yes, Frau Ringer answered angrily, but I usually don't go to demonstrations, for surely you know, Frau Ringer, the Boss also invited me once, years ago, when he and his comrades were taking part in something like this, but—Florian raised both his hands as if to ward something off—I said no, and he looked at Frau Ringer proudly, expecting some recognition, I don't go to demonstrations, I wouldn't know what to do there—well, aren't you at all disgusted by what those wicked people are up to? Frau Ringer asked accusingly with her own sharpened tone, I don't understand, Florian answered, I really don't understand, because both the Boss and I don't see any point to the whole thing, and we don't know who's doing it, why they're doing it, or how long they'll be doing it, we have no idea, you know, Frau Ringer, it isn't such a good feeling to be cleaning up that graffiti exactly at those places where the memory of Johann Sebastian Bach is preserved, because for me, Bach—I don't know if I've told you already, but before I was deaf, I simply heard nothing from his music, even though, as you know, every Saturday I had to sit there at the rehearsals, and no, even though I sat there—Florian looked at Frau Ringer with his unchangingly radiant gaze—I sat there, but how should I put it? I sat there in the midst of Bach, and all around me were these beautiful sounds, and nothing, I didn't open up my ears at even one of these rehearsals, only now, of course—he explained to the increasingly ill-spirited Frau Ringer—it didn't occur gradually, but like a bolt of lightning, like when someone blocks up his ears, and he doesn't hear anything, and suddenly his ears are unblocked and he hears everything; that's what happened to me, and ever since then I always hear the music of Bach even if it's not playing just then, I hear it in my head, just imagine, Frau Ringer, when I sit on my little bench by the banks of the Saale, and I listen to the splashing of the river, even then it's as if I were hearing a piece by Bach, although I'm only remembering the sounds, or how could I put it, the melodies, or if I'm sitting in the car with the Boss, and we're going to work, even then, and even when I'm working, and when I'm spraying chemicals and I'm scraping off the graffiti, even then I remember it, I hear it in my head, I always remember it, and even when I wake up, it's my very first thought, the main thing is that ever since Herr Köhler came back, I remember the music of Bach all night, even when I'm asleep, that's what's going on with me, and I only don't remember it if there's a lot of noise: once I went to Jena, and I was watching a demonstration, but there was so much noise that it was frightening, and just as earlier I didn't go to any demonstrations because I accepted your counsel never to do anything with the Boss's friends that could lead to problems later on, now I don't go to demonstrations because they're too noisy, and then I can't remember Bach, and Florian would have continued, but Frau Ringer just shook her head, and she kept shaking her head until Florian had to stop trying to explain everything about Bach and demonstrations to her as

thoroughly as possible, she saw that Florian was never going to understand why he should have been there, and certainly, Florian did have a
few pangs of conscience after their conversation, but he never mentioned it again, as the problem with demonstrations wasn't just the
noise, but that he didn't want to draw the wrath of the Boss onto himself by going to one, because the Boss had told him earlier, of course
earlier, that people like these shifty Ringers were bringing problems to
Thuringia, and they had to be rounded up again, all of them, get it?!
rounded up again, and taken out to below Leuchtenburg, and we will
not allow any of their demonstrations, because a demonstration like
that was shameful, shameful to anyone who felt himself to be German,
so that no, it never occurred to Florian to go to Erfurt, although there
would have been room in Herr Ringer's car, but God forbid, that was
all he needed, for the Boss to know that he had gone to the demonstration there, he couldn't do that, and moreover—Frau Ringer and her
husband weren't aware of this—the Boss himself was against the
sprayer, he wanted the exact same thing as they did, for the sprayer to
be caught, and therefore, in Florian's view, a great misunderstanding
had occurred, and because they didn't speak to each other, Florian had
been wishing for a long time to reconcile Frau Ringer with the Boss,
and the Boss with Frau Ringer, but both were obdurate, so that lately
Florian hadn't even dared to mention that perhaps it would be good if
they could discuss their differences of opinion, so that now, after the
demonstration in Erfurt, Florian was continually on guard so as not to
say anything if somehow the subject came up, but the subject no longer
came up, or at least not in such a way that he would have to say something—Bach remained, and now Bach was in his head all the time, in
his head, in his ears, in his heart, that was exactly how he put it when
he started writing a new letter to the Chancellor, as he considered it
only fair to inform her of the latest developments, and primarily her,
as Herr Köhler had been released, and he, Florian, knew full well who

he had to thank for this, and therefore he asked the Chancellor to kindly accept his most sincere gratitude, as it possibly could be difficult for the Chancellor to imagine what he, as Herr Köhler's faithful devotee, had gone through until this decision was put into effect, rendering Herr Köhler once again a free man, of course Herr Köhler wasn't talking about it, he inspected his instruments in the yard, he managed his website and did other things on his computer, one didn't know what exactly, only that he was doing something, Florian had realized that Herr Köhler did not want him, Florian, to know *about that*, and so Florian never asked Herr Köhler *about that*, and, well, otherwise he acted as if nothing had happened, so that he, Florian, didn't force the issue, maybe later on Herr Köhler would tell him the whole story if he wanted to, but Florian frankly admitted that he wasn't even so interested in where Herr Köhler had been, what he had been doing, what happened to him before and what was happening to him now that he was released, the only important thing was that he had been released; Herr Köhler was once again among them, and he never, but never, would ever be able to thank the Chancellor enough, would never be able to repay her enough, but if Mrs. Merkel would ever have need of anything at all, then he stood happily and willingly at her disposal, all she had to do was write a few lines and already the matter would be taken care of, so many people here in Kana asked him for his help in taking care of smaller matters, because he knew how to repair everything, he could saw, file, screw something in, unscrew something, mount and dismount, nothing was a problem, he could lift trees, cut and prune anything in the garden, he was good at carrying things, in a word, Mrs. Merkel could count on him if she needed a helping hand with any kind of work at home, and even this, on his part, was not true repayment for her kindness, because in reality he could never repay what the Chancellor had done for Herr Köhler in all of its magnitude, and Florian put all of this down on paper, but for the time being he didn't send the letter as he was still waiting, he was watching to see what was happening at the Security Council; as often as he could, he went to the Herbstcafé and with the help of an online dictionary, he looked at the UN website and the relevant menu items at un.org to see when the Security Council sessions, either live or upcoming, would be taking place, and he was ever more confident that the matter would soon be made public, of course he suspected that it wasn't quite so simple, most likely everything was still in preparation and this could take a long time, but obviously, closed negotiations were being held in back rooms, he thought, as he shut down his laptop at the end of this or that day at closing time in the Herbstcafé; he no longer had to take his laptop home, because Frau Uta, the owner, had suggested to him that if he was using his computer only here, then there was no point in carrying it home and back here again, she would set the laptop aside for him in a safe place, and she put it somewhere in the back, and this worked splendidly, Frau Uta was also very fond of Florian, she always referred to him as her nicest regular customer, here comes my nicest customer, that's how she always greeted Florian when he stepped into the café, and she trusted him so much that from time to time she even asked him to help her out in his free time at the peak of ice-cream season: namely, on the first or last days of the school year or other holidays, because then the children came charging into the Herbstcafé in much larger crowds than usual, and of course it filled Florian with joy to complete this task, he loved serving out the ice cream, and he got the hang of it in no time, so that after a short while Frau Uta even suggested that she would pay him as much as he was getting from that horrendous person if he could take on a four-hour shift off the books, but Florian answered that it would be better to help out in his free time because he couldn't leave the Boss all alone, so that he only served out the ice cream sometimes, on certain occasions, and if Frau Uta wasn't looking just then, he served big scoops, namely, he didn't smooth the scoop down with the ice-cream scooper as Frau Uta had strictly instructed him—in a word, Florian remained with the Boss, of course, they cleaned graffiti at addresses in districts near and far, until the large explosion happened in the shopping street in Jena, nine people were wounded, and the Boss said they deserved it, then when they heard a second explosion in Suhl coming from next to the market square, and the car radio announcing it almost as soon as it occurred, the Boss only noted: so they're paying attention now, goddamned motherfuckers, and Florian didn't understand until the Boss explained that these two explosions had been carried out by the same anti-national terrorist group, the same ones who wanted to destroy Thuringia, the same ones who were contaminating decent Germans with their liberal claptrap, and now—the Boss raised his voice—maybe now people will come to their senses, fuck it, and realize we have something to protect here, not even to mention—the Boss banged on the steering wheel in rage, his cigarette falling to the floorboard, so for a few seconds he had to drive holding the steering wheel with one hand as he reached down for the cigarette and tossed it out the window—not even to mention that maybe they would finally be willing to do something, got it?! finally to do *something* against these ass-scraping fag children and co., because a little unit, such as the Boss's, on its own power, could not achieve the desired result; but then a few days later, the Boss said that didn't mean that they were shutting things down, oh no, not only are we not shutting it down, but we're ramping things up with ever greater purpose, ever greater purpose, do you understand, and Florian just nodded, because of course he didn't understand, and then once again they heard a radio report as they were driving to Ilmenau where they had a job to complete, as usual, the radio was continually on, and there was an announcement that in Jena, some members of an illegal graffiti gang had been seriously assaulted by another group, the Boss immediately turned up the sound, and they heard that the previous night, somewhere near the University of Jena, unknown individuals had attacked a group of youths suspected of defacing buildings with illegal graffiti, well, now we'll see what's going on, the Boss snarled through clenched teeth, and from this point on, work came to a halt, the Boss told Florian to practice the national anthem every blessed day, fiddle in peace with Herr Köhler's weather-measuring instruments on Oststraße, or serve out the ice cream as he pleased, because for a while now they weren't going to be cleaning any walls, for you this means paid time off, you get forty euros, and I have a task, because the nation has greater need of me elsewhere, and he looked at Florian, and Florian had seen this expression on the Boss's face—resolute and secretive—only very rarely, the Boss often liked to pretend he had a secret, but it always turned out that he was only pretending, or if there was something he didn't tell Florian right away, it was always the Boss himself who couldn't bear not to divulge it—although given the latest developments, the Boss announced one Friday evening in the Burg, I'm not telling Florian anything, it's too dangerous, Florian, well, you know him, he's harmless but unpredictable, and he'll blurt something out, to which the others unanimously agreed, because they had no trust whatsoever in Florian, despite his being a muscleman Godzilla, as Jürgen mocked him: he wasn't the type who belonged among them, and, moreover, they found him to be pretty repulsive, because what kind of person has no father or mother? Fritz noted during that time when Florian, thanks to the Boss, moved into the Hochhaus, we don't need anyone like that, someone who will never make a good patriot, dammit, they said amongst themselves, that was their opinion on Florian, so that now the Boss put Florian into a drawer and turned the key in the lock, and although he didn't toss away the key, he carried it in his pocket, and that was all, the subject was closed for the time being, and from this point on Florian had little idea of what was happening around him, he no longer had to attend rehearsals, he didn't have to work, he could do whatever he

wanted, and what he wanted was to be next to Herr Köhler just as often as he could, to spend hours in the library with Frau Ringer, during
the day as well, to look in more frequently, and stay for longer, at Frau
Hopf's, who said that as far as she was concerned, and this also included her family, she was seriously afraid, until now—she shook her
head and sighed deeply, while clutching a handkerchief—until now,
you know, I just worried and worried if I started thinking of what was
going to happen, if this happened or that happened, but now, Florian,
whether you believe me or not, what I'm feeling now is unadulterated
fear, because of course I'm afraid of the wolves, of course I'm afraid
of the Nazis, but in actuality, my fear is that the terrorists are going to
start blowing everything up around here as well, just imagine, as soon
as the postman delivers the *Ostthüringer Zeitung*, I snatch it up and hide
it away, I don't even let myself turn on the TV if I'm in the living room,
because I never know when they're going to start talking about that
Chemnitz trial, and I'm really worried about my husband, because you
know him, he only wants peace and quiet, and my only job is to ensure
that my beloved has this peace and quiet, because I'll touch wood—
she touched the underside of the table—thank God I'm healthy, and
I can stand the work, to be honest, said Frau Hopf, there already isn't
that much to do, just take care of breakfast and keep the rooms in order,
the cleaning lady does the physical part of the work for me, but you,
Florian, what do you think? Frau Hopf looked at him questioningly,
me? Florian answered cheerfully, I don't think anything in particular,
and I don't think that we have to be afraid of any explosions, ah, no,
and he looked with an even more cheerful gaze at Frau Hopf, we're
too small for that here, of course it could happen in Erfurt or Jena or
Leipzig or Plauen, those places are different, maybe there, but here in
Kana? for me that's unimaginable, although if you wish, I could ask the
Boss about it, because he'll certainly say we have nothing to fear here,
and that will reassure you, if there's anyone whose word you can trust

it's the Boss's, oh no, anyone but him, Florian, Frau Hopf clasped her
hands together, don't let that person even come to your mind, no, no,
it would have been better if I hadn't said anything, don't you dare! and
she waved her index finger threateningly at Florian, don't you dare say
anything, not a single word, ah, she stood up suddenly, I'm sorry I even
mentioned this, forget it, and she saw Florian out, who said nothing,
he wouldn't even have been able to as she showed him out the door so
quickly, so that as he left he wasn't at all in as cheerful a mood as when
he'd arrived, and he went down along Jenaische Straße, and he mused,
wondering how he could reassure Frau Hopf the next time he saw her,
maybe, it suddenly came to his mind, he could convince her to start
listening to Bach as well, of course, this would be the best solution, because there was no greater magician than Bach anywhere in the world,

he served big scoops

and he had already turned back, and he had already rung the bell at the
Garni, and he'd already said into the intercom: oh, I'm sorry for the
trouble, I only wanted to ask if you, Frau Hopf, might have some device
for listening to music, what? asked a reluctant voice, and Florian slowly,
and more loudly, repeated his question, and the reply came: we have a
hi-fi tower in the living room, but what do you need that for? ah, it's
not about me, Florian answered, I'll explain later, and he said goodbye,
no reciprocal greeting was heard from the intercom, because Frau
Hopf was upset, just as she was generally upset these days, and now
this Florian, because all she needed was for him to start blabbing about
something, and then before too long they would come at midnight
from across the street, and—as had already happened once before—
kick apart the Garni's gate, Frau Hopf decided that she would not stand
idly by waiting for this to happen, so she went to Ringer's repair shop
on Friedrich-Ludwig-Jahn-Straße, because he was the only one she

knew who had unconditionally stood up to the residents of Burgstraße 19, and more than once; she'd also heard that he helped anyone in need, and she was not disappointed, because Ringer immediately put aside what he was repairing, invited her into his repair shop, offered her a seat and a glass of water, and he said: dear lady, please do not worry, for I am not one to sit with my hands idly in my lap while these scoundrels behave with ever more impunity, and you are right, he said, his face clouded over, without a doubt, the horrendous events of recent times underline the unconditional need for a civilian alliance, and believe me when I say that such a civilian alliance—one that will put an end to these horrific events—already exists, and with that Ringer said goodbye to Frau Hopf who, after this conversation, returned home in an even more perturbed state, not only did she lock the gate, she barricaded it with an iron bolt which the Hopfs had never used before, while Ringer called up an acquaintance of his from the Federal Office for the Protection of the Constitution, and he reported that every day now, ordinary citizens were coming to him because they feared that everything they had worked for, everything that they had built up and which, until now, they had believed to be secure, would all come to naught in the current chaotic political situation, then he went back to the repair he'd been working on, installing a new filter in a 2010 Ford; Florian, making use of his newfound freedom, traveled to Jena on the 11:30 bus and went to the Mr. Music shop on Kahlaische Straße, and in the one-euro sales bins immediately found what he'd been looking for, because he felt that Frau Hopf should not begin with the great Passions, not with the great organ concertos, nor with the great violin concertos, but with a CD containing the Brandenburg Concertos, as well as *Wo soll ich fliehen hin, Bleib bei uns, den es will Abend werden*, and *Denn du wirst meine Seele nicht in der Hölle lassen*, he found a CD with these three cantatas, the cover was a little ripped in the upper-right-hand corner, the plastic case was cracked in one place, but the CD itself looked intact, so that he purchased it with another discount CD—the Brandenburg Concertos for 2.50 euros—and he traveled back home happy, and already he was on Jenaische Straße, and already he was happily announcing into the intercom: hello, it's only me, Frau Hopf, don't be angry, I only brought two CDs, please listen to them, I'll toss them into the mailbox, and Florian tossed them into the mailbox, carefully so they wouldn't get damaged, then he cheerfully headed back to the town center, and he wondered if Frau Hopf would immediately fall in love with what she heard on the CDs, or if she would need time to get closer to the music of Bach, because that is what had happened to him, when not only did the individual pieces remain in his mind, but he began exploring them ever more deeply, and there were works that immediately found a place in his heart, there were works that didn't affect him at first, only later, when, after many attempts, he understood them all at once, namely he grasped how deeply was concealed within them that which he could never reach, and of course the word "grasped" did not, in his case, express the actual situation, because he felt incapable of speaking about anything like his own relationship to Bach, he did not have a personal relationship to Bach, because whenever he listened to Bach, he himself became nothing, that which was exactly he himself disappeared, Bach took dominion over him: if Bach was speaking it didn't matter who was listening, because if Bach spoke, he listened, but more precisely, if Bach spoke, there was no need of any listener, Florian was of the opinion that Bach also spoke even when no one was listening, Bach was continuously saying something, and sometimes people listened to him, but Bach was speaking, he was speaking all the time, at one point it had begun, Bach had begun to speak: and ever since then he hadn't stopped, ones like Bach, thought Florian, begin to speak at one point, and they never stop, and for them, and all the others here in Thuringia and everywhere in the world, the only task was to listen as much as they could, and it was always like this with geniuses, he thought, and he wrote this down too on a piece of A4 paper kept on his kitchen table (although not intended for future letters to the Chancellor), however, feeling the need to explain more precisely what he'd been thinking of earlier when he had recommended that Mrs. Merkel should also include Johann Sebastian Bach in her negotiations, he began writing on another piece of A4 paper to confirm that he still held to this view, and he started this new letter just like all the others, beginning in the upper corner of the A4 sheet, although this time he began writing completely at the top, at the uppermost edge, leaving no blank space, he even wrote the address—Angela Merkel, Chancellor of the Federal Republic of Germany, Willy-Brandt-Straße 1, 10557 Berlin—on the upper-left edge of the paper, he completely filled the entire A4 sheet, leaving no extra space in the left-hand margin or on the right, and that is how he proceeded to the lower part of the page as well, his handwriting running across the A4 sheet until he got to the lower edge, and he only continued on the next sheet of paper when it seemed he was about to start writing on the surface of the table, then, however, he would always take out a new piece of paper, and this is how things occurred this time too, because while he could not claim to be acquainted with every masterpiece in the musical literature, nor could he even claim to be too well informed, because, frankly speaking, he knew no one apart from Bach, before Bach he'd been deaf, and after Bach he became deaf to everything else, he admitted that he had no need of any kind of music which was not composed by Johann Sebastian Bach, for him this encounter had granted him an experience which seizes a person in the presence of greatness and he had been seized by Bach, seized by genius, and he considered it simply superfluous to try to sample any other music, that is to say that for him Bach was not even music but heaven itself, and he was certain that the Chancellor would understand this just as precisely as she'd understood everything he'd written heretofore, he was not a religious person, and this wasn't how he thought of heaven, he admitted, even if he was aware that the Chancellor saw things differently, but still he hoped she wouldn't be angry at him, he'd had no opportunities in childhood to have any connection with religion, and then when he was brought here to Kana as an adult, there was no chance to get close to any religion, but now he had gotten close to Bach, and that meant that he had grown close to every religion as well, at least every kind of religion in which there was a God, but this didn't matter either, because what was necessary now was for the Chancellor to clearly understand the necessity of the involvement of Bach in the negotiations which, he presumed, were taking place, although as of yet behind closed doors, he could hardly wait for the discussions to be publicly announced on the Security Council's public agenda, but he did not want to emphasize this now, but rather the question of Bach, and why he was of the opinion that the lifework of Bach, continually and eternally audible—that realm, in which the music of Bach could not only be heard but experienced—was a *truly existing* realm, which perfectly contradicted any view that did not recognize such realms, moreover that denied that any such realm could ever exist, but it did exist, comprising that world in which it had been given to them to live, alongside plants, animals, inorganic elements, and the phenomenon of events appraised by the human mind as unique; and how did he know this? Florian posed the question, hunched over the piece of A4 paper in his kitchen, namely how did he know that the universe was much more capacious—he would specify the meaning of that word in a moment—than what the human mind accepted as extant? well, from him!!! it was precisely Bach who had shown him, it was Bach who could show anyone, and it was Bach who showed this in every single fraction of time in the everyday sense of the word, he'd gotten it from him, because anyone who listens to Bach would sense that realm—Florian got to this part in the letter, but this was only the first thing that he wanted to write, because the second thing was: inasmuch as this was true—and it was true—then the universe was a much, but much ... not even bigger, not even more capacious, but, and *now* he would specify what he meant! ... it comprised a much more abundant wholeness, itself only apprehended by means of another viewpoint, radically differing from the conventions of science, although not unscientific or antiscientific, not some kind of mystical or transcendent or other foolish gobbledygook, but instead an image of the real obtained via a different view, only that the construction of this reality, its logic, is not yet before us, because we cannot know, here, what exists there in place of a causal system, and this is what he wished to say: the decisions of the Security Council must emphasize the fully justified concern over the catastrophe that might ensue at any moment, and yet as we stand in the dreadful shadow of this total catastrophe, we must yet realize: the experiential world as sensed by ourselves, from the viewpoint of this veritable realm, is only an *idea*, a mere *idea*, Mrs. Chancellor, of what reality truly is, hence this dear Earth, and everything that we think about it and the universe that surrounds us, is perhaps but a mere *misunderstanding*, a *misunderstanding* of that veritable realm for which he could not find, at the present moment, a more precise designation, only "realm," but even this term communicated nothing, because it was difficult to describe something the vocabulary or grammar of which is unknown to us, but this vocabulary and this grammar is in all of Bach, and it didn't matter if he designated this God or Faith, it doesn't matter, Mrs. Chancellor, Florian wrote with growing enthusiasm, as long as we listen, and if we listen to him, to Bach, then we can be certain not only that this realm truly exists, but that there is a path leading to it; whether there is more to be said is yet another question, but still—Florian wended his way to the end of his letter— from this point on, there can be no doubt: the most suitable way of handling the looming catastrophe is for the Security Council to listen to Bach, you must listen to him, Mrs. Chancellor, and not only must the Security Council listen to Bach, but Bach must be introduced with universal validity, on every television station, every radio broadcast, in every school, every department store and sports stadium, every factory, on every train and plane and bus and boat, on every cell phone and on every screen of every computer starting up, the music of Bach must be played, no matter what the billions of people are doing at that moment, they must always listen to the music of Bach, let Bach be something like the air, and Bach will not bore them, for surely we do not grow bored of the air, let Bach be invisible, an unceasing part of our life here on Earth, but I will stop for now, as this was all that I wished to write you, Mrs. Merkel, only that I greatly await your visit to Kana, I only ask for a sign and I will be there waiting at the train station, or at any other location, because Kana needs you, the people in Kana need the infusion of your strength, because people do not fear what they should fear, instead they fear what they shouldn't fear, but Florian had already reached the bottom of the last page he had intended to write, and unfortunately, the words "people do not fear what they should fear, instead they fear what they shouldn't fear" slipped onto the kitchen table: in that trance which Florian had fallen into during writing, he simply didn't notice, only when he pushed the letter away from himself, leaning back against the chair, he suddenly noticed the piece of paper from a distance, and that the last line of his letter was written on the surface of the table—now what should he do? continue on another piece of A4 paper? but then how would the whole thing look? with the last line at the very top of the last page? followed by the words "with respectful greetings, Herscht 07769"? no, he decided, instead he would copy out the last page anew, reducing the space between the lines, and he did so, and he brought the letter to its conclusion by the bottom of the page, then he leaned back again and closed his eyes; in his mind's eye he reviewed everything he'd written to make sure it was satisfactory, and he found that it was satisfactory, then again in his thoughts he underlined the most important words: "deaf," "to everything else," "experience," "seized"—he underlined this last word twice—"involvement," "realm," "truly existing," "anyone who listens," "wholeness," "image of the real," "idea," "misunderstanding," "path," and "air," and at last he folded the paper in two, but this time there were so many pages in the letter that it wouldn't fit into a regular small envelope, so he unfolded the sheets of paper and tried to make the fold marks disappear; then the next morning, he stood in front of the post office right at opening time, and he was fairly anxious as to whether Jessica would have the right size of envelope for his letter, but there was no point in being nervous because Jessica did have it, we have everything here, she smiled at him proudly, and once again when Florian handed her the envelope, she didn't look at the address but only tossed it onto the scale and said, one euro and fifty cents, then she took the euro and fifty cents and said: it's good to see you again, and already she was calling the next person to the counter, because just then there were a lot of people, the door could hardly be closed even though it was already fairly cold outside, too cold for the door to stay open, so the line snaked off to the left, Volkenant also came out to organize the queue, because this is a post office, please don't stand around in one big jumble, he said, stand a little closer together and right behind one another, well, that's it now, he praised the waiting people who obediently formed a neater line, and he went back to his office while Jessica continued to diligently stamp letters, she counted change and issued receipts and took money or credit cards, I don't know what came over them, she looked at her husband uncomprehendingly when they were finally able to put out the lunch-break sign, and they went up to their apartment for lunch, no holiday, nothing, and they just start trooping in here like an army, I'm telling you this seriously—she took a sandwich from the paper bag and gave it to her husband, because they always had their sandwiches delivered for lunch; they only had time to cook a proper meal in the evenings, during the one half-hour lunch break there was no time for anything, only a sandwich and a coffee and that was all, still they ate at a leisurely pace—Herr Volkenant only said "hmm" and didn't voice his thoughts as to why there'd been so many people in the post office, but

Jessica didn't leave him in peace, her mouth full, she asked him once again, what do I know, he brushed her off, there were a lot of people today and that's all, I think it was a coincidence, and he swept the morsels on the table into the sandwich wrapping paper, old auntie Ingrid brought the sandwiches and the coffee for them, auntie Ingrid who lived not too far away on Margarethenstraße near the Demokratieladen; once, when the post office was being relocated to a new building, and overhearing the Volkenants talking about how short their lunch break was, auntie Ingrid had suggested, namely, she stepped forward with the idea, that since she had nothing to do and was bored to death, she'd be more than happy to bring whatever they wanted for lunch from the Hubert Bakery downstairs, and that's what happened, they all approved the idea, and ever since then auntie Ingrid was like a clock to them, because, as Jessica put it, auntie Ingrid was always on time, the clock didn't strike noon above their heads, but instead auntie Ingrid set the clock moving every noon, because she was the one who, exactly at twelve noon, pressed down the door handle of the post office, at first carefully unpacking the two plastic cups of coffee, then putting the plastic bag on the counter, and taking out the two sandwiches, and all she would say was *Mahlzeit*, and then she was gone, because she knew there was no time for chitchat, although that realization filled her with regret, because she could talk about something every day, there was always something going on she wished to converse about, and, well, she couldn't always be bothering Frau Ringer in the library, although it would've been good to talk to her, especially now with these explosions which were on her mind just like they were on everyone's, because that's all you hear about nowadays, she told Frau Ringer, when she had her library day, you hear about this and that, about how they have their nest here in Kana, and all of our Thuringia is full of potental terrists, she always said "potental terrists," and no one ever corrected her, everyone always let auntie Ingrid say whatever she had to say, for everyone knew how hard the solitude was for her to bear, my husband died, she would swoop down on this or that unsuspecting tourist when they asked her for directions, the poor thing has been gone for seventeen years now, ever since then I've been all on my own, and with these legs of mine, and exactly me who was always such a sociable person, every day we had guests over, because that János of mine—that was my husband's name—he too loved company, and ever since then hardly anyone comes to my door, only the doctor, because I have a thousand problems, auntie Ingrid complained to the person endeavoring to continue on their way, my leg, look at it, full of varicose veins, but that's nothing, because the problem is here, and she pointed at her stomach, if I eat anything I bloat up straightaway, and it doesn't go down, for the love of God it doesn't go down, only the next day, so how am I supposed to eat anything? can you tell me that, but the discussion was concluded because the tourist had succeeded in getting away, and auntie Ingrid stood there alone with her problems, and could only wait again for the post office or the library, she was able to collar Florian only rarely here on Roßstraße, well, that Florian, he's a proper young man, she would say to the Volkenants, he doesn't immediately run away, he doesn't say, oh, sorry, I have to do this or I have to do that, he listens to an old person, such a good-hearted boy, no? and what could the Volkenants reply, except to say that Florian, yes, he's really a good-hearted boy, and that was it, of course Florian tried to avoid auntie Ingrid like everyone else, and not because he didn't like her, he did like her, she was a sweet old lady, only that when he couldn't help it and he inevitably ran into her, auntie Ingrid didn't want to let him go, she just kept on talking and talking and Florian just nodded and nodded, then, when he made a movement as if to go, auntie Ingrid grabbed his hand and wouldn't release him, moreover, even as he tried, very cautiously, to free himself, auntie Ingrid's grip got even tighter, don't go, don't run away, where are you rushing to so much, and she just kept saying that the doctor came by so infrequently lately, even though they agreed he would come by, because her legs couldn't carry her down to the clinic anymore, and certainly not back again, and what did Florian think about that medicine she was prescribed, because she read on the information leaflet that it might be bad for her liver, so should she believe the doctor or not believe him? and when Florian counseled her, better to believe the doctor, auntie Ingrid started in with: still, but that last time as well ... and there was no exit until auntie Ingrid finally gave up and let Florian go, saying fine, my son, you go on your way if you have so much to do, I don't want to keep you, and there really was a lot for Florian to do, because not too long ago Herr Köhler had asked him to paint the instrument shelter, reinforce the steps, and paint those as well, because ever since Herr Köhler had assembled these items in his yard so many years ago, these repairs had never been done, and apart from that, Florian had to see about the winter woodpile which had completely dried out and then out of the blue collapsed, and he had to stack it up nicely again for the Feldmanns, Herr Feldmann lived in a beautiful old villa on Hochstraße, and he was always very busy; he explained to Florian that he couldn't get around to stacking the wood himself: you know, I have no time right now, since there are no rehearsals with the Boss, I can finally finish up my orchestral arrangements of those classics, you know, those wonderful old hits from Eberhard and Stefanie Hertel, you know, Frank Schöbel and Brigitte Ahrens and Ute Freudenberg, but of course, you don't know, you didn't even exist at that time, but I'm telling you, they're worth it, the public will go berserk, Herr Feldmann's eyes glimmered, I'm planning a concert of classics, I'm hoping we can start rehearsing in the spring, but please—Herr Feldmann lowered his voice—don't talk about this to the Boss, you know what he's like, for him there's only Bach and Bach, and he doesn't appreciate these sweet, catchy little gems, and Florian promised, and he stacked the wood, piling it up nicely by the side of the house, because the Feldmanns had an elegant fireplace, even though they, like everyone else, used central heating, still, for the sake of ambience they

213

kept the old fireplace, it's such a good feeling, my Florian, Herr Feldmann's wife said to him smiling, it's so good to snuggle up by the fireplace when the wind is howling outside, the warmth from the fireplace is different, you know, of course, central heating is good, but when there's a fire in the fireplace, there's a kind of atmosphere, it's so ... how should I put it, so human, you understand, Florian don't you? and Florian nodded, and it was very difficult to get him to accept the five euros that Frau Feldmann tried to shove into his pocket, and now Florian had a total of 220 euros, generally speaking he didn't take any money from people he felt close to, but he wasn't that close to the Feldmanns, in fact he hardly knew them at all, sometimes there was work to do at their house, that was all, they also lived outside of the neighborhoods he usually frequented, so 220 euros, he thought, he wouldn't have to wait too long now for that new laptop, and he asked Frau Feldmann what the time was, good heavens, he said, quickly taking his leave, because it was almost four fifteen, and before he went over to Herr Köhler's he had to stop off at the Herbstcafé to see Frau Uta, stop by if you can, Frau Uta had said to him the previous day as she was putting away his laptop, I'm rearranging something in back of the kitchen, but I need to move those heavy pieces of furniture, one over here, the other over there, and already Florian was running along Hochstraße to complete this task, and he pushed one of the pieces of furniture over here and the other piece of furniture over there, then he ran to Oststraße, oh, Herr Köhler, he said, out of breath, when Herr Köhler let him in, please don't be angry that I only got here now but I've had so much to do today, and he told Herr Köhler everything he'd had to do while Herr Köhler showed him into the house, the upper floor of which no one ever used ever since its owner had been living alone; Herr Köhler had locked it up, left everything as it was, and never went up there; sometimes for weeks on end it never even occurred to him that his house had a second floor, for him, that second story meant the past, and Herr

Köhler did not want to deal with the past, or at least not with that part of his past connected to his wife, he had resigned himself to her loss and in time he'd gotten over it, just as he'd gotten used to his solitary lifestyle, moreover, today—he'd been saying to Dr. Tietz just yesterday evening, who, after many telephone calls, finally came from Eisenberg to visit him—he couldn't even imagine his life any other way, he liked to cook and he liked to shop, he also liked to clean, he was of the opinion that even when Eva was still alive, the house hadn't been as tidy as it was now—but tell me already, Adrian, Dr. Tietz interrupted him, what was this whole thing anyway? you told me this and that on the phone, but really, tell me now: where did you disappear to without a word, and for so long? to which Herr Köhler replied: I'll tell you about it one day, but don't expect any kind of bizarre story or adventure, it was nothing in particular, and that was it, although when he said this, Dr. Tietz felt that his friend was ill at ease and perhaps more than a bit irritated, and so Dr. Tietz didn't pry further, Adrian can tell me later if he wants to, in the end it's his business, and that's it, he said to his wife, we can't pressure him, and on this they both agreed, only that the whole thing was strange, Frau Tietz decided that if her husband was dealing with this so inanely, she herself would try to draw Adrian out the next time he visited them, but so much time passed until that point that she herself had forgotten about it, and when she did remember the incident, it didn't seem so important or baffling anymore, in fact she didn't find it to be important or baffling in any way at all, because everything had returned to the old routine, they spoke frequently on the phone just like before, they met up frequently just like before, and Adrian was exactly the same as he had been before, Dr. Tietz and his wife also hadn't changed a bit, what would be the point of trying to force it, so they didn't force it, just as Florian didn't, even if his reasons for doing so were different, namely, he thought that he had to respect the obvious fact of Herr Köhler having to keep mum, he clearly couldn't say even one word when he'd been involved in such a life-and-death matter, and anyway, who was he to expect Herr Köhler to initiate him into his most private affairs, as, for example, what Herr Köhler was writing so diligently on his laptop, Florian was a nobody, it was already such an enormous honor that Herr Köhler was so friendly to him, and that was true, Herr Köhler welcomed Florian into his house even more warmly than before, if that was possible, of course there was an implicit precondition, or at least Florian thought so, that he should never again mention the destruction of the universe which could ensue any moment now, and he should not discuss how he was still in contact with Mrs. Merkel, because this was his own matter, Florian concluded to himself, and thus equilibrium was maintained, Florian painted the instrument shelter, he repaired the staircase that led up to it, which was in fact really only a kind of ladder, only that Herr Köhler called it a staircase for some reason, Florian replaced four of the steps that were already a bit rotted, you'll certainly find something in the attic, Herr Köhler said to him as he sent Florian up there for materials, and Florian found the planks, and the ladder was better than new, Herr Köhler said appreciatively, and now there only remained the painting of the staircase, although it wasn't white oil paint that had to be used, but a kind of weather-resistant varnish which would prevent the stairs from becoming slippery, and they weren't slippery, and Herr Köhler was satisfied, so much so that one day he asked Florian, if he had so much free time now, could he climb up the stairs to the instrument shelter, open it up, and take the readings himself, and Florian was desperately happy, because now he felt that he too played a part in the operation of the famous Weather Station, and Herr Köhler even referred to him as my little meteorologist, well, my little meteorologist, dictate the results to me, because to note down the results, to know what and how to read from the instruments in the instrument shelter, was child's play in the company of Herr Köhler, and Florian was proud that he knew how to take the right readings, and when in the Herbstcafé, looking at the Weather-Kana website, his heart throbbed as among the readings he saw "his readings" as well, and he couldn't stop himself from looking at the website over and over, and he even showed it to Frau Uta, this is really something, Florian, she praised him, you see, my boy, if you pull yourself together and leave that criminal behind, how much good you can do right away? which of course did not really make Florian happy, and he didn't even react to this statement: he only closed the program he was using, shut down the laptop, and silently gave it to Frau Uta, then he said goodbye, because it distressed him, it distressed him a great deal when people spoke this way about the Boss, he should have gotten used to it already, but he never did get used to it, only that usually it didn't distress him quite so much anymore, and he didn't know why exactly now it was distressing him more today, because today it felt much more distressing how no one knew the Boss's true face, and if Florian frequently blamed himself for the accusations that surrounded the Boss, recently he had been blaming himself even more, because why wasn't he doing anything to get people to change their opinions about the Boss?! he had really hoped, at the time of the first wolf attack, that the earlier harsh judgments of the Boss would change for good when he suddenly became a hero in people's eyes, but his newfound positive reputation only lasted for a short while, and even just a few days ago people had started speculating as to whether the weapon the Boss had used to shoot the wolf was even registered, followed by even cruder insinuations: well now, the Boss was the one who shot that beast, who else, who else around here is good with weapons, only he and his gang, Ringer added, namely, from the beginning of the beginning he only acknowledged the Boss's merits in the story through gritted teeth, through gritted teeth, meaning that he never saw the Boss as a hero, he had to admit that yes, maybe he and his wife owed their lives to him, but this was exactly the bitter edge to the truth, because why did it have to be him?! the Revierförster could have come along, or a policeman, but no, it had to be exactly that cursed Boss with his rifle, this whole thing was not to Ringer's liking, he was incapable of feeling gratefulness or any kind of true gratitude toward the Boss, in addition when the whole thing died down, he even found a good pretext to feel no gratitude whatsoever, namely he'd realized—and he told his friends at the first opportunity: not only were the Boss and his crew more than suspect in this graffiti scandal, but the Boss almost certainly had a hand in those two explosions, but Ringer couldn't convince anyone, his friends from Jena knew the Boss, and that was exactly why they thought he wasn't involved, fine, said one of them, he recognized that the Boss was a contemptible, underhanded Nazi, but those explosions, well, that was something else, there's no way he could engineer something like that without the authorities getting suspicious, and indeed the Thuringian Bundeskriminalamt had not considered him a suspect, even though Ringer, right after his first conversation with his friends, had reported the Boss, I don't understand, Sebastien, one of his closest friends, said to him in the Café Wagner, how did you come to this conclusion, what is your proof? because the Boss and his gang have been lying low, Sebastien is right, Irmgard, one of the oldest friends in the group, joined in, the most we can suspect the Boss of are those graffiti at the Bach sites, that really fits him and his mentality, as you put it, he is obviously the perpetrator, and he acts if he were trying to catch the perpetrator, namely his own self, that makes sense, but these explosions?—she wrinkled her nose—no, these are attacks against migrants, and you yourself said that the Boss is an anti-Semite who deeply resents anyone who pushes the migrant question instead of going after the Jews, really now, it can't be the Boss or his crew, we know this, they haven't done anything for years—well, that's exactly it, Ringer raised his voice in annoyance, and he shifted in his chair because it was making the wound on his back itch, for years now they've been quite clever, it might seem like they haven't been doing anything, and yet the Boss founded this nightmare club known as the Kana Symphony just so he could cast Thuringia in an ignominious light again, because he only wants trouble, only chaos, because chaos is what he—and all of them—need, chaos is their natural medium, they move in it like fish in water, because in reality they don't want anything, just this chaos, so you should think about this Kana Symphony just as you think about everything else that this repugnant monster has come up with in the past few years, and moreover what is this even, the Kana Symphony!!! what a deeply cynical move that could correspond to no one but him, rotten to the core, building up this pitiful orchestra to hide behind, because they're all hiding behind it, I can only repeat: hiding behind it like wild animals, but I know exactly who the Boss is, and I know exactly who they are, these ones are the most Nazzi of them all, and they don't go marching and they don't wave flags, they don't call attention to themselves with Nazzi provocations, no, and that's exactly it—they haven't called attention to themselves in years, and that's precisely why this group is so suspicious to me, especially here in my hometown, Ringer went on ever more stridently, but he couldn't persuade the others, his companions were expecting more convincing arguments, besides the fact that everyone knew Ringer was motivated by personal revenge: he spoke about Burg 19 and the individuals camped there as if each one were his own personal enemy, Fritz and Jürgen and Karin and Andreas and the others, I feel like throwing up, Ringer remarked sometimes at home, before they turned on the TV—and all the while the Ringers had no idea that a pretty big change had happened in the Burg, because apart from Fritz, who was registered to live there, and who did live there, the other members of the unit canceled their sublets elsewhere, and after a truck transported their nonessential belongings to a warehouse leased under the Boss' name in Im Camisch, the entire unit moved into the Burg, this had been the Boss's recommendation which they had taken up unanimously, in this way we will be more effective, he explained, better able to focus on our goal; the Boss was the only one who kept residing in his own house, his own property, as an unspoken agreement had been formed, if only for reasons of security, that the unit leader should reside separately, also granting him the solitude required for working out his plans, not to mention as an appropriate concealment strategy, because no one is going to notice any of you, the Boss said, all living together, up till now you were all together anyway, that's how people around here know you if they know you at all, but I would stand out like a sore thumb if I were living here, so it will be good like this, and it was good like that, only that the members of the unit didn't count on how residing together could sharpen the old tensions, because there were tensions, partially from soccer, partially because their characters were fairly different, especially Karin's, but Jürgen's and Andreas's too, it was hard for them to agree on who would clean the bathroom and when, this proved the most serious problem at the beginning, cleaning up the shithouse, as Fritz said, calling things by their name, Karin wanted to pay Andreas when it was her turn, because, she said, the mere sight of shit made her nauseous, and when she felt nauseous she felt like killing someone, and she didn't think that anyone really wanted this in the Burg, and at the same time Fritz also completely withdrew from cleaning the shit as he claimed that since he had previously been the only true renter, he was always cleaning up after everyone else, but now that everyone was living here it would be fair for everyone to start cleaning up their own shit, and his as well— this was his opinion—since you all owe me from before, he said as if he were joking, but he wasn't joking, and then the problem with Jürgen was that his digestion was really bad, he was regularly tortured by diarrhea, and he shat out whatever it was that was inside him like a cannon, and he was incapable of understanding that it wasn't only the bottom of the toilet bowl that had to be cleaned, but the upper rim had to be thoroughly checked, and the bottom of the seat, because it was always splashing up there, but Jürgen didn't feel like cleaning the toilet, and he always waited for others to do it, if that's what they wanted, and this was only the toilet, because there were other similar problems in the room they used as a kitchen, because the question here was why whoever made coffee never cleaned out the Moka pot and kept dumping the coffee grounds down the drain, who would take the empty beer bottles to the bottle return, who would sweep up the broken beer bottle on the floor—at the beginning everyone was waiting, as previously, for Fritz to do these things, they waited for him, because until now he had been the Burg's only official tenant, and it was difficult, now that they were all together, to get used to how Fritz didn't want to do these things anymore, but the worst was when Fritz himself dragged the mud in, because he was indifferent to conditions in the Burg, if someone started grumbling, he considered it a trifle, shouting down the others: much greater and more serious tasks stood before them, everyone should leave him in peace already about the toilet and the kitchen and the garbage and the coffee grounds and the beer bottles, who cared, when the future of Germany and the Fourth Reich were at stake, and this was hard to argue with, the only problem was that he himself, and in general, the others too, didn't want to use the toilet if someone before them had left it a mess, nobody wanted to drink coffee if they had to clean out the Moka pot after someone else, not even to speak of taking out the garbage or redeeming the beer bottles, everyday life had to go on, unfortunately, and within a few weeks tensions had really increased, they kept reminding each other in vain of their common goal, the importance of which superseded anything else, that huge piece of shit, or Jürgen's more speckled variety, often had them jumping at each other's throats, the Boss could hardly keep the peace, and in the end, he was forced to write down a set of house rules, obligatory for everyone, well, this worked for a while until the whole thing started up again, although this time they didn't turn against each other, they had accepted that living together meant compromise, they didn't reproach each other, saying: why didn't you wash that out, why didn't you sponge that down, why didn't you mop that up, why didn't you wipe that off; they focused their attention on their alliance, so that if the Burg had hardly been a palace before, fairly soon it really began to look pretty bad, as, for example, one day when Florian had to walk by the front entrance, left open during the day, and he didn't want to look inside, and yet he looked inside, and his heart sank, because, through the opened door, he could perceive a narrow hallway, so dark that only the first few meters were visible, the light coming in from the outside already somehow breaking down after those first few meters, the bare light bulb hardly gave off any light, and this bare, filthy light bulb, hanging from the ceiling, crooked and orphaned, at the end of a wire, as well as the musty, sour smell of poverty emanating from within obligated Florian to take a step toward the doorway, but then he quickly reconsidered and he hurried onward, troubled, and all he could say to himself was: *those poor Nazis*, even though he himself hardly came from one of those villas on Hochstraße like the one where Herr Feldmann lived, and his own apartment in the Hochhaus was hardly a castle, moreover the elevator—it now appeared—would never be repaired ever again, the Deputy seemed very nervous whenever the residents asked him about it, I keep trying to get them on the phone, but to no avail, he explained, they don't pick up, referring to how he could not reach the usual repair company and the Hochhaus had no connection with any other company, and the truth was that

in the presence of greatness

the elevator could no longer be fixed, but of course the Deputy couldn't tell the residents this, he only talked to Florian about how he couldn't talk about it, well, he could hardly stand in front of them and say: my dear fellow residents, the elevator will never work again, don't even dream of it, I am powerless in this matter; Florian, the Deputy said to him, the superintendent of this building, whose name is written on the sign on the outside wall, hmm, he doesn't exist, and the Deputy asked Florian please not to blabber about what the two of them had discussed, not at all! put a lock on it, please, I'm asking you, not a single word, of course, said Florian, I would never say anything, Mr. Deputy, who just shook his head—he really liked to shake his head—and he said: how many times have I already told you not to call me Mr. Deputy, we're already rather close, aren't we? feel free to call me by my first name, well, yes, Florian answered, troubled, it's just a little difficult for me, I'm already so used to calling you Mr. Deputy—well then, call me whatever you want, the Deputy gave up, and that was it, he let Florian go on his way, who had indeed been on his way out when the Deputy had caught him just now in the doorway of the Hochhaus, Florian was on his way to the Boss, wanting to be of help to him, namely the Boss had rung his buzzer at around noon and yelled up to the seventh floor to come over to his place at four p.m., and it was getting very close to four p.m. now, so Florian was relieved when the Deputy let him go, come in, the door's open, the Boss called out, in his undershirt with a towel around his neck when Florian rang the bell, but the dog, Florian pointed at the Rottweiler, barking with its habitually foaming mouth, the dog is no problem, the Boss said in irritation, turning back, it's on the chain, and he disappeared behind the door, so that Florian could relish his rare piece of luck in being able to enter the Boss's house, the Boss almost never invited him over, and on the one hand, Florian was truly happy he'd been asked in, on the other, as he opened the gate, he was already half-dead with fear as he was terrified of the dog, and he wasn't at all sure that the chain would hold back the Rottweiler, leaping toward him, as he passed by, but the chain was short enough, creating a protective strip of about one meter, although for Florian it was more of a death strip, he never dared go anywhere near dogs; if he had something to do in the yard, as now, holding his breath, he slipped along in front of the dog and headed toward the door, but the Boss just laughed when he finally got inside: well, fuck it, how do you think you look?! it's only a fucking dog, I'm sorry, Florian said, his mouth trembling, but I'm afraid of it, you don't have to be, well, whatever, listen to me, and the Boss looked at him very seriously: the situation is this ... he began, but he couldn't continue, because right at that moment somebody pressed the doorbell, the Boss cursed, looked out, then he let Fritz in who hardly looked any better than Florian, and the Boss even noted: well, fuck it, how do you look?! you're shitting your pants too over a fucking mutt? what the fuck is going on here?! because he thought Fritz was also frightened by the dog, but no, because Fritz began saying: Jürgen was picked up by the police, because it's not even enough that that idiot assaulted Nadír, but he also got in a fight with Rosario, Rosario hit him over the head with a bucket full of sand and called the Polizei, and all of this was essentially true, only that Rosario hadn't hit Jürgen with a bucket full of sand, but with a fire extinguisher he'd grabbed off the wall, and he threw it at Jürgen, running away, and he hit the target right on the head; Jürgen fell to the ground, for a long time he didn't know where he was and what had happened, not even when the police came out to the Aral gas station, although it was a pretty long time until they got there, it was always like that, Kana is Kana, but it was still nineteen kilometers, explained one of the cops when Rosario demanded: what in God's name took you forty-five minutes?! calm down, you're not chatting with your pals here, buddy, the cop said, and they took one look at Jürgen, took down the necessary information from Rosario, and questioned him, and Rosario pointed to the corner of the gas-station building, this criminal—Jürgen didn't look like a person, but like a sack propped up against the wall—this

224

repulsive freak, Rosario repeated through clenched teeth, and he shook his fist, but in vain, because Jürgen still hadn't come around, the blood dripping down his back from his bald skull had congealed, the policemen standing in front of him only saw a head slumped over to one side, and although they tried to question him, Jürgen could pronounce no intelligible words, and moreover his trousers were still down around his ankles, Rosario had left him that way when he tied him up and leaned him against the wall, waiting for the Polizei, because this is how I caught him, Rosario pointed at Jürgen, with his trousers around his ankles, his shirt unbuttoned from the bottom, my wife was screaming and trying to get away, this beast, he pointed again at Jürgen, he attacked my wife, dragged her into the office, and raped her, and here his voice choked, and he motioned to one of the policemen to follow him into the building, where he sat him down and he sat down across from him, and his hands were trembling, and he told the policeman that he'd already seen this Jürgen looking at his wife for a long time now, and it was obvious he was going to try something, and that was why he, meaning himself—Rosario pointed at himself—was always alert, ready to strike him down as soon as he tried something, but this one was clearly watching to see when he went with the receipts to Jena, and he took advantage of that, but still, the piece of luck in all this bad luck, Rosario continued, wiping away a drop of sweat about to start dripping down his forehead, was that he'd forgotten one of his receipt books at home, halfway to Jena he had to turn around, and he caught the perpetrator in the act, he heard poor Nadír calling out from the office, heard her cries as he was getting out of his car in the parking lot, well, fine, the policeman interrupted him, holding his pen above the report, but slower, slower, and he posed a few more questions: at exactly how many hours and how many minutes had Rosario called the ambulance, when did it get here, when did it leave, and why wasn't Nadír taken to the hospital instead of being treated here, then the policeman made a phone call, agreed with someone on something, finally he finished up his report, he went over to get Jürgen, took the duct tape off him, and dragged him into the police car; Jürgen still hadn't come to, he still didn't understand what was going on, no one had called an ambulance for him as they had for Nadír, Fritz said indignantly, even though he had serious injuries, and when a police car pulled up in front of the Burg and the cops questioned its residents about Jürgen, they said nothing about if he had been taken to the hospital, the cops only asked about this and that, as if they would have anything to do with what this idiot was up to, how many times had they told Jürgen, Fritz shook his head agitatedly, to leave Nadír alone, because that Rosario was not joking around, these South Americans only stop once they're pissing on your grave; in any event, the Boss sent Florian home immediately, and Florian never found out what the Boss wanted from him; that same night, though, he found out from the Deputy that there had been another explosion which he himself had actually heard, as he hadn't been able to close his eyes for a second, he was fretting if it wouldn't be a good idea for him to go to Rosario and Nadír the next morning to ask if he could be of help with anything? or perhaps, given the nature of the incident, that was a very bad idea? Florian was ruminating on this when he heard the explosion: he immediately ran to the window, opened it, leaned out, and down below he saw the Deputy in his pajamas and striped dressing gown, and the Deputy called up: there's been an explosion, the flames are coming from somewhere on the A88, because it's burning, the Deputy pointed somewhere to the right, do you see it? but Florian didn't see anything, his window looked out from the other side of the building, he saw nothing, although he heard the fire engine sirens, although neither he nor the Deputy could determine where the sound was coming from, it was as if the sirens were echoing above the entire town, so they had to wait for news; the porter, whose name, amusingly, was Pförtner, had walked from the Porcelain Factory

to the Deputy and said: the Aral gas station blew up, the Aral?! the
Deputy was incredulous, that's impossible, he quickly called up to Florian via the intercom: do you hear, it's the Aral, yes, Pförtner continued, out of breath, because he had run all the way here in order to share
the news as soon as he could, because he was all alone on the shift, he
wasn't even employed as a regular porter but instead as a kind of nighttime porter, meaning he only worked at night, and he had never hidden
his willingness to take this on when a good three years ago he'd been
discharged from the Army; he immediately reported to the Porcelain
Factory where he was told that at the most he could work as a night
porter, what about as a security guard? he tried to ask; not that, came
the reply, fine, he said quickly, I'll be a porter, and he took the job, in
the end, as he explained at times, namely to the Deputy when the Deputy was having a worse night than usual, and who, after they'd first met
up, regularly walked over to the porter's booth at the Porcelain Factory
for a chat—I was always a night owl, when I think about it, always able
to sleep better in the morning or before noon, namely, in the Army I
would have but I never had the chance, because in the Army I was on
day duty, but here, whether you believe it or not, he nodded, to convince the Deputy—although he didn't need to, because the Deputy
believed the porter even before he told him he was happy—I am
happy, this is a happy man who stands before you, because ever since
I have been employed here as a night porter, I can finally get all the
sleep I need, and if it isn't God's truth, at five in the morning I call it a
night and get into bed and I snuggle in those comforters and sleep like
a little teddy bear, do you understand? like a little teddy bear, and the
Deputy did understand but preferred not to reply, because what was
the point of complaining: ever since Christine was gone, whether it
was day or night, it was all the same to him, he couldn't even say what
garbage his sleep was, he was woken up by every stupid piece of dreck,
then he lay there torturing himself to go back to sleep, and God knows

it didn't work, so why should he complain now to Pförtner, it was enough for him if he could complain to Florian who seemed more understanding, and Florian even encouraged him: if he was having such a hard time sleeping, Mr. Deputy, please feel free to come up to my place, and the Deputy would have done so, but, well, seven floors were seven floors, so instead he went over to Pförtner if he was on duty in his little booth in front of the Porcelain Factory, there was even a notice posted stating his hours for the next week and the week after, and so on, and Pförtner always gave him a copy too so the Deputy would have someone to talk to, because it was fine if the Deputy liked to come over, Pförtner tolerated the night shift very well, his head never nodding off to one side, and although he was decidedly very happy during those hours when he could browse through all the TV channels, finish off the *Ostthüringer Zeitung*, and end up in that state where he was no longer thinking of anything, but really nothing at all, still though, it was good to talk to the Deputy who understood what he had to say, and he too understood the Deputy, Pförtner himself was originally from Mecklenburg, and the Deputy, as he had revealed, was from Sachsen, but what was really important—the Deputy slapped Pförtner's back—is that we're both Ossis, it's no wonder we understand each other so well, no? and the Deputy agreed, for him too, it was good to know he had somewhere to go when he couldn't fall back asleep, but the Aral gas station?! he was appalled, and he was waiting for an explanation from the porter who, however, could not provide one, as that was all he knew, the police still hadn't said anything, he added, I tried the 5:15 *Thürigen Journal* on MDR, but nothing, maybe there'll be something on *Aktuell*; and the situation was no different for the other residents of Kana, the explosion woke everyone up and they were frightened, and now it was already past eight a.m., and no one dared come out onto the street, even those who needed to go somewhere, what they had feared had finally come to pass, and now in Kana as well, the Volkenants didn't even dare go downstairs, and so they didn't even open up the post office, because there was no one to open it up for, Frau Burgmüller was too fearful to shuffle over to the window, and Frau Schneider felt the same, the Feldmanns ate their breakfast behind closed curtains, and of course this happened in every single house in Kana, because no one had the courage to make even the most insignificant decisions when they still had no information, no one wanted to play fast and loose with fate, not even Herr Köhler, because after all this what was going to happen today, how could he go out in the yard to his instruments? would it be better to postpone his readings? better to postpone them, he decided, and made himself some coffee, he sat down in front of the TV set, which he'd switched on as soon as he'd heard the explosion, waiting for news from either MDR or the Jena TV station, or Erfurt TV from his phone, so that when at about nine a.m. the report reached everyone at once that the Aral gas station had blown up—the police weren't making any statements yet, investigations were ongoing as to the cause of the accident—Frau Burgmüller couldn't stand it anymore, she opened the window and knocked on the windowpane (this was the signal between herself and Frau Schneider when they wanted to talk to each other), Frau Schneider immediately heard the knocking and leaned out the window: well, what do you say, Frau Schneider—there are several dead, answered a tomb-like voice, what?! Frau Burgmüller cried out, where did you get that from?! there are several dead, repeated Frau Schneider in a voice that brooked no contradiction, and she just looked at her to see what the other had to say about this, but Frau Burgmüller shut her window, several dead, I also watch TV, and not only that, she raged, I watch the same channels as she does, but nobody spoke about any dead, not only not on MDR, I have Jena TV too, she groused to herself, and she went to the kitchen to make another pot of coffee, and she was right, because there had not yet been any mention of any victims, Herr Köhler thought that no matter how much one might wish to know the truth, at such times one must wait and resign oneself to waiting, he called his friend in Eisenberg, but Dr. Tietz was already seeing patients, and his wife seemed so frightened that Herr Köhler thought it better, after a few reassuring words, to say goodbye to her with the comment that if he found out more later on he would call again, but for a long time there was nothing, the news reports were broadcast on various stations every half hour, but still only reporting an accident at the Aral gas station in Kana, nothing else, the police were investigating with the help of expert investigators, as nothing was clear, neither the fact of the explosion itself nor its cause, the Boss stayed put at home after they'd all split up in the middle of the night, and the Boss advised the unit to do the same—it sounded like a command, and it was a command—at times like this, the Boss thought, discipline was the most important thing, and no one else doubted this either, but no one felt like sleeping, they all sat in the kitchen for the rest of the night and the entire next morning, they could hardly see each other through the cigarette smoke, no one spoke, the essential thing had been taken care of, they drank coffee and more coffee, but it was already getting on to noon when Fritz spoke, and he informed them that he was giving up his rental lease on the Burg, and who wanted to take it over in his place? but no response came, because it wasn't clear what Fritz was trying to do with this, then Karin got up, slowly walked over behind Fritz, and she stood there until Fritz turned around, and she said: the rental stays in your name; Fritz didn't reply, only turned around, but on his face it could be seen that his announcement of a few moments ago was null and void, so that Karin, just as slowly as she had walked over to Fritz, strolled back to where she'd been sitting and sat down, and it was clear that out of all of them, she was bearing up the best, she seemed completely unchanged, exactly the same as she'd been yesterday or the day before yesterday, so that when MDR announced that there were two victims in the explosion, the

Boss jumped up, dialed a number on his phone, jumped into the Opel, and drove to Jena, where Jürgen had been taken to the university clinic, his head injuries were serious but not life-threatening, the doctor on duty conveyed when the Boss found him (which hadn't been easy), announcing himself as next of kin; it was hard, very hard, to look at poor Jürgen lying there, even if, thought the Boss, it was his fault, because he was really a half-wit, but this was brutal, very brutal, the Boss didn't ask the usual questions—how long it would take until Jürgen came to himself, how long till he got better, were there permanent injuries and that sort of thing—he merely exited the hospital, made another phone call before starting the ignition, then drove back to Kana, he wanted to drive by the gas station to see what was going on, but traffic was diverted, going toward Grosspürschütz he had to take a detour up into the mountains, then take the L1062 back down, that was the only way he could get back to the town where, in the afternoon, people were out and about already, Florian was out too because he wanted to see Herr Köhler and make sure he was unharmed, then when Herr Köhler saw Florian and how the boy had been crying his eyes out, he tried to lighten things up with a joke, and affecting amazement, he asked: did you think that the explosion blew up Oststraße as well? but then Florian explained with some confusion: he only wanted to make sure the instruments hadn't been damaged, and no, they weren't, said Herr Köhler, and he made Florian drink a glass of water, and he tried to detain him, but Florian said he still had many things to take care of, he put down the glass, and rushed off with his cried-out eyes, and he ran—not for the first time—to the Aral gas station, but now they weren't letting anyone get near, a police car closed off the road from the Altstadt, so that there was nothing else for Florian to do, he sat down on a stone, and once again cried his eyes out, he knew that Rosario and Nadír were the two victims, who else could it be, and he couldn't even conceive of it, he struck his head with his hands and he wept, and he couldn't bear to sit there any longer, and he ran to the library, but Frau Ringer, seeing his state, spoke of everything but the victims in the explosion at the Aral station, and to calm him down somehow, she began complaining that her voice wasn't getting better, and really, it still was very raspy, my voice, Florian, it's not getting better, briefly put, she did not want, under any circumstances, to talk about, not even to mention, the attack—which she considered it to be—to Florian, seeing the state he was in, her opinion was the same as her husband's, there's no way this was an accident, Ringer said in his repair shop, utterly crushed; after what happened to Nadír, this is no accident, and at first he didn't even want to let his wife go to the library, but after she'd left anyway, saying: a fifth-grade class is coming today to visit, and they didn't cancel, and what if they show up and find the library door locked? Ringer went back to the repair he'd been working on, because the Ford with the bad radiator had been brought in yesterday evening, overheating again, he leaned over the radiator but couldn't concentrate, and it was like that for almost everyone, they couldn't concentrate on what they'd been working on the day before, only auntie Ingrid came out of her apartment on Margarethenstraße, and the first place where she looked in was the post office, which was open, as the Volkenants feared an unexpected visit by an inspector who might find the post office closed, because anyone can report us, Herr Volkenant noted with a worried expression on his face, but that didn't happen, because nobody dared to go to the post office anyway, only auntie Ingrid, radiant with joy because she'd heard absolutely nothing, she had special earplugs that no one else had, she'd told everyone about them for a while: I have special earplugs that no one else has, believe you me, and really, she hadn't heard either the explosion or the ensuing bedlam last night, although in the morning her plan was ready, because her doctor had advised her at her last appointment: auntie Ingrid, you're in good strength, and you have no health problems unexpected at your age, so you should find some kind of activity, and auntie Ingrid thought about this a great deal, she was relating now to a pale-faced Jessica, and she had figured out what the activity would be, she was starting a movement, what? Jessica looked at her above the empty counter, well you know how much I love chrysanthemums, right? yes, came the muted response, well, Jessica, get ready, because very soon the chrysanthemum competition will be starting, chrysanthemum competition? Jessica asked, although it came out as a statement, yes, my dear, a chrysanthemum competition, and maybe that will even be its name: Auntie Ingrid's Chrysanthemum Competition, I still haven't decided, and she described how the number of chrysanthemums in Kana had visibly decreased, if you go to the cemetery do you see any chrysanthemums? hardly any, my Jessica, hardly any, although the chrysanthemum, how should I put it? is one of the most beautiful flowers to exist on this earth, what a fragrance it has, and, well, it blooms in so many different colors, that I almost feel like crying sometimes when I see those red and green and pink and blue buds beginning to sprout and … I understand, auntie Ingrid, what a charming idea, Jessica stopped auntie Ingrid's enumeration, people will be jumping at it, she added with just a hint of sarcasm so that auntie Ingrid wouldn't notice, but Herr Volkenant did notice, and no matter how oppressive the atmosphere was at the post office, he couldn't stop himself from laughing out loud, this is the last flower to bloom in the autumn, auntie Ingrid continued enthusiastically, and you know, my Jessica, it's a perennial, and you can get it so cheap in the spring, anyone can afford one or two euros for a chrysanthemum bulb, I'm going all around the town and I'll get everyone involved, do you hear, my Jessica, everyone, and I'm thinking of you too, because you also love beautiful flowers, true? what woman doesn't? well, you see, my dear, you'll take part in it too, I already have my first competitor, yes? yes, came the reply, even more muted, from behind the counter, Jessica couldn't stand chrysanthemums, she always called them "death flowers," but she couldn't betray that now, auntie Ingrid traipsed outside with her bad leg and rang the bell at the door of everyone she knew, because who wouldn't know her, especially here in her own neighborhood, and she told them all about her competition and made them promise that they'd sign up, and she became ever more enthusiastic as she went along Jenaische Straße up to the intersection, she was already ringing the bell at Frau Hopf's, who genuinely liked chrysanthemums, although she didn't open her door for a long time, but then she did, and she listened to why auntie Ingrid had rung her bell, which meant that auntie Ingrid evidently hadn't heard the news; Frau Hopf was happy for her, and she not only said yes in a more friendly manner than usual, but immediately ushered auntie Ingrid into the house, auntie Ingrid made excuses in vain that she had so much to do, but Frau Hopf sat her down and asked, what can I get for you? and auntie Ingrid sat straight up, smiled, and tilting her head to one side asked: do you have any of that fine cherry liqueur, my dear? and there was still some left, and after the events of the night before, Frau Hopf thought a wee sip could certainly cause no harm, so she immediately got two small liqueur glasses, they both knocked back the liqueur with one movement like two people who could have done with this quite a while ago, especially Frau Hopf, she had been so terrified last night by that horrific explosion that she hadn't dared move in her bed, her husband slept with earplugs because supposedly Frau Hopf snored, and this snoring could ruin Hopf's entire night, so that she'd gotten him a pair of earplugs from the pharmacy, and ever since then my darling doesn't hear a thing, she related at times to this or that returning guest of the Garni, and this time too he heard nothing, only she heard it, and she heard it most acutely, every single one of her muscles tensed, and she curled up beneath the comforter, after the first explosion she didn't believe it, then came the next explosion, and she didn't believe it, but then came the one following that, and she still

234

didn't believe it, but even that wasn't the end, there were ever louder, ever deeper, ever more terrifying explosions, they went on for quite a while, she thought there'd never be an end, when suddenly it did come to an end, although the clamor stopped echoing in her ears only very slowly, gradually becoming fainter and fainter, and everything was covered by a horrific silence which was even more terrifying, and she didn't move until she began to hear the sirens wailing, and she didn't even know how many she heard, so that she sneaked over to the window on tiptoe, but the street below was completely deserted as always, she withdrew a little to the side, just enough so that no one could see her but so that she could see everything going on down there, if there had been anything to see, she stood there for a long time, and nothing, but nothing, and she was about to go back to her bed when she noticed—it was only a quick flash—a car driving at great speed along Burgstraße toward Roßstraße, but really tearing along so she couldn't even make out the color, only that a car was tearing along Burgstraße, she heard as the car braked, came to a stop, the slamming of doors, and then complete silence, it's those Nazis, thought Frau Hopf, who else would drive around in the middle of the night except for them, and especially at such breakneck speed, in such a hurry, in such a hurry, she murmured to herself, and she quickly lay back down, she pulled the comforter up to her chin, and she didn't move because she didn't want to know what had gone on, she didn't want to know about anything, she only lay there for long minutes and waited to see what would happen, but nothing happened, and then her body gave up, she fell into a deep sleep, only waking up when her husband brought her coffee, because that was their routine: the day started with Herr Hopf appearing with a steaming cup of coffee, and Frau Hopf liked this so much that she couldn't renounce it, although she had already decided several times that she herself would take over this task so that dear Herr Hopf could continue to rest in peace and quiet, but it was so good, so good, while she was still slumbering, to sense the fragrant aroma, so nothing changed, Herr Hopf continued to make coffee and bring it up to the bedroom, as he did today, and as usual, they sat up in the bed with their backs against the headboard, the comforter pulled up to their knees, Frau Hopf didn't say anything about what had happened the night before, not wanting to ruin Herr Hopf's mood, he always seemed very happy at the beginning of their day, they bought the coffee in Jena, generally enough for one month, and only the finest and tastiest coffee, as that was important for them, they could never make do with the coffee that was sold in Lidl or Netto or PENNY, and they didn't get on too well with the Hunger Bakery across the street—that stuck-up Herr Hunger who, for some incomprehensible reason, saw them as rivals, not wishing at all to partner with them, as in, for example, procuring coffee jointly when the Garni restaurant was still in full operation—and so they continued to get their coffee from Jena, for which otherwise they'd found another family on Hochstraße to join in on the purchase with them, but as the Hopfs also needed other items, it was usually they who handled the order, and otherwise Frau Hopf would not have been happy to entrust the purchase to someone else, because she only trusted herself, because she did not make errors, she was proud of this, and she even said so to Florian when he appeared with his cried-out eyes at their house, and they spoke about what they knew about the explosion; until now, she said, I've kept everything under control, but now, when things are like this, I don't know, I really don't know what's going to happen; and Florian, after a long silence, pulled himself together and tried to reassure Frau Hopf, although he wasn't too convincing, as it was more than clear what he himself was going through as a result of this tragedy, in addition he had to hold something back, moreover something that he unconditionally would have liked to mention, but with Frau Hopf in this frame of mind he thought it better not to do so—namely that, beyond these inconceivable explosions, there was something wrong with Herr Köhler, for two or three days now he had become unexpectedly and conspicuously silent, he seemed just as balanced and calm as before but he hardly spoke, if someone asked him something, he didn't always answer, and he seemed incapable of longer conversation, although Florian did tell this to the Boss, when, after leaving Frau Hopf, he rang the bell at his house to find out if he'd heard any news about last night, Florian imagined that they would talk over the fence in the yard as usual, but once again the Boss called out from the front door, once again he was only in his undershirt, with a towel around his neck, which meant that he had been working out, come in, he said and waved to Florian to really come in, once again there was the fear of the Rottweiler, once again the color drained from Florian's face, but this time the Boss didn't joke about it, as if he didn't find the whole thing even worthy of comment, because he wanted to start talking about something, but Florian started talking first, saying that in his view, there was a pretty big problem, because it was strange to him, something was not right, namely Herr Köhler sat him down in the armchair where he usually sat, but he didn't sit down in his own chair across from Florian so they could have a thorough discussion about those things they could touch upon only briefly when outside in the yard taking readings or doing other tasks, no, Herr Köhler remained standing, and what was the strangest was that he just stood there, leaning against the back of the armchair, but he didn't even look at him, and yet Florian had the feeling that he wasn't looking anywhere else either, he just stood there and said nothing, of course Florian tried to start talking about something, but nothing, with Herr Köhler it was as if you were talking to a wall, no reaction, only at the end when Florian himself got up to leave, well, then he said something, but it was so noncommittal and banal, as if he hadn't even heard anything otherwise, and this, Florian explained to the Boss—who was counting to himself while lifting the two dumbbells, trying to figure out how much longer to one hundred—this had never happened between them, the day before yesterday, and above all! Florian rubbed his eyes, he couldn't stand it, and when he left, he explained, he waited for Herr Köhler to close the still unrepaired gate and go back into his house, and Florian pretended he was walking to Bahnhofstraße, but no, after a few seconds he turned around and he slipped back to Herr Köhler's house to peek in through the window, and as the shutters weren't closed, he saw Herr Köhler stepping into the room and walking over to his laptop, sitting down and writing something, but with horrendous speed, and always, ever since he had known him, Florian had been amazed at how quickly Herr Köhler could type, moreover, he could type with all ten fingers, and, well, he saw that now too, Herr Köhler typing with all ten fingers as fast as the wind, of course, he was typing the same thing as always, Florian said to himself, sighing deeply, clearly he was inputting the data from the instruments in the yard, but still, the whole thing was quite peculiar, everything taken altogether, for example, Herr Köhler had ignored Florian's suggestion to finally fix the lock on the gate and the front door, he just waved him off saying, there'll be time, there'll be time for that, it's no wonder he was so worried, Florian added; I'm not worried, the Boss lowered the two weights onto the bench, and the sweat was dripping off of him, the sweat is dripping off of me, fuck it, he said, panting, I'll take a shower and be right back, sit down here, and he pointed at a chair, and disappeared into the bathroom, because he still wanted to talk to Florian, and he did talk to him after his shower, he sat down across from him in his bathrobe, and the Boss said that the night before, he'd been at home, I was here at home, he stared fixedly at Florian, and Florian answered: yes, why wouldn't you be here at home, Boss? you're always home at night, well, of course, the Boss continued, irritated at the interruption, only if anyone asks you—anyone, got it?—if anyone asks you, I was here at home last night, that's what you say, just like I'm home at night

238

every night, and you just happen to know this because I called you last night, I called you at around eleven, then at around twelve, then at around one, then at around two, at around three a.m. as well, I called you five times last night, because when I'm tallying up the accounts, when I'm doing the monthly mileage and all the other shit—the Boss leaned closer to Florian—it's always like this, we always do it at night, and I call you, if I can't remember this or that piece of information, you tell me what it is, because you always have the list, but especially now, you always have the list, and last night I called you every hour just like I always call you every hour at night when we're doing the monthly statements, got it? Florian, this is important, and I'll tell you why, it's because—he cleared his throat while taking a cell phone out of one of the pockets of his bathrobe, but it wasn't one of the Boss's own cell phones, Florian noticed this immediately, only he didn't dare to take a proper look at it, because he suspected something, but he still didn't dare believe that … ! and the Boss pulled his chair closer to Florian—because I can't exclude the fact, and his eyes suddenly grew cloudy … no, not at all … that with this huge mess—he nodded to somewhere outside far away—that someone is going to try to smear the whole thing on me, you know how many people hate me, and with no reason at all, yes, Florian agreed nervously while now daring to look at the cell phone, because the Boss had started to gesture with it forcefully to give each one of his words greater weight, do you get it?! it's possible that someone is going to try to smear that whole Aral gas-station thing and everything on me because of Jürgen, oh come on now, Florian laughed, nervously, and he was still following the movements of the cell phone as it grew nearer and then more distant in the Boss's hand, and all the while he was thinking: IT'S A NOKIA, and he stammered: Boss, are you talking about the explosion last night? that was an accident, wasn't it? everyone says it was an accident, it's being investigated, well, so we understand each other, the Boss lowered his voice and the NOKIA, then he raised both of them again, and he pressed the cell phone into Florian's hand with a solemn gesture, and he said: you've had this phone for at least six months already, and you got it from me, got it? six months? yes, fuck it, at least six months, and ever since then we've called each other every single day, every single day? yes, every single day for at least the past six months, and you only speak with me on this phone, that's why no one else has ever seen you with it, you only speak with me and no one else, and yes, at night too, when I call you five times, the Boss repeated, and he repeated it nice and slowly to make sure it sank in: five times! got it? then, from his other pocket, he pulled out a charger, and he placed that into Florian's other hand, who from this point on could simply not look at either one of his hands, only at the Boss, and forgetting everything else, his face became radiant with happiness, it's a NOKIA, he mumbled, yes, a NOKIA, the Boss answered, irritated, and you already have five calls on this phone, got it, yes?! but Florian still didn't dare look at his hands, although with his entire body he showed how much he understood, and how much he wanted to engrave into that stupid head of his whatever had to be engraved in it, and he did engrave it, now he en-gra-ved everything thoroughly into his brain, and you can have perfect trust in me, he said, and it was even good to hold the cell phone and the charger in his hands, and so these are mine now? he asked, for six months already, fuck it, the Boss answered impatiently, and then he got up from his chair, he rubbed his body with the bathrobe, then took it off, threw it to the back of the room, and as Florian saw that he was stark naked, he leapt up and began to slip away, but the Boss stopped him, and threatened him with his index finger, and for the last time he put the question to Florian: did you really take note of everything?! of course, everything is clear, Florian nodded, turning red, because the Boss hadn't even covered up his cock, and Florian left, and the path in front of the dog was just as frightening as it had been on the way in, although if anyone were passing by at this point, they would have seen that the Rottweiler not only didn't bark, it didn't even choke itself by continually yanking on the chain, it didn't even get up, but just growled, but this too was enough for Florian to feel the same as he'd felt going into the Boss's house, and Florian didn't even have a chance to close the gate behind him, because auntie Ingrid appeared from the direction of the neighbor Wagner's house and called out energetically and waved for Florian not to shut the gate, my dear boy, don't shut the gate, because I think, she added, out of breath as she reached Florian, I think the bell isn't working here either, just imagine, my dear boy, she related to Florian, I have been going around the town for hours now with this bad leg of mine, but so many doorbells aren't working at all, I would never have thought there would be so many houses with broken doorbells, I don't understand how people don't need a working doorbell, do you know why, Florian? and Florian didn't know why, and he didn't even understand what she was talking about, he let auntie Ingrid take hold of the gate handle and he set off for home with the cell phone in one hand and the charger in the other, he held both of them at a little distance from himself as if they might scald him, and he didn't even *want* to look at them till he got home, till I get home, the words throbbed within him, then as he entered his own apartment, he very carefully set the cell phone down on the kitchen table, turned it on, and immediately on the small display a background image of light-blue crystals lit up, but Florian didn't sit down in front of the cell phone, moreover he even took a step back and closed his eyes, then he opened them again, and said to himself aloud: light blue, he stepped forward and put the charger next to the cell phone, he stepped back again and continued to look at the phone and the charger—the Boss, he thought, and his heart was flooded with warmth, my God, and his eyes filled with tears, because when a person felt that they were about to collapse beneath the weight of a tragedy, along came the Boss, because he understood what was going on within Florian ever since Rosario's and Nadír's horrific deaths, and the Boss had given him a real Nokia so that it would be easier for him to bear what could not be borne, and Florian stood there, not touching the cell phone or charger, he just stood and stared at them, and then he was outside again on the street about to go somewhere, only he didn't know where to go, his instincts led him in the direction of the Boss, but then he turned around suddenly and went along Bahnhofstraße, and he kept on walking all the way to Oststraße and already he was at Herr Köhler's house where he happened to bump into the Revierförster who realized he could just walk in as the lock on the gate was still broken, but out of courtesy he pressed the doorbell, do you think he's at home? he asked Florian, and he pressed it again, because he isn't coming out, I ring and I ring and no one comes out, but then Herr Köhler appeared, he opened the gate wide for Florian, but then he invited the Förster in as well, I brought you some honey, the Förster explained, I don't want to bother you, I've come with the honey, that's fine, said the owner of the house, please come in, today a half liter will be enough, he pointed at one of the jars, but the Förster offered him a larger one: are you sure that'll be enough? he looked at him hopefully, but Herr Köhler pointed at the smaller jar and said: yes, that will be enough, he paid, and he asked the Förster to shut the gate behind him, which he did as best he could, he got into his car and he went on with the honey, more precisely a large bag filled with jars of honey, wanting to make use of the increased demand which he hoped would be sustained; for years he'd hardly sold any honey, sometimes he was left with an entire year's yield, but now because of the wolves, demand had risen, although this demand had also suddenly dropped in the past few days, so that now, as he'd heard from the retired fireman who lived by the L1062 access road about what had happened at the Aral gas station, he quickly filled his largest leather bag so as to unload all the honey he could while it was still possible, he didn't even dare think of the remaining jelly or syrups, but at least the honey, because honey was still honey, it still yielded the most profit, although the Förster had a feeling that from now on it would be difficult; when all this wolf fever started, he thought that he was going to have to start diluting the honey, well, so much for that, he muttered to himself as he came out of the Köhler Weather Station, he too just bought a small jar, what the hell am I going to do with all this honey, once again I'll be stuck with it, he turned on his blinkers and set off, because he'd decided to drive over to Hochstraße, maybe he'd get some takers in those big villas, and a minute later he was ringing the doorbell at the first house, but to no avail because no one opened the door, just as no one opened the door at the following house or the one after that, although he saw a curtain fluttering here and there, everything was as silent as the grave, only at the Feldmanns' did someone answer over the intercom to say yes, they wanted some honey, Frau Feldmann liked honey very much, especially when the weather started getting cooler as now, and she even bought three large jars, you always overdo it, my heart, Herr Feldmann rebuked her, and he put two of the jars back into the leather bag; they invited the Revierförster in to ask him if he had any information, then they looked at him with long faces when it turned out that he'd just come down from the mountain himself and he had just now heard the news, so nothing, after a few minutes they showed him out the door, but there were still seven jars of honey in his bag, what should he do with them, he wondered, take them home? the Förster tried every doorbell, he would drive five or six houses' distance, park the car, and walk back, he rang every doorbell, then he drove five or six houses' distance, parked the car, and tried again, but for God's sake, it wasn't working, he complained on his way home to the retired fireman, because he stopped by at his place, feeling very sad, because the honey isn't selling anymore, at home I have at least two full shelves, the fireman gave him a beer, alas, those two shelves, the Förster sighed, finally he said goodbye and drove home, and he decided that for a while he wouldn't even set foot in Kana, why, he said bitterly to his wife, why should I humiliate myself? I'm no itinerant tinker, no miserable peddler, this is the finest honey they could ever buy, and he was right, because Herr Köhler couldn't stop eating it, just as soon as Florian left he unscrewed the lid, and at first, eyes closed, he just sniffed it, then he gulped down a teaspoon, then he thought for a moment and he took out a soup spoon, just as Florian might have wanted to, but he could not permit himself because a small jar of honey cost six euros, oh, Mr. Förster, he once said to him, this would be an expensive indulgence for me, because that was indeed his asking price for a small jar of honey, the Förster thought to himself, because if that Rinke could sell his dubious honey for eleven euros a kilo, then his honey was certainly worth twelve, no? of course, his wife agreed with him, and that's how small jars of honey ended up costing six euros, and at the beginning people bought it along with the jellies and the syrups, but now they were buying almost nothing, stop repeating yourself so much, his wife grumbled, so the Revierförster stopped talking, and then the same thing happened, only in a different sense, with Herr Köhler as well, this strange silence, because Florian had to observe that from one day to the next the situation got worse and worse, because apart from the two days he had spent with the Nokia when—as a counterweight to the sorrow pressing so dreadfully on his soul—he tried out everything on the device and learned everything about it, now he came to visit Herr Köhler not only on Thursdays, but every day, and he had to observe that Herr Köhler only greeted him when he arrived, and greeted him when he left, but in the meantime he hardly spoke, and when, later on, he told both the Boss and Frau Ringer how things were going, he had to acknowledge that Herr Köhler now only nodded when he came to open the gate for him, and he only nodded when Florian left, and in between he said nothing at all, and it wasn't that he couldn't speak

244

anymore but that he didn't want to, and it was impossible to understand why, and now he did not seem as tranquil and as balanced as when this whole thing started, although Florian also wouldn't say that he seemed depressed, instead he seemed ... apathetic, like someone who was indifferent to everything, so take him to the doctor, fuck it, the Boss brushed off the subject, because he didn't have any time for this chickenshit crap, as he called it, because what had happened was that the Revierförster said he'd seen the wolves again, this time at Ölknitz, and the Boss was called in, and not the police, the Boss and those goddamned morons from the Naturschutzbund, and on top of that there was another smaller explosion in Eisenach, not so far away from the Bachhaus, so that I have more than enough problems, the Boss growled, inhaling on his cigarette, then blowing out the smoke for a long time, then he changed the subject: he himself hadn't seen any wolves when, after he got the call, he drove out with the Revierförster to the alleged location, he'd have to go back at night sometime, but there's something else, he said to Florian, and I'm counting on you, because it looks like—Aral gas station or not—we have to round up these spineless pants-crappers for a rehearsal in the gym again this Saturday, but, as the Boss explained, he had no time to be there himself, so it would be Florian's task to supervise the rehearsal, and it took Florian some time to understand what the Boss was saying, namely, the Kana Symphony rehearsals were starting up again, and someone was needed to keep things in order, you're good at Bach now, you have the mind and the experience for it, not to mention your stamina, because if you see anything that doesn't pertain, then you just go and stand in front of them where the conductor's podium would be, if there were one, and that will be enough—but it wasn't enough, because on the next Saturday, when the rehearsal began at eleven a.m., out of the twenty-one members of the orchestra, only eleven showed up, and Florian thought that there was no point in standing in front of them, he wouldn't be able to do anything anyway, so altogether he just asked them to practice what they could, all of them together, and to stay there till one p.m., because that's what the Boss had asked him to do, although nothing came of it, because the string players who'd showed up squeaked out something and the lone trumpeter blew a few notes on his trumpet, but the two double bass players announced that they didn't want to rehearse like this: they packed up their instruments, at which point they were followed by the two remaining cellists, and the bassoonist and the two oboe players looked at Florian so imploringly that Florian just stood up and wandered over to the wall bars and sat down, leaning his back against them, and he watched, as one after the other, the members of the Kana Symphony sneaked out from the gym, he got up to go after them, but then in the doorway he thought better of it, he sat back down, and so that he would not have to think about Rosario, Nadír, or Herr Köhler, he practiced the national anthem to himself a bit, then he tapped here and there on his phone and waited for one p.m. to come, and he knew what was going to happen, and it did happen, the Boss was in a rage and gave him a proper tongue lashing, although he didn't hit Florian, that happened only rarely these days, of course nothing was the same as it had been before, he didn't go to work with the Boss anymore, there were no regular rehearsals, everything had changed with the exception that the fear was exactly as great as when the wolves had first appeared—they're here again, and this is how it's going to be: women raped, explosions, wolves sent into our midst, that's where we are now, the situation was summed up, by Herr Heinrich at Ilona's buffet, the Volkenants in the post office, the Deputy in the IKS pub, or by Frau Hopf, and they just waited for someone at the state or even federal level to strike down whoever it was who was responsible for all of this, Florian's head was buzzing, everywhere he heard the same thing, everyone was afraid, everyone but him, namely, apart from his great sorrow over Rosario and Nadír, he was preoccupied with Herr Köhler, devoting all of his strength and time to him, because of course he suspected an illness, and at one point he picked himself up, and, since he considered it discourteous to discuss such a matter on the telephone, he personally traveled to Eisenberg to ask Dr. Tietz to come have a look at Herr Köhler, because the situation was pretty worrying, Dr. Tietz traveled to Kana, and he did have a look at his friend, Florian waited outside in the kitchen, they were together in there for at least an hour, unfortunately, Florian couldn't hear anything, although he kept sneaking over to the closed kitchen door and pressing his ear up against it ever more frequently, but he only heard Dr. Tietz speaking, he couldn't make out what was being said, and when Dr. Tietz finally came out, and Florian looked at him questioningly, Dr. Tietz, frowning, just shook his head, as if Herr Köhler were incurably ill, but he isn't! a voice cried out in Florian, this was completely absurd, and he exhorted Herr Köhler—until now he hadn't dared, but now the time had come—and he asked him: Herr Köhler, for the love of God, please say something, why won't you speak with me?! and Herr Köhler looked at him in astonishment, like someone who didn't understand at all what Florian was so worked up about, then he smiled, turned away, sat down at his desk, and opened his laptop, and before he continued with what he had been working on, he remarked offhandedly: I'm only counting something, Florian, I'm only counting, there's no problem, Florian stood there for a while and he watched what Herr Köhler was doing, but he couldn't figure it out because he had never seen anything like what he was seeing on Herr Köhler's laptop screen before, numbers and letters running quickly downward, Herr Köhler immediately became immersed in them as if he weren't even there, Florian just watched as those numbers and letters kept running down, and as Herr Köhler sat there, it became clear that he no longer cared about his website, he no longer cared if the residents of Kana knew that tomorrow there was a chance of fog, or if they knew it was going to rain, Florian saw nothing else on that laptop screen—as he stood behind Herr Köhler day after day—only a black background with white or green or sometimes red letters and numbers and signs rapidly plunging downward, Herr Köhler never went outside, or at least not when Florian was there, he was no longer interested in the yard, or sending Florian out to the instrument shed to take the readings, and Florian didn't know how to do these things by himself, because he wasn't sure, apart from the thermometer, he couldn't manage any of these instruments without guidance, in vain did he ask Herr Köhler for just a few minutes of his time, Herr Köhler did not want to leave the house, and after a while Florian also noticed that Herr Köhler wasn't changing his clothes, even though earlier he always used to scold Florian and ask him when he was finally going to change his overalls and get rid of that Fidel Castro cap already, now, however, Herr Köhler was wearing the same brown cardigan with gray flannel trousers and tasseled slippers every day, the shirt beneath the cardigan was looking ever dirtier, Florian was certain that he was no longer changing it for a clean one, as well as what was beneath, and, well, Herr Köhler began to smell, although Florian felt it would be indiscreet to make any allusion to this, but still he had to do something, he sat one morning facing Frau Ringer at the library counter, please tell me what I should do, but Frau Ringer was just as perplexed as Florian, well, the way you're telling it, she began uncertainly, the whole thing seems as if he's going into ... decline, but it would have been better if she hadn't said anything at all, because once Florian heard this word he burst into tears, leaning forward, he buried his face in his hands, and within him all the tension that he'd suppressed ever since Rosario and Nadír had fallen silent forever was spilling over, and now Herr Köhler was becoming ever more silent, Florian could no longer bear to hold it all in, he had to cry, and Frau Ringer was very sorry about what she'd said, and precisely this, but that was how things were, it was the only explanation, she said to her husband with a worried look on her face, her husband, though, wasn't paying attention, being oppressed by much more serious problems, namely that there was no explanation for anything, it's too mystical for me like this, he shook his head sitting with his Jena friends in the Café Wagner, and the residents of Kana were thinking and saying the same thing as well, as it all seemed very suspect to them how no one seemed to be in control, they weren't used to this and never would have thought it possible: no hands holding the reins, but of course, someone is holding them, they reassured themselves, absurd to think otherwise, after all this was the *Bundesrepublik Deutschland*, now, at the state or directly at the federal level, something must happen, and they waited for something to happen at the state or federal level, because now the entire country was talking about it; Florian, when he was not sitting in Herr Köhler's living room, was in the Herbstcafé tapping on his cell phone or his laptop, as he searched, he searched for an explanation to the current state of affairs, writing the rough drafts of his letters to Mrs. Merkel in Word now, as he had not stopped writing his letters, moreover, he was writing to her ever more frequently, he set down his ideas in Word, and then he printed everything out at the Print Shop, one page cost only a couple of cents, and this presented no burden to Florian because he was stopping in at Ilona's much less frequently, he bought his food in the Netto where the prices were the cheapest, because he was saving, and finally he'd saved up 280 euros, and then he didn't even need the Print Shop anymore, and he had already gotten the knack of these things so well that he didn't ask the Boss to help him this time, because ... the Boss ... seemed very busy ... so he looked for a cheap laptop all by himself, and along with it—and this was the big news—a home printer as well, he paid a firm in Leipzig for both items, 280 euros was enough, they wrote him back when he was negotiating the final price, so that from this point on his only expense was printer paper, he could somehow manage that with his household budget of forty euros a week, of course he would eventually have to refill the toner, but only rarely, he told the Deputy, well, it's good if your budget can handle that, said the Deputy, and he was amazed at how Florian was able to take care of such matters in these frightening times, because that's how he termed it, "these frightening times," and the porter from the Porcelain Factory agreed with him, the two of them were meeting up more frequently now, as the Deputy was sleeping even more poorly than before, moreover, he confessed to Pförtner, he wasn't sleeping at night because he didn't dare sleep in the darkness, preferring to do so when it was light outside, he could sleep in the morning, then at noon a bit more till two p.m., and then he had his requisite number of hours of sleep: even though at his age even five hours could be considered enough, it wasn't enough for him, unfortunately, he needed at least seven hours, but if he wanted to be thorough and include his sleep for the entire day, then probably it came out to about eight, well, that's how it was, and yet even during the day outside there was always some kind of noise, cars going here and there, and everything, that calmed him down, but at night, there was that deafening silence when a person pulls the comforter on top of themselves and listens for the sound of something being blown up again, because things were degenerating here—and it wasn't only the Deputy, but almost everyone in Kana was in agreement, the explosion at the Aral gas station was no accident, somebody had a hand in it, just like everything that was happening in Thuringia—while in more distant federal states, people were saying that the pandemic was becoming ever more unmanageable—these obscure events, now occurring at least every two or three months, continued to startle the residents of Kana, you can take your pick, they muttered at night beneath their eiderdowns, unable to sleep, so that Florian was virtually the only one getting a good night's rest, because on the one hand he always slept with the Nokia, and on the other, he was able to banish the image from his mind of the Aral gas station exploding in one single ball of fire, thanks to a meditation exercise he'd found on the internet, because his mind had been continually assaulted by this image, so that afterwards, at most he was disturbed by Herr Köhler occasionally standing next to his bed, looking at him, but of course Herr Köhler wasn't standing next to his bed, and he wasn't looking at him, but sometimes, Florian admitted to the Deputy, I feel I'll keep on seeing this until one day, he really will be standing there, oh, don't you worry about Köhler, the Deputy said, this town has much bigger problems than your Herr Köhler, I suggest instead you try to find out from that Boss of yours what's going on—he, the Deputy, was convinced that a shady character like this Boss (the Deputy thoroughly detested him, stemming from an old incident), would certainly know much more than any upstanding citizen, he loathed the Boss, only he couldn't talk about this to Florian because he was afraid, once having argued with the Boss by the Hochhaus dumpster, namely, the Deputy had politely requested of the Boss not to throw his garbage into the Hochhaus dumpster, then this specific criminal—the Deputy always called him "this specific criminal"—almost clobbered him as he spat out that if he ever saw the Deputy again when he was throwing out his garbage into the Hochhaus dumpster, he'd crack his skull open on the lid, well, ever since then, if the Deputy saw the Boss coming with his garbage, he didn't dare step out of the building, and he really didn't want to talk about this with Florian, because what could he expect? well, of course, Florian would defend the Boss, and he simply couldn't understand why Florian always stood by him, obviously he too was afraid of the Boss, as the postman had confirmed to him, as well as Pförtner and everyone to whom he'd mentioned this absurd situation between Florian and the Boss, and everyone agreed with the Deputy, because of course it would be all too easy for him to crush this child, people opined, whereas Florian didn't feel at all that he was being crushed by the Boss, of course he knew what the general view was, only that he—who had just now been gifted with a cell phone, inherent proof of who the Boss really was—didn't accept this opinion, and when the wolf was shot down by the Boss (and not by the police or the Revierförster), Florian was convinced people's opinion would change, but he was disappointed, so that when the news spread that once again a pack of wolves had been spotted near Ölknitz, and despite all of Florian's good intentions, the general opinion concerning the Boss had not changed, Florian decided he would talk to people, convince them that their view of the Boss was mistaken, namely, he took it to be an old error which had somehow remained in them, they weren't paying enough attention, because if they had been paying attention, they would have had to notice what the Boss was really up to, and not judge him on the basis of a presumed involvement with that shooting incident at Leuchtenburg years ago; afterwards, the Boss had been under police observation for a few months, clearly this had only been a youthful lapse, even Florian knew of it from hearsay, because at that time he wasn't living here yet, but he was of the opinion that others too only knew this incident from hearsay, and were therefore misled, because just look at everything the Boss had done and was doing for Kana since then, look at how his efforts and enthusiasm would soon result in Kana having its very own symphonic orchestra, well, who could even say, in East Thuringia, that they had their own symphony orchestra? and if that weren't enough, then people had to consider how it was no wonder if this person, obliged to live in near ostracism due to unfounded gossip, practically banished by the residents of Kana, sought out friends who were similarly cast out, if people would only consider that even so, the Boss did nothing else but fight for Thuringia, and of his own accord—don't forget, of his own accord—because did he ask for money as his company removed all that scandalous graffiti? no, he did not ask for money, and this was a statement that Florian could make, for he had been there and he was there when the Boss received the orders to complete this work, or: was anyone considering the Boss's strong commitment to catching the perpetrator? to put an end, once and for all, to these acts of vandalism? and if this still weren't enough, then at least people should reflect upon the passionate devotion of the Boss for Johann Sebastian Bach and all the treasures of Thuringia, this is what Florian said to the Deputy, and he also said this to Ilona, and Ilona's regular customers, he also peddled this narrative to Frau Hopf and Frau Ringer and Herr Feldmann, and everyone Florian spoke to was surprised, because this was the first time they'd seen him like this; there was a new quality in him which they'd never experienced, namely Florian wasn't trying to convince them in his usual serene or naive or gentle manner, but there was something slightly despairing about him, perhaps because he sensed that the noose was tightening around the Boss's neck, and this was the opinion of Frau Ringer, whom Florian especially tried to convince as he knew—specifically from her—that Herr Ringer had the Boss in his sights, and zealously so, and this was too much for Florian, such a great misunderstanding must be put right no matter what, he felt strongly, and he did not tell the Boss, who, when he found out that Florian had launched a campaign on his behalf, immediately tried to stop it, but he couldn't—Florian immediately rejected this idea and stuck to his guns, but the Boss noticed that if Florian was sticking to his guns, he was doing so in a strange manner, as if he were precisely doing so, as if this previously unknown stubbornness had emerged within him, precisely because Florian had his doubts about him—the Boss—moreover, perhaps this even explained why he had launched into this entire campaign, as if he were trying to convince himself that he really didn't know what he did indeed know very well, and that is why he was so confused, because he was confused, if the Boss started talking to him, Florian no longer really looked at him, not only that, but he was ever more conspicuously avoiding the Boss's gaze with those shining eyes of his, what is going on with you, fuck it?! the

Boss asked him suspiciously, don't you even shave anymore, but Florian hung his head and he didn't explain, he didn't make excuses or protest, which was completely unexpected from him, but what really got the Boss thinking was that time when he rang Florian's intercom— even though he'd given Florian the Nokia, they never used it to contact each other—the Boss had rung Florian on the intercom and called him down to tell him he was expected on a sortie against those little cocksuckers at the original crime scene in Eisenach, that's what the Boss had started calling them, those little cocksuckers, and Florian didn't come downstairs, he only leaned out the window and that was all, then the Boss pressed down more forcefully on the intercom, and he yelled: do you understand what I just said, fuck it?! yes, came the response after a while, in a soft, reserved, and yet not at all uncertain voice, and the Boss understood: Florian no longer feared him for some reason, what the fuck has happened with him?! he grunted, but he had no more time to dissect the question, Florian was relieved to be freed of the Boss, he went back to the window and he watched as the Boss stormed across the yard to the Opel, got in, and sped off toward the town center, he almost knocked down auntie Ingrid turning out of the Hochhaus parking lot; and auntie Ingrid immediately told Florian through the intercom—as he was the only one who responded after she had pressed all the buttons, auntie Ingrid was fairly baffled by the fact that even here no one answered the buzzer—you know, my little son, I don't understand, how is it possible that only you answered, well, where has everyone gone? to which Florian had nothing to say, nor did he wish to say anything, how could he possibly know where everyone had gone, he wasn't interested, he didn't even care about auntie Ingrid, he stopped pressing down on the intercom button and put the receiver back and sat down again in front of his laptop like someone who was about to start writing a new letter, but he did not write any letter, he had stopped writing any letters in the past few days, because why should he write any more letters? they already knew everything; instead he selected a Bach cantata which he had been returning to frequently of late, and which he'd been able to download, along with many others, so he could listen to it at home without the internet, he clicked on the play button, leaned back in his chair, closed his eyes, and the opening chords of *Falsche Welt, dir trau ich nicht!* began to sound, he could have gone over to Herr Köhler's place, but no, he could have gone to Frau Ringer, but no, he could have gone over to Ilona's buffet, but not even there, he didn't feel like going anywhere, he was neither thirsty nor hungry, the intercom buzzed again and he didn't care, he didn't move, and in the meantime the cantata came to an end, he played it again, once again he leaned back in his chair and he closed his eyes, and auntie Ingrid didn't understand, well now, this one too? even he's not answering the buzzer? or perhaps it wasn't that all of the doorbells were broken in Kana, but that people were pretending not to be at home when they were at home? unfortunately, auntie Ingrid, here at the front entrance of the Hochhaus, began to be convinced of this, because where could they have gone, and she had come up with such a lovely idea, the Chrysanthemum Competition, although she still wasn't sure what to call it, she said later on after she'd left the Hochhaus and gone along Ernst-Thälmann-Straße, and at one of the houses, where Dr. Henneberg lived, Ruth, the cleaning woman, came out and asked her: well, auntie Ingrid, what are you doing wandering around here? you know, my dear, answered auntie Ingrid, I still can't decide if I should call it Auntie Ingrid's Chrysanthemum Competition, or the Chrysanthemum Festival, or simply the Chrysanthemum Competition, because in reality she hadn't decided yet, but the main thing was that the most beautiful chrysanthemums would be competing against each other, no? and Ruth just looked at her the way that everyone else did as auntie Ingrid continued on her way, and sometimes people came out of their houses to see who it was, and they also thought that she was clearly confused, which was no surprise in these times, and they said goodbye and closed the door on her, and then auntie Ingrid heard not only one lock clicking in the door, but sometimes as many as three, even so, there will be a Chrysanthemum Competition, she muttered to herself and went on, she rang at the doorbells, but nothing, until her legs grew sore, but there was hardly anyone for her to tell of her plans, and as she arrived home, she felt as if her legs were falling off, especially the bad one, she quickly removed the compression stockings, put her feet up, and all afternoon she looked at her list, arranging the names in alphabetical order, the names of those she'd been able to speak with, the ones who all considered her idea to be "truly marvelous," and they had signed up, so I can add you, my dear? she'd asked, and they had all said yes, although she was still taken aback because she had been counting on many more names, well, never mind, it will come together, she reassured herself, she had dreamed of hundreds, and so far she had seventeen, but that was no problem, she said, resting with her legs up, and really she did not give up, she went out the next day too, she went and she rang doorbells and she knocked, and her list began to round out, even if slowly, you see, my dear, she said to Jessica when she brought lunch to the post office, I've already got twenty-two, and I have a feeling that this is only the beginning, and Jessica replied in a lackluster voice: of course, now that's really something, she wasn't in a good mood, to put it mildly, I'm not in a good mood, she said, as one of her customers asked: well, what's up with you, Jessica dear, you're not usually in this kind of mood, to which Jessica said, almost harshly, as if it were the questioner's fault, why, is this how you imagine life here in Kana, with people too scared to go out in the dark?! although, Jessica herself was not from Kana, as she once explained, answering a customer's question with a roguish expression, but born in Sachsen-Anhalt, in such a tiny village that obviously you here never heard of it, but nowadays she never mentioned the small village, she never mentioned anything, she merely acknowledged the customers' greetings, she stamped the envelopes mutely, she took the checks and the money and the debit cards without a word, not wishing to lighten up the atmosphere even a bit, even though before she'd always said, and especially before they moved into this nice new post office: if we are a post office, then it doesn't have to be like a queue at the Ausländerbehörde, why, she would retort to Herr Volkenant, when he teased her about this, why not cheer things up a bit, a person isn't a machine for stamping envelopes; Herr Volkenant had his own opinions about this, he was a born postmaster, yes I am, he stated, if they were quarreling and he wanted to hurt her feelings, but not you, the post office is no cabaret and it's no revue, I'm telling you, people aren't coming here for entertainment, and we are no entertainers, and Jessica really didn't have the temperament of a postal worker, she loved being with people, and as their entire lives were determined, for the most part, by work, and at the end of the day, they hardly had the energy to droop their heads in front of the television and then dizzily collapse into bed, Jessica always tried at least to have a bit of fun at the post office, as Herr Volkenant put it, meaning a casual remark here and there or the occasional question, such as: did the cat turn up, or is the medicine the doctor prescribed yesterday helping? that was all, nothing more, but that was enough for Jessica, and people were happy to chat with her until the apocalypse began, because the evangelical pastor had been talking about that in church, and he asked the faithful, whose number was increasing from day to day, to look deeply into themselves and reflect and so on, to which, earlier, they would have replied: okay, fine, but don't start frightening us, especially not in a church, and immediately the attendance numbers would decrease, yes, that's how it would've been before, but now attendance was not dropping but growing, really, the congregants asked if the pastor could hold the evening service at an earlier hour so as not to have to walk home in the dark, the pastor merely held his hands apart, indicating an upward direction with his head: it was not he who made these decisions, namely, this wasn't something he could change, so that everything in the church remained as it was, and after the evening service the newly minted believers scurried home fearfully in the dark, including Frau Hopf, although things were easy for her as the church was located *directly opposite* from the Garni, but even so, those few steps, she would say, if someone was visiting her, were more than enough, because the gate of the Burg, also *directly facing* the Garni, was continually open, do you understand, any one of those hooligans could jump out at any moment, attacking her and Herr Hopf as they unlocked their front door, and then what would become of them, and the situation had only been made worse—since the Aral station explosion—by the ever increasing numbers of police in Kana, moreover, the Deputy noted with satisfaction, almost no matter where you go, you bump into one of them, this is the beginning of a new dawn, although no one else shared the Deputy's opinion: indeed, the effect on the other residents of Kana was precisely the opposite, the indisputably heightened police presence only alarmed them even more, because this heightened police presence did not indicate security but its opposite, it indicated that someone here was not in charge of things, and not only that: nothing happened, nothing came to light, these police merely poked around and probed, people noted with disapproval, but the identity of the perpetrators, their motives— what would be the end of all this?— was never found out, nothing, but nothing had happened ever since those cops had started poking around here and asking questions; Florian himself had been questioned twice, each time about the inhabitants of the Burg, but chiefly about the Boss, but to no avail, because Florian didn't talk, he just looked at them—a broken, confused person looked at them, and even the Deputy said one evening to Pförtner that something had happened with this Florian, I'm telling you, he's like a different person, and everyone noticed the change, but they attributed it to how Florian, of course, would feel even more oppressed than the others by the overall dreadful atmosphere, it's no wonder, with his sensitive temperament, this was Frau Ringer's opinion as well, and she deliberately brought up the subject of Florian to her husband at home, but Herr Ringer was silent and just looked at his wife, and in his eyes a furious light, hitherto unknown, glimmered, Frau Ringer immediately stopped talking about Florian, and she tried to calm her husband down with a few reassuring words, but with no effect, Herr Ringer kept looking at her with those same agitated eyes, then he stormed out of the house, but he didn't get into his car and drive to Jena, instead he drove all around the town, he went to the Altstadt and he sped down Bahnhofstraße like a madman, as whoever saw him reported: he doesn't speak, he stares and says nothing, but with eyes which bode no good, in brief, it was clear to the residents of Kana that something was going to happen, and yet when they heard the news about the Boss, found dead in his own house—beaten to death with a single blow to the head; no object was used, the assailant killed him with his bare hands, Hoffmann told the others in a low voice at Ilona's—still, they did not dare to mention who they were thinking of, although it was clear to everyone that only very few were capable of such a deed, they did not pronounce the name of the person they suspected; but when, one day later, as Andreas came running out of Burgstraße 19 to the police car stationed in front of the house, motioning for the policeman behind the wheel to lower his window, he said that there were two dead in the Burg, both of them beaten to death with a chair while the others were out, only these two had stayed behind, and one of them was Jonathan Fritz; the cop, hurrying into the Burg, noted down the name, the other dead man was the goalkeeper coach for the Kana Soccer Association, Eberhard Kossnitz, and Andreas didn't know why he'd been in the Burg—well, at that point more than a few Kana residents were alluding to one single individual, even if they still didn't dare pronounce his name, because everyone was thinking of Ringer, who else had that kind of brute strength, everyone knew his sheer physical force, and chiefly, Ringer had been blaming the Boss and Burg 19 for all of Kana's problems for years now, and indeed, what other name would have come to their minds, when his passionate loathing for the Boss and his associates was so evident; the common verdict formed quickly, no matter who the police questioned, everything pointed in one direction, and at the end there stood Ringer—earlier generally respected, but now, practically from one day to the next, people sent him to the devil, Ringer became a target at whom anyone could freely shoot, and a few people clearly would have shot at him if they'd only known where he was, because Ringer had disappeared, of course he knew what was happening, he knew he was wanted for questioning and that he was a suspect, and therefore he had fled, and it could not be said that the residents of Kana weren't shocked, they were shocked that Ringer, until that point enjoying great respect, was a murderer, but since he was—surely he betrayed himself by fleeing—everyone hoped he would be caught as soon as possible and locked away, take him away, there were more than enough horrible things here, and supposedly this pandemic was headed their way now too, in a word, they didn't need to be chasing after a butcher, because what else could they have called Ringer but a butcher, to kill someone with your bare hands on Ernst-Thälmann-Straße, to thrash two men to death with a chair, even saying the mere words was horrific, where have we gotten to?! Frau Hopf asked in the Garni, where have we gotten to?! asked Frau Burgmüller and Frau Schneider, where, for the love of God?! asked every single resident of Kana, and he wasn't there, he's not at home, Frau Ringer said to the police in a metallic voice, sitting hunched over in the living room facing two policemen who were questioning her, I haven't seen him ever since he stormed out of the house, when did he storm out of the house? one of the detectives asked, examining Frau Ringer's face suspiciously, when? you're asking when? but the two policemen couldn't understand what she was saying, because Frau Ringer burst out in sobs, she couldn't stand it any longer, she realized her husband was a suspect, which was absurd, but the police forcing her awareness of that fact broke her completely; she really didn't know where he was, and it would have been hard to say what weighed on her more heavily: the suspicion, or Herr Ringer not coming home for an entire day, both were incomprehensible, and how could her husband be a murderer?! this was sheer insanity, but if it wasn't true, and he wasn't the murderer, then where was he?! she leaned forward on the sofa, burying her face in her hands and sobbing, motioning to the policemen to leave her in peace, to leave her house, but they, sitting across from her in the two armchairs, did not move, they waited for her to calm down, to presently give them comprehensible answers, but she didn't calm down, she just kept on mumbling incomprehensibly, the policemen asked more questions, she just kept on mumbling, and that sobbing, which burst out at each question aimed in her direction, grated unbearably on the policemen's ears, until finally they mentioned that they would go for now but come back later, but they didn't come back, in fact they never even left but remained sitting in a police vehicle in front of the house, Frau Ringer crept into the bathroom, grabbed the sink, slowly raised her head, and she did not recognize the face she saw in the mirror, blindly, she felt for a jar of face cream on a shelf behind the mirror, and after she had cleaned up her eye shadow, smeared from weeping, she rubbed some of the face cream right above her eyes, then a little below, then she applied it to her forehead and cheeks, she began fixing her hair, but she stopped because she felt her hair couldn't really be fixed, once again she leaned against the sink, bowed her head, and waited for the weeping to break out once again, she was incapable of understanding what had happened, incapable of believing that her husband could be accused of something like this, not only was this accusation not true, but it simply surpassed anything that any resident of Kana could be capable of, and yet Frau Ringer knew exactly that is what the two police officers had been thinking, and that's what people in Kana were thinking as well, which was deeply wounding to her self-esteem, her sense of justice and pride, it was gravely wounding to everything that mattered to her, she made herself presentable again—cleanser, face cream, everything—then she staggered out of the bathroom and went over to the liquor cabinet and she reached for her favorite, the cherry liqueur, then she thought again, and she opened up a bottle of strong plum brandy from which, until now, she had hardly taken a sip, because before his disappearance Herr Ringer had been visibly dipping into it, she knocked back a good dose, shuddered, finally she sat down on the sofa and she waited, she waited for him to come back, she waited for him to explain, to explain the inexplicable, because nothing like this had ever happened, him staying away and not breathing a word to her: when he used to go see his friends in Jena because of daily tensions and the general situation, that was fine; Frau Ringer took it as natural that her husband had his own little private sphere just as she did, but for him not to sleep at home, nothing like that had ever happened, she stepped over to the window and looked out through the curtains, but outside she only saw the police car and the policemen sitting in it, otherwise the street was completely deserted, as it usually was at this hour, but now things were different, now this street indicated to the person standing behind the curtains that it would never be what it had been before, this street would never be the same, nothing would ever be, just as for Frau Hopf who sat alone in the reception area, not even turning on the light, her afternoon coffee cold in the mug, and she didn't feel like drinking the rest of it, because it didn't matter, because nothing mattered anymore if gas stations could be blown up here, because if people could be murdered here, then nothing mattered anymore, and it didn't matter anymore what happened to the cold coffee in the mug, namely she never wasted anything, ever since childhood, it was her habit to never pour anything out, never to throw anything out, she wouldn't even throw away the last little plastic bag, because it always turned out that that little plastic bag, exactly that size, would be good for something, in the pantry next to the kitchen there was a large plastic garbage pail which they had scoured thoroughly when they first bought it years ago, even though it was perfectly clean, and since then, she had been collecting plastic bags in it, for years, even for decades, but not only plastic bags, but every kind of bag: string bags, tote bags, grocery bags, the large garbage bin was continually full, and she was always able to make use of its contents which were always needed for either this or that, and it was the same thing with bottles, because apart from the beer and wine bottles, which, of course, she always made sure to return, she saved every other kind of bottle or jar, and not only jam jars, but every bottle of champagne or liquor received as a present, moreover, her booty included gifts made to the hotel by foreign guests as tokens of their satisfaction, her collection enriched by unknown labels and liquor bottles of never-before-seen shapes, which of course, for the most part, did not merely comprise a collection, because Frau Hopf always sought a use for each and every one of these items, and in good time she did find a use for each one of them, either when she had bought a larger quantity of tomato juice, or when the syrup concentrate delivery came, the instances were innumerable when Frau Hopf happily went into her pantry and took down a row of bottles which, from that point onward, gained their true value, for nothing was without use, this was the motto of Frau Hopf, she confessed: not only was squandering the sign of weak character, but there wasn't even any point to it, not that I'm some penny-pincher, she would explain to one of her neighbors when they stopped by, don't think that I am, it's only that this is my connection to things, because I don't believe in the kind of life that's being forced on us, always buying new stuff and then tossing it out, well what kind of behavior is that? what kind of thinking is that?! and she spread her hands apart, I'm not like that, and I'm not going to be like that, I hang on to things, I put them away, and the things are grateful, because this is the only way to lead a proper life, and no other way, and that's it, she concluded her explanation, and every visitor or relative or acquaintance agreed with her, especially when her advice was dispensed with a brandy glass, a mug, or a large box containing so many bottles of tomato juice (for the grandkids in Dresden) that it lasted them a good long time, until she gave them another box, this was the order of things, this was her principle, so that, normally, she wouldn't have done anything differently with the cold coffee, she either would have reheated it or drank it cold, only that now extraordinary circumstances prevailed, and because of this Frau Hopf felt that she had no more strength to keep up the veneer of peace, even upstairs in her own apartment, because how could she hide from her husband that everything had been in vain, that they would not be able to live out their lives as planned, because there was no peace anymore, and after all of this—she shook her head bitterly in the dark room—there would never be peace, because they would have to live here among murderers and terrorists, and a person didn't have to look at these murderers and terrorists on the TV news but instead had to live among them, murderers and terrorists!! it was horrific!! Frau Hopf sighed and got up to go upstairs and see if everything was in order up there, and everything was in order upstairs, Herr Hopf was peacefully dozing off in his favorite spot, a couple of years back the children had given them a rocking chair for Christmas, and of course she, Frau Hopf, had paid for half of it, then she padded it with thick blankets and pulled it over next to the window where Herr Kopf could enjoy the sunlight the longest, and now her dear husband sat inert, head tipped over to one side, dozing, yes, and Frau Hopf's heart sank as she wondered when that moment would come of something exploding or collapsing or keeling over right on top of them, something aimed directly at both of them, I'll close the curtains, she decided, observing her husband's breath, I'll close all the windows, and now, with bad weather coming, I'll make him nice and warm, I will lie down on the bed, and we'll stay like that and we will pray and hope, because what else is there to do except to stay and pray and hope, even if there is no point, but that's what people are like, she said the next day to auntie Ingrid whom she had let in once again, and she offered her something to drink, as long as people are alive, they hope, well, certainly that's what things are like, her guest nodded, but she admitted that she herself did not see things as darkly as all that, therefore she advised Frau Hopf not to give up, because, for example, there will be the Chrysanthemum Festival, do you know how far we've gotten? we now have twenty-seven competitors!! and in auntie Ingrid's view this could be enough, because with this number she could hold the competition the following autumn, auntie Ingrid gulped down a full glass of liqueur, then she asked Frau Hopf for her advice concerning her competition's name, but Frau Hopf just stared right past her, she didn't even hear what auntie Ingrid was asking, just as Herr Köhler didn't hear the doorbell ringing, it was only when Dr. Tietz knocked on the window that he looked up from his laptop, closed it, and let his friend in, who began by saying that he and his wife had made a decision in Eisenberg and that he had come to Kana today to let Herr Köhler know the decision they had reached, because they had decided that it wasn't good for Adrian to be here by himself, they'd heard about what happened in Kana, and they were convinced things weren't good for Adrian here anymore, it wasn't safe; they'd decided that Adrian should move into their house in Eisenberg, because nothing ever happened there, and especially nothing horrific like here in Kana, and you know we have that little shed in our backyard, our older kids used to live there, but they've flown the nest and it's empty, well, we've set it up nicely for you, it's all ready, you can bring over whatever you want, a cabinet, your bed, anything you like, even the Weather Station, well, that's where we stand, what do you say? but Herr Köhler said nothing, he only looked at his friend and asked him if he'd like a cup of tea, Dr. Tietz didn't want a cup of tea, so Herr Köhler strolled slowly into the kitchen and made himself a mug, adding two spoonfuls of honey, he came back, and Dr. Tietz noticed for the first time that Adrian seemed to be shuffling a bit, is everything okay? he asked, and he stood up as Herr Köhler sat down in his usual place, of course, everything's fine, Herr Köhler mumbled, stirring his tea indifferently, then he adjusted his eyeglasses, took a sip, screwed up his face, and asked his guest to please bring him the honey jar and a tablespoon from the kitchen drawer, but do you understand me? Dr. Tietz asked, you can move in with us, even tomorrow if you like, of course, that would be good, muttered Herr Köhler, and clearly he was watching to make sure the doctor didn't trip on his way to the living room with the honey pot and the tablespoon, as he wasn't so young himself anymore, his movements visibly somewhat uncertain, Dr. Tietz's wife sometimes jokingly noted: you always look like you're about to start fainting on me, it's more than high time you went to the doctor, because as I see it, you have a problem with your balance, but Dr. Tietz brushed her advice off by saying, it's only because a woman made me dizzy with love, and that woman is you, my dear, and other such witticisms, which didn't reassure his wife, and she didn't laugh, so that after a while Dr. Tietz really had to go to one of his old classmates in Jena and get himself examined, but they didn't find anything serious, it comes with age, his colleague said to him, with age, Dr. Tietz explained at home as well, and he was only delaying the inevitable, namely that he had to start taking medicine for these ever more frequent problems of balance, medicine which only slowed down the problem, but whatever his problem was, he still was more nimble than his friend, and to see this was not a good feeling, Dr. Tietz was not the sentimental type, not least for professional reasons, but still it took something of a toll to see how much Adrian had aged—from his point of view: suddenly!—and clearly a kind of mental decay had also set in, and Dr. Tietz was surprised by the velocity of the process, and so with his wife they'd begun to think of what they could do for Adrian, and in the end they decided that they would try to bring him closer to themselves to take care of him, it was only what a person owed his best friend, Dr. Tietz noted, and his wife agreed, convinced that she could handle taking care of everyone, yet, as she remarked to her neighbors with good cheer, they were not expecting—especially not Dr. Tietz— the entire thing to go so smoothly, they were expecting resistance in Kana, for Adrian to say this or that, that he was used to things over there, and that Kana was Kana, and his Weather Station was there, but no, he offered no resistance, and although Dr. Tietz was full of uncertainty, when, on the next day, he showed up with two trucks in front of Herr Köhler's house, Adrian, with his laptop beneath his arm, sat down next to the driver in the first truck with no further ado, and someone had to ask him to go back into the house and tell them what he was taking and what he was leaving behind, at which Herr Köhler compliantly trudged back into the house and pointed at this or that item as if at random, he had a few things carried out, somewhat haphazardly, Dr. Tietz felt, and Frau Schneider remarked, standing in front of her doorway so that Frau Burgmüller would hear: hey, there's lots of activity over here at the neighbor's, although she was really stalling for time so she could hear what Frau Burgmüller had to say about this turn of events, but the latter merely stood in front of her doorway, arms crossed, and watched the movers, dumbfounded as they came out of the house with this or that cabinet, bed, table, and other items, packing up the truck, until finally: well, what's going on here?! is he moving away because of the pandemic?! Frau Burgmüller asked, like someone who very much wished this were not the case, but it was the case, this could not be denied and there was no point in debating it, the dear neighbor certainly is moving away from here, Frau Schneider pursed her lips bitterly, she had been suspecting this for a long time, she'd even predicted it would end like this, and now they too would have to leave, but where? could she tell her that? at which Frau Burgmüller was flooded with rage, and she bawled at Frau Schneider: well, that's you, because you're always watching TV where they keep frightening everyone and scaremongering with virus this and virus that—what?! Frau Schneider raised her voice, I always watch TV? and, offended, she went back into her house, but then she didn't think about their quarrel, instead she thought about her dear neighbor, because she truly felt sad as she looked out of the window and watched the two moving trucks, what would happen to her street now, Oststraße was inconceivable without him, Herr Köhler represented the highest value of this Oststraße, and now he was leaving? Frau Schneider watched the movers, and her heart told her: yes, this hurt like every other loss, but she did not want Frau Burgmüller to see this, because that old witch would only think she was meddling in the affairs of others, but there it was, she couldn't hide it before her own self, and why would she, it was evident what was happening when the backs of the two trucks were closed up and they drove off toward Bahnhofstraße, then she saw Herr Köhler getting into the car of that doctor from who knew where, and they drove off, she just looked at the building across the street and she felt as if her dear neighbor had died and his coffin had just been carried out, and she no longer wanted to look out the window that day, she didn't care what that withered old hag would have to say; Herr Köhler sat next to his friend, his laptop in his lap, clutching the door handle tightly while Dr. Tietz chatted to him cheerfully about his future accommodations, how good it would be for them to be so close; Herr Köhler, visibly afraid, never took his eyes off the road, so that after a while the doctor noticed, and he slowed down from 140 kilometers an hour to 90 and they drove on toward Eisenberg, that was always the problem with Dr. Tietz, he drove too fast, he was always getting warnings for speeding, if the policeman knew him, he got off sometimes, but if the policeman didn't know him, he didn't get off, his wife was of course very angry, I'm very angry at you, she scolded him, because you

268

drive too fast, but why, tell me already, but Dr. Tietz couldn't tell her why, because he himself didn't know, it simply felt good to drive as fast as circumstances would permit, what could he do, that's what he was like, but his wife did not accept this, and more recently, she was decidedly worried about him, because you're getting old, my heart, do you understand, you have to wear glasses, and especially at your age you have to slow down a bit, and that was it, everything remained as it was, although for the sake of his friend, Dr. Tietz slowed down to ninety kilometers an hour and kept on talking about their shared future life, his wife was waiting at home with a light meat broth, prepared especially for Adrian—the little one, their grandchild, couldn't have this— as well as a nice little Arabic meat dish, because once she had served that when Adrian was over for dinner, and he really liked it, so she decided to make it again, she had informed her husband yesterday as they discussed everything, but she was still a bit worried, because to take in an ill Adrian wasn't the same as inviting him over for dinner, although Adrian himself was a decisively amusing kind of person, she even sometimes admitted that he pleased her as well as a man, but of course no one took any notice, Dr. Tietz was happy to see his wife so galvanized when Adrian came over, it never occurred to him that there might have been another reason, and now he was especially happy that their cheerful dinners together would become a regular occurrence, and they did in fact regularly dine together, even if the earlier cheerful character of these repasts wasn't revived; Dr. Tietz did not admit this to himself for a long time, and he brushed his wife's comments aside when she tried to allude to this, and of course he too knew that Adrian was no longer

Falsche Welt, dir trau ich nicht!

the person he'd been, everything about him had changed, still he felt, even months later, it had been the right decision to have Adrian move

in with them as he was truly in need, a need which—little by little—
was becoming ever more evident: at first they merely had to get used
to Adrian wandering around here and there, and then sometimes at
night they started awake to find him standing next to their bed, hair
disheveled and his gaze fixed somewhere above, Herr Köhler would be
talking about how it was not the case that during the great annihilation
at the time of the Big Bang, after the emergence of one billion particles,
due to a breach of symmetry, a surplus of a plus one particle of matter
emerged and this is what created the world, but instead that in the great
annihilation at the time of the Big Bang, an antiparticle *did not* arise,
and this was what led to the creation of the world—the antimatter
simply vanished without a trace, no one knows where it went, only the
antimatter itself knew, because in Herr Köhler's opinion, due to the
instability in its structure, this antimatter immediately collapsed into a
black hole, and now all the antiparticles were concealed in these black
holes, it was only necessary to measure their total weight, and all that
had disappeared to such an enormous extent would exist again, Herr
Köhler explained as they sat here, leaning against the headboard, the
comforter pulled up to their chins, as they stared, terrified, into the
dark, and they understood none of this gobbledygook, and they especially didn't know if this meant that Herr Köhler had gone completely
mad?! although neither Dr. Tietz nor his wife dared ask about these
nocturnal apparitions, which, after a while, stopped of their own accord, and with that the spectral nighttime lectures also came to an end,
namely they came to an end because every kind of fundamental initia-
tive had died out in Herr Köhler, and why deny it, he had also lost all
interest in the little one, a sacred gift to them in their old age, the little
one whom Adrian used to coax to himself with such disarming simplic-
ity, he played with the child and the child grew so fond of him that they
could hardly get him to go to sleep after dinner when Adrian had left,
the child just kept crying, and cried himself to sleep, and now it was as

if Adrian didn't notice him, the child tried something every day, he
crept over to Adrian and nudged his elbow, and Adrian didn't chase
him away, he accepted that the child was there, right by his elbow, but
he kept on working, whatever that meant, so that after a while, the little
boy would simply steal into the little house in the back, he stood in the
doorway and watched from there, because he too now took it as natural that uncle Adrian was no longer the same, Adrian, who one time
turned to him and said: do you know that there is nothing else that is
perfect, only the world? and the little one stood in the doorway and
watched Adrian, then he ran off, sometimes returning to peek inside,
but never daring to come close again, and Adrian no longer noticed the
child, but he was like that with everything if no one was urging him, he
never would have gotten up from his laptop, he had to be reminded to
come have lunch or dinner, because he didn't even budge when told
for the first or second time that the meal was ready, he had to be helped,
if doing something in the garden, to recall what he was intending to do,
and his hosts knew what the problem was, and Dr. Tietz began to treat
him, but you know, my dear, what a treatment like this means, Dr. Tietz
sat hunched over on the sofa next to his wife as they turned the TV on
to *MDR Journal*, we can only slow things down, slow things down, but
still it's worth something, his wife encouraged him, and these were the
key words for Ringer as well, slow things down, stop this headlong
rush, only that for a good long while Ringer was incapable of slowing
down even though he really needed to, because he sensed that he
wouldn't be able to hold out too much longer, now I will stop, he decided over and over, but he kept on running, he was in Ilmenau, in
Meiningen, in Suhl, then in Sondershausen, and finally he called a
number and said into the receiver: I want to be brought in for questioning, and he repeated his request as he sat in a bare room in Erfurt, albeit
with a different emphasis: I want to be interrogated, write it all down,
I insist, he said to the officer sitting in front of him, and he gave a full

271

account, leaving out not even the smallest details, including names and addresses proving the veracity of his words, because it wasn't him, it wasn't me, he said, I know that's what everyone is saying, but no, he sat in the bare room in Erfurt, his gaze sincere, and already feeling calmer, he looked at the detective questioning him, but when the detective asked: fine, then, but who did it? Ringer had no answer, that's not my job, Ringer shook his head, that's for you to find out, leave me in peace now, I have more than enough to deal with as is, and truly that was the case, things were fairly difficult for him, because if Ringer was asking for his name to be cleared of all suspicion (which in any event he termed absurd) and if his name was indeed cleared, thanks to the assistance of the Federal Office for the Protection of the Constitution, he still didn't talk about how he still partially blamed himself for how everything in Kana had gotten so out of control, how they hadn't put a stop to all of this when they still could, they themselves who were right on the scene, what a sad, dismal failure, but Frau Ringer didn't agree with her husband when he turned up and finally came home, she agreed with everything but not with this, because why, she spread apart her hands, why are you responsible for things degenerating here, why blame yourself, you did everything you could, no, Ringer shook his head, I was just running off my mouth, I didn't do anything, because against these ones, against such developments, demonstrations are not enough, my heart, and lectures and manifestos and television debates, and Frau Ringer patted his hand, they sat across from each other in the living room, they didn't turn on the light even though it was already dark outside, she just caressed his hands and tried to console him, and now they were speaking in very quiet tones, and she asked him: tell me, what should I cook? what would you like, a Biersuppe? that would be nice, her husband smiled at her, completely exhausted, but it's already too late for that, why, why would it be too late? Frau Ringer jumped up from the sofa and she was already in the kitchen cleaning the vegetables, she took out a frozen portion of the meal from the freezer, put it into the microwave, set it to defrost, set the dial to ten minutes, then she changed her mind and set it to fifteen minutes, she felt how much she wanted to sigh deeply but didn't want her husband to hear, so she sighed a few near-silent sighs, then the vegetables were ready, she steamed them with a bit of sugar, then took the Biersuppe from the microwave and stirred it into the pot, adding a bit of water, no spices yet, those only came at the end when Ringer came into the kitchen, enticed by the fine aromas, he plunked himself down at the table and rubbed his face as if he were trying to wake up from a nightmare, because it had been one, what he had gone through in the past few days now seemed like a true nightmare as he ran and fled, he who had never before had to hide from anything or anyone, and it hadn't even started with him hiding—he had simply snapped, unable to take it anymore, and although he had realized that they were living in a different world now and he didn't understand this world, now for the first time he truly didn't understand what was going on in Kana, what was going on in Thuringia, what was going on in the entire country, it was disturbing to him; he didn't even know how long he had been running all over town until somebody told him confidentially that he should make himself scarce because he was a suspect, he who would have been more than happy to somehow eliminate those damned sick Nazzis if that would have solved anything, only that even in his distressed state, Ringer was aware that it wouldn't solve anything, impossible to return evil with evil, so that he gave himself up voluntarily, because he wanted to put an end to this senseless hide-and-seek, and now he no longer worried about Kana, but he was immeasurably disappointed in Kana, no one had stood up for him—in the first possible moment, people had turned against him, but he didn't bother with that anymore, he didn't bother with anything, he fell into complete apathy, he no longer even wanted to see his friends from Jena, when they came to visit he told them explicitly not to come again, because he felt he was no longer useful, which rather frightened Frau Ringer, and she did everything she could to make him feel that she stood with him, she took his hand, caressed it, but she frequently left him alone if she sensed that was what he needed, and she would have liked very much to speak about this situation with someone, but there was no one in Kana she felt like talking to, the library still wasn't open, she spent every minute at home, she didn't want to be far away for even a moment in case her husband might suddenly need her, well, but what to do? she couldn't keep sitting idly at home?! so she began working on something that had been weighing on her mind for a long time, namely the pantry, well, there was so much chaos in there that it was more than high time to straighten things up, she was always planning to start working on it, but it never happened, she and her husband would spend the weekends together, they went on outings or to the theater, they went to the movies either in Jena or Leipzig, there was no time, and during the weekdays, even though she hardly had anything to do in the library, afterward she was always just a trifle too tired to start working on the pantry so she kept putting it off, but now she began, at first she took down all of the innumerable preserve jars and brandy bottles and the boxes and bags from the shelves, countless spices and flour and sugar and oil and and and, she took it all into the kitchen where she inspected everything at length to see what to throw out and what to keep, then she washed off the shelves, wiped them dry, then put everything back, everything she could still make use of, but that was hard to determine, she was not a spendthrift, but if she decided to throw this or that out because of the expiration date or condition ... she was plunged in thought as she put things back, the scales kept tipping in one or the other direction, even as she took out the things she'd deemed to be of no use, she knew she'd never really be able to throw them out, instead she gathered everything up and put all the items into a big, strong garbage bag, dragged it over to her car, took it to the evangelical pastor's office, it could come in handy for the poor, she said to the pastor, and this calmed her down, she hurried back to her husband although she knew that he almost certainly didn't need her right now, Ringer's state was unchanged, moreover, if possible, it seemed even more hopeless than before, and that made everything else seem more hopeless to Frau Ringer, so that now she really had to talk to someone, to share her burden, beneath which, she felt, she was going to break, but not with any one of her girlfriends, because they were exactly the ones—just as with the other Kana residents—who immediately turned away from her as soon as Ringer had fallen under suspicion, so that now, if only from pride, she did not return to them, although they tried, very cautiously, to send her this or that signal, it's been so long, let's get together, a little coffee or something, but no, Frau Ringer needed a different solution, and a different solution emerged when she went to the Shopping Center to get some flowers, and maybe a pot too, she told the saleswoman, just to cheer up the apartment a bit, and there, in the florist's, she bumped into Frau Feldmann, who, with her own youthful enthusiasm, was able to shift Frau Ringer away from her hopelessness via a simple everyday chat, she suggested, namely Frau Feldmann suggested to Frau Ringer, in her own dear way, that since they hadn't met up for so long, they really should sit down for a coffee, Frau Ringer hardly knew Frau Feldmann, but even so, she felt a kind of self-evident, natural goodwill emanating from her words, so she accepted the invitation, and they sat down for coffee, and she wasn't meaning to, but suddenly she realized she'd poured out her heart and soul as she gazed into Frau Feldmann's friendly, smiling face, and it was already too late to consider if this was the right person to pour her heart and soul out to, she'd already done so, the two families—the Feldmanns and the Ringers—hardly knew each other, although they ran into each other now and then, for example at the May Day celebrations in the Rosengarten when they always exchanged a few friendly words, but nothing more, they didn't visit each other, didn't go out to dinner together, nothing like that, I don't even understand, Frau Feldmann noted, why we never got to-gether more seriously, you—and she grabbed Frau Ringer's arm—you should both come visit us one weekend, and Frau Ringer was happy, although she knew that due to her husband's condition she wouldn't be able to accept this invitation for a long time, if at all, but it felt good, it warmed her heart, at last there was someone who spoke exactly the words that would comfort her, my dear, Frau Feldmann said, it's like this everywhere, don't think it's only our specialty here in Kana, it's the same everywhere, people are afraid, so easily influenced by gossip, that's why I don't judge them, so don't you trouble yourself about it, it's natural, everyone here has something to be afraid of, no? because what kind of horrors are we surrounded by, all of a sudden? am I not right? yes, you are right, Frau Ringer acknowledged, with the sense that she had a new girlfriend in Frau Feldmann, and so it was, when it be-came clear that the Ringers weren't going to come over to Hochstraße together anytime soon, Frau Feldmann came over by herself, *directly* to Frau Ringer, and said to her in the doorway: look, I have come over here *directly* to you, I know what the situation is, so that I came here even uninvited, if you let me in, you let me in, if not, I understand, and they sat down in the kitchen, and the lady of the house brewed good coffee, happy that Frau Feldmann was so lovely, you are so lovely, Bri-gitte, she gave her a cup of coffee, I don't even know how to thank you, and Frau Ringer was truly full of gratitude, and once again she poured out her soul to Frau Feldmann, and she was relieved, and she felt she'd gained a new strength, new energy, and the following weekend, after a fruitless attempt to get her husband to go on an outing to Saaleblick she said to herself, well then, there's always the summer kitchen, be-cause the Ringers also had a back kitchen for cooking in the summer—practically no one else had this kind of summer kitchen because almost all of them had sheds in the Kleingartenanlage, and if the sun was shin-ing, people in Kana liked to concoct their meals there—the only problem was that Frau Ringer needed a little help with this back kitchen, because if she was going to start cooking there again, it had to be repainted, a necessary step, and yet Ringer had only one local housepainter friend, whom they couldn't call because times were just as hard for him as for everyone else, Florian hadn't been coming around lately, so what if she went to the Baumarkt? and handled it herself? yes, that seemed the best solution, and why not? she could do the repainting herself, couldn't she? of course she could, and so Frau Ringer set to work painting and cleaning and sorting and washing and she put things in order, she hardly knew herself, once she got to the end, what to do next, so engrossed had she become in this task, so she washed off the large ceiling beams, and all the while Ringer sat in the living room, the television was on but he wasn't watching it, he wasn't watching anything, Frau Ringer determined, but then nothing was like the old days when there weren't cops or who knew what kind of civilians everywhere, when there were no explosions or murders or anything like that, before, no one in Kana could even recall a murder taking place; there had only been that single, dark, criminal nest, as they termed it, Burgstraße 19, but that was finished now, the residents of Kana noted among themselves, relieved; the door to the Burg was firmly shut, sealed off with yellow tape, indicating that no one could go inside and that no one lived there anymore, not Karin or Andreas or Gerhard or Uwe or any of the others—who, on that day, did not remain in the house but dispersed, that would be the smartest, they nodded, upon hearing Karin's advice, and that's what they did: Karin went to Mattstedt, Gerhard to Saalfeld, the others dispersed throughout Thuringia and Sachsen, only Andreas tried to stay in Kana, but this decision promised nothing good, so he soon gave up and went to Jena, and it was the same with the others who dispersed, one here, one there; they ended up meeting up for the first time at an important soccer match, we shouldn't be meeting up, Karin said immediately, not even for a moment, her ice-cold gaze roaming over the small stadium in Gera, they'll take pictures of us, I'll signal where and when to meet later on, and she left the match, only Andreas and the hard-core Gera fans stuck around, of course they had the internet, as they stayed in touch on a daily basis using certain secret websites as they'd done before, and this is how they found out the date of the funeral, they called Andreas in Erfurt to let him know that the autopsy was finished, the corpse could be retrieved, Andreas put out the alert, and that evening he went to Mattstedt to find out if the Boss had any kin, but then they decided that since the Boss himself had never mentioned any relatives, they would assume this to be his last will and testament and bury him themselves, the situation was different with Fritz, whose mother was still living in Meuselwitz, Gerhard went to Meuselwitz to inform her, but the woman was so drunk that she didn't understand, your son is dead, do you understand? Gerhard raised his voice, and in the end he started shaking her to make her realize that she had to bury her son, he dragged her into the burned-out bathroom reeking of smoke, opened the shower tap, waited for the rusty water to become clear, he held the woman's head under the showerhead, then dragged her back into the living room, pushed her into the old armchair with its stench of old vomit, grabbed her and kept on slapping her, until the woman somewhat came to herself, then she asked: what's going on, what's going on?! her tongue heavy and thick, your son croaked, fuck it, then go get the priest, the woman faltered out, and as this seemed to be the best solution, Gerhard went to the local parish and rang the bell, the reverend knew Fritz, I held him under the baptismal waters, what a tragedy, I tell you, and he knew Fritz's mother as well, that too is a tragedy, I tell you, but it's all in the hands of the good Lord, I couldn't care less, said Gerhard, fed up with all this rigmarole, if it's in God's hands or someone else's, I'll give them your address and they'll bring Fritz here, okay? of course, the reverend answered, the church takes back every sinner, and so it was, the sinners have come back from Erfurt, exactly like the wolves, Uwe wrote on their secret website, Uwe, who was Andreas's half brother, because they have appeared again, the Revierförster announced to the Rathaus in Kana, a new pack consisting of five members, three males, including both the alpha and a young cub, and two she-wolves, how do you know this is a new pack, the Revierförster was asked in the Rathaus, because it's not the same one that was here before, answered the Förster, offended, and he explained, as he had countless times already, what they needed to know: the wolves were not dangerous, they had already moved on toward Schiefergebirge, most likely seeking a larger expanse of territory, so that once again there was no reason to be afraid, but of course the residents of Kana were just as afraid as before whenever they heard of a new wolf-pack sighting, and NABU decided they could not come to Kana often enough to give public lectures regarding the true nature of the wolf, they can explain to me all they want, Herr Heinrich shook his head in Ilona's buffet, they can talk all they want, a wolf is a wolf, and a wolf is a monster and that's all, and everyone at Ilona's agreed, especially Hoffmann, who was running up a big debt at Ilona's and was looking for Florian, maybe he could get something from him, but Florian was nowhere to be found, so that at Ilona's Hoffmann cowered and only spoke very rarely, but now he did speak up, and he said that he was of the same opinion, because a wolf was a wolf, that's exactly correct, a wolf does not know mercy; although as Tamás Ramsthaler—his own importance emphasized by the white mask on his face—said to the sparse audience in the room made available to him by the Rathaus, more precisely to those four Kana residents who thought they might learn something from NABU about what to expect from these mountain visitors: the fear of wolves is as old as humanity itself, or at least so they say, because I must admit, he raised his voice, when I began to deal with this theme, I myself was utterly shocked by the naivete and ignorance surrounding it, because before the Middle Ages and after the Middle Ages, whatever, no one ever took the trouble to get a little closer and get to know this magnificent, this exceptional, animal, no one was interested to find out what we were facing in reality, because the fear was so strong that it would have only been disturbed by the truth, because it is easy to renounce truth but difficult to renounce fear, so that the words of the first learned minds espousing a scientifically acceptable view regarding these magnificent creatures were nothing more than phrases shouted in the desert, the myths and legends and fairy tales about the bloodthirsty wolf were always more credible than the wolves that truly—I must emphasize—lived together with us until we exterminated them, all down to the last wolf, Tamás Ramsthaler from NABU raised his voice, because this is what happened, by the end of the nineteenth century not a single wolf remained in Germany, and only since the 1980s and 1990s—in no small part thanks to the goodwill of organizations such as ourselves at NABU—have we begun to counter this situation, but there is still much to be done, he said, but he did not convey what was to be done because the four people who comprised the audience simply left the room, one after the other, so that there was no longer anyone for Tamás Ramsthaler from NABU to talk to; and as for Florian, he didn't even see the point of talking because who was there for him to talk to, not only that, but he would have only been able to talk about a very personal matter, as he still slept with the cell phone, although not next to his pillow, he placed it a little farther away, then a little farther away and a little farther away beyond that, so that one morning it fell onto the floor, and finally he didn't even take the cell phone to bed with himself, he didn't even reach for it, but took it into the kitchen and put it in the cabinet above the gas stove, way in the back behind a bag of sugar, then even this didn't seem far enough away, so Florian put the phone beneath the sink, behind the cleaning supplies, that is to say, he didn't put the phone there but threw it, he threw the phone behind the sink as if it were burning his hands, and he quickly closed the cabinet door, and that was it, he reached for the phone no longer, although it hadn't been that way at first, no, not at all, because the joy he had experienced when he got his first laptop wasn't even comparable to this, the Nokia was different, because he hadn't been expecting the Nokia at all, he had accepted the Boss's explanation that previously he'd had no need for a cell phone, no need, because only the conversations that took place between him and the Boss in person were the real deal, as the Boss put it, and this must never be destroyed by any technical means—with the exception of the Hochhaus intercom—the two of them together formed a separate world, said the Boss, and the fact that everyone else had a cell phone was different, completely different, just as it was different that he, the Boss, also had a cell phone, moreover, more than one, although the Boss never used those cell phones for personal affairs, because for him there was just this personal affair, and that was Florian, and it gratified Florian to hear this, so that he had banished the thought of having his own cell phone, he accepted the Boss's argument, but then the unexpected moment arrived, the phone pressed into his hand, and the reasons for him to get a Nokia were suddenly just as convincing as the reasons, previously, for him not to have had one, but who the devil cared why he hadn't gotten a phone before, and now he suddenly had one, here it was in his hands, that was the main thing, and Florian carried it home holding it at a distance from his body as if he were afraid he might drop it if he held it any other way, and he placed it carefully on the kitchen table as if he were afraid even the smallest movement might break it, but the cell phone didn't break, Florian closed his eyes a few times and opened them, and the Nokia was still there on the kitchen table, so it was true, he wasn't dreaming, I have a Nokia, he thought, his brain buzzing, then he ran over to Herr Köhler, then he ran back home again, and for the next two days he discovered as many secrets of the cell phone as he could on his own; he'd known much less about cell phones than about laptops, he'd seen, for the most part, how cell phones were used, but he never really paid any attention, so that now he had to learn to recognize the functions of the touch screen, the buttons on the side and at the top, of course he began by charging the phone, because he saw on the display that the battery was almost out of charge, and he knew it needed to be charged—the Boss had at times entrusted him with charging one of his cell phones—but now, when he plugged the end of his own charger into the socket, and the other end into the small jack he located at the bottom of the telephone, and the display lit up, indicating that it was charging, he nearly yanked the cord off the kitchen table in his excitement, and he only had his own good reflexes to thank that nothing worse happened, as he caught the cell phone in time and placed it cautiously back on the table, but to avoid endangering the phone any further, Florian didn't sit next to it while it was charging but remained standing at a respectful distance, watching the phone as it just charged and charged and charged, sometimes he took one pace toward the phone, leaning over the display to see how much it had charged, and this was always the most difficult, that first step; what came after didn't seem so complicated already, even though Florian had no idea how the fingerprint reader or the icons worked, and since he couldn't decipher the English words and abbreviations popping up here and there, he used trial and error: he pressed on this and he pressed on that and waited for something to happen or not, and he kept on pressing things as much as he could and he waited, then something happened or something didn't happen, and nicely and slowly, the entire world of the Nokia was revealed to him, and from that point on Florian only had to practice, because until this point he wasn't actually using the phone but merely practicing on the touchpad, he turned the phone off and he turned it back on, he tapped out a number and erased it, he typed out something in the notes app and erased it to see how it worked, and so he kept taking these small steps forward, until finally in the middle of the second day he was so hungry that he had to stop and go down to Ilona's, but then he didn't know what to do, take the phone with him? leave it here at home? there were arguments to be made for both sides, so in the end Florian left the cell phone on the kitchen table, only that before he stepped out into the corridor, he thought things over, went back, and covered the phone with a tissue so it wouldn't get dusty while he was out, and he wanted so much to say what had happened, he was flustered, everyone at Ilona's was scaring each other with the latest rumors, and somehow Florian couldn't find an opening in the conversation to tell everyone about his Nokia; in the end what happened was that he never even got the chance to say: hey, people, I have a Nokia, and

there is nothing else that is perfect, only

he hurried back to the Hochhaus, still having to keep the exciting news to himself, the Deputy wasn't home or he'd already gone to bed, in any event, he wasn't answering his doorbell, so Florian couldn't tell him either about the big news on the seventh floor, although the Deputy was at home, he just didn't feel like getting up, he was lying in bed fully clothed, covered with a plaid blanket and watching TV, of course it's just Florian, he thought, and he didn't move, he'd buzz him on the intercom later on, and he kept on watching MDR-Thuringia, the Deputy never watched anything else, at the most sometimes RTL, but in his opinion, RTL was just seeking attention, the only station that sincerely was what it was, was MDR, that was his station, here in the East, only MDR, because he felt it spoke to him, not only because of Thuringia and everything, but because it reminded him a bit of the old times, which, no matter what anyone said, he thought were beautiful, he didn't hide this opinion, and particularly not from Pförtner, he preferred not to talk about these things to Florian, but Pförtner understood what he meant, there was a kind of complicit understanding between them, especially in these larger matters, because of course they

283

had their smaller differences of opinion on, for example, the best beer, was it Lübzer or Rostocker Pils, Köstritzer or Hasseröder, but on the most important questions, their agreement was complete, so that no matter what anyone said, noted one or the other in the great silent night of Kana, whether the subject was our industry, our housing situation, or our labor market, and so on, there was never any subject lacking in the conclusion that everything had been so much better in the old days, so much better, well, either Pförtner or the Deputy would add, apart from the quality of the roads, because the roads! you couldn't even compare them with these new ones, and they didn't compare them, although Florian was himself a little rattled by a comparison when, the next day, he went to the Herbstcafé to download more music, and to also have a look and see how his Nokia compared to other devices from the same manufacturer, but the designations and the data were too complicated for him to figure out, so that when he went home, he only pressed the settings icon, and he changed some settings he was already familiar with, for a while that was all that happened, he practiced what he knew, and he only began venturing into unknown territory when he began to get bored with what he had already figured out, and in this way he ended up at the menu showing incoming and outgoing calls where he found a list of other calls besides the five incoming calls the Boss had told him about: there were, to his great surprise, five other calls, five outgoing calls placed from this phone to the Boss, and this was when he asked himself for the first time if it might be a good idea to look into this a little more closely, but even before he might have engaged with this thought, he had already dismissed it, he chased it away, because what was the point of trying to understand this in more detail, there was already so much about the Boss he had never understood, why did he need to understand anything about those five outgoing calls, so that after somewhat troubled hesitation, he decided not to bother, and instead his finger slid over to the camera icon to see how to use it, at first he pressed a button on the display at random, but since he was holding the Nokia downward, he only photographed a kind of crimson-brown spot, but the second time he took a photograph looking out of the window, and Florian was very proud when he saw how well it came out, he spent the entire day taking pictures from the window from every possible angle until it was dark outside, then he carefully set the phone on the table and he waited for it to cool down so he could wrap it up again in the tissue, because he had decided that it wasn't enough to cover the phone to protect it from dust, instead he wrapped it up nicely and thoroughly in tissue and left it there; he sat and waited and watched while the phone cooled down, then in a certain moment he got up, he unlocked the phone with his fingerprint, he clicked on the incoming and outgoing calls and looked at them again, then he closed that menu, and as the phone had cooled down enough, he wrapped it up in the tissue, and he went over to Ilona's, but he couldn't say that there wasn't a bad feeling within him, because there was, and because of that and mainly because he found himself in the middle of a debate on the question of the Boss's responsibility—as Heinrich was saying, and Hoffmann was agreeing with him, the Boss was the one who brought all these problems on us, he was the one raising up these little Nazis on Burgstraße, and so on— Florian ordered a Bockwurst and a Jim Him and he was quiet, but everyone kept talking about the Boss this and the Boss that, the Boss was like this and the Boss was like that, so that when Florian finally spoke, it was not in his usual tone of voice, but instead it burst out of him: well, of course Heinrich and Hoffmann are twisting everything!! why were they always distorting everything?! why weren't they talking about who had founded the Kana Symphony Orchestra, about who saved the life of Herr Ringer and his wife?! and of course everyone fell silent immediately, and not only because of the sudden dissenting opinion, but because this voice, Florian's voice, was so unusual, because there was rage in it, and there was something else not easy to determine, they all just looked at him, Hoffmann immediately got up and moved to another bench, Florian turned red because of his sudden emotion, he bowed his head and stared at the table, his hands were shaking as Ilona brought him his Bockwurst, and he ate it like that, his hands shaking, the others, after a short silence, began to speak again in quiet tones, but they did not bring up the topic of the Boss again, so surprised were they at Florian's unexpected and incomprehensible outburst, they had never seen him like this—I, said Hoffmann, after Florian paid and left, have never seen him like this, Herr Heinrich, there's going to be a problem with him, I'm telling you, because something happened, he added, but he didn't continue the thought, he just hemmed and hawed like someone who knew more than what he was saying, but he didn't, he knew nothing at all, Ilona cut him down from behind the counter, you be quiet, Hoffmann, you're saying things like that about someone you're constantly hitting up for small change? and her voice, Ilona's voice, sounded strange now too, it was unusual for her to shout at anyone, only if someone had had a few glasses too many, but even then it was without real anger, as opposed to now, when it was clear she was very angry at Hoffmann who immediately regretted his words, he asked for the key to the toilet and left, then when he came back he sat down in the corner and said nothing, he was subdued, because Ilona, as ever, was right, Hoffmann was always trying to mooch off everyone, but no one ever gave him anything, only Florian, and moreover he always did so if he had some extra cash, so Hoffmann held his tongue, sipping his beer or smiling if somebody told a joke, or nodding and consenting with a gloomy face when something more serious came up, because this was his only society, the only company in which he'd found his place, and he feared only one thing, that they might one day turn away from him, cast him out and never let him in again, so that he truly regretted speaking against Florian, he would have taken back his words if he could, but he couldn't; then Ilona closed for the night, and the regular customers dispersed from the parking lot in front of the Baumarkt and no one said anything to him, he wished the others good night but no one returned his greeting, and so Hoffmann trudged home like someone who'd been beaten, the wind was blowing, the first icy wind of early autumn, the rain began to drizzle down like a thousand sparks hitting him in the face, he pulled down his hood and kept on walking with one shoulder thrust out, almost blindly, although he knew the route well, never once stumbling, at least when he wasn't drunk, as he wasn't now, he knew every single centimeter of this distance between his apartment and the Grillhäusel so well, he knew every hole, crevice, every protuberance in every meter, he knew by heart where the sidewalk was perfectly smooth, where he had to step down, where he had to step across, where he had to lengthen his stride, his leg raised, because in the entire blessed world this was the route to which he truly belonged, because this path also knew him well, it knew his every step, whether he was staggering along or stepping smoothly, the path knew whether he was raising his left or right leg, when he stepped to one side, when he had to lean to one side for support and which leg he used to try to gain his balance when he was about to topple over, and that's how it was this evening as well, as Hoffmann sidled his way back to his apartment, turning off from the Wagner repair shop, down through the small underground passage to the other side of the rail tracks, then to the right up to his house on Ölwiesenweg where he rented a room in the back for sixty-five euros a month, and if he had gone a little farther he would have been able to say he was sorry to—and perhaps even scrounge a bit of change from—Florian, because Florian, in his emotionally heightened state, did not go straight home to the Hochhaus, but after leaving Ilona's and walking in this or that direction, he also found himself on Ölwiesenweg, and if he was already there, then, despite the bad weather, which he hadn't noticed anyway, he decided to go to his bench on the banks of the Saale, where he didn't sit down, instead, he stood for a long time beneath one of the chestnut trees, he watched the raindrops plunking into the rushing waters, and he was still so agitated that he wished he could have gone back to Ilona's to explain everything, newer arguments were forming in his mind, because, well, no, he decided things couldn't go on any longer like this: until now he had only hinted at the truth concerning the Boss to the others, but it was time for him to step up more forcefully, someone had to protect the Boss, Florian determinedly stepped away from the tree, but there was no one to talk to, nowhere to go, it was too late, nothing else to do but for him to walk home where he went up to the seventh floor, took off his clothes, hung everything up, he hung his coat from the window handle, placed his overalls on the drying rack in the bathroom, put his cap and pullover and shirt on the radiator, but he spread out his underwear and socks on the edge of the bathtub, everything was completely soaked through, and not only that, but he started sneezing, so that after he had put on dry clothes, he quickly made himself a coffee, then sipping his coffee, he sat in the kitchen, watching the raindrops hitting the windowpane, better to look at the raindrops and not at the Nokia, somehow he didn't want to look at it now, there was some kind of problem with this Nokia although he didn't know what it was, something wasn't right with it, better to look at the windowpane and the raindrops rolling down, but no, in no way not at the Nokia, there were no five conversations, there wasn't even one conversation; before, Florian couldn't have a cell phone and now he could, a used phone but light blue, used but so beautiful, and it worked perfectly, you could take wonderful photographs with it, it had a fingerprint reader and everything, only that something about it wasn't right, and his brain kept doubling back and back to this something, he tried to impede his own train of thought, but to no avail, he tried to pay attention to the raindrops rolling down the windowpane,

but he couldn't hold out too long, his thoughts kept returning to the
Nokia, he sensed his body flooding with heat, and it wasn't from the
coffee, he knew his face had turned red, he knew that when something
bothered him his face always turned red, and now something was really
bothering him, only it wasn't clear what it was, but definitely, he
thought, it has something to do with those five conversations, why
were those five conversations bothering him so much? Florian asked
himself, well, because there weren't five conversations, he answered his
own question, and then he repeated to himself several times over that
not only were there not five conversations, there wasn't even one conversation, nothing of the sort had occurred, and yet the Boss had told
him: there were these five conversations, and of course he had said yes,
and he would say yes today as well if anyone asked, but nobody was
asking him, and nobody had asked him before, so why was this being
asked of him now? ah, no, he shook his head, there's something else
going on here, he would ask the Boss about it tomorrow during the
funeral, but he didn't ask the Boss, because there were only two other
people there, and the Boss thought they had come to the wrong funeral, so now what, the Boss said, followed by a long series of fuck its,
there's only one cemetery in Kana, or did I miss something?! and he
looked at Florian, but Florian stood beside him as if he were made of
stone and said nothing, then the priest arrived, and he too was fairly
surprised that only two people, that is to say hardly anyone, had shown
up for the Brazilians' funeral; the announced time of the funeral had
already passed a quarter of an hour ago, yet the priest acted as if he fully
understood: I understand, he leaned over to the Boss's ear, because
nothing is more self-evident than people being terrified after such a
weighty trauma, and so I owe both of you a special thanks, he turned
toward them, and I will mention tonight, during the collection, that
there were two brave and honorable people among the fearful, there
are always two righteous ones, as the Gospel says; well, that's enough

now, the Boss, who didn't feel frightened, brushed him off in irritation, let's get this over with, he said, tell us where to stand, and start already, you know what you have to do, at which of course the priest was offended, and he no longer looked at the Boss, he only looked, if necessary, at Florian, from the Credo to the Dismissal, he recited the entire liturgy to him, Florian, whose behavior was rather confusing; not that he was behaving inappropriately, the priest determined; rather, it was as if he wasn't even here, but somewhere else, and in reality Florian was somewhere else, he didn't even cry, although the priest saw, at the beginning, that Florian had been crying, but then nothing, nothing during the Invocation, the Psalm of Confession, or the Herald of Grace, they started walking with the two cheaply made coffins—nothing, Florian remained stone-faced—the priest was not consoled—after the gravediggers shoveled the dirt back onto the graves, dug fairly closely together to save space and expense, and the three of them began walking back, and it emerged that the coffins and everything had been paid for by the Boss, and Florian, standing halfway between the graves and the cemetery gate, suddenly began to sob—the priest was not consoled, he saw this more as the voice of conscience of a guilty soul rather than as grief felt for the deceased, although he was mistaken, Florian's grief, from the beginning, was deep and it was sincere, only that the chaos in his head was complete, and he needed all his strength, now expended, to keep it from showing, and when they drove back in the Opel to the corner of Ernst-Thälmann-Straße, and Florian got out, he didn't even say goodbye to the Boss or anything like that, and when the next day the Boss rang his intercom, Florian just opened the window and looked down and then closed the window, and he asked himself out loud: why is he buzzing me, why doesn't he call? I have my own cell phone now, don't I?! and when the intercom rang again he didn't answer, the Boss gave up and he drove off in the Opel, Florian collapsed in the living room onto the stone-hard bench, the Boss had gotten this for him too, even before he had brought him over here and told him: well, goddammit, this is yours, it had always made Florian so happy when he recalled how he'd realized that everything here was his own personal property, even the stone-hard bench, the bench he'd just collapsed onto, because *now* the exact opposite occurred, *now* it completely bothered him that this too was his, because it wasn't his, everything here was the Boss's, Florian jumped up and went into the kitchen and began to walk around, then he ran down first to the Deputy, then to Frau Hopf, then to Frau Feldmann, then to Ilona's, and finally he went over to Frau Ringer as well, and he said that he was asking her greatly to please leave the Boss out of everything, and he enumerated the entire list of the Boss's good qualities, but to no avail, no one seemed convinced, although everyone could clearly see the state he was in, so tense he was about to explode, and they didn't understand why, but they—and not just Frau Ringer, but everyone else to whom Florian spoke on behalf of the Boss—attributed it to his having become troubled after the horrific events, and that's why he'd become so agitated, so frightened, so aggressive, because yes—and Frau Ringer mentioned this to her husband—she had never seen Florian so aggressive, but now he was: just imagine, his eyes nearly turning in his head as he just kept saying and saying that the Boss was like this and the Boss was like that, I think that brute has frightened him, Frau Ringer shook her head angrily, he's frightened that poor child with something, although he hadn't, the Boss couldn't get in touch with Florian, because Florian didn't want to meet up with him, or precisely, he couldn't bear to, he couldn't explain to himself why he couldn't but he couldn't; if the Boss buzzed the intercom, Florian didn't pick up the receiver, didn't even open the window, if the Nokia rang, he didn't even react, five calls from that night, it kept running through his head, but he only thought of those five calls from a distance, he didn't dare go any closer because he sensed a great problem in connection with those five calls;

after his first attempts he gave up trying to get everyone to see the Boss in a different light, namely he himself began to see him in a different light, but that form into which the Boss was changing in his eyes had not yet crystallized, he was still viewing the fact of those five calls made that night from too great a distance; and yet the Boss was no longer the same person that he'd previously known and for whom he would have given up his heart and soul to protect, and then the day came when he didn't even take the Nokia into his hands, but instead he put it into the cabinet above the gas stove in the kitchen, behind a bag of sugar, then in the cabinet beneath the sink seemed the most suitable, the dark, dirty space between the cleaning supplies, and Florian didn't place the phone there but threw it there, quickly slamming the cabinet door shut as if his hands were burning, even now when he wasn't even using the phone, moreover, he knew that from now on he would never use it again, he had to calm down, I have to calm down, he told himself, and he bent his head beneath the faucet and drank a few sips of water, he sat down at the kitchen table and he started playing *Was willst du dich betrüben* on his laptop—he'd just downloaded it—he listened to it on his earphones until he started awake, because he had fallen asleep, leaning forward on the kitchen table, the edge of the laptop crushing his arm; he turned the laptop off, lay down in bed fully clothed, and immediately fell asleep, a statement that could be made by very few that evening, because ever since the explosion at the Aral station, the inefficacy of the police had become obvious to all; the news had been spreading—even this afternoon—that it was definitely no accident, someone had blown up one of the gas stations on purpose, and poor Nadír and poor Rosario had burned to death in it, but, well, who? people asked, not each other, but themselves, and they didn't dare go to the funeral, they only kept asking themselves at home: well, who was this monster, who was so despicable, who would descend to committing such a horrific deed, and why?! who could those two have hurt?! and sleep did not come to them, for a long time they didn't even dare turn over in bed, because they were afraid that as they turned over they would fail to hear that suspicious rustling sound alerting them to leap out of bed and run down to the basement, because this was the plan of most of the residents of Kana when hell broke loose again, to jump out of the bed and run down to the basement, because if there had been one explosion, there was going to be another, the general opinion was ever more decisive, everyone was preparing for this or something similar, but no person of sound mind could have prepared for what actually happened: the murder of first the Boss, then the two others in the Burg, it was simply inconceivable, the residents of Kana said to each other with sleepless eyes, murders didn't happen here, never, as even Torsten, the school janitor, kept asserting to his wife, although he didn't really have to because his wife knew this too, Torsten was stating the obvious, and although he could not deny that he had pangs of conscience, from that day on, he didn't go back to work, he didn't even open up the high school building again, because after what had happened at the Aral station, no teachers were coming in to school and no parents were letting their children go to school, only he, the school janitor, kept coming in until the news of the murders—to turn on the large boiler, because he hadn't wanted to risk not coming in, and he waited alone, he sat around in his basement room, sometimes he went upstairs and strolled up and down the ground-floor hallways, he looked at the group graduation photographs on the walls and the children's drawings that had been awarded prizes, he reread the latest announcements that had been put up: the time of the Friday basketball match was rescheduled, and someone had tried, somewhat sadly, to press back the lower-left-hand corner of the paper which had come loose, but it no longer stuck in place, so the janitor just kept on strolling down the hallway, he went up to the first floor, then he went up to the second floor, and everything seemed so ghostly, empty, and fallen into complete muteness, and it was strange that although nobody was coming in to the building anymore, he still heard, in this muteness, a kind of

uninhibited din, as if it were always recess, he heard the students rushing out of the classroom doors, and the school bells were deafening as
well, especially like this, when they were no longer ringing; but then
news of the murders came to light and from that point on his wife
wouldn't let him out of the house, they argued over whether he should
go in or not, but in the Torsten household, it was his wife who made
the decisions, and his wife wouldn't let him, she said: no, and that's it,
you're staying home, that's all I need, for you to ...! and Torsten stayed
home, but at home he wasn't doing anything, there was nothing to do,
because if he started something, for example if he started dismantling
the dripping faucet, his wife immediately grabbed the wrench out of
his hands and said: you'll break it even more, or if he wanted to
straighten up the basement, his wife immediately appeared, looking at
him sternly, so he stopped that too, he just sat idly in the kitchen, not
knowing what to do, not knowing whom to call, it's the end of Torsten,
he said to himself, but in reality he was thinking that it was not only the
end of Torsten but the end of all of them, and there certainly was a
good dose of exaggeration in that, because after the murders, the police
showed up with even more force than they had before, and this time
they stayed, continually patrolling the roads, Kana was full of police,
more police than after the Aral explosion, and they were clearly intent
on finding the perpetrator, holding mass interrogations, and they appeared to agree with the residents of Kana, there was a connection
between the Aral station explosion and the murders—at first the police didn't think so, largely due to Jürgen, who, having somewhat recovered, could now return from Jena, namely he could have returned from
Jena and awaited his trial under house arrest, but then he said he didn't
want to go back to Kana, so where do you want to go? the police asked
him as they placed an electronic bracelet on his ankle, to my mother's,
he said, and as he didn't have enough money for a taxi, they transported him in an ambulance to his mother in Mücka where they

checked the ankle monitor and told him he couldn't leave the house until he got the court summons, but when the summons arrived, Jürgen was no longer at his mother's, I have no idea where he is, his mother, in a wheelchair, blew the cigarette smoke away to one side as she rolled up to the policemen standing in the doorway, the cut-off ankle bracelet in her hand; her son, she added, as she looked at them with ice-cold eyes, had never told her where he'd gone, or what he was doing ever since he was fourteen, and he wasn't going to change, he doesn't listen to his mother, but the policemen didn't let her keep on talking, they just took the electronic bracelet from her hand and put out the arrest warrant for Jürgen, although Jürgen had disappeared, they couldn't find him, and they couldn't have found him; for a while, the residents of Kana discussed how much time he'd get and suchlike, but when the murders happened everyone forgot about Jürgen, because the murders in and of themselves erased all other earlier, more minor events, and the residents of Kana didn't understand, why exactly them?! it would have been logical—Herr Wagner, who had gone to get four Bosch spark plugs, elaborated in the Baumarkt parking lot—if those beasts had murdered someone, because they are beasts, but for them to be murdered?! well, I can't wrap my head around that, and what could Herr Heinrich do but nod in agreement, he'd only come here to see if he could find someone he might know in need of some odd job done, and Herr Heinrich continued to analyze the matter in this light to the regulars in the Grillhäusel, while Ilona, although horrified by the events herself, paid them no attention, for a while now she had been disconnecting from her customers' conversations, it bored her, frankly put, it really bored her, because they always talked about the same things, how horrific this or that was, how this or that had never ever happened before, they just chew the cud the entire day, she complained to her husband, when I'm opening up and when I'm closing down, it's the same thing from beginning to end: this and that, this one was the perpetrator, that one was the perpetrator, Nazis this and Nazis that, cops this and cops that, my head is buzzing, don't even talk to me, I want an hour of silence; this happened every night when she went home, but what could she do, she had to keep the Grillhäusel going, every morning she had to open it up, every evening she had to close it down, although at times it did occur to her and her husband that given the state of things here, it might be best to move on, what would you say to that, her husband put the question to her every now and then, if we just took the whole thing, closed up, and got the hell out of here—where?! Ilona yelled at him, which was fairly unusual for her, she nearly exploded, betraying that she'd also had this thought at times, things were getting to her as well, but where?! and she looked at him angrily as if he were cawing out doom with no concrete idea of where to go, because were they just supposed to leave everything that they had built up here?! when they were fully settled in?! when business was going fairly well, soon they could start working on accommodations for tourists to stay over! Ilona's husband didn't utter a sound, for days they didn't speak to each other, and everything proceeded along the old track, only that the tension remained in the air, Ilona's husband ruminated on where they could go, and Ilona ruminated on how they could stay, and only Florian did not take part in the nervousness of this nebulous general state, he wasn't afraid of what would happen, he wasn't worried about the turn events would take, in brief, if he was tormenting himself, it wasn't because of this murky general state of things, but exclusively because of the Boss, he simply didn't know what to do with those five calls, about which of course he was silent when the police questioned him, they were standing there again in front of the Hochhaus chatting with the Deputy, they've come for you, the Deputy called out to Florian, here for you again, he added with a little edge in his voice, but what could Florian say to the police? he sat in the Deputy's living room—the Deputy had convinced the police to use his apartment, partially because it was on the ground floor, meaning they didn't have to climb the stairs up to the seventh floor, partially because the Deputy wanted, with this gesture, to demonstrate his own willingness to be of assistance; Florian, however, was not a good subject for interrogation, the Deputy quickly recognized this, as did the police, as Florian sat in one of the sagging armchairs in the Deputy's living room and gazed at the police with a fair amount of incomprehension when they asked him what he knew about Jürgen, if he recognized him, of course he recognized him, Florian muttered, but he didn't know anything, looking like someone who couldn't bother to conceal his agitation, why were they asking him about Jürgen?! his mind was on other things completely, fully preoccupied by other matters, so that after one half hour, the police stopped questioning him, like someone who was useless, we'll come back later, they said as they left, and the Deputy didn't even know how to make any excuses for Florian or how to save the situation, he called after them: come back, another time, of course, my apartment is always open to the authorities, because the Deputy was very angry at Florian for not having been more cooperative, and he even said to him, fairly resentfully: why weren't you even a little bit cooperative? can you tell me why? cooperative? asked Florian, but how? and the Deputy just waved him away, saw him out, and angrily closed the door after him, because Florian truly did not understand what the devil they wanted from him, he didn't know anything about Jürgen apart from who he was, he never spoke to him, just as he usually never spoke to the others, but especially not with Jürgen or Fritz as he feared them the most, apart from Karin, of course, so what could he have said? that he feared him as he did fire? the next time he would tell them, he decided, if there would be a next time, and there was a next time, because the two same policemen buzzed his intercom, and this time they came up to the seventh floor, and after they caught their breath they had to deal with an even more reticent Florian, namely he did not reply at all to the questions of (1) could he describe the characters of Jürgen and Fritz and the others who resided in the house at Burgstraße 19, (2) was he aware of the nature of the activities that had been carried out in the past few months by the residents of this building, and (3) how would he characterize the ring-leader of this group of people, his own employer as well—Florian didn't answer, he just looked at them, into the eyes of one policeman or the other's, and he was very sad to see nothing in these eyes, the policemen waited for a response, but no response came, so they changed tactics, and now, in more threatening tones, they bombarded Florian with questions about the Boss, at which Florian became even more reticent, and even if he had wanted to, he was no longer capable of replying as he was completely disconcerted, he didn't even get up when the two policemen left his apartment, he just sat there facing the bench they'd been sitting on, then he went into the kitchen, he took out the Nokia from the back corner of the sink cabinet, and he once again looked at the list of incoming and outgoing calls—the five in-coming calls were still there—Florian quickly navigated away from that menu and tapped on the camera icon, then, to calm himself down a bit, he started looking at all the photographs he'd taken, and then when he reached the end, or more precisely, the beginning, he realized that there were also photos from before that day when he'd started tak-ing pictures out of the window, more precisely, he'd realized that at the time, but he hadn't even glanced at these earlier photos, he hadn't looked at them because these were the Boss's, and he had no desire to stick his nose into something that wasn't his, but now everything had changed, and he saw that there were not only photographs, but pic-tures with a triangle in the middle, at first he didn't know what this was, it was only after he had touched one and the picture started moving, and he saw them—Andreas running ahead, Fritz right behind him, and a little farther behind, Karin and Gerhard, each holding a metal canister, at this point, the hand of whoever was holding the Nokia trembled, the picture jumping back and forth, then one of the figures came into focus again, and it was Andreas as he spilled some kind of liquid from the canister onto a wall; Florian tensed up as he realized what wall this was, it was the Aral station, no doubt about it, then the Nokia jumped again, and it showed Fritz, as, stooped over, he ran away from the building toward the Nokia, and he was smirking, visibly smirking, and he said something to the hand that was holding the Nokia, but Florian couldn't understand what he was saying over the buzzing sound in the recording, then the camera jumped again, and Karin's face was visible, seen from up close as her hand reached out to the Nokia and turned it away, and she said, slowly, emphasizing every syllable: no document is needed here, then Florian heard a voice that was very well known to him: but it is needed, fuck it, it'll be good for Jürgen, cheer him up a bit, and then Florian stopped the whole thing, but unfortunately, he wasn't quick enough, as Florian also saw how the video showed burning flames from afar, yes, the video showed the ARAL GAS STATION BURNING, Florian let the Nokia drop into his lap, and he felt that his muscles were hurting so much that everything within him was going to break apart, because his muscles couldn't withstand what he'd just seen, his brain wasn't working, but his muscles understood everything, his brain wasn't connected, it had switched off, but the exact opposite had happened with his muscles, they were convulsing and spasming, then they were contracting so violently that it was clear that they were going to tear his body apart while his brain remained in mute operational mode, namely above, there was complete paralysis, below, complete chaos in the most painful intensity imaginable, Florian wanted to stand up, but he couldn't, he felt he would shatter to pieces if he tried, unconsciously he picked up the Nokia and he went to the photos app, and he found the gallery where he had just been browsing, and he found the next video which only showed a series of explosions, enormous flames, from beneath the earth, then the sounds of smaller explosions, his muscles understood everything, and his muscles made him stand up, the Nokia fell out of his hand, and every single movement hurt, but he started pacing around and around the kitchen table, he wanted to drink water, but he felt that if he touched the faucet he would break it, instead he kept walking around and around in a circle, then he sat down on the floor, throwing his back against the sink cabinet, and Florian just sat there, and it got dark so quickly, as if someone had suddenly turned off the lights, his brain still wasn't working, only his muscles were working, which, hours later, made him stand up, because to them, everything was clear: what had happened, who was who, what was what, why, and when, and already Florian was throwing his laptop into his backpack and whatever items of clothing his hands happened to come across, and already he was out of the Hochhaus, and this time he did not ring the bell, he just pushed in the gate, the dog didn't even whimper, but Florian didn't care because he broke its neck with altogether two movements and he threw it somewhere away into the darkness, then he kicked in the door and he struck down the Boss who never even had a chance, everything happened within a few moments, the Boss was lying on the training bench, because that's what he used if he didn't have time or wasn't in the mood to go down to the Balance Fitness Center on the other side of the rail crossing, the blow found him like that, lying on the bench, and it was as if several hundred kilos had fallen on his head, and he stayed there, really as if several hundred kilos had fallen on his head, but it wasn't even a head anymore, just bloodied bone and flesh, but Florian didn't even look because he was already running outside, his brain was buzzing, he was still being led by his muscles, and there wasn't much for him to strike as he ran into the Burg, so he grabbed the first chair he saw and immediately knocked down whoever lay in his path, he didn't care who they were, only that it was them, and already Florian was on the second floor and Florian was searching the entire building upstairs, then he was downstairs again, but Florian found no one else, so Florian went out of the gate and ran down to the banks of the Saale where he placed his backpack on the bench and washed his hands in the river, but the blood wouldn't come off, and Florian's brain only knew that he was running, his muscles could handle it, and Florian ran in the night, he ran out of Kana, and he ran out of the world, then, late at night, Florian ran back, no one saw him, of course, because the streets became deserted much earlier these days, and now it was half past three in the morning, and Florian pushed in the gate quietly, he slipped across the yard past the instruments of the Weather Station up to the front door, and he knocked softly, but inside there was only silence, no one stirred, Herr Köhler was clearly sleeping deeply, he'd always been a pretty good sleeper, moreover, as Herr Köhler himself sometimes noted to Dr. Tietz, do you see what a good conscience does? this was the subject of recurring playful banter between them, Herr Köhler would joke about the well-known amorality of psychiatrists, and Dr. Tietz would retort that only gym teachers were hated more by their students than physics teachers, and the reason for that was their cold hearts, which sounded particularly funny, because if there is one thing that could not be denied, it was Herr Köhler's sympathetic attention and his inborn goodwill toward everyone, Herr Köhler hadn't changed since he was a young man, and Dr. Tietz truly prized this quality in him, Adrian is really a good man, he and his wife noted at times, but his wife always added that one day he would get the worst of it, because he almost always allowed himself to be used by others, and in this they both agreed, and this was why— alongside their relief that he finally had a closer bond with someone— they had, for a while, been somewhat suspicious of the young student whom Herr Köhler had described, and how this student, Florian, was paying him regular visits, yes, at first Dr. Tietz and his wife were somewhat concerned, because this was the first time since the death of Adrian's wife that he had let someone come close to him, but then, as they heard more about this young student, the suspicion within them died away, and it turned into a kind of gratitude, because after a while it became clear that the presence of this student—despite the pangs of conscience his exaggerated passion might be causing Adrian—only indicated the depths of the affection that Herr Köhler, getting on in years and alone, had for him; any friend of Adrian's who cared about his fate could only be grateful, because even though Herr Köhler liked to joke about how psychiatrists were heartless and amoral, that was exactly what made it so funny, because no one could ever say that Dr. Tietz was like that, Dr. Tietz had a blessed good heart, he hadn't gotten so far in his profession, and yet he harbored no grudges, he had opened up his private practice in Eisenberg instead of staying in Jena and rising through the ranks with Leipzig or even Berlin in his sights, no, he had moved to this small town and buried himself alive here because he wanted to enjoy life, and he enjoyed it because he loved Thuringia, and he wouldn't have left for anything in the world; he loved his friend, the one single friend remaining from his youth, and with him, he felt that life was full, especially now when they could live together due to the sad turn of fate that had turned Adrian into a person marked by rapid intellectual decline, because Dr. Tietz and his wife perceived nothing else in the new Adrian now, only a patient who needed care, who had to be given everything they could give, and that was all, and so they were happy if something captured his interest, if already he had lost all interest toward the Weather Station, because that had happened too, and from this point on, if with nothing else, then Adrian was visibly happy to preoccupy himself with some kind of new computer programming software, or at the very least he spent hours with his laptop upon which, against a black background, white and green and sometimes red numbers and letters and other signs kept running down the screen densely and with tremendous velocity, Dr. Tietz didn't understand anything about computers beyond the average user, but he was able to make out that what Adrian was spending hours with might be some kind of new programming language, or who the hell knows, he told his wife, when she asked him what he thought Adrian was doing, the main thing is that it occupies him, his wife sighed, and Frau Ringer was thinking exactly the same thing, namely how would she be able to get her husband's attention and break off his dark thoughts, because the situation hadn't improved, moreover from time to time the police were still showing up, and although they emphasized that they weren't there to question Herr Ringer, only to get some information, and they were very polite, it only pushed him down further into those dark thoughts, so that his wife tried however she could to help him, but, well, this Ringer was clever, and no matter how she tried to divert his attention, he would not allow himself to be torn away from the grave facts, and, as his wife clearly saw, his self-accusations; the new bottle of Hungarian plum brandy had long since been emptied, because recently, Ringer had been hitting the bottle pretty strongly, he drank in the afternoons and in the evenings, even in the mornings, and if one of his friends from Jena showed up, despite Ringer's request that they no longer visit, they always came with a new bottle of Hungarian plum brandy, clearly this had been planned in secret on the phone once Ringer realized they wouldn't stop visiting, and they'd agreed on a time, and well, why deny it, why should I deny it, Frau Ringer complained to Frau Feldmann, I can tell he's been drinking, in a word, he drinks, her new girlfriend sighed, and she searched for comforting words, but she couldn't really find them because her husband Feldmann had frequently been staring down the bottom of the liqueur glass recently as well, before, nothing! Frau Feldmann burst out, but now I keep noticing one or two fingers missing from the bottle, from my liqueur bottle! and not only that! but Frau Ringer wasn't consoled by the fact that someone else's husband was drinking too, she never, but never could have imagined Ringer's life taking this direction, because it has turned in this direction, she said very sadly to Frau Feldmann, he's not doing anything, not going down to his repair shop, he doesn't go to Jena, sometimes his friends come to see him, they watch videos of Nazis marching here or there, he stares fixedly at those horrific flags waving above and those heavy boots stepping below, he just watches, the entire day he just cowers, he stares into space, and ... and ... well, he drinks, and at this point Frau Ringer began crying, this had been happening pretty frequently with her recently, but only in the company of Frau Feldmann, before others she controlled yourself, well of course! she sighed when the subject came up, the others! all my old girlfriends have betrayed me, and I don't care for them anymore, so that I only have you, my dear Brigitte, I'm not ashamed before you, she sobbed, well, I've reached this point now as well, and then Frau Feldmann found the right words, and she was able to console her new girlfriend, at least during those hours while they sat together either in her house on Hochstraße or in a café somewhere in the Shopping Center, as lately it hadn't seemed such a good idea for Frau Feldmann to visit Frau Ringer at home, although Herr Feldmann would have happily come along, as he found Ringer to be decisively sympathetic, because I—he noted, slightly red from the liqueur—I always liked Ringer, I always trusted him because if he says something then it is like that, you can trust him, because if he says five o'clock, then it is five o'clock, well, where has that Ringer gone, brooded Frau Ringer at home, alone, because Ringer was no longer who he used to be, a mere shadow of his old self, she acknowledged, and nothing wanted to change, somehow everything was just getting worse, although, ever since the murders in Kana, there had been no more criminal cases, yet people did not draw the conclusion that things had ended, instead they drew the conclusion that things were only just beginning, because something has been unleashed, the Deputy noted with a gloomy face to Pförtner, because he too had now joined those who expected nothing good after these events; the Deputy, for a while, had trusted that the increased police presence would yield results—the only problem was that after weeks, even months, there were no results, nothing to be seen, moreover, no indication of a motive, not a single arrest by the cops, no one has been arrested, the Deputy said to Pförtner disappointedly; for him, an arrest would have indicated that the police force and the state were reliable, functioning as they should, but, the Deputy lowered his voice, leaning in closer to Pförtner, nearly whispering, this police force isn't worth shit, excuse the expression, not even a piece of shit, because why can't they arrest anyone?! have they arrested anyone?! no! no! and with that he straightened up, and looked into Pförtner's eyes asking to be excused, although Pförtner's face clearly expressed approval, the Deputy didn't have to say anything, he knew Pförtner agreed with him, and that was also why he had never became a regular customer at the Grillhäusel, well of course sometimes he went over there for a good Bockwurst, Ilona knew her job, but he had to confess that he didn't feel at home there as the others did, and this was never, but never going to change, he explained to Pförtner, they're all either Wessis, like Heinrich, or messed-up useless Ossis, they buzz around that Heinrich like bees, so was it any surprise he felt like a stranger there?! Pförtner nodded, but this was not enough for the Deputy, he wished he could have talked to Florian, to talk with Florian about anything at all, he missed Florian and he had no idea where he could be, he'd already been gone two weeks, good God, and the Deputy climbed the stairs to the seventh floor, caught his breath, rang at the four other tenants' doorbells up there, and inquired, but they hadn't seen Florian, just as no one else had seen Florian, because new abilities were being born in him, Florian was able to move so that no one ever saw him, he was able to obtain food or water so that no one ever noticed, because he took the rolls and other food items from the crates in front of the stores' loading docks in those dawn moments after the delivery trucks had

driven off and before the staff came out to unload the merchandise, he
drank water from cemetery faucets or from fountains on main squares
in larger towns at night, and he never got on a bus or train, he didn't
even hitchhike, Florian made his journeys exclusively on foot because
he didn't want anyone to see him, he didn't want anyone to identify
him, and he did not want anyone to impede him, because there was
something he had to finish

and light blue

and it didn't really occur to people in Kana that Florian wasn't around,
apart from the Deputy no one thought about it, just as Karin didn't
think about it after she got rid of her Jeep for security reasons and
started looking for Jürgen, it would be hard to find him, because Jürgen
was clever, she acknowledged as she searched for him in vain in Mücka,
she knocked and she knocked, but no one answered the door, she left
and came back an hour later, but even then she found no one at home,
or at least that's what she was thinking when one neighbor opened the
window a crack and called out to her to pound on the door more
loudly, because someone was at home, but watching television, finally
the door opened and she was let in, I have no idea, the old woman declared, he never tells me anything, it's been like this ever since he was
fourteen years old, but Karin raised her hand and stopped her: didn't
he tell you where he was going, I'm a friend, said Karin, and she looked
at the woman, her gaze icy, but the old woman just scratched her bald
skull, straightened up in the wheelchair like someone who'd been sitting there too long, then she took a deep puff on her cigarette, waved
the smoke away, and told Karin to speak louder, and after Karin repeated her statement, she only said: you're really his friend? and she
made a face like someone whose disbelief that Karin was her son's
friend was equaled only by her disbelief that her son could have any

friends, because he'd been taken away by the cops when he was fourteen, right into the slammer, but she didn't continue because Karin
interrupted her: he didn't mention any other friends? what he was up
to? work? anything else? he's in Kana, the old woman said, he's definitely not, because I just came from there, well then, he's in Suhl, the
old woman retorted, in Suhl? asked Karin, why in Suhl? because he
couldn't stand it here in Mücka, came the answer, ever since his two
childhood friends danced the Chicken Dance in old Army fatigues at
the House of Culture, he said he couldn't stand it here even another
hour, even though this is his birthplace, but if only it weren't; the old
woman made a face, put out the cigarette on the arm of her wheelchair,
threw the butt onto the floor, and she began to roll toward the front
door, indicating it was time for Karin to leave, and Karin left, she didn't
even say goodbye, Suhl, she said to herself, and she was gone, the old
lady tried to observe her for a while from behind the curtain in the
window, but Karin disappeared so fast, like some kind of evil appari-
tion, then the old lady noted to herself, well, there are lots of people
looking for this felon nowadays, then she rolled back into the living
room, back to her spot in front of the TV which she hadn't turned off
while Karin was here, she only turned down the sound which she now
turned up again, and she kept on watching *Violetta*, her favorite series,
and it was hard to get into it again, although she wanted to see if León
and Violetta got back together, but this strange-eyed woman had spent
too much time in her house, or at least enough that it felt too hard to
pick up the thread, but then she picked it up, León and Violetta got
back together, all's well that ends well, she sighed, and she turned down
the volume when the ads came on but didn't turn off the TV, why
should she, because the next part would be coming up right away, and
before it started, she wheeled herself over with her cup and her teapot
and made another pot of tea because the tea that was in the teapot had
grown cold, adding a splash of Deutscher Rum Verschnitt, then she

added another splash, she rolled back to the TV, and put up the sound, because the series was beginning again—just like Karin's hidden rage, because it always happened, she said to herself, if she looked into a face, if she watched someone for more than a moment, a nerve twitched in her jaw, and then, because of her bad eye, the other person always started watching her, as was occurring now, she moved to the next train car and sat down, she sat there for a bit, then she went to the toilet to hear if the person was coming after her, but no, she heard no movements, the door wasn't hissing, she waited a moment, went back and sat down, and looked out the window, but there was nothing to look at, only raindrops hitting the glass and dripping down, and it was raining in Suhl as well, although not as heavily as during the train ride which had been pretty long with three transfers, first in Hoyerswerda, then Leipzig, then Erfurt—and she was exhausted, although she felt no fatigue, only impatience, she wanted to get things over with, because once again she was starting from zero and there was nothing else, only this one thing she had to take care of; it was dark by the time she got to Suhl, she knew the city somewhat as she'd been here many times before, although she'd never taken part in any operations here—the Suhl group was only a self-promotion circus for her, as for everyone else in the unit—she went to where she thought he would be, and as always she'd reckoned well, because she found him in the Sportpension, she assembled the silencer on the stairs after the porter told her where her "little brother" lived, knocked softly, and when the door opened she stepped in, closed the door, two quick shots to the head were enough, Jürgen realized what was happening, although the expression on his blasted-apart face resembled wonder more than anything else, Karin didn't see it though, she was long gone, although it was thanks to this that Florian realized he was on the right path, because when he found out in Mücka that Jürgen's mother only knew that her son might be in Suhl, it became clear to him that things wouldn't be so simple: Florian had been in Suhl previously on wall-cleaning jobs, but he really didn't have a concept of the place; he recalled a large residential area and the city center where he'd cleaned walls, nothing more, so that he had to make a lot of inquiries until finally he got to the Rifle Shooting Center Park, where he crisscrossed the terrain, then realized that the person he was looking for wasn't there; he made his way to the Sportpension, picked out a spot where he could hide with a perfect view of the building, put down his backpack, and on his laptop he began playing Book 1 from the *Wohltemperiertes Klavier*, he didn't have to put his earplugs in his ears because he never took them out, he heard the first bars of the Prelude in C Major, and he waited, he waited to see when she would come out, then, when darkness had fallen, Karin suddenly appeared wearing a hat, a red wig, and eyeglasses, he recognized her immediately, even from this distance, behind her fake glasses; impossible not to recognize Karin's rigid movements and her fixed gaze, he watched her scurrying into the building, and he didn't hesitate for a moment, the *Wohltemperiertes Klavier* was at the Fugue in E Major, Florian immediately began running after her, he couldn't see her in the entrance hallway, he asked the porter about Jürgen, but he didn't know the name, although if he was looking for the same person as a woman was just a moment ago, he'd sent her up to the room of a sports shooter from Mücka, but it was already too late, Karin was gone, Florian immediately saw the open door on the third floor, and as there was nothing for him to do there inside he dashed back down the stairs, looking for another exit as he reached the ground floor, Karin must have used a different staircase, left the building by a different exit, because he didn't see her, and yes, the building had a back door on the other side, Florian caught no glimpse of her but sensed she must be headed toward Schützenstraße, I'm closer now, he said to himself, and he was closer, because there was one less of them now, although he couldn't get on Karin's track, Karin had disappeared, there was no point in looking any further, he knew he was no match for her, for now he didn't even want to try, he stayed in Suhl that evening, huddling in an abandoned-looking industrial plant, he got to the end of Book 2 of the *Wohltemperiertes Klavier,* he withstood the cold and the rain, but now, because he was freezing a bit, he looked for a spot of relative shelter in the dilapidated hall, he had a dry pullover and a dry T-shirt, underwear, and socks in his backpack, so he changed his clothes, spread out his drenched clothing on an iron banister, and even though he picked out another piece on his laptop, he fell asleep as soon as the *Goldberg-Variationen* began, then hearing some noise, he started awake, immediately he was watchful, raising his head, he turned off the *Variationen* and listened, but nothing, in the hall there was complete silence, he couldn't fall back asleep because he was freezing, he gathered up the clothes from the banister, crammed them into his backpack and already he was on his way out of Suhl, not directly, for the most part walking along the B71, making a wide detour around Ilmenau, then he headed toward the A4, and it was beginning to grow light outside, he was hungry and thirsty, although mainly he was thirsty, so that next to a sports field in Martinroda he looked for water and he found a tap, then he approached the outskirts of the village cautiously, dug potatoes out of the garden of one house and ate them raw, his stomach was strong, nothing could ever harm this stomach, because ever since he'd left the Hochhaus, everything within him was transformed, just as his sense organs had completely transformed, he relied on them instead of his brain as his brain still wasn't working, and he avoided anything that might bring him into contact with human beings, with animals, on the other hand, he met up frequently: deer, rabbits, foxes, squirrels, mice—he observed them from up close, because none of these animals ran away too far when they noticed him, the deer jumped a few feet away, then they stopped and looked at him, the deer and Florian looked at each other: just as with the other animals, it was as if they sensed that Florian posed no danger to them, because truly he posed no danger, and especially not to them if just at that moment he was cutting across a wooded area, and this happened frequently: he and the animals drank and ate the same things, because not only could his stomach withstand raw potatoes and other garden vegetables, but he could eat, with no worries, almost anything that he found in the woods, and he could drink with no worries from any kind of brook, lake, or stream, he had no problems whatsoever, the only worry was that the real frosts were beginning at dawn, Florian was starting to feel extremely cold at higher elevations, and so he had to prepare for this, so he began stealing, whenever he happened upon any kind of thicker fabric, he immediately put it into his backpack, he went into every backyard where there was laundry hanging and took down whatever he needed, later on he also went into churches where he hunted for anything he could use as a blanket or outerwear, and, for example, one night, he pulled down the tarpaulin from a café terrace in Erfurt, but Florian no longer lugged these and so many other items around all the time, but instead built hiding places for himself located in the vicinity of various towns, concealing his plunder there, until finally he accidentally picked up a trace in Jena: he had been washing up in a cemetery, cleaning off his clothes inasmuch as he could, and after he had turned off the laptop in his backpack, he sat down in a café, which was actually a pub, on the town's outskirts, he asked for coffee and water but only as a pretext, because his real reason for being there was to recharge the laptop battery and he needed his laptop to dry out, he was afraid it had stopped working in his sodden backpack, but no; he took the laptop and put it onto the table, he asked the waitress if he could plug the cable into the socket next to his table, and he wasn't conspicuous either in this or any other way because the café was a kind of free Wi-Fi place on the edge of town, almost everyone was busy with their phones, laptops, or iPads, and while Florian was drying off his laptop, he heard, in the small café, although they were speaking very softly, two men talking about how there would be a gathering in the Braunes Haus, and it wasn't difficult to learn that the location was Lobeda-Altstadt, not too far away by tram, he'd only have to watch the entrance, although he was expecting someone else, not Andreas, Florian saw Andreas going in—he waited outside, then followed him into a small, deserted street from where he would never again emerge, Florian didn't even bother to hide the body but left it next to a dumpster, he didn't care anymore, whatever was behind him was of no interest now, as it no longer existed, whereas whatever was before him had yet to exist, he strove only for complete emptiness; he could not be stopped, because it was not possible to stand before him; he could not be impeded, because he moved as if he were invisible, we simply don't know where he is, the Deputy wrung his hands together, when a new plainclothes detective came to his door asking questions about Florian, the Deputy wrung his hands as if he could have done something about it, but there's nothing I can do, he defended himself when he saw the detective's dissatisfied expression, because what can I do? I'm not his father! I'm telling you everything I know, I'm at your service, but I have no idea where he is, he never went away for long periods of time before, even if he did go somewhere, let's say to Leipzig, he was already back by evening, look, the Deputy leaned closer to the detective in his living room, Florian is a child with weak nerves, but a child nonetheless, and I would like to emphasize that, no matter why you're looking for him, he is most certainly harmless, I've never seen such a harmless child in my entire life, so that ... and here he grew quiet, and just shrugged his shoulders and saw the detective out, and the Deputy had no idea why they were looking for Florian; as far as he knew, Florian had stopped writing his letters to the Bundeskanzler a long time ago, he couldn't even imagine why they were looking for him, just as no one else in Kana would have been able to, that is, if they had been aware that the police were looking for Florian and still hadn't found him—but no one knew, Frau Ringer didn't know, not even Frau Hopf or Ilona or Frau Burgmüller or Frau Schneider, no one knew, but it seemed strange, it's strange, said Frau Ringer, he never stayed away for so long before, if there was someone I poured out my heart to it was him, of course, I also pour out my heart to Brigitte, but that's different, I've known Florian since time immemorial, and I really wish I could look into those big blue eyes of his right now, Frau Ringer said to her husband, but Ringer pretended not to hear, he had no interest in Florian or Kana or anything else, Frau Ringer sighed, although more recently, in her view, Ringer had calmed down somewhat, or at least it seemed he had resigned himself to what he could not change; there had been no newer horrific events, and even the Nazzis, in their own way, had disappeared from the town, all of this began to look like a good reason for him to be drinking less and less, namely, the wounds of his soul seemed to be healing, or at least that's how Frau Ringer explained the difference in Ringer to herself, and she began talking to him more than previously, because up till this point she'd only dared say: come, dinner's ready, or come, my heart, and bathe, you haven't showered in two days, and things like that, but now she spoke to Ringer about this and that, telling him how good the pantry and the summer kitchen were looking, that tomorrow she'd be starting on the attic, and she did start on the attic the next day, although, unfortunately, first she had to bring everything down into the yard, and with the rain, this step had to be delayed, so what could she do? she asked herself, and she began sorting all the items accumulated in the attic over the years, sneezing from the dust, but she didn't care, if she wasn't doing this, she wouldn't be able to find her own self, she said to Frau Feldmann, whom she preferred to visit at her house, even though it was fairly distant, you know, if I stop, I start thinking about everything, and that's why I don't stop, all day long I'm doing something so I'll get tired, and I am really tired, I nearly fall into bed, but it's good that way, because if I don't keep myself busy I'll go mad; Frau Feldmann tried to convince her to slow down, let it go and stop driving yourself so hard, things will work out, because everything always works out in the end, things fall back into place and time heals all wounds, and she said this among other similar sentiments, but Frau Ringer did not believe that the wounds would be healed and certainly not by time, and although such banal turns of phrase usually made her skin crawl, she not only tolerated them but even wished for them, they were something like a balm, they have healed me, my dear Brigitte, she said, we both know what's going on, but I confess that your words help me so much, you can't even imagine how grateful I am to fate for bringing us together, and the tears came to Frau Feldmann's eyes; bravely, she squeezed her new girlfriend's hand, then she made two caffè lattes, because she couldn't get herself to stop when something tasted really good, and the new coffee from Jena was really good, before, Frau Feldmann had been teaming up with Frau Hopf for the grocery shopping, but even though the Garni had no guests and she only needed coffee beans from Jena, they still made the trip now and then, and Frau Ringer joined up too, it was well worth it as the gas money came to almost nothing, of course, none of them would deny that the Markt 11 coffee was expensive, because it was expensive, they looked at each other, only that one got used to good-quality ground coffee, and the three of them had gotten very used to it, and sometimes, these days, Frau Ringer also bought the Hausmischung, she said, whereas Frau Hopf swore exclusively by the Rica Tarrazu, as did the Feldmanns, who earlier, for years, had only been drinking Santos, but they came to agree with Frau Hopf, and it was very good coffee, very good, Brigitte noted, as she sipped from her cup, because the fragrance, my dear, she said, and she closed her eyes in pleasure, as it hits my nose, it's divine, isn't it? yes, it is, Frau Ringer had a sip as well and nodded in recognition, and she smiled, and this is new, my dear, because I haven't seen you smile ever since we met, Frau Feldmann looked at her with glimmering eyes, my God, the smile immediately disappeared from Frau Ringer's face, and even she felt that everything was getting better, and she cried, she usually wasn't the weepy type, but the sufferings she'd had to endure had broken her soul, it was so hard in the first weeks, she explained again to Frau Feldmann, and Frau Feldmann didn't mind hearing over and over again about how it had been so, but so, difficult to maintain her soul within, difficult, horrifically difficult to realize my own powerlessness, and that I can only trust in patience, Frau Feldmann had a heart of gold, and of course she knew whom Frau Ringer was referring to, her sympathy was complete, you can pour out your heart to me, she squeezed her girlfriend's hand, you can tell me everything, my dear, and Frau Ringer did pour out her heart and she did tell her, and slowly but surely a close connection formed between them, so close that Frau Ringer really only missed Florian now, she even went one time to the Hochhaus and buzzed the intercom, but Florian didn't respond, although after she had buzzed the third time the Deputy jumped out of the door and said: perhaps you don't remember me, but I am the Deputy of this building, and Florian isn't at home, there's no point in buzzing him on the intercom, we don't know where he is, no one has seen him for weeks, and we're worried about him, and the Deputy puckered his mouth, pulled his neck in, shrugged his shoulders, and held his two hands apart, indicating that no one knew anything about Florian, which—he then explained—he truly regretted, because we both get on very well, I know, nodded Frau Ringer, I know, because he spoke of you many times and I'm grateful for the attention you paid to him, but where could he be, nothing like this ever happened before, true? true, said the Deputy, even the police are looking for him now, the police? Frau Ringer raised her voice, yes, certainly, the police, they questioned him several times and then they came back again, and then our Florian simply vanished into thin air, and Frau

Ringer was not pleased at how the Deputy was speaking, this "vanished into thin air" echoed for a long time afterward in her ears on the way home, because it was all too obvious why the police had been talking to him—Florian knew more than anyone else about that beast—but with this "vanished into thin air," the Deputy had, in her view, gone too far, as if he were insinuating that there was a reason for the fact that Florian couldn't be found, if it were even true, she added, as she related the incident to Ringer at home, but he didn't reply as he still wasn't interested in anything, and the topic of Florian decisively got on his nerves, as it had done earlier as well, so he disconnected and just let his wife talk and talk, and at some point she'll stop talking, thought Ringer indifferently, these days he was also watching television, which earlier his wife had just left on, but before he'd never been able to concentrate on the program, but now he could, if they were announcing the news on MDR, then he listened, even if superficially, and he was getting stronger, Frau Ringer sensed this as well, and she began adding more spices to the meals that she placed before him for lunch or dinner, because at the beginning she had spared him this as well, but now as she saw—or wished to see—an improvement, she tried to slowly guide things to their original state, even in such trifling details as food, because she wanted him to get his strength back, to pull himself together, to be the old decisive, vigorous Ringer, the Ringer whom people followed blindly, just as Florian was following the traces blindly, the traces leading him to the next one and the one after that; that particular sense which had awakened in him was making his instincts ever sharper, and now much time had passed ever since he had left, but he still wasn't thinking, not because he couldn't think, as at the beginning, but because he was no longer interested in thought, he had no more need for thought, moreover, if it seemed at times that a thought might be forming in his mind, his stomach clutched up in spasms, because only his instincts mattered now, and he was led by those, blindly, and

316

he always reached his goal, and no one stood in his way; he avoided those places which could be dangerous for him with ever more adroitness, only occasionally exchanging a few words with passersby, waiters, with this one or that one, when he needed to charge his laptop or get some information, but nothing more; he felt himself a stranger among them: of course, he'd always been a stranger among them, with the difference that now things were going in the direction that he wanted, now he clearly saw that he had been born for this, only that before, he'd been misled, but now he knew himself for who he was, and now he moved with familiarity in this strangeness, among the trees in the forests, along the shoulders of highways, but never too close, at night he lay low in thickets of shrubs or abandoned locales on the periphery, then by day, he crawled, ran, walked, in a controlled way, whatever was necessary at that moment, if he found a well, he washed up, or if he found a public toilet where he wouldn't be disturbed, but he didn't even consider this to be so important, because he knew—although he didn't care—that washing up didn't change his outer appearance very much, and it was precisely because of that, his outer appearance, that he was asking people for directions ever more infrequently, which meant that he had to find what he was looking for in a different way, as now, for example, when he had to wait for the Gera soccer team to play a home match, but then he waited in vain, because he didn't find who he was looking for among the screaming fans, so he headed off toward Saalfeld, not along the A9 or B2, but via a detour, a large detour from Dürrenebersdorf through Markersdorf, Bocka, and Lederhose, either along traversed roads or beaten paths, next to brooks, and always proceeding near forested areas until he reached Pößneck, while in his earphones the *Matthäus-Passion* was playing, then it ended and he listened to it again, he set out from Pößneck, following the B281 from a good distance until he reached the northeastern periphery of Saalfeld, he had left at dawn, but it was late at night when he staggered up to a shipping container in the rear yard of an ironworks, somehow he climbed up onto its roof, then, without even shutting down his laptop, he immediately fell unconscious into a deep sleep because he was exhausted by the journey, his foot was injured, as if he'd broken a toe when he jumped across the ironworks fence, he only looked at it the next morning when the sound of voices awakened him, he hadn't been vigilant enough, the workers had already arrived, so that he had to stay there until evening, he waited for everything to quiet down, then he climbed down from the container and crawled to the nearest fence, the dogs, who'd been let out, caused him no problems, they hadn't even barked when he'd gotten here the previous night, just as they didn't bark now, they only watched his every movement from a respectful distance, mutely and motionlessly, as if they recognized someone within him; the Saale was much wider here than in Kana, for a while he went along the bank, but avoiding the town center, then he turned off, avoiding the train station in a large arc, and he went on further along the tracks, he drank from a faucet in the yard of a factory, but he found nothing to eat, so that now he looked for a garden where he could dig up something from the ground, but for a long while there was nothing, only an industrial wasteland, finally he noticed a bakery, a light burning inside, and by the back of the building, next to a door, two workers smoking cigarettes, he waited for them to go in, then, among the crates piled up on two sides, he found one filled with dry baked goods and loaves of bread, he stuffed his backpack as full as he could and retreated from where he had come, and on the other side of the road, behind a service building, he began to devour the bread, tearing at it, stuffing one roll into his mouth after the other, he wasn't even really chewing but devouring them whole, famished as he hadn't eaten anything during the entire journey, he'd wanted to get here as quickly as possible, and finally he tied up the remainder of the baked goods into a shirt, stuffed the shirt in his backpack, put the whole thing on his back, and then he was walking next to the Saale again, and for a long time he did not find a bridge to cross to the opposite bank, to the town, so he started walking back, once again avoiding the train station, then he thought again and went inside as the main entrance was unlocked; there were a few loafers and homeless, no one was waiting for a train here, he sat down on a bench, reached into his backpack, found the *Matthäus-Passion* and started listening to it again, and he waited; then after a while he went over to a Döner stand about to close down and through the open window he asked: where are the Nazis here? at which the kebab seller, just then slicing off chunks of cold mutton from a metal skewer, threatened him with his knife, but Florian reached in through the window and grabbed his neck—they're in the Lab, the kebab seller stammered, his eyes starting to bulge out, Florian loosened his grip, and he asked again: where? the Lab, in Silberberg, then he let him go, and Florian made the kebab seller tell him where this Silberberg was, and already he was gone, he didn't know Saalfeld any better than any other town in Thuringia, but at least he had a vague idea, so he quickly found the road leading to the district known as Gorndorf, then he went farther on along Geraer Straße, but the building where the Lab was located was shrouded in darkness by the time he got there, seemingly with no one inside, only when he had surveilled all the entrances did he hear some sounds filtering out from one of them, he couldn't tell if it was a human voice or something else, but it was a human voice, it emerged immediately, where's Gerhard? Florian asked three boys in combat fatigues, with earrings and shaven heads, sitting in the corner of a large room behind the door, they were next to a coal stove drinking beer, Gerhard who? said one, and Florian headed toward them; the three immediately stood up, so he was forced to strike two of them down, he pushed the third one back into his chair beside the stove, and he asked: Gerhard, where is Gerhard?! what fucking Gerhard?! the boy answered, looking at him with frightened eyes,

I don't know any Gerhard! and Florian grabbed his neck, pulled him to himself, and for a second, just looked at him, then he let him go, are you a cop? the boy whimpered, while pulling back in the chair as much as he could, no, answered Florian, and when he realized Florian was looking for someone from Kana, the boy became more accommodating, massaging his neck with a painful expression, he's living with Berndt these days, where is this Berndt? I don't know, answered the boy, but as Florian reached for him again, he immediately stammered out: in Gorndorf, then he explained exactly which street and building, Florian was still looking at him and not moving, the boy biting his lower lip, he looked at his companions still lying there motionless, then he lowered his head, Gorndorf wasn't far, Florian had to go back a bit toward the town center, and he found the house quickly, already it was very late, there were hardly any houses with lights on inside, he tried the intercom in case somebody might open the door at random, but if anyone had even answered, after a few seconds of hissing, the line broke off, so he circled the building looking for the yard, and he found it, and right in time too, because just at that moment Gerhard was coming out through a small chicken-wire gate, trying to disappear into the darkness, but he wasn't able to because his head was smashed apart by a concrete column at the top of which a bare streetlight bulb — like the lantern on Charon's barge — was faintly flickering, but this weak light illuminated nothing of what happened beneath it, because in that murky, grimy daybreak there was not much to see, for Gerhard was no longer Gerhard, and Florian was already far away, and for a long time nobody knew he was the one they should be looking for, the pieces of the puzzle weren't falling into place even though there were reasons for suspicion, only that nothing was decisive, and chiefly no one made the connections, because this only occurred when they started focusing on the perpetrator's modus operandi, namely the same mode of attack had been used in Saalfeld and Jena as in Kana, and only the Suhl murder didn't fit into the sequence, because there the perpetrator had used a 9mm Parabellum, and this once again confused the cops in Erfurt assigned to the case, let's split it up, said the lieutenant leading the investigation, but they could've split it up however many times they wanted, for a long time no one saw any connection between Florian and the murderer, winter was raging in earnest, all Thuringia lay under its domain, every morning at dawn, people struggled with strong frosts and fog, snow fell frequently in daytime, and transportation was growing ever more difficult: train and long-distance bus connections were reckoning with serious delays; at the beginning, of course, as during every winter, the extent of the chaos was fairly great, but then, as during every winter, the general mood slowly calmed down, everyone got used to the strong frosts and fog at dawn, the frequent snowfalls in daytime, but the greatest cause of concern to Florian was the wind: he could no longer spend the day, when he needed to rest, in any inhabited area, so he withdrew to the denser sections of the forests, the bone-penetrating, ice-cold wind exhausted him, he could almost no longer use his hands, so frozen were they, and although he tried several times, he hadn't been able to steal a pair of gloves, so he either wound his hands into an undershirt, or he tried to wind a sweater around them, solving this problem only for an hour or so, because there was still his face, nose, and ears, because if he wrapped up his entire head with something, after a while he couldn't get any air, but if he didn't try to warm up his head somehow, he felt, by the next morning, that his nose or ears were going to break off, so it was difficult, he sought refuge on solitary farmsteads, crawling into haystacks, into anything, just to survive another day, but this was dangerous because somebody could come at any time, as they did come, with a pitchfork to the haystack or wherever he was planning to rest for a moment, and then he had to escape again, but it also happened—even if very rarely—that he was seen, which meant that either he had been reported or not, this could not be determined, but he felt that things couldn't go on like this much longer, in addition, because of the weather, he couldn't traverse greater distances, and for a while he had not come across any new traces, because he hardly knew anything about Uwe, even when they'd been in the unit together, he'd hardly ever seen him, Uwe was considered a murky figure, murky and insignificant, which also meant that he had no true contours; if Florian had had to describe him, he wouldn't have been able to come up with anything in particular, so average was he, neither tall nor short, fat nor thin, his face expressing nothing, he never drew attention to himself and he almost never spoke, always in the background of the unit's operations, so that now, when he was the next one up, Florian didn't know where and how to get information on him, Andreas would have been the next logical step, but unfortunately, he hadn't asked Andreas when he still could have answered, never mind, too late for that now, he must find Uwe by tracing Andreas's footsteps; he only knew from the Boss that both comrades had ended up in Kana after their respective stints in the youth detention center, but as to what had happened with this Uwe, in the adverse conditions of this raging winter, he had no answers; as for Uwe himself, the possibility of him paying back the person who had finished off Andreas seemed just as hopeless, at first he suspected Karin, but that made no sense, of course to suspect Karin was self-evident, because she had always been the most unpredictable, the most unfathomable member of the unit, no one ever knew what she was thinking, why she said or did this or that, it was enough to look into her eyes and a person already realized: don't approach her, too unpredictable, she was the one person in the Burg feared by all, no one said so, but all knew it, Uwe always sensed it, everyone, even the Boss was afraid of her, so that at the beginning, Uwe really did think that the whole thing was in Karin's hands, only that it made no sense, he thought it over again and again, it was already weeks after Andreas's funeral, where, in any event, Karin hadn't shown up, although she knew about what happened to him, just as she hadn't come to the Boss's funeral either, which, however, had been organized fairly well through secret channels, because people came from Plauen, from Erfurt, from Dresden, from Berlin and Dortmund, and they also came from the Czech Party of National Unity and the Légió Hungária, it was a truly beautiful memorial, and it had given them strength, even though they had to confront the loss, but strength, because such speeches were heard drawing upon a newfound strength from this sacrifice, and Uwe was turning the matter over this way and that, and it just didn't make any sense, because what, why would Karin finish Andreas off, well, and?! not only that, but how could she have done it, she weighed only fifty kilos, Uwe brooded in his parents' house which was in fact just a small, one-room ground-floor apartment where his mother's older sister had moved after she had completely fallen apart because of drugs and she lost the parental home, Uwe's only choice had been to move in there once the unit decided to go their separate ways after the explosion, absolutely no hiding out with sleeper cells, instead they should bunk up with their own families, that was the plan which they all accepted, also meaning that Uwe couldn't stay with Andreas, although if he had, he would have protected him, he felt, would have fended the attacker off, no matter how strong, clearly Andreas had been ambushed, Uwe thought, because how could they have gotten him otherwise, he was convinced of this, but he still didn't understand, he simply couldn't call to mind any internal or external enemies who would make such a move against his brother, unless—it had come to his mind at some point at the beginning of the winter—unless it had been that lumbering Jew who for years had been riling up the population and the authorities against the unit, who would do anything to wipe them off the face of the earth, but somehow he didn't seem like the type who would get into illegal operations, contravening his own laws and all that, ah, no, Uwe thought, discouraged, it's not him, but since he couldn't think of anyone else, he decided to go back to Kana, it was the beginning of December, Bahnhofstraße was already decorated with grotesque strings of lights and blinking garlands, fucking piece of shit town, Uwe snarled, then he looked for Archie, he sat down among the people in the waiting room, then he called the master tattoo artist over and whispered into his ear that it was urgent, motioning everyone else out of the basement studio, because this was important and it couldn't wait, and Archie began speaking to him in a deep voice, huh, they sure taught you, where the fuck have you been at, university? and what's the goddamned fucking rush?! enough of that, Uwe continued quietly, although there was hardly anyone left in the tattoo studio, and he told Archie he needed a lead, he told him what happened in Saalfeld and Jena and Suhl, and no one in the unit had any idea of who the fuck it could be, but since they bumped off my brother, I must seek justice, you understand, and now for the first time in their acquaintance, Archie looked at Uwe as if he were someone who could do what he was threatening to do, and in general, Archie looked at him for the first time as if he were really seeing him, because to tell the truth, Uwe never mattered to him, even if he was there, he still wasn't present, if someone photographed them together, there was just a blank spot where he was, because no one ever noticed him, and yet—Archie lowered his head, while he thought about what to say—this was the next generation, and so they put together what they knew, and separated it from what they didn't know, and Archie closed the shop, sat down in front of the computer, and started searching on the web, but there were no good results, Uwe became more and more agitated, and when he saw Archie getting nowhere, he slammed his fist down on the table where Archie kept his needles, disinfectant, and spare grips so hard that everything flew off the table, then Uwe knocked down the shelf where Archie kept his tubes of paint, Archie tried to save what he could, but he wasn't in as good condition as Uwe, so that it was difficult, but in the end he was able to push him out of the shop, and Uwe was only thinking, well of course, fuck it, it was her, that's why we didn't find anything, everyone's scared shitless of her, but I'll find that motherfucker, yet he didn't find her, just as he hadn't before when he had to; no one knew anything at the address he had for her, although he was certain that it was her, it couldn't be anyone else, no one else was as smart as she was, no one else as murderously clever as she, but even so he was having trouble finding her, and she didn't come to the funeral, although it was her place to be there, because the Boss also respected her, he never dared match his strength against her own, as was clear to everyone in the Burg, so that the burial went ahead without Karin, still, it was a beautiful funeral, many people, for the most part unknown to Uwe, showed up, the Kana Symphony played "Yesterday," and it was beautiful, they kept cranking it out, playing it over and over again, in the funeral chapel, during the procession to the grave, and by the grave pit; they had asked for a simple funeral and they got one, they threw their money together, but no priest, they couldn't risk that; after the out-of-towners had spoken, from among their number only Herr Feldmann gave a speech by the grave, they had asked him to keep it short, but it was long, Herr Feldmann enumerated everything that came to his mind: spring was in flower and fate was inscrutable, the reward of heroism was only found in heaven, the weight of unexpected tragedies, and so on, finally he concluded with a quotation in Latin, and they just stood there shifting their weight from one foot to the other, they didn't know what the hell they were supposed to be doing, the gravediggers pulled the Reichskriegsflagge off the coffin, which, due to their not being fully informed, they almost tossed into the pit, but the flag was grabbed above the pit in time, then they folded the flag up nicely and returned it to its place, and that was all, this had happened three times now, there was hardly anyone left from the original unit, the great ones have left us, said Uwe, standing by the cemetery gates, to a few other mourners, and they dispersed, they finally dispersed, Uwe felt as if he were enter-ing a space where the air had been sucked out, he hid for a while, but then he couldn't take it anymore, now he was here with Archie, then he wasn't with Archie, because he too was just a useless motherfucker, and Uwe traveled back, and for days he tortured himself in the small, one-room, ground-floor apartment, his aunt lying nearly permanently ensconced in one of the beds, nearly permanently out of it, Uwe slept on the other bed, clasped his hands beneath his head, and stared at the ceiling, but that ceiling oppressed him so much that he preferred to close his eyes, and he could not and not find the reason as to why it would be Karin, when one day it suddenly just occurred to him that perhaps it was her after all, perhaps she wanted to liquidate the entire unit to eliminate every trace of them, and that would be like her, he thought, that kind of foresight; he jumped up from the bed, there was a horrific stench coming from somewhere, the stench of shit, and it was coming from his aunt, he didn't want to look and see if it was really coming from her or not, so he gathered up his things and left the apart-ment without a word, he went back to Jena, although in Jena, there wasn't very much for him to do, so he strolled to the cemetery and stood by Andreas's grave, the weather already turning to spring, but still a fairly chilly wind blew, and facing the grave, the wind struck Uwe's face, so he couldn't stand there too long, he pulled his jacket zipper all the way up to his neck, then pulled the hood onto his head, and he leaned into the wind and began walking toward the cemetery gate when suddenly the world in front of him grew dark and after that it never grew light for him ever again; the birds chirped on the branches of the bare trees around the cemetery gate, although they seemed com-plaining rather than cheerful, because even if spring was coming, they did not have much reason for joy, but Florian realized that there were birds nearby, so that for a short while he stopped playing *Wo soll ich fliehen hin* on his laptop, and he listened to the birds chirping, then he continued listening to *Wo soll ich fliehen hin*, and that was how he set off, and now he had only one task, even if the most difficult, because the difficulty didn't lie in having no support, he hadn't had that until now either and he had still achieved his goals, but that Karin seemed to him to be so dangerous, and he must reckon with this danger, so that from this point on he proceeded with more caution than ever before, and this was also why, from this point on, he withdrew almost completely, giving no sign whatsoever of his existence, and if he didn't have to charge his laptop every day, he would not have met up with any other human beings at all, but it was a necessity, although—despite his wild exterior—he was still able to pass himself off as insignificant, so that even if someone gazed at him for a second, they immediately assumed he was homeless, for example, if he went into a pub, train station, or computer business, and so on; in order to charge his laptop, he only went to crowded places, and where, with his neglected appearance, he aroused no suspicion, and in this regard he was very lucky, because someone could have been looking for him: the Deputy had reported to the Jena police station—where they knew him well from the old days—that Florian Herscht, Ernst-Thälmann-Straße 38, 07769 Kana, had not been seen for months, not weeks, he emphasized, but months, he dictated the details, and then went home and waited to see what would happen, but nothing happened, Florian did not show up, of course, nobody informed him of any more developments because this wasn't even a development, just one report among many, and, as they put it at the Jena police station, they had neither time nor energy to deal with some civilian who kept coming back and asking questions, look, they said to the Deputy, when he went back to the police station about two weeks later, we can't say anything, but we're on the case, you've done your job, and that was it, and the Deputy was not reassured, just as Frau Ringer, Frau Hopf, Ilona, or any resident of Kana who'd known Florian well wasn't reassured, but no one was dealing with this in the great chaos of events, he'll turn up, clearly he's afraid, hiding out somewhere, they thought, if they thought about it at all; but now, there had been no more explosions or murders, nothing from the previous horrific chain of events, and Florian's disappearance became not only conspicuous but decisively alarming for them, only auntie Ingrid reassured the Volkenants, when they informed her that Florian still hadn't been found, and she said, well, he's such a scatterbrained child, he'll turn up, there's no reason for worry, as auntie Ingrid was completely reassured that her list was in order, she also told them this almost every morning when she popped in to the post office: the list is in order! and the Volkenants were happy to hear her voice, as there weren't too many voices to hear at the post office, people just mumbling a greeting as they walked in, then silence as they mutely stood in line, waiting to pay their bills or mail the postcard they were sending to invite their children back for Easter, although those children had no intention whatsoever of coming back for Easter, who the hell wanted to come back to this dark province, if at one point they had succeeded in escaping from there, so the postcards were duly mailed, but the children did not come back either for Easter or later on, winter dragged on, in April there were days where the MDR reported ground frosts, but then in May, everything settled down, spring, as the residents of Kana said to each other in the Shopping Center, spring had finally come, it's finally here, and although earlier this realization always occasioned them great joy, now there was very little of this joy, only a fleeting sense of relief that spring was here at all, although for Florian the coming of spring meant much more, because finally he didn't have to struggle against the frosts every day and every night, moreover, his instincts told him that he had been hiding for long enough; now he had reason to come out, and he did come out, and he was no longer perturbed by that enormous golden eagle appearing in the air above him, the eagle that had started tagging along with him in the winter, as if it had a solution to this winter, and now it was as if the eagle were waiting for him again, and as he set off, the eagle accompanied him, circling slowly overhead; when Florian stopped, the eagle, spreading out its enormous wings, alighted, with slow circling movements, on a nearby branch or fence, just as it had done when it had first emerged in the air above Florian, it always followed him, always remaining close by, so much so that one time, when Florian, in Friedrichroda, took refuge in one of the abandoned Marienglashöhle caves relatively close to the surface, the eagle tried to follow Florian into the cave, but he chased it away, although he did so in vain, because the eagle stayed near the cave, it persevered, and for a while Florian was uneasy when, as he went out for food supplies every second or third day, the eagle immediately soared up and followed him no matter where he was going, so that after a while, he stopped worrying about it, moreover, after two or three weeks Florian began stealing baked goods, or whatever he could, for the eagle as well, before he went back into the cave, he always left the eagle a roll, or whatever he'd been able to get, by the mouth of the cave, so that now, when he was leaving this hiding place for good, his first order of business was to look up and search the sky, but he didn't have to search too long, because within a few seconds, the eagle rose from the top of a tree, and began circling, according to its wont, high above Florian's head, Florian said not a single word, never gestured to the eagle indicating this or that, but the golden eagle always precisely understood what it had to do and what not to do, so that when they got to Kana that night, and Florian effortlessly pried open the lock at Archie's tattoo studio, walking down the steps—as he had done in his nightmares a few times—then retreating behind a curtain covering the toilet door, the eagle waited outside high above with its broad, mute, enormous, extended wings, together they lay in ambush until he came, for a while Archie examined the broken lock outside at the top of the stairs, then he headed down the stairs uncertainly, hesitating after each step, but then, when he saw that there was no one in the studio, and that nothing was missing, no sign of damage, he shrugged his shoulders like someone saying to himself, well, so that's all, only he didn't understand why somebody had broken the lock, but Florian did not explain this to him when he stepped out from behind the curtain soundlessly, slamming the side of his hand into Archie's throat, he wanted him to talk, he didn't want to finish him off, because he didn't belong to the others, he only wanted to know where he could find the last one who did belong to them, he heard the bird screeching from outside, he sat down across from Archie, put the earphone that had fallen out back in his ear,

only for complete emptiness

waiting patiently for Archie to come to, and at first he said he didn't know where she was, but then he forced the words out and said that as far as he knew, Karin had moved to Mattstedt, but he didn't know if she was still there, but she definitely wasn't here, Archie whimpered, clutching at his throat, as if that would help the intense pain, but it didn't help, he was able to get some air, but his throat was hurting so much that he could only take small breaths, he was very dizzy and felt like he had to throw up, but Florian didn't stick around for this, dawn was breaking outside, the outlines of everything becoming clearer, houses, streetlights still burning, cobblestones luminous in the mist, and that's exactly what she saw as well in the rented apartment on Margarethenstraße above the pizzeria, how long will you need it for, the owner of the building had asked, to which she only said: I'll see, and she immediately went to the window facing the street, looked out, and she said, I'll take it, because she had no doubts as to Florian's course of action, she knew precisely that he would have to show up at Archie's studio, and so day after day she sat by the window in the apartment on

Margarethenstraße above the pizzeria, waiting for him to show up, and her wait was not in vain, because Florian did show up, and it was as if he sensed something, because as he left Archie's studio, heading toward the pizzeria, he thought twice and turned back, with the eagle circling above, for some reason it was shrieking crazily again; Florian ran out of the Altstadt at Karl-Liebkneckt-Platz and by the time Karin got there, he was nowhere to be seen, clever, she thought, then she went back to the rented apartment, changed her red wig for a black one, and put on nonprescription glasses, then she covered all the directions leading from Burgstraße, and finally, although she wasn't giving up, she renounced the idea of getting him right away, she could do this because she had no doubts as to what was going to happen next, and that evening she got her chance, but she missed it, she walked for hours back and forth through the narrow underpass leading from Ernst-Thälmann-Straße to Ölwiesenweg, on the other side of the rail tracks and parallel to them, because she had a feeling she'd find him somewhere between the Boss's house and the Balance Fitness Studio, and that was the solution, only that Florian was no longer the Florian she knew, this Florian was something like a trained guerrilla fighter, she didn't know what happened to him, and she didn't care; it's either him or me, that was the only thought in her head, when she realized that the person who had wiped out almost everyone could only be him— preempting her own similar plan to eliminate the entire unit, erasing each and every trace the authorities might have picked up on; she didn't search for a reason, she had never been interested in reasons and circumstances and explanations and opinions and deliberations, so that, as was her way, and without emotions, she determined to find Florian and remove him from the face of the earth, and she had to be patient, partially because it took her a while to realize what was going on, partially because she had no leads, and that was why—as she attempted to strategize, as she imagined that Florian would strategize—

she chose the tattoo studio, as she realized that Florian wasn't finished, and that what he wasn't finished with was exactly her, so that she had to show herself, she'd decided not too long ago, draw attention to herself, lure him out, wherever he might be, and that was why she had come back to Kana, because she knew Florian also had to come back here, as only Archie, and no one else, would know where she was, and this is exactly what happened, the likelihood wasn't too great, but it was the only likelihood, and so it occurred, and so Florian was here, thought Karin, and he's not going to leave until he's finished, and at that moment she glimpsed him at the rail crossing, it was just a glimpse, someone disappearing behind the fitness studio building, but her good eye identified him immediately, certain it was him, she took out the Parabellum, releasing the safety lock, running toward him, she jumped across the closed railway crossing, and now she wasn't running but circling the building cautiously, moving from one corner to the next, when from above, so silently that she heard neither hissing nor flapping of wings, an enormous bird swooped down, its claws digging through her hood, hat, and wig, only once but with two clawed feet and with such force that in the first moment she thought she'd lost consciousness, although she'd only lost the Parabellum; the beast was enormous, and during that second moment, as its claws dug into her scalp through the thick wig, it spread its wings, covering her completely with them, and she thought, well, it's the end, this beast was going to grab her and lift her up into the air or tear her to pieces here, but the whole thing happened so quickly and came to an end so quickly that in the third moment Karin was able to thrust herself to one side; her fake glasses shattered and cut her forehead as she fell to the ground, she held her head in her hands and didn't move, the bird flew off with a whoosh and could no longer be seen in the dark night, Karin didn't lose her presence of mind, namely she did not move right away because she knew this wasn't over, she waited for her head to clear and groping, carefully searched for her weapon, clutching it in her hand, and then she rolled

on like lightning; she crawled until she reached a patch of densely overgrown weeds and bushes where she could hide temporarily, but not for
too long, because that beast—some kind of vulture or eagle, judging
by its scale—hadn't vanished into nothingness but seemed very real
indeed, because it had its plans for Karin, at first only circling above the
weedy patch of ground, Karin saw it exactly, because lying on her back
and even holding her breath, she was concentrating on the sky, and she
could dimly make out the bird in the town light filtering over here, then
it swooped again and again with relentless strength, but this time it
only struck the top of the bushes, Karin turned over on her stomach
and pulled her hood over her hat and lay there unmoving, it was only
when the beast attacked for the third time—by that point Karin had
formulated her plans, or at least as much as she could, she wasn't worrying about being scratched by the twigs—that she rolled in the other
direction beneath the bushes and as the bird came swooping down on
her again, she jumped up, and as she had dropped her weapon again,
she tried, with her bare hands, to grab its neck, but she couldn't, the
beast flew up again screeching violently, sharply, and this time it did
not return, or at least Karin didn't stick around to see if it had returned
or not, because she grabbed the Parabellum and began running back
toward the town, through the narrow underpass beneath the tracks,
then out onto Ernst-Thälmann-Straße, out by the Baumarkt, up Franz-
Lehmann-Straße, and up the hill toward the residential area, she still
wasn't thinking clearly, she knew where she was going, she only didn't
know why one road would be better than another, she kept turning her
head to look back, turning it to look up at the sky above her, but nothing, and although she could have taken it as certain that the beast
wasn't coming after her, she was still so much under the influence of
this surreal attack that anything seemed possible, so for a while she just
ran, sticking close to the buildings, and she got back to Margarethenstraße where she dashed up to her room and threw off her wig and the
red coat which she had gotten after she'd been in Suhl, because she

knew people would recognize her in Kana without this disguise; she sat down in a chair next to the window, for minutes only panting, then she went into the bathroom and examined her wounds in the mirror, although since they were, for the most part, on the back half of her skull, she couldn't see them, so she palpated them, judging them to be big and deep, but not requiring stitches, disinfectant was enough, she went back into the room, and took a first-aid box out of the side pocket of her combat trousers, dabbed some alcohol on a strip of gauze, and rubbed the wounds, then disinfected the gashes on her forehead, pressing down good and hard to get them to properly bleed out, finally she licked the blood off her fingers, rinsed her mouth out with water, and sat down at the rickety table where with one finger she pulled up her upper eyelid, then pulled down her lower eyelid with another finger, and popped out her glass eye, she took it over to the faucet where she waited for the water to warm up a bit, washed off the glass eye thoroughly, and placed it into a small box for the night that she kept for this purpose, and finally she lay down, and she just lay there, unable to fall asleep, starting awake at every sound, sitting up, then lying down again, and she was only able to sleep a little bit toward dawn, but then, as a truck barreled down the street below, she immediately awoke, jumped up, went to the window, opened the curtain a crack, because it was already growing light outside, but there was not a soul to be seen, she took the artificial eye from its box, rubbed her eye socket with eye gel, then rubbed a bit onto the prosthesis as well, then popped the eye back in with a practiced movement, and after she had more or less sewn up the gashes in her hat and the torn-apart wig, she put the black wig aside and took the red one, donning her hat on top of the wig, she put on her coat, and she was ready; she hadn't washed, she couldn't have cared less about the pungent smell of perspiration emanating from her armpits through her clothes; before leaving, she drank a glass of water, closing the door after herself quietly so as not to wake up the landlady who would ask her for the rent money due today, because clearly the woman who owned the house did not trust this person in a red coat, as they called her, and rightly so, because she had no intention of paying the rent, she didn't even have anything to pay with; usually she carried the Parabellum—retrieved from the unit's secret grenade stock—tucked into the back belt of her trousers, underneath her coat, but now, still affected by the previous night's events, she put it in her coat pocket, continually gripping the pistol, not letting go for a second, and it was only as she started walking down Margarethenstraße toward the Hunger Bakery that she began to think about how clumsy she'd been with the Parabellum: nothing like that had ever happened at training, and if what never happened before had not happened twice, namely her dropping the pistol, then she could have taken aim at it, even into the air, well, into the air, and she'd also had a knife, she had her pistol, what the fuck happened, and even more importantly: *what the fuck was that whole thing?!* she didn't think this was some mysterious or mystical occurrence, because she had no beliefs, especially not in anything like that, however, with a sober mind, which was all she had, it was difficult to explain this bird in the dark suddenly attacking a person, by mistake?! or maybe the bird was crazy?! is there even such a thing?! she'd never heard of anything like that, and then she thought that it had been trained, there was no other possibility, certainly it had been drilled, yes, because no bird of prey would do something like this no matter how wild, it was simply absurd, the thought kept circling in her head just as the beast had circled above her last night; the Hunger Bakery was open already, she got two sunflower seed rolls for herself, and walked to the side of the Sankt Margarethenkirche where she sat down on a stone pillar and ate one of them, putting the other in her left pocket for lunch, and not waiting for passersby to start showing up, she ran down Jenaische Straße, just as Frau Hopf looked out the window and saw her, oh good Lord, she called out to her husband from the window, who still hadn't completely woken up, they're back here again, who's back again? the Nazis, Frau Hopf answered in fear, I recognize her, she drew the curtains somewhat more apart, pressing her head against the glass in order to see the woman as well as she could, even though her hair and coat were red, and she was wearing a hat, but I recognize her, Frau Hopf called back toward the bed, it's that woman, the woman with the tattooed head, she has that thing in her mouth, they're all tattooed, my dear, answered her husband from beneath the quilt, and all of them have some kind of ring inserted in their mouths, noses, ears, or their eyelids, that's what they're like, come back to bed and go to sleep, and what else could she do but lie down again, pulling the comforter onto herself, but she couldn't fall back asleep because what she had seen was fairly disquieting: she knew that the police were searching for the ones who hadn't been killed yet, namely her task was to immediately report what she'd seen, but no, not that! she chased the thought away, because all she needed was for those hooligans to start smashing her windows again and breaking in like before, she and her husband needed peace and quiet, not for police to be coming and going again, she'd had enough of that, they were keeping their mouths firmly shut from now on, they already regretted that when, after the murders, the two police-men had shown up to interrogate them and they'd told them every-thing they knew, they shouldn't have, but too late, they couldn't take it back now, because what would happen if they knew?! if it came to light?! if somehow this woman found out that they'd filed a complaint here in the neighborhood, which, by the way, was their civic duty?! no and again no, moreover, when they decided to get up, and her husband came back after a few minutes with breakfast as he usually did, so that they could have their morning meal sitting up, leaning against the soft headboard, together, they didn't mention anything to each other, as if the whole thing had vanished along with the previous night, and Herr Hopf said nothing, as if it had only been a stupid dream, and so things were like the old times, inasmuch as you could say that, because although the entire day they did the same things they'd always done before, they were full of fear, because the fear hadn't passed ever since things in Kana started going downhill, as Frau Hopf expressed it, things had started to be that way and they remained that way; the Hopfs did not speak of what was going on in the depths inside them: they spared each other, because they loved each other, never as much as in these times when it turned out that only they were there for each other, so much were they as one, as much as two people could be, two bodies, one soul, that is how Frau Hopf characterized it once, but only once to one of her children visiting at home, you know that if something happened with your father, I would be no more, believe me, my girl, she said to her; and the daughter, herself the mother of two small boys, understood what her mother was talking about, because the situation wasn't too much better where she lived, there weren't too many reassuring things to say about Dresden, either, don't even ask, she deflected Frau Hopf's questions, who of course never neglected to ask: well, and how are things by you? complete chaos, the daughter explained bitterly, nobody knows what to do, migrants, Nazis, demonstrations, clashes, and, you know, that inner agitation, that atmosphere of tension on the verge of cracking, but everywhere, believe me, mother, if you're on the tram, everyone is just quiet, sunk into themselves, if you go to the store, nobody talks to anyone, the whole city is such that I would be more than happy to move home, but, well, Kana isn't any better, better?! Frau Hopf burst out in fear, clasping her hands together, don't even think of such a thing, my dear!!! come back home?! here?! have you gone mad?! the most dangerous place is right here, *I've* been thinking that we should leave because people are afraid for their lives here in Kana, no matter how idiotic or exaggerated it may sound, but that's what it's like, don't even talk about it, my girl, that's enough, and now, from mother to daughter and daughter to mother, only words of comfort remained: take care of yourselves, call us, send a text, anything, let us know what's going on with you, these words sounded out again and again in the doorway as they said goodbye, then the daughter and her family drove off along Roßstraße toward the B88, the Hopfs stood for a while in the doorway, listening to the droning of the car's engine, then they went back inside, locked the door tightly, that day they only ate leftovers, just enough for the two of them, Frau Hopf had cooked noodles with cabbage because her daughter loved that, but only when she made it, although the little ones didn't even touch it, because while the adults were talking they'd found the key to the drawer, hidden away in vain, where the sweets were kept, and by the time they sat down at the table they had no appetite, but as far as noodles and cabbage went, it was a favorite dish elsewhere as well, Frau Feldmann liked to make it, and Frau Ringer served it to Ringer a few times a week, so that they wouldn't always be eating only meat, only just meat, but while Frau Feldmann made it with salt, Frau Ringer prepared a sweet version, because Ringer, having a decidedly sweet tooth, would only touch it then, and this too had not changed, even though he hadn't been able to come out of his deep depression, as the general sense of powerlessness, and thus his own powerlessness, became ever more manifest, and he could make no exception for noodles with cabbage; he wouldn't eat them savory, as he hadn't before, so there remained the sweetened version, although Frau Ringer wasn't happy to add sugar to anything, but what could she do, one had to eat, and Ringer would only eat it like that, although this was not an issue for auntie Ingrid, just let there be noodles with cabbage, she even said so to the Volkenants as she brought them their lunch, she could eat it even twice a week, savory or sweet, it was all the same to her, she said, because the main thing was the inimitable taste of noodles and cabbage, overshadowed for her by neither salt nor sugar, and she would be more than happy to eat it without either salt or sugar, but well, still, you need to add something, no? and with this she flounced out the door, there was no sign of her having comprehended any of the changes in the town or Thuringia, worry—over any subject at all—did not fit into her worldview, of course she was appalled if she heard from the TV news that there had been a fatal collision here, a fire breaking out there, a murder somewhere else, and then the demonstrations and the deteriorating statistics, not to mention that the Große Koalition had fallen apart, auntie Ingrid was the only one who was staggered by that, but then the next day, MDR announced that Chancellor Angela Merkel was concluding her political career—for her, Angela Merkel was the epitome of stability, circumspection, and reliability, and now what would happen without her? auntie Ingrid asked the Volkenants with frightened eyes, but Herr Volkenant reassured her: don't be nervous, auntie Ingrid, it was time for Merkel to go, because just think of how long she's been doing this, now she really deserves some peaceful years, that was how Volkenant expressed it, because he still had a good sense—as his wife always said to their acquaintances—for finding the most succinct and clear words in any given situation, and he did so with auntie Ingrid, because auntie Ingrid suddenly looked at him and it was as if she had really calmed down; do you really think it's time already? at which Volkenant nodded reassuringly, and the anxiety disappeared from auntie Ingrid's eyes, because, well, really, that Angela Merkel, she's worked so hard for us Germans, she too deserves some peaceful years in the end, no? she held her hands apart, but of course, of course, I agree, Volkenant concurred, and he showed her out the door, then when he came back into the office, he remarked curtly, because no one else was in the post office at that moment: whew, I thought she might stop bringing us lunch because of Angela Merkel, although auntie Ingrid had been thinking no such thing, she only regretted that the years had passed so quickly, and now the Chancellor too was retiring, well, yes, she sat at home in her rocking chair, time passes for us all, one day there's a knock at the door, and she began weeping, she rocked in her rocking chair, and for a few more minutes, she sobbed, then she got up from the rocking chair, took out her papers, and in accordance with her daily habit, checked if she'd managed to arrange the names on the list correctly, that is in the proper alphabetical order, and they were in the correct order, correct, as was the case every time, this time too she found every single name in the greatest of order, she sat back down, leaned back, closed her eyes, and began to rock again, and while she was thinking that soon it would be time to go to the kitchen and brew her afternoon vitamin tea, she slowly fell asleep, and then the rocking chair, nice and slowly, stopped rocking, but no one was shaken by her death, moreover there were people who—when the news had spread how she had departed so beautifully, so peacefully, and in a rocking chair too—were a little jealous of her, although many of the older residents would not openly admit it; granted such a beautiful death by heaven above, but I don't envy her, they said to each other at the funeral, all the while greatly envying her, hoping that life would grant them an even less painful death than hers had been, and that is exactly what the Deputy was thinking, he wouldn't say, he said to Pförtner one night, that he didn't think about it sometimes, how the hell could he not think about it, but still it was new for him, how he was thinking of it day after day, but that's how it was, a day didn't pass that he didn't wonder about how much time he had left, and he said this with all sincerity, and as that day got closer, he was ever more fearful, and living alone, he added, didn't help at all, but there you are, if my wife were still alive, things would be different, and Pförtner just nodded and said nothing, he still counted as a young man, especially in comparison to the Deputy, so he didn't pay too much attention to such matters, not even to mention the fact that thanks to his porter's booth he never felt alone, he said to the Deputy, the porter's booth was his wife, and moreover one who didn't talk back, and he laughed—it doesn't cook, though, the Deputy replied with a constrained smile for the sake of saying something, but really, the Deputy felt very constrained, because he didn't like joking about this topic, he didn't even understand what his nighttime companion was getting at with these allusions, how could the porter's lodge explain his not being alone? nonsense, he thought; although it was true, Pförtner didn't like being at home, because there, on the contrary, he did feel alone, very alone, he moved about ill at ease, apart from a good night's sleep, there was nothing about home he liked, not the walls or the door or the door-knob or the door key, and if he were calling it a day, as he put it, he couldn't wait to get back to work, he himself didn't know why, but the porter's booth, with its own small dimensions, and how, despite its scale, everything was in its place, even when sitting, everything in reach or a mere step or two away, made him feel as if the whole thing had been completely tailored for him, and the nights were good too, he loved the nights when there were no people coming and going, when the silence was undisturbed, he liked listening to the barking of the dogs rising up from time to time from the town, and if he wasn't going over to see the Deputy, or the Deputy wasn't coming over to see him, then Pförtner just leaned back in his chair and he thought of nothing: this, for him, was the most agreeable feeling in the world: to sit in his chair behind the window of his porter's booth, and to think of nothing, and in that, in Kana, he was not alone, because Herr Feldmann also truly liked to do so, even if he himself wouldn't have called it "thinking of nothing," he spoke to his wife about how, on a pleasant afternoon, he would sit down in his favorite leather armchair, lean back, close his eyes, and to him this was Paradise itself, nothing happening, his thoughts, as he put it, came to a stop, moving in no direction, it's like that Zen state of yours, he said, referring to Brigitte's favorite pastime, as she had been doing Zen meditation for years now, and she tried to get her husband into it as well, but he just dug in his heels and just laughed at this whole Zen thing, seeing it as an activity aging hucksters had come up with to relieve middle-aged women of large amounts of cash, Brigitte had started with this in the old post office building, where one of these charlatans—he really grated on Herr Feldmann's nerves—had set up shop, he was from Hamburg, but of course who knew where he was really from, people like that can't even open their mouths without lying in their unbearably sanctimonious voices and this one did too, lurking around any suitable female, and already, after two weeks, Brigitte came home with the news that she'd had a satori, Herr Feldmann didn't even ask what the hell a satori was, he resigned himself to the fact that he wouldn't be able to beat this out of his wife's head for a while, and anyway, he had his music, so why shouldn't Brigitte have her satori? he thought, and he placed no obstacles in the path of his wife throwing herself ever more deeply into searching for this satori; for him, his satori was the Beatles, for him, the Beatles rose above everything else, he knew everything about the Beatles, ever since he'd been a young man, he followed everything about them fanatically, and he had a passion for everything connected to the Beatles, oh, George, oh, Ringo, oh, John, he often sighed as he played his own arrangement of one of their classics, but he loved Paul the best, in his opinion he was the sole genius, and no one else, because of course the others were still Beatles, but Paul, musically speaking, towered above them, Paul had never wished for anything else than to write music, and he practiced this art on such a high level and no one could ever overtake him, and, in Herr Feldmann's sacred conviction, no one would ever overtake him, not even to mention the fact that Herr Feldmann found Paul's personality to be extraordinarily engaging, he was no rebel, never getting himself mixed up in the great turbulences of the 1960s, as Herr Feldmann summarized that period, he truly held Paul to be a congenial person who simply wrote and wrote music that was getting better and better all the time, and his ORCHESTRATIONS!!!

PEOPLE!!! his unparalleled sense for and knowledge of MUSIC, manifest in his orchestrations, were inimitable, and when he got to this point, Herr Feldmann's eyes filled with tears, and to calm himself down, he would play "Blackbird," and sometimes in the summer, not exactly accidentally, he would play "Blackbird" by the open window with one eye on the passersby outside, to see if they might stop by the open window of this house to listen—but what would be the point of opening the window when the situation was enough to drive one to despair, especially now when it was spring, he thought, and the window was still closed, waiting for better times, but these better times were no longer coming, Herr Feldmann sensed this, and everyone in Kana sensed this, people's habits had changed, if not completely, they were altered, the residents of Kana went to the Shopping Center, the doctor's office, the pharmacy, or the massage therapist in other ways and at other times and for other reasons, and to be sure, the renowned May Day celebrations in the Rosengarten were looking different this year as well, oh dear, said Frau Uta, who, husband at her side, had been among the first to arrive, these are supposed to be the May Day celebrations?! and she looked around at the nearly empty benches and tables, then picked a table with a good view, sat down, and pulled her husband over to herself: what are you staring at, sit down already; her husband flopped down by her side, but kept turning his head more and more toward the beer stand, where the servers would have drawn a beer, but there was no one to draw it for yet, Frau Uta had found a spot the farthest away from the beer stand as the most suitable, thinking to impede her husband in the too easy and frequent acquisition of his liquid plunder, but, well, it's May Day, the man groused, and he would have set off for a small stein, but Frau Uta immediately and unequivocally pulled him back: you stay here, you're starting with that damned drinking already? but after ten minutes of silence, during which they listened to three Omega songs from the loudspeakers, she gave up, released her grip, and called after him: only one glass!!! and she let him go, it was May Day after all, and then, from the mouth of the underpass that led here beneath the rail tracks, the local celebrants of May Day began showing up, at first smaller families, clearly finding their charges somewhat hard to bear, but then the lonely, older people began to drift in, and the married couples, nicely dressed up as was suitable for the occasion, the music bellowed, the terrace filled up, beer flowed from the kegs, the first Bockwursts were being thrown onto the cooker, in a word, the usual activities started up, but the music was still only coming from the loudspeakers, the so-called Enlarged Kana Symphony had still not appeared on the stage, but what was delayed was not lost, and so when the stroke of eleven rang out from the bell tower of a nearby church, the members of the orchestra in their lovely red uniforms began to climb up onto the stage, took their seats, here and there the tuba or the trombone or the saxophone honked, the musicians in the first string section mewled on their violins and began to tune their instruments which filled the audience with pleasant shivers while they finished tuning and then they were ready, so that, at the gesture of Herr Feldmann, the first beats sounded, now everyone was looking at them, the steins were clinked together, the first Rostbratwurst went down the hatch, of course with Bautz'ner mustard, only with Bautz'ner; but where was that atmosphere, the Deputy grumbled, shaking his head, he was here by himself, and he only muttered his comment into the air lest anyone sitting at the neighboring table answer him, but if anyone agreed with him, they didn't reply, so that after a short pause, he grabbed his stein, downed half of it, wiped his mouth, leaned with his elbows onto the table, and waited to hear what would happen next, and what happened next was that the orchestra played "Yesterday," because according to Herr Feldmann, this always went down well, the members of the orchestra seemed enthusiastic, the wind players' veins bulging, stage fright clearly visible on all of their faces, almost the exact same expression of the faces of the audience watching them, as if each were waiting for the other to launch the May Day celebrations with their inimitable atmosphere, but this inimitable atmosphere did not begin for quite a while yet, for that, it was necessary for the first stein to be consumed, then the second one, although by the second one it was no longer possible to stop, because it was exactly with this second one— it'd been this way now for centuries, and not only on May Day—that a certain bleak atmosphere set in with the Kana public, the men stared in front of themselves, clutching the handles of their empty steins, and they nodded slowly, they didn't know why, they just nodded, and what else could happen but for them to head off for the third mug of beer, and they sipped away at that third mug of beer, and it was as if those ill-omened clouds above the terrace had been swept away, somehow the first sip of the third stein always brought about the miracle: the men's gazes cleared up, the conversations no longer seemed as if gagged and stuttering, but suddenly came to life, laughter was heard to the left, then to the right, and within minutes, the crowd was buzzing like a beehive, Hoffmann seemed in particularly good spirits, walking back and forth among the tables, a wide grin on his face as he greeted anyone he could chat with, remaining until his interlocutors turned away; then he went on and tried to chat with others, moving in this way through the bustling crowd; on the stage, Herr Feldmann and the orchestra were playing "Blood of My Blood," but to tell the truth, nobody was really paying attention anymore, although Herr Feldmann had begun his movements, his own inimitable acrobatics that he always employed on May Day when the atmosphere—in his opinion—had reached its height, he directed the rhythm, and before each essential cadence, he moved his body one quarter note in advance so that by the end of the measure he was throwing one leg out to the side, but leaning in the opposite direction, holding this position until the last note, then, with a single, enormous, enthusiastic sweep of his arm into the air, he concluded the piece, and this time as well the applause was not lacking, and it was clear that Herr Feldmann counted this as his own personal success, although, as the public applauded, he never neglected to acknowledge the Enlarged Kana Symphony, at times himself clapping for this or that section, but still, it could be seen from his face that this undoubtable triumph was his alone, and he thanked the audience with a deep bow after every number, and truly, their acclaim was sincere, although, with their faces red from beer, they were in fact celebrating their arrival to a more elevated realm, because although there were still the worries, the cares, it was clear they were thinking: what's the point in being gloomy here today when the orchestra is playing so well, the men said so as they headed off for another stein, the women stood in line for a bottle of beer and some Wurst, and when the Symphony announced an intermission, and Hoffmann, in unparalleled good spirits, began singing between two tables *Wenn Mutti früh zur Arbeit geht*, at first only a few older women, eyes shining, joined in, then more and more people joined, so that within minutes there could only be heard the song booming out:

Wenn Mutti früh zur Arbeit geht
Dann bleibe ich zu Haus
Ich binde eine Schürze um
Und feg die Stube aus

and now the men also raised their steins, and the bass voices rang out:

Das Essen kochen kann ich nicht
Dafür bin ich zu klein
Doch Staub hab ich schon oft gewischt
Wie wird sich Mutti freu'n

and then they began again from the beginning, because they somehow couldn't recall the next verses of this dear little ditty from the old times, and maybe the repetition did them good as well, because they were singing, mainly Hoffmann, but neither Torsten nor Wagner nor the Deputy neglected to bring up the rear, they sat hunched over, banging their steins on the table, by the end they were yelling, so that nobody could complain about the atmosphere, and there were no complaints until the early afternoon, and the railroad crossing proved to be the only reason for the sudden silence of the celebratory crowd, even though they'd heard it innumerable times before—only now they were slightly drowsy as they heard it—they'd heard it thousands and thousands of times, as, twenty-five or thirty meters to the left of the tunnel, the mechanism that signaled approaching trains began ringing with its own peculiar timbre, of course, from here below, in the Rosengarten, they couldn't see it, they only heard it, but they knew what was going to happen: namely that the rail-crossing gate would creak enormously and lower, and the wait would begin for the train, and they too now began waiting for the train coming from the north or the south, either from Jena or Saalfeld, to come rumbling past—slantwise, but at a higher elevation—they waited and waited, two minutes went by, three minutes, five minutes, nothing happened, the orchestra stopped playing and came down from the stage, but the revelers were still waiting for the train, although they waited in vain, because no train arrived either from the south or the north, and what happened next was merely what always happened these days: the rail-crossing gate, after eight or ten minutes, as if it too had been waiting in vain for something to arrive, began to rise with a somewhat sadder creaking than before, well, and that was the end of May Day, people struggled to their feet, and they slowly began to walk to the underpass, making their way beneath the tracks to Töpfergasse, then to Heimbürgerstraße on their way home, home, where they were greeted by cold, because most people didn't have the heat on at this time of year, especially during the day, they had to save, they didn't know exactly why but they had to save, so instead they wound blankets around themselves, if anything, collapsing onto their beds to rest, Frau Hopf watched them from the window, because she never, but never went down to the Rosengarten, it's not for us, she always lifted her head a bit if someone asked, well, why don't you go there, there's such a good atmosphere, and after all, it's May Day, to which Frau Hopf never replied, she and her husband just looked at each other and warded off the mere suggestion, because it was enough for them, when the time came for this popular celebration, to say to each other: it's not for us, and it really wasn't for them, because when they were still young they used to go to the theater in Jena or Dresden or Leipzig, and they would still go to the theater if such a plan, these days, weren't so exhausting, indeed, it was evidently dangerous to step outside, they had stopped going shopping in Jena, they really didn't care to do that anymore, they were fine at home, if they wanted company, they had guests, especially as long as the restaurant was still in operation, for now there were enough customers, those few foolhardy travelers passing through the Garni were more than enough! Frau Hopf raised her voice, and sometimes there were visits from family, and they didn't need anything else, Herr Hopf sat down, after eating, in his comfortably cushioned rocking chair pulled up in front of the TV, and he dozed off for an hour or two, Frau Hopf, after washing up, sat down next to him in the armchair and leafed through *Barbara*, her favorite magazine, because *Barbara* was intended for someone of her age, because well, she considered herself to be a modern woman, and *Barbara* addressed her in precisely such a way, yes, it spoke to her, because in the course of years it had almost become her best girlfriend, she had no need to travel here and there anymore, because she traveled everywhere with *Barbara*, oftentimes rereading this or that article, but if she was already very bored, there were always the pictures, and in *Barbara* the pictures were really good, she explained to her husband if he asked her if she wasn't in the mood for something different, just look at this or that, she showed him this or that, and her husband nodded in agreement, and he suggested no change of magazines for a certain time, namely, *Barbara* was present in more than a few households, exercising its own strong influence, but still, such long-term subscribers as Frau Hopf were extremely rare, Frau Feldmann had tried, one or two times, to convince Frau Ringer to subscribe, but she said: a subscription, no, because no, but still, sometimes she would pick up a copy in the Shopping Center, and now she was looking through one of those copies, but really just kind of flipping through the pages, because she couldn't really concentrate as the situation with them had decisively worsened, her husband's state—despite all earlier hopes, and truly unexpectedly—had once again begun to disintegrate, even though she had restored his regular special diet, and in vain did she announce to him every new development in the extensive house renovations, because they were extensive, because this involved not only painting the walls and cleaning up afterward, but a genuine renewal, things inside were getting lighter, even if everything outside was so dark, and the spring didn't mean anything to him, Frau Ringer tried in various ways to smuggle back in their old passion, the weekend outings, but she was not successful, Ringer always just shook his head: not today, and that was it, as if he wished, with this curt and pithy refusal, to alert his wife that there was no need to return to a place where wolves attack people, although there hadn't been news of wolves in their immediate area for quite some time, the MDR only gave reports, from time to time, of sightings of this or that pack between Coburg and Schiefergebirge, which lay to the south of them, so it seemed quite likely that the wolves were not going to return, because, as had been mentioned in the bulletin issued by NABU, Kana and the surrounding region no longer formed a part of the wolves' range of interest, that's how the bulletin put it, humorously, so as to further reassure the local residents, but that was in vain, because, needless to say, it only made people in Kana even more nervous, although everyone was happy that at least now they could sleep at night, and they didn't jump up in fright at every trifling sound in the great Kana night; no one wanted to hear anything about NABU, because those ones, led by that medical-mask-wearing Tamás Ramsthaler, had only stirred up more trouble ever since they'd started coming around here, trying to calm people down by giving public lectures, but in the end what happened was that the so-called mayor of Kana—having zero significance to the life of Kana, no one took him seriously anyway—asked them to stop coming, and from then on, NABU never set foot in Kana again; Tamás Ramsthaler was offended, thereafter only posting monthly notifications in the form of an Open Letter to the Residents of Kana on his own website, but no one read it, so that at least one small chapter in this series of horrors had now closed, because people did not conceal that the wolf attacks had now blurred into a mere small chapter in the mirror of the horrors that followed, remaining a ghastly memory largely for Herr Ringer and Frau Ringer, but the wounds healed, and after a while, Frau Ringer's physiognomy bore no more trace of what had happened; look at you, there's almost nothing on your face, Frau Feldmann would say to her as they sat down for their usual coffee and pastries, at the Feldmanns', or in the Herbstcafé, and Frau Ringer smiled confusedly, with a kind of defensive shame, and she reached involuntarily for her silk scarf covering her neck, because she felt the scars, she felt them very much, and she knew that for her they would never fully disappear, as was true, for the most part, of the horrific events themselves, moreover, the residents of Kana tried to hurry up the process of forgetting, because how could anyone live with all of this? the Deputy asked Pförtner one night, it's normal to want to file away the whole thing, because just look now how they're trying to scare us with this pandemic, life will return to normal, only that it wasn't returning to normal, even the Deputy suspected this, chiefly because certain things, as he formulated it to Pförtner, had yet to be cleared up, because if I think about it, nothing has been cleared up, he stated bitterly, because why? do we know anything about who blew up the Aral station and poor Nadír and Rosario in it?! we don't know, and do we know who killed the Nazis?! we don't know, or do we know—if I may refer to something that personally affects me—Florian's whereabouts?! I don't know, the Deputy spread his hands apart, and, standing in the porter's booth at the Porcelain Factory, he looked around accusingly, the entire universe is an enigma, he shook his head, disillusioned, like someone who didn't believe in enigmas—because the Deputy had faith only in the work of the authorities, organized, rigorously focused—and, he concluded his remarks, this is something about which we simply cannot speak any further, it's a debacle, my Pförtner, the entire investigation and everything, I keep submitting reports, telling them everything I know about Florian, down to the smallest details, but nothing, they don't even bat an eyelid, which was not entirely true, because an investigative division in Erfurt had been assigned to the case, and particularly to Florian's disappearance, and who would have known this any better than the Deputy himself, because they'd come back to the Hochhaus twice already, and he had led them up to Florian's apartment, where he opened the door for them with the master key, the Deputy had to wait outside as he wasn't permitted to see what they were doing inside, then the cops came back into the hallway but said nothing, which pained the Deputy, they could have said something to him as he was a kind of official himself, particularly as he was assisting their investigation so much, but they said nothing, merely motioned to him to lock up the apartment; then they appeared one more time, and everything happened in the same way; the Deputy didn't know if they had come back a second time hoping to find something else besides the cell phone trampled on the apartment floor, from which, however, thanks to the work of the Erfurt special lab, the memory card data had been retrieved, including the two videos, so when the video analysis was completed, an arrest warrant, featuring a relatively recent ID photo from the Jena Job Center, was issued for Florian Herscht and distributed nationwide as it was suspected that, being at large, the wanted man had already fled Thuringia and was hiding out in a different federal state; in short, there was a fair amount of excitement in Erfurt, because they finally had something in their hands: almost certain proof that this Herscht was the one holding the cell phone which meant he was deeply involved in this unsavory affair, now they just had to get a lead on him, only that there were no leads anywhere, which was not so surprising, because Florian, within the past few months, had not only begun to resemble a predator, but there was nothing at all in his appearance that would remind anyone of his most recent photograph: his exterior was fundamentally altered, he had metamorphosed; instead of his Fidel Castro cap, which he'd lost somewhere, he wore a stolen fur cap with earflaps, from which his hair hung down in clumps, his beard had grown feral, his eyes were red, his face covered with scars and scratches, he had gathered innumerable pieces of clothing which he wore day and night on top of his overalls, but everything now so tattered and reeking that homeless people chased Florian away if he wanted to spend the night in a residential area—although this happened rarely—namely the other homeless were always wearing relatively good, or even high-quality clothing—coats, trousers, sweaters, shirts, and shoes—which they received from organizations providing such items, whereas everything that Florian had was ruined, and it never even occurred to him to find out where these clothes distribution places were located and go there, no, nothing like this ever even occurred to him, he held himself far apart from any such institutions, and, in general, from any place where he might come into contact with those for whom he had undoubtedly become, sometime in May, an enemy, for there was no question that he had broken every conceivable law: he was a murderer, he was hiding out, and he wasn't finished yet, so that it wasn't even just that his exterior had changed, but inside, he was no longer the person the residents of Kana had known, he was no longer gentle and shamefaced, no longer uninformed in daily matters, no longer practically a half-wit, but as dangerous as a land mine: if his brain had stopped functioning when this new chapter began in his story, and did not start up again, from the depths of Florian's being another being burst out, a being no one would have recognized anymore, and this being was now spending the night in Eisenach, because, due to an image that had been reoccurring to him over the past several days, he'd felt the need to see the Bachhaus again, because there was something there he'd always passed by, but that remained in a blind spot in his memory, he didn't know what it was, but he had to go back there to survey the place, and he did; the two benches located in the narrow semicircle known as the Frauenplan, off the tiny square with its Bach statue in front of the Bachhaus entrance, were, as usual, occupied by two homeless people, but he didn't allow himself to be chased away, although they tried, he grabbed one of them by the shoulder and flung him farther on, at which the other sneaked off, and they left him to do what he wanted, they moved higher up the square and watched him, but this didn't get them too far because they didn't understand what this guy was doing, examining the walls on either side of the museum entrance: at first he began running his hands over the wall, then rubbing ever more forcefully, as if trying to scrape off the plaster, but he's a lunatic, one of them remarked, and they remained with that conclusion, carefully sneaking back to their benches where they adjusted their coats, turned on their sides, and went back to sleep, Florian continued examining both sides of the museum entrance, finally he stopped, and went up toward the Frauenplan, passing in between the two benches with the two homeless sleeping men and he went up to Domstraße where he looked to the right, then looked to the left, but he didn't see anyone, it was the middle of the night, he didn't know the exact time, maybe between two and three a.m., once again he looked to the right, and it occurred to him why he had to come here, he realized what had led him back here, he saw it: twenty meters away from where he stood, there was a large dumpster, that's what he was looking for, because when he used to come here with the Boss, they had only cast the merest of glances at this street, Domstraße, they had overlooked this dumpster because they'd been searching for someone and not for something, namely they hadn't examined everything thoroughly, although they should have, as Florian did now, he went over to the dumpster, but as he was about to open the lid, it suddenly flung open, hitting him on the chin, he was unsteady on his feet for a moment, but only just, so that he was able to pull out the figure hiding in the dumpster, a boy of maybe fifteen or sixteen years old, Florian twisted his hand and pushed him to the ground, then he took the bag off him which was filled with spray-paint cans in three different colors, and now Florian recalled how the sprayer had used exactly these three colors, he put the cans back in the bag, tossed the entire thing down to the ground, and with a few movements trampled on the bag until it ripped apart, until the spray-paint cans exploded with loud bangs and the paint was flowing out onto the ground, the boy thought that he could use this opportunity to escape, but he was mistaken, he only knocked the earphones out of Florian's ears, but he couldn't escape, because Florian was holding him so tightly by the neck that he had no chance, and he understood this now, and he began stammering out: I'll explain, to which Florian replied: I don't care, the boy looked at him with enraged eyes, and he didn't leave it at that, he stammered out again that he would explain, at which Florian loosened his grip somewhat, and he asked if he had acted alone; the boy nodded, inasmuch as he could; Florian pulled the boy closer to himself, looked into those eyes sparkling with rage, and he asked: who are you? the boy stared back, and he groaned ... the school ... no, at NABU ... this and that, but ... here his voice faltered, Florian loosened his grip a bit again, because the child was wheezing and gulping for air, then, after a desperate inhalation he said he would explain if Florian didn't hand him over to the cops, and he began babbling that he'd dropped out of school and was volunteering, but he didn't agree with how NABU was treating the wolves, because they said they loved them, but they didn't love them, for them, the wolves were just some fucking data, and all they cared about was getting the fucking dough, subsidies, state money, grants, and Florian shook the boy, but in vain, because the boy wasn't afraid of him anymore, his entire being burned with rage, so that when Florian asked him what the hell all this had to do with Bach, at first the boy didn't give him a comprehensible answer, because all of his words were choked in coughing, then Florian really let his neck go, and he held him by the collar of his jacket, the boy coughed for a while, and, his face darkened in anger, he almost spit into Florian's face: and Bach?! how the fuck should he know?! he had only done what they told him to, but by now he was hissing, his face completely distorted, and Florian asked: who was telling you to do this? how the fuck should I know, the boy said, they just call, tell me the place, and I finish the job, or I finished half of it, because they wanted it to say WE ARE COMING, but he'd only been able to get as far as WE because he also had to add the tag, the WOLF HEAD, without which he wouldn't have even taken on the job, and it was taking too long to spray ARE COMING, so they agreed on that, did he get it now?! how much? fifty for one graff, and why you?—this was the last question—and the answer came: because I'm the best, and with that the conversation was over, the boy just kept shaking his head bitterly, as if everything were all the same to him, and whatever had to happen, he would let it happen, although he wasn't expecting this guy to pick him up, and to look into his eyes for a long time, a very long time, like someone who was trying to discover if he'd been telling the truth, because it never could have occurred to him that

Florian was instead asking himself: how can there exist so much coincidence? that he had just happened to find him here?! the boy had just decided now to try again, to come back here again, and Florian opened the dumpster lid just at that moment, what kind of coincidence was this?! how much of a chance was there?! such coincidence only happens in novels, but this isn't a novel, thought Florian as he gazed into the boy's daring, proud eyes, glittering with hostility, the boy who withstood his gaze, and only wanted now for the other to know that he wasn't afraid of him, because it was really all the same to him, because as far as he was concerned, the entire world could collapse, he had settled his accounts, and he didn't even fucking want anything at all from this fucked-up world, but this wasn't entirely true, because there was one thing he did want a great deal, and he even forced it out through his lips, and now he did so for the second time, when he was on the ground again, and he said: fuck it man, don't hand me over to the fucking cops, then, as Florian said nothing, he added that otherwise ... the clients are actually pretty good guys, they actually don't want to destroy anything, no way, because he had figured out that they were doing it out of respect for Bach, because supposedly there was some kind of higher goal which he himself never understood, but that wasn't his business, although the boy received no answer to this last statement, his head was beaten into the puddles of paint spilled everywhere on the ground, then he was picked up and thrown back into the opened container, and the lid was shut closed, because this is what happened, even if he didn't exactly understand what the boy had been talking about here, Florian didn't want to bother him anymore, he shoved his earphones back into his ears, and he left the dumpster, and with noiseless steps he went along Domstraße, then, avoiding the hill at Kreuzkirche, he left the town, and all traces of him were lost, and when one of the two homeless men who had a cell phone called the police, they didn't even find the boy in the dumpster, so that the cop who showed up didn't seem to really give any credence to the jumbled explanations of the two homeless men, although he threw him over there like a sack, they said, interrupting each other, and they both gave evidence, each one frequently contradicting the other, the cop, after a while, stopped writing it down, closed his notebook, waved them away, got back into his car, annoyed, and left them there, and in any event, there was at least a personal description of the alleged troublemakers, who, according to the witnesses had been brawling, and at the end of which allegedly one had thrown the other into the dumpster, but of course, apart from the smashed-up spray-paint cans, there was no evidence, no point to the entire thing, no criminal case, so that the policeman, when he got back to the station in Jena, didn't even feel like giving the officer on duty the personal descriptions, according to which one of them looked like a beast of prey endowed with superhuman strength, and who didn't speak at all, only growled, and for reasons that could not be more precisely deduced, before his attack, was closely examining the walls of the Bachhaus, yes, that's right, one of the witnesses added, and he was wearing a backpack and had an earplug stuck in one of his ears, well, and the other one was just a kid in a hooded coat, a gangly kid, said the other homeless man, and he showed how scrawny he was, well, and that was all, and the cop really almost threw out his notes, but then he thought again, and he tore out the relevant pages from his notepad, put them down on the desk of the officer on duty so that they could be typed up to at least create some kind of record as to where he'd been and what he'd been doing in Eisenach, and it was good that he didn't throw them out, and it was good that the officer on duty typed them up, because this ended up becoming the first usable lead, namely the written note was sent to Erfurt, and one of the Erfurt investigators reported to his superior that in his opinion this current case was connected to the earlier acts of vandalism committed by that sprayer or sprayers in Eisenach and other locales in Thuringia a few years ago, so it wasn't so difficult for the cops in Erfurt to decide that they had to look into the earlier set of events, and they did look into them, and from the data of the earlier case, they now had something to work with, because it immediately emerged that the most important suspect of all the people they were following at that time was murdered in Kana only a few months ago, namely—noted the head of the Erfurt murder investigation commission, as he reported these developments to the group—he was assassinated, or, if he wanted to put things more precisely, and he did want to put things more precisely, he was murdered with one blow, and this one single blow already led them to another murder case in Kana, because even though in that case an implement had been used, the two victims there had also been killed with one blow, well, and with that they were already on his trail, but it was as if Florian sensed this, because now he was even more cautious than before, already—when living in the cave—he had kept his distance from residential areas, but now he avoided them more than ever, only quickly grabbing a few provisions from this or that back garden in the outskirts; drinking water was more difficult because the fountains in the main squares were, for the most part, not working, so he had to be ingenious; the surest thing seemed to be for him to observe deliveries being made to this or that village shop, and either scurry to the delivery truck and steal one or two crates of water, or to lie in wait, ambush and incapacitate the driver, and make off with one or two crates, but it was a complicated and risky operation no matter how good his timing was, although once he was finished he could be tranquil for a while, and at those times he sought out a suitable place for himself in the woods or on hillsides abundantly overgrown with shrubs where he could also pay more attention to what he was hearing at that moment; ever since he had found his winter hideout, going out every day or two for provisions, he had given up recharging his laptop, he knew that with his appearance, his raggedy clothes, unkempt hair, and reddened, hunted eyes, made so by his escape, he could no longer enter a bar or any public place without drawing attention to himself, not even a train station, so he no longer charged his laptop, but he didn't take his earphones out of his ears, because, as it turned out, not only did he remember music as he had before, but he heard the music clearly, he heard it clearly even when his earphones were completely mute, because ever since the ending of his involvement with the Boss this music played continuously: it had saturated him so much, hearing these sounds became as natural to him as breathing, and there was no need for them to come from his laptop, the music played even when his laptop was off, so that during winter, or now in the woods or on hillsides abundantly overgrown with shrubs, in these tranquil hours or at night when he woke up, he could, with full concentration, devote himself to this music, because his brain, albeit with difficulty, was working again, and this brain realized, in connection with his earlier thoughts concerning the horrific danger lying in wait for the universe—the danger against which he had not been able to warn the Bundesregierung, first and foremost the Federal Chancellor Angela Merkel—that elementary particle physics gave no answers, because it probably could not give any reassuring answers at all; he didn't know why it could not do so, but during the winter, during his complete withdrawal from the world, he'd had time to think about this, and he'd reached the conclusion which, it is true, did not take him very far, but nonetheless told him that elementary particle physics either was not able to give an answer, or would never be in the position of being able to give an answer, simply because particle physics was always placing barriers before its own self, barriers it could never overcome, because these barriers ensued from the system of human logic, and at that point thought became, as it were, entangled in its own self, consuming its own free strength, only seeking an exit, always just seeking an exit and again an exit from the newer and newer snares set by its own self, and precisely because it proceeded on the basis of scientific logic as it could do nothing else, so that now, at the beginning of May—Florian knew it was the beginning of May because he saw maypoles everywhere—with his brain functional once more, he stepped back to an earlier train of thought, no, not a train of thought, merely a feeling that he must step back, and that he must step back to Bach himself; before, he'd had a rudimentary idea of what he was finding, and he'd shared this with Mrs. Merkel, but now, in May, he was approaching the matter from the other side, and the music continually reverberating in his brain, the continuous presence of Bach in his brain, was an indication of how Bach had become, for him, a *personal state of being*, namely, he was no longer hearing Bach, he was inside Bach; in his own brain, he could no longer separate himself from the music he heard continuously, and so he no longer had any need to start playing the *Matthäus-Passion* or the chorale themes, because the *Matthäus-Passion* and the chorale themes resounded in his head regardless, every work of Bach's he'd ever listened to, all the music he'd downloaded, never stopped resounding in his head, merely because he wasn't pressing the play button on his laptop; he lay in the gentleness of May on the hillsides abundantly overgrown with shrubs, or deep in the woods, well hidden from the world, and he listened to all of the *Matthäus-Passion* and the chorales and the *Wohltemperiertes Klavier* and the *Goldberg-Variationen* and the orchestral sonatas and the suites and the partitas and the cantatas and so on, and he thought that the remedy for the Last Judgment perhaps did not lie in science or the politics it had given rise to, but that the remedy lay wholly and singularly in Johann Sebastian Bach, the path to Bach led through the structures of his works, and these structures were perfect, and therefore if the structures were perfect, then the themes built upon them were also perfect, and if these themes were perfect, then the harmonics embodying these themes were also perfect, and if the harmonics embodying these themes were perfect, then every single note was perfect, that is—the conclusion that Florian reached in these tranquil moments, minutes, and at times hours was that in Johann Sebastian Bach there was NO EVIL, well, and this could be set against inevitable-seeming danger; the art of Bach simply was lacking in EVIL, it had been created by Bach and it could not be destroyed, as opposed to the universe, and there was nothing in the work of Bach that was accidental, not in that period before these works were made, but from the moment that they arose, no and no, there was no contingency here and there never would be, no change, because Bach was a STABLE STRUCTURE and would remain so for all eternity, something like an ideal, like a fairy-tale crystal, like the surface of a drop of water, its stability indecipherable, its perfection indecipherable, and of course this could be described, but it could not be grasped, because its essence sidestepped the movements of the spirit that attempted to grasp it, because there are things of which we are not capable, thought Florian's brain, and that is natural, and yet for us to understand why there is no essence of the perfect, this is why we must say that the perfect merely exists, but if it lacks essence, then only wonder remains to us, this is what Florian's brain was thinking, then once again his muscles took over, he came out from the depths of the woods or from among the hillsides abundantly overgrown with shrubs, and he returned to Kana, and from there he did not leave again, he waited, just as Karin was doing, she couldn't go to Margarethenstraße, moreover she couldn't even show herself too much in that area, so instead she chose Ilona's pension, located not in the center of Kana, but a few kilometers northwest of the town, she could get there by foot, and that's how she got there, and no one there caused her any problems, two shots and they were gone, she buried them not too far away from the house, but outside of the village, then the next evening she walked back to Kana so that by complete onset of darkness she had positioned herself at one of her ever-changing observation points, for a while she watched the fitness center building, but then she gave up on that, and from the vantage point of the abandoned gas station, she observed the small patch of green in front of the entrance to the Hochhaus, she removed the wooden plank covering the windows and put it back in place undamaged, and so, she could spend the night here as well, completely protected, as well as keeping an eye on the Hochhaus, the Ernst-Thälmann-Straße intersection, the parking lot in front of the Baumarkt, the narrow path near the Boss's former house which led beneath the railway tracks to the Ölwiesenweg, but she also spent hours in the Burg, cordoned off and sealed by the police, it was child's play for her to get in without damaging the seal, and from the upper floor, which the unit had never used that much, she had a pretty good view of Jenaische Straße and the two parallel streets leading to the Rathaus in the Altstadt, but she also had another observation point from the plot of land next to the high school where she could see who was going into and coming out of the Herbstcafé, but Florian neither went in nor came out, as he wasn't going anywhere as he had found a suitable spot directly across from Burg 19, in the tower of the Sankt Margarethenkirche, as only from there could he see, clearly and undisturbed, what was going on at night in front of Burg 19, he could observe, clearly and undisturbedly, who was going in and who was coming out, but on that one occasion when he could have struck her down, Karin was moving so quickly that he didn't even have a chance to get down in time from the tower and throw himself on her, but as he tried, he suddenly heard a faint rummaging sound coming from around the altar, and he stopped for a moment at the bottom of the stairs, and listened into the silence in the church, he was too late, and it wasn't difficult to figure out that Karin had been hiding out in the Burg for a long time—who knew since when—and she was leaving it now, so he wasn't getting off to a lucky start, although he wasn't too surprised at how hard it was, because he knew it would be difficult, Karin was hunting him, and Karin was a very good hunter, she had proven this already at the Sportpension in Suhl, and she was proving it now, in brief, it was obvious that while he was looking for Karin, Karin was also looking for him, namely, Karin knew that she was next—knew she was last one who would have to pay, just as it was clear that Karin had realized who her enemy was: him, and it wasn't too difficult for him to realize that Karin knew everything, and therefore she wanted to get ahead of him: sadly, and with this recognition, Florian climbed the narrow stairs leading to the tower, but he didn't know why he was suddenly overcome with sadness, it had happened to him before too, and he had never been able to deal with it, either previously, or now, perhaps this was the only feeling left in him from his old life, although he was always surprised that there was any feeling left in him at all, he wasn't expecting it, in any event, when caught unawares he could do nothing against it, he had to allow it to fill every one of his pores, helpless in the face of this particular, metallic, cold sadness, and so he remained here now as well, he sat down in the tower on one of the beams next to the bell, leaning forward with his elbows on his knees, waiting for it to pass, for his brain to clear up again, the strength to return to his muscles, and this may have been why he wasn't paying attention when the mechanism that operated the bell began to buzz, indicating that the bell was about to start ringing, and he neglected to do what he had been doing ever since he had stolen away up here, namely, instead of running down the stairs to a lower level, and withdrawing into an alcove to protect himself, this time the first striking of the bell was so close, and hit him with such force, and with such dreadful volume, that it nearly knocked him over, he fell to his knees and threw himself away from the bell onto the floor while grabbing his ears in vain, although before the next strike of the bell, he still had enough presence of mind to roll over to one side and he threw himself onto the stairs, his body ricocheting back and forth as he rolled down the stairs, then, still clutching his ears, banging against the wall, he tumbled down into the nave, everything within him was rumbling terribly and hurt, his head wanted to split apart, and he was very dizzy, it was a while until he came to himself, fortunately, though, the noise he'd heard coming from around the altar had not been made by a person but by a rat that had climbed up here, perhaps, from the banks of the Saale, a harmless rat, Florian sat down on the nearest pew, and, still holding his head, he watched as the large animal tried to pull down the light lace covering placed atop the heavy altar cloth—and with it the piece of bread, left there scandalously—he watched as the animal finally succeeded, and fell on the piece of bread; it had only been able to pull down the lace covering by pulling down everything else along with it, including the desired morsel: the cross, the opened Bible on its stand, two candlesticks and four vases, everything, but the rat didn't care that all this was covering it now, it yanked out both itself and the piece of bread from beneath the white lace fabric covering it, never leaving off eating for a moment, it chewed and chewed on the bread, and it wasn't interested in anything, from time to time turning its head here and there, but visibly uninterested in anything else, only devouring the food, displaying no interest in Florian either, although Florian, even in the midst of his great dizziness, knew that the rat had noticed him, but it didn't care, just as Florian didn't care what it was devouring and how it was being devoured, he was struggling still with the nausea and dizziness, which was not easy, he lay down on a pew and he had to stay there, because that first strike of the bell kept on roaring in him for a long time, the rat was almost done with its meal, its tiny mouth—especially compared to the rest of its large body—had gathered up the last crumbs, and jerking its head back and forth, it chose a direction and bolted away on its tiny legs, speedy as the wind, in that direction, Florian lay on the pew until he felt enough strength returning for him to scurry away; a caretaker of the church might come in, having heard the noise, to see if there was some problem, so that before that could happen he staggered out the side door which he had forced open before he started feeling better, and this was not a bad idea because the fresh evening air helped him, and after a few minutes the nausea and dizziness had considerably lessened, and although he did not dare sit down on the ledge of the wall that surrounded the small hill the church stood upon, he did sit down next to it, and he stayed there, protected somewhat from the strong and chilly wind, because there was a chill wind, even though it was May, here in Kana, the mountain air made the evenings and the mornings bitingly cold, and tonight there was a full moon, and the sky was so clear that there wasn't even one cloud above, so that anyone who wished to proceed along the streets unseen would have to think carefully about how to proceed, while Karin hadn't moved from her observation point: she was afraid that if she moved, Florian would become aware of her; she was aware that her plan to lure him out with her presence hadn't worked, as the other was now possessed of uncommon skills, who knew how he'd managed this, this was a fairly surprising development in Florian, who had always come across as blundering, but looking back now, she had to admit that maybe this had always been a part of the package: from this clumsy but hefty figure, the Warrior would one day break out, as she expressed it to herself, so she remained very cautious, thinking it best for the time being merely to observe, to register where Florian was moving, if he was moving around the town, and only to attack when she knew his routes precisely—only that Florian no longer had any routes, he changed his position with complete unpredictability, and he was even more cautious than Karin, at least he seemed to indicate that by spending several days not coming out as she hid in the attic of an abandoned building on Jenaische Straße, she'd used it a few times already in the past, and she took her post up there now as well, because she could more or less follow, from there, any movement in certain sections of the Altstadt, but also the vicinity of the Shopping Center and the Bahnhof, and there seemed to be no trace whatsoever of Florian in the town, it even occurred to her that Florian might have changed strategies, he might be lying low somewhere in the surrounding area as he too was waiting, and only this could explain her relative lack of caution when one day at dawn, she came down to the area behind the Shopping Center, and as she had forgotten to bring any food, she pilfered a few things from the delivery trucks parked there, then, walking toward the train tracks, she intended to leave the area, she was lacking in caution, meaning that she was not as attentive as she should have been, and this was why she only noticed the wretched beast that had already attacked her once when it was already above her head, already plunging down onto her; in the last moment, she jumped away from the blow, once again, it almost dug its claws into her head, Karin knew that was its intent as she jumped to the side, but this time she wasn't completely frozen by shock, she grabbed the pistol from her pocket, undid the safety latch and took aim: she didn't hit the target at first, only on the second shot: the eagle quivered in the air, fell back slightly, then continued to climb, Karin took aim again, expecting to see the eagle plunging to the earth, this time dead, after a few final flaps of its wings, but it merely drifted off to one side, as if avoiding her field of vision, so she could not see it plunging, no, because while it was true that the eagle was losing strength from one meter to the next from its bullet wounds, it held out, it spread its wings, and it began hovering, expending the smallest amount of energy needed for flight, because it had to fly, and it had to fly up, because it wanted to find, as it did find, the place where it could finally descend, Florian didn't budge an inch when the eagle alighted a few meters away from him, and sprawled onto the ground, not even retracting its right wing: they were up on the Dohlenstein, with a clear view of the town, and even though, from this altitude of more than three hundred meters, the movements of the people below could not be followed precisely, it was still good, as Florian could not be seen up here in this area full of caves, in which, due to the favorable weather, he did not have to suffer during the nights as in wintertime in the Marienglashöhle, by day he sat outside as he was doing now, by a lookout point, and he tried to see what he could not see, still he felt that the attempt was worth it, as he was certain that Karin was about to make a significant move, he could sense it, and he would respond, he cast a glance at the eagle bleeding to death by his side, its wounded legs stiffly held out from its body, he saw the lacerated claws on one leg, he saw the blood as it spread out, releasing a small pool around the claws, but he also saw a much larger pool of blood gathering elsewhere, from somewhere around the wings, perhaps the bird's crop had been injured, and from there, with every breath, this puddle grew larger and larger, he looked at it, he turned his gaze back to the town, and he remained there until it had grown completely dark, Florian found a different cave that night, the bird was no longer moving, that was how it spent the night, dead, by the morning it's body was completely stiffened, rising no longer, its crop no longer throbbing, everything around it was mute, and when Florian came out of the cave and sat down next to the eagle, he didn't even look at it, because he was looking at the town to see if Karin was moving around down there somewhere, but he sensed she was not moving, and he was right, because Karin was having breakfast in the pension, Ilona and her husband had fitted it out quite well, she found everything she needed, even antibiotics she could use to prevent the wounds on her head from becoming infected, then she pulled a cap onto her wig, she walked into Kana, once again she slipped into the abandoned house on Jenaische Straße, she had no better ideas just then so she waited, which was not unusual for her, even before, when they were still together in the Burg, if the unit was initiating a sortie, then patience was always needed, and Karin was good at being patient, the others were always rushing ahead to the goal, always champing at the bit like that one time when they had to nab those six scumbag sprayers in Jena, but Karin remained calm and waited until exactly the right moment, and it came together in the end, because she'd been able to round up the six frightened faggot children, of course the Boss handled the interrogations, she wasn't a part of this because it wasn't up her alley, she wasn't good at interrogations but at attacking—not open, helter-skelter missions led by feelings, rage, anger, and muddy thinking, but precision attacks, suitably timed, and for this, patience was required, deliberation, so that she stood to the side, and literally so, the six little sons of bitches were tied up in chairs in the basement of one of their armories, but only after they'd all been thrown on the concrete floor so that the Boss could expend his rage on them, and he kicked them until they couldn't move, water was splashed in their faces to wake them up, they put them on the chairs and tied them up with duct tape, and the interrogation began, if it could be called that when one side poses questions and the other side can't answer, because with each question, a blow was dealt, mainly it was Fritz asking the questions, and Jürgen, the Boss stepped to the back, his face clouded over, wanting to attack again and again, but Karin and Andreas stood in front of him, gently impeding him, and Fritz asked: why did you besmirch everything?! and Andreas dealt a blow, then Andreas asked: what were you doing in Eisenach, *whack*, and in Ohlsdorf, *whack*, and in Wechmar, *whack*, and so it went on, the first one asked, the second one hit, then the second one asked, and the first one hit, until they got tired, the six boys propped up more or less only by the duct tape, then they rested a bit, splashed water on their faces again, and now it was Karin's turn, as she stepped out from the back of the room, she walked in front of the six boys, she looked at them well, as it caused her no problem to examine them and to engrave the features of the six boys into her brain while the blood gushed from their faces, noses, and ears, then she posed questions to the one sitting at the end of the row, but quietly, so that no one else could hear, only the one she questioned, then she took a step forward, and in this way she interrogated each one of the six boys, then she turned around and said only this to the Boss: it wasn't them, she left the basement, she sat down on a stone, lit up a cigarette, and waited for the entire unit to do the same, because in reality patience was her single strength, so that now too her tactics were built on that, and now the only question was: who would hold out longer—Karin knew this would be the decisive factor, and in her opinion, Florian would be the first to show himself because he would want to bring an end to this whole thing, at one point he would suddenly become enraged and try to attack her, but for now he was alone and birdless, no longer with that trained beast at his side, because, as she had strongly presumed, that beast could not have survived: it belonged to him, and without it, he wouldn't have the strength to play this waiting game alone, he would betray himself, walk straight into the trap of time which she, Karin, was setting for him, a trap made out of time, which, as she thought, could only work in her favor, because she still didn't know that Florian had stopped functioning within time a long time ago, and there was no deliberation in his acts, he did not think at all, he had no plans whatsoever, he sat above on the mountain and he looked at Kana, he watched the movements of the cars, and he only had to look to the side to chase away this or that animal trying to approach the golden eagle which had now turned into prey, it was enough for him to cast a glance and they understood: this plunder could not be theirs, the cadaver had shriveled, the large body didn't even look as if there had ever been life within it, and the generally weak, and yet sometimes biting wind caught up the feathers of the right wing, and, if the wind was a bit stronger, it even lifted this wing slightly, as if the wing were beckoning, but then it fell back down next to the cadaver, always back in the same position from which it had just slightly risen, spread out, stretched out, as if it were flying there, one wing stretched out on the ground next to Florian, so that it could still be of assistance to him, protect him, chasing away anyone who might put him in danger, this human being who had only become aware of the eagle in his own way, namely he had accepted its presence alongside him, alive, and he accepted its presence alongside him, dead, and that was all, Florian had other matters to attend to, and he could only focus on that, and when he determined—as did occur one evening—that he would go down to Kana, he already left his backpack in the cave where he had last taken his retreat, because what did he need a backpack for, what did he need a laptop for, he no longer needed anything, he hurried down the L1062, visibly unconcerned whether anyone saw him, and this became ever more obvious as he crossed the bridge into the town, a few cars even slowed down, the people in the cars staring at him, wondering who this hirsute vagrant was, but they didn't recognize him, although it seemed prudent to call the police immediately, even from their cars: a stranger, some kind of enormous forest barbarian, had been sighted at such and such a location, and it seemed he was up to no good, but the police force, ever since they had reduced their numbers in Kana, weren't too interested, and moreover it was Monday, when, according to the old custom of the town, there was no one on duty in the small Polizeistation on Gabelsbergerstraße, there were the two police cars parked in front of the police station with no one inside, the police station was open on Tuesdays and Thursdays, meaning that there were police officers in the town only on these days, not including holidays, and if their presence was absolutely needed at an important soccer match, then they showed up, but now, just because some kind of weird character had sauntered into town, come on already, they put down the telephone, and they made a note of it, but the officer on duty didn't think it necessary to alert anyone, so Florian was able to walk along the streets undisturbed, not counting, of course, the suspicious glances cast his way: old ladies stood there after he had passed by, staring at him for a long time from behind, but he didn't seem to care in the least, clearly, if this was a game, his cards were all on the table, although it wasn't a game, he was deadly serious about exposing himself to Karin, he was offering himself to her, he offered her the possibility of having enough time to deduct his strategy, and Florian didn't stop, he walked all along Bahnhofstraße, casting a mere glance at the Hochhaus, then he turned in front of the Baumarkt, and, as if nothing would be more natural, went into the Grillhäusel, sat down in his usual place, and when a young lad of maybe twenty or twenty-two years asked him from behind the counter what he wanted, he said a Bockwurst and a glass of water, altogether there were four people inside, Florian knew who they were, but he didn't care, just as they clearly had not recognized him, because it so happened that they had not recognized him, they stared at him for a while, but none of the regulars realized: this was Florian, it never would have occurred to them as there were no resemblances at all between the old Florian and this unknown customer, even though the strapping frame—the enormous shoulders—might have given them a clue, but it didn't, because in the eyes of the regulars this figure was strapping in a completely different way, it couldn't be Florian, the face was different, the posture was different, the way he sat, with his legs spread out, as he propped himself up, was different too, there was nothing in this figure that reminded them of Florian, and they didn't even dare to ask who he was, as he didn't create the impression of someone who welcomed inquiries, so they left him alone, once again they began muttering to each other about the Hartz IV benefits being late again and other such matters, Florian was served his Bockwurst and his glass of water, and he ate like an animal, as Hoffmann related later on, but really like an animal, he tore his food apart, and after a couple of bites it already disappeared in his mouth, he panted, and drank up the water in one gulp, then he went over to the server and said he couldn't pay; the boy swallowed once as he said: what?! and he began wringing the tea towel, he wasn't prepared for anything like this; originally, the idea had been that he would only temporarily take over running the Grillhäusel: he would prepare the sausages and fry them if he had to, serve the drinks, and collect the money, but not anything like this; his plans did not include becoming a bartender, he had different plans, he wanted to be a painter, and he wanted to live in Holland, but when his cousin and her husband were found dead outside of Kana, not too far from the town of Altenberg— the authorities had closed down the Grillhäusel, then once again issued permission for it to open—the relatives back home in Transylvania designated him to take over the buffet for now, they put him up with Herr Heinrich, because there was no question of the child living on the premises where that horrific incident had occurred, of course he agreed, but he was unprepared for a provocation like this, because what was he supposed to do now?! the question was written all over his face, he just kept on clutching the dish towel, he puckered his mouth, then he unpuckered it, then he puckered it again, so that while he was trying to figure out what to say, Florian slowly walked out of the Grillhäusel, and nothing happened, the regular customers, especially Hoffmann, immediately began assailing him, why did he let that happen, he was the boss now, everyone pronounced their opinions loudly, this was no way to run a business, if someone orders, they have to pay, what would happen if they did the same thing? what would happen to the Grillhäusel then? which made the boy even more nervous, it was clear that he would be more than happy to throw his tea towel at them and leave for Holland immediately to become an artist, but he just kept on clutching the dish towel, while Florian continued his route, he went all the way to the end of Christian-Eckhardt-Straße, turned to the left, and for a while he continued on the B88, passing through the town, walking next to the cars occasionally honking their horns at him, then he walked up to the Altstadt, and he walked the streets for hours, and here no one recognized him either, no one, but no one thought that this might have been the lost Florian, because if they saw him, they were afraid, and if they had enough time, they quickly crossed to the other side of the street, then they kept looking back to wonder who that was; Herr Volkenant, as people told him what kind of character had passed in front of the post office, ran out to have a look, and not only did he not recognize Florian, he stated directly, as he went back into the post office, expressing his displeasure by shaking his head: well, things are looking really good here, people, because now it seems that not only are they scaring us with this pandemic or whatever the hell it is raising its head in our own protected Thuringia, but now we have wolves in human skin, a comment which was not unconditionally appreciated as it reminded everyone of the latest NABU newsletter addressed to the residents of Kana, in which they were informed: there was no reason to be afraid, the situation was such that in Germany, presently, more than one hundred complete wolf packs living in X number of pairs and as X number of solitary wolves had been sighted, all of them coexisting peacefully in the vicinity of humans; and no one realized why NABU was suddenly so focused on Kana again—coming around, giving their lectures, writing their newsletters, and exclusively for them, the residents of Kana—of course, people suspected something behind all this, but they couldn't discern the real reason, which was a bad conscience following a badly botched experiment: NABU wanted to hush up a failed research project in which they planned to collect new data concerning the wondrous auditory and olfactory facilities of wolves, and the Erfurt NABU team—three researchers, including Tamás Ramsthaler—had kept the project with its modest budget under wraps, namely they had decided to catch two wolves, whose identification chips were switched, and their eyes were bandaged shut, so that with the help of electronic tags, NABU would follow and observe the two wolves to see how they would orient themselves by means of only hearing and scent, but during several phases of the process, mistakes were made, one of which the researchers only discovered after the project had been initiated, the more serious errors only becoming evident a good while later: of course, they had been counting on the animals, who'd been tranquilized and then woken up, to try to remove the simple medical eye patches, but they hadn't counted on how—because they'd used an extraordinarily strong adhesive on the depilated bones around the eyes—the two wolves would scratch off the adhered eye patches *no matter what it took*, precisely, they wouldn't give up until they had gotten rid of them, so that when they were released, and had gotten a certain distance from their torturers, they began to scratch wildly from their eyes with their claws that which wasn't supposed to be there, because it was horrific to them not to be able to see, and they wanted, with horrific force, to see, although the adhesive also turned out to be horrifically strong, so that they scratched and they scratched, and despite the ever more horrific pain, the two wolves scratched their eyes bloody, with the end result that the both of them were blind, but for now NABU only knew that the planned tracking hadn't worked out as the two animals had also scratched out the new electronic tags from beneath the skin of their left cheekbones, so the wolves were lost and although NABU searched for them, they couldn't find them, and when they realized what had happened, they gathered in Erfurt and vowed to keep it all under wraps, but Tamás Ramsthaler, due to his scientific conscience, as he expressed it, and in the hopes of a possible later intervention, recommended that since the two animals had originated from a wolf pack originally under observation in Kana, they should try to reinforce the connection with the residents of that town, provide them with information, and perhaps it wouldn't seem so strange to be showing up regularly so that they could, in this way, survey the area to see if the wolves had returned, although the chief unspoken cause of their worry was the prospect of the specter of the wolves' bandaged eyes appearing before the residents of Kana, Tamás Ramsthaler did not mention this to his two colleagues, he didn't have to, they were all aware that this had been a primitive procedure, unscientific, using bad methodology, so that they feared exposure of having employed unauthorized procedures in an experiment, in short, they were silent as the grave on this matter as they went to Kana, surveying the surrounding mountains and collecting their data, and of course they wrote their newsletters intended for the locals who weren't too happy to see them showing up again, because each individual communiqué left them feeling frightened, just as now a similar feeling ran across them having heard the postmaster's half-joking comments, which, in a short amount of time, were already being transmitted from mouth to mouth, and everyone who heard it added their own two cents, as did Dr. Henneberg, who remarked: well now, that's all we needed, werewolves!!! and he carelessly mentioned this to his wife in the dining room as they were finishing up lunch and he called his practice to tell them that there would be no consultation hours this afternoon while he checked to make sure that the smaller windows looking out onto the Porcelain Factory were shut tight, which until now had only been fitted with bars, and no, the windows weren't shut tight, he repeated, even more carelessly, to his wife, who, wringing her hands, followed him, and she kept asking him: why, my dear, do you think they're here already?! she kept repeating, but hearing her idiotic and exasperating questions, he stopped saying what he wanted to say—unfortunately this was his life, he never could discuss what he wanted to at home, but not only at home, he had no true friends with whom he could discuss these matters, and such occasions cropped up the least of all in his dentist's office, where, from the frightened eyes of his patients waiting to see him, he never read anything good; let alone have a conversation with them?! he cried out within himself, pour out one's heart to them?! everyone just always wants to run away from me, this goddamned life with these pliers and drills and excavators and spatulas and root lifters and scissors, to hell with all of that, sometimes it burst out of him, and only

Melanie, his assistant, was the witness to these outbursts, because Melanie understood, she understood the doctor deeply, but this only made him even more ill-tempered, because darn it, it was exactly Melanie that he didn't want to understand him, anyone else, just not Melanie with her sorrowful, sympathetic, and moist eyes; bulging, they gaped at him from behind her nine-diopter glasses, and when the doctor had one of his outbursts, she was overtaken by a motherly feeling, she would have been happy to stroke Dr. Henneberg's head, take him into her lap, and she would have just caressed and caressed him until the end of time so that at the end she would confess that she felt more toward the doctor than was strictly permitted, but she didn't want any trouble, she didn't want to be a home-wrecker, well, and that is why all this remained shut up within Dr. Henneberg throughout the years, nay decades, he drilled teeth, he filled them and filled them, he treated decaying, stinking roots, and he pulled teeth and he pulled them, but nothing or no one ever helped him in his solitude, and now—thanks to a patient that ill fortune had brought into his path on his way home from lunch—now that he had suddenly heard about these werewolves, he was filled with such vehement bitterness that, after he closed the small windows facing the Porcelain Factory, he escaped from his wife into the living room where he immediately poured himself three fingers' worth of Rhöntropfen, the famous stomach bitters, in his view a truly excellent calling card from the past, because Meininger Rhöntropfen is the peak, my dear, as he would explain to his wife in one of his more cheerful moments, he screwed the top off and poured himself a few more drops, then knocked it back in one gulp, he sat down in the nearest armchair, an imitation of a Chesterfield, and he tried to do so as if he didn't realize that his wife was standing behind the door to the living room and waiting, because she didn't dare come in, because she knew what would happen: she stood there, crying softly, waiting for him to say something, well, what kind of a life is this?! Dr. Henneberg asked himself, overcome by bitterness, then he leaned forward to pick up a small hand mirror from the small table beside the armchair, which, just as the armchair itself, evoked the Victorian age—the epoch most dear to his heart—he pulled up his lip and bared his teeth, grinning into the mirror, then with his index finger, he tapped the upper fifth, because it seemed to have gotten more sensitive recently, but no, nothing, he leaned back in the armchair, and he poured himself another glass, this time about four fingers, he took a few sips and then leaned back again, he sighed and looked toward the window, and he determined, sadly, that Maytime or not, it was still getting dark too early, and in truth the sun was setting quickly over the winding path of the Saale, perhaps because of the mountains which certainly let the light in so tardily coming from the east, and just as surely shut down the light too abruptly from the west, they hadn't had a May like this ever before, Frau Ringer established, but only to herself, she didn't dare mention this to her husband, because remarks such as these had an invariably deflating effect on him; as for Ringer's view of the situation—and he did speak to his wife about this, if he spoke at all—and he meant this not merely in a political or societal sense, but in the overall sense as well—his view was that they had lost the battle, and not only that, he added, but maybe even the war as well, because they were coming up from the sewers—as always occurred in these historical pauses, they emerged, ruining everything, destroying and debasing whatever they touched, degrading everything that was valuable, fouling what was sacred for others, spreading a disease against which there was no vaccine, because it was not the pandemic that was the danger, but instead this infection, the main symptom of which was that people showed the worst side of themselves, and they were weak, immeasurably weak and immeasurably idiotic, and what can we do about this, Ringer pointed at himself, and usually, at this point, he did not continue his thoughts, like someone who couldn't say anything more than this, and didn't even need to, because if what he was speaking about wasn't clear before, it wouldn't become so now, and he sank back into that apathetic frame of mind, and on his face was that vacant expression which worried his wife so much, because it seemed to indicate that he, Ringer, was not really alive anymore, because this wasn't life, Frau Ringer said to her girlfriend as she sipped her coffee in the Herbstcafé, it's more like, you know, when a person is spending their last days in the crypt, I don't see an exit, and she just shook her head bitterly, of course Frau Feldmann tried to cheer her up, and although she would've been more than happy to say that her life with her own husband was no piece of cake, she held her tongue, because why should she lament, why should she burden her friend when this friend had so much more cause for complaint than she, because she really did have so many more reasons: she and her husband were the first ones to be attacked by that beast in the mountains, then Ringer was suspected of murder, and finally he was having this breakdown, because he blamed himself for everything that had happened in Kana and everywhere else, although there was no reason for that, Herr Feldmann objected at home when his wife told him about the situation, why Ringer, he said, he is purely a man of principle who, during his entire life, only sought the good, just as I always only seek an adequate harmony when I am transcribing a difficult piece by the Beach Boys, because look—he showed her the score on the music stand on the piano—here, for example, is the famous "I Get Around," I've been working on that, my heart, for two days already now, and I really don't want to boast, because I can deal with Bach, but not with these complicated, refined, wondrous harmonic progressions, characteristic only of the greatest; no and no, because you know, I somehow try to build in what the chorus is doing while preserving the melody, but it's very difficult, Herr Feldmann pursed his lips, and once again he was immersed in his work, because he considered music to be work, for he loved everything that was music as others loved their work, and for him it could be anything from classical to pop, he saw no difference between them, sitting down at the piano with the same devotion as if he were designing a bridge or a matchbox, and he said: I am starting work now, and that's what he called it when his wife, around noon, informed him in a cheerful voice that lunch was ready, and he would say, oh, my heart, just one minute, just one minute, I'm working, and Frau Feldmann waited happily and patiently, and she did not scold him for having to keep the meal warm—for it would surely cool off—but she waited and she kept the meal warm, and so they lived in the greatest of harmony by which Frau Feldmann meant to say, when she brought this up from time to time at the end of one of their loving everydays, that perhaps there were harmonies in Herr Feldmann's piano and in his scores, but certainly this harmony was present in their lives as well, and as long as there was a lock on their door, she would announce, as another frightening rumor reared its head, then I'm not afraid, because for her this was the guarantee that nothing could ever happen to them, she loved the lock on their front door, not only that, she could speak of how it wasn't just one lock, but a thorough, well-thought-out locking system installed by a clever locksmith from Bad Berka, a master of his trade, and when they had renovated the villa they were able, to their greatest fortune, to call upon him, and this locksmith installed a combination of locks in place of the old such that, as she put it, even a Soviet-made T-34 tank wouldn't be able to break through, and Frau Feldmann, after the horrific events at the gas station and especially after news of the three murders, sometimes crept out of bed at night, she always waited until Herr Feldmann began snoring, and she crept out, and at first she pulled on the locks to see if they would hold, and they held very well, then she caressed them, she loved them, well, and that was all, but the importance of locks was overestimated in Kana, because now the amateur locksmiths were showing up, but the old professionals showed up as well, who, making convincing arguments, installed locking bars—vertical and crosswise—into the residents' doors, thus assuring them complete protection, as these had become the bywords in Kana and all of Thuringia—"protection, personal security"—and this is also what the police officers advised to everyone who turned to them; although the police were unconvinced that these locks would protect anyone, psychologically, they were important, and so this is what they advised, for the sake of personal protection: have modern locks installed, forget about the old ways, install such-and-such a precise, modern locking system on every door and window, and turn to the future, because it was here already, the residents of Kana were told on the information hotlines, because the traffic on these hotlines was ever increasing, at first in Erfurt, but elsewhere too: Jena, Suhl, Gotha, and in Weimar, even in smaller towns such as Eisenach or Ohrdruf or Wechmar and so on, the number of people giving advice on these telephone lines had to be increased, as the usual staff couldn't cope with the onslaught, weekend shifts were made mandatory, but even so, that wasn't enough, they had to take on people not trained as police officers, employed only to staff the hotlines, so that while they managed, they were palpably overburdened, people living in Thuringia were used to having to wait, although they were less used to having to listen to one ad after another as they waited on the phone, after which the line usually broke off and they had to dial the number again, well, never mind, said the Deputy, as he dialed the number again, because he had something to report again, and his persistent calls did end up bearing fruit, because he was summoned to Erfurt where he stated that Florian's particular character had always given him pause, because the two extreme poles of this character were somehow never in harmony with each other, namely— he leaned in closer to the female police officer in the Erfurt South police station—between Florian's extraordinary physical strength and his seemingly gentle nature a precipice gaped, it gaped, he repeated, I'm telling you, which was something he'd always reflected upon, but to tell the truth, he'd never been suspicious of Florian as it had never occurred to him that he was dealing with a two-faced man, a so-called Janus, a fact he now saw clearly, and that is why he considered it necessary to fulfill his responsibilities as a citizen, namely that he wished to call the attention of the authorities to the fact that they should not be looking for an inveterate, coarse, aggressive, red-handed murderer, but exactly the opposite—he hoped his comments would have some impact on the direction of the investigation—because no, they should be looking for a child-faced, good-natured, seemingly thoroughly harmless boy, a little afraid and a little ashamed, and the Deputy would have said more, but the policewoman lost her patience, cutting him off: we're talking about a serial killer here, she said, and she finished taking his statement, the Deputy signed it, and the policewoman sent him away and told him that they might need him later on, so he should pay attention, keep his eyes open, and contact them with whatever he saw, but only if it was something concrete, the policewoman emphasized, the police force needed concrete facts, not opinions and not intuition, only pure, tangible facts, well, she said, you can report to us again but only then, and the Deputy promised he would do so, and he went home deep in thought, and already on the train he greatly regretted not having been able to express himself as he should have, the sentences he had uttered whirled around in his brain, as well as those that expressed the essence of what he had to say with so much more precision; he would have been genuinely happy to get off the train and go back to Erfurt to emend this or that part of his statement, if the authorities might be so kind, but then he gave up the idea, not wanting to overburden them, as he'd also overheard, at the beginning of his statement, the rather voluptuously endowed policewoman mention that they had a good lead, which was not too far from the truth, namely that in addition to receiving reports like the Deputy's—unfortunately worthless—another resident of Kana had shown up at the Jena police station not too long before the Deputy did with new information as to where a certain

Florian Herscht could be found; his whereabouts? the officer on duty asked, yes, came the answer, are you certain? yes, came the reply, and with that the person was led into a smaller office where it was registered in the police record that a certain Thomas Hoffmann, resident of Kana, claimed, pertaining to the whereabouts of Florian Herscht, who was subject to an arrest warrant, to have knowledge of his current location, that namely the wanted man was in Kana, where he had been for days, his appearance completely altered and in a state of disguise, the person making the report stated, and yet he had recognized him with one hundred percent certainty, which was not entirely true, as he was the one designated to make the report, because it had been Herr Heinrich who had first noticed there was something familiar about that stranger who came into the Grillhäusel one day, but Herr Heinrich did not identify him at first, it merely occurred to him he hadn't seen that face and that kisser—as he expressed it—before, no, but the eyes yes, he'd seen those eyes before somewhere, the first thing that came to his mind was a TV series, as he told the others, he was honestly thinking of the eyes of Gojko Mitić, well, but then when that stranger started walking around here and there in the town, and he bumped into him again, there was something in his gait that was not reminiscent of Gojko Mitić, the famous German Winnetou, but even then it didn't occur to him, but only that evening or the next day, he didn't exactly remember as he was getting ready to lie down, stretching out his limbs, he groaned, turned over on his side, closed his eyes, and then! then, he said in the Grillhäusel, it came to him all at once why those eyes and that gait were so familiar, well, because they were the eyes and the gait of Florian, he raised his voice, and the customers in the Grillhäusel burst out as one: come on now, not Florian! it couldn't be him! but, but it was, Herr Heinrich insisted, he wasn't mistaken, and he had a special ability: once he saw a pair of eyes, he never forgot them, and on top of that there was the gait, in a word, he raised his beer, that strange character was Florian himself, and he took a gulp of the beer and fell silent, not being the wordy type, while the Grillhäusel turned into a beehive, at first filled with incredulous voices, and as Herr Heinrich maintained his silence, at first only Hoffmann came and sat closer to him, saying that he'd also had the same thought, then others began to join in, so that within a few minutes a unanimous opinion had formed around Herr Heinrich, and, as no one had any work to do just at that moment, it only remained to decide who should tell the authorities, and Herr Heinrich suggested Hoffmann, who undertook this task with pride and modestly accepted a beer in exchange, after which there was nothing else to do than to travel to the city, as they called Jena—as opposed to Kana—and convey these latest developments, once again the police showed up in Kana—they hadn't been there for a while—at first blockading the town, stationing police cars with two officers at every exit leading out of Kana, then they began to trawl through Kana in three stages, the first time without result, as they simply had no luck, although once the residents saw the police presence, especially in such large numbers, they disappeared from the streets; Florian, just at that moment, was not moving, although he wasn't even hiding, he was sitting in front of the fitness-center entrance on a chair that had been left behind when the owner had shut down the business for good, he sat there eating a piece of bread stolen from the back entrance of the Netto, he broke off a piece and chewed it thoroughly and swallowed, then he broke off a second piece; from here, where he was sitting, he had a view of the rail-crossing gate, this rail-crossing gate was one of two on the tracks running through the town, the first one was by the Rosengarten and the second one was here, although recently, both of them operated on a similar principle: from time to time both would begin to make a buzzing sound, then, creaking, the gate would be lowered, and then they waited and waited for a train to come either from this direction, that direction, or either direction, it didn't matter, although generally nothing at all came passing through, the rail gates waited and waited, then after a while, after eight or ten or who even knew how many minutes—sorrowfully, because no train had come from anywhere—the gate would begin to raise, as it did now here too, and Florian was watching this; the closest police unit, however, did not come out this way because they were combing through the area in the vicinity of the house of the first victim, then they took up an observation post in front of the house, the Deputy, seeing them, hurried out: the entire day he'd been watching from his window, and he told them who he was, held out his ID card, and even though they weren't interested, he mentioned that if they were looking for Florian Herscht, the wanted murderer, this Florian Herscht had been a resident in his building, and he had much information to impart about him, although there was no point as the two police officers didn't seem interested, because after he responded negatively to their query as to whether or not he'd seen the wanted man now, they sent him home so as not to impede their search; the Deputy returned to the Hochhaus in an agitated state, and he didn't enter the building immediately, but then they motioned to him not to remain outside in the yard, so obliged to comply, he went inside and quickly seated himself next to the window from where he had a good view in two directions from his corner apartment, but nothing was happening on Ernst-Thälmann-Straße, the two police officers just stood around, a police car pulled up and brought them coffee, that was it, and for the most part this was the situation at other points in the town as well, the dragnet was wrapped up for the time being, and because they hadn't found the wanted man, more observation posts were set up, the Deputy having a good view of one of them, although the hours passed and Florian was seen nowhere, because he was just sitting on the chair by the entrance of the former fitness center, sitting motionlessly, the rail gates tried again, raising and lowering themselves a few more times, but no train arrived from either the south or the north,

Florian gazed in front of himself and he waited, and all of Kana was waiting too, to see what would happen, because if from nothing else, they could tell from the altered demeanor of the police officers—now visibly nervous—that they suspected something big was going to happen, although nobody knew what, opinions were shared that were vague on the details, most residents betting on packs of wolves about to attack the town, they called NABU, but NABU had no information about this, although when more than fifty calls had been logged, Tamás Ramsthaler decided that he would not go out to Kana tomorrow as planned, but today, so many people were calling that there must be something afoot; his first stop was at the Revierförster's house, who opened his door happily to him, thinking he was here to buy honey, but Tamás Ramsthaler, after handing the Revierförster a medical mask, divested him of his illusions when he said that the residents of Kana were convinced a pack of wolves was about to attack the town, and did the Revierförster know anything about this? no, he didn't know anything about this, came the reply, he'd not seen any wolf traces since the sighting of the last pack, and not only that, but perhaps NABU themselves would have a better idea of where to find the wolves as they supposedly were publishing, on their website, exact and updated information concerning the most recent sightings, and, the Revierförster added, if he remembered well, in their last bulletin, NABU had reassured the residents of Kana that although there were wolves present in Germany, they were decisively not present in Thuringia, or very sparsely, the closest large territory where packs might be found was Sachsen, or was he mistaken? the Revierförster asked sharply, and Tamás Ramsthaler shook his head, no, of course not, his information was correct, and he was happy that the Revierförster read their bulletins regularly, he was merely following up after having received many reports to see if there was any, and he would emphasize this—any basis to the rumors, because he had to investigate, at NABU they always had to investigate as their task was to peacefully supervise the newly resumed connection between wolf and man, well, you just keep on supervising that, the Revierförster turned his back on Tamás Ramsthaler and he closed the gate, then, grumbling, he went back into the house: he wasn't even here to buy honey! then, almost immediately, he turned around and went to the back building to count how many jars were still left from last year, even though he had done so only three days previously, and well: there was still *a lot*, the corners of the Revierförster's mouth turned down in dissatisfaction, he recounted the jars: in addition to the seventeen half-liter and the five liter jars of honey left over from last year, he had to face the sad fact that there were more than eleven jars of blackthorn jelly, although it wasn't good for the jelly to sit there for so long, because the Revierförster preferred natural methods, and so did not use any chemical substances for preserving, although this entailed a certain danger—as he knew well—that sooner or later, no matter how thorough and clean and careful he was, that damned mold would start forming on the surface of the jam, already once last winter he had removed all the mold nicely, but clearly it was just a matter of time, because the mold would not keep a frightened distance, but reappear, and then he could toss out the whole lot, it was no wonder if he sat dejected in his kitchen all day; in his sorrow he drank four bottles of beer, his wife hovered around him as if her presence might somehow reduce the number of beers he was consuming, because she couldn't say anything, this was the unspoken agreement between them, they could have different opinions on Marx but not beer, although it was pretty impudent how that woman was hovering around him today, although what could she do, too much was too much, four bottles! beer wasn't for free, her economizing soul screamed within, and what would happen to them if he drank four bottles of beer or even more every day, she flared up, and her husband heard her: what's that, now? he snapped, nothing, nothing, the woman mumbled, walking out of the kitchen and leaving him alone, because what could she do?! meanwhile the Förster took out a fifth bottle, because those twenty-two jars of honey were really a lot, they had already gotten cloudy, moreover, the process of crystallization had already started in some of the jars, if he couldn't sell them, he buried his head in his hands, the honey would turn rock solid, and then no one would buy it, and to be sure the residents of Kana were not in the mood for buying honey right now, many still had the jars they'd bought from the Förster in previous years, they wouldn't say it wasn't tasty, it was tasty, they noted, if it came up in conversation, it was just *a lot*, he kept foisting his honey on them, this was the general consensus, the Revierförster took advantage of how we needed to get news from him to palm off all this honey on us, and now here it is, and what are we supposed to do with all this honey? we can't stuff the children full with it every single day, and now it's spring, and it will be winter again, when all the same a little bit of honey is good against a sore throat or a cold, but until then it might solidify, and indeed, it was going to solidify, so that no one knew what to do about this honey, although it was good to deal with these questions at least for a few minutes, and not with what was truly threatening them, because the rumors—why were there police again in the town, and why were they so agitated?—once again the rumors took off in the most variegated directions, the wolves slowly withdrew into the background as the majority assumed the police were operating with new information, meaning they'd set up camp here again because there was something they wanted to *prevent*, but the residents of Kana still weren't too pleased about this renewed police presence as it tended to create the impression that no matter what these police were planning, it wasn't going to lead anywhere, meaning that anything could happen to anyone at any time and for any reason, as if the police were always only trudging after events when it was already too late, when the Aral station had already exploded, the Nazis were already murdered, the wolf had already mauled Ringer and his wife, and so on, conjecture was abundant, only the Deputy wasn't conjecturing, he knew what was going on, but he uttered not a word to anyone, he did not betray whom the authorities were pursuing, he kept it to himself so that in this way too, he could aid in the investigation, only that it was difficult to consider with whom he had lived here under one roof, if living in the Hochhaus could be described as being under one roof, but never mind, the main thing, he thought, was that he had let himself get so close to this two-faced psychopath, exposing himself to such danger that it made his skin crawl, he sat next to the window the entire day, watching the events outside, although well, these weren't events, and he thought about how this Florian could have even murdered him, how many times had he been in his apartment! how many times could he have thrown him out of that seventh-floor window if he had wanted to! he was strong enough for that, no question, and yet he had treated him as one of his most intimate friends!!! how could he have been so unsuspecting?! the Deputy tried and he tried to see the red-handed murderer in Florian, but somehow it didn't work, so he did what he had to do, namely he had reported him to the authorities in a proper and timely fashion, but to think about him, to imagine him in his mind's eye, to invoke his bearing, his gait, his smile, his gaze, his voice, and to reach the conclusion that this Florian was a doctorjekyllandmisterhyde was difficult, it is decidedly difficult for me, he explained to Pförtner, shrugging his shoulders to show how difficult it was, and no, in my opinion, this child could not be a murderer, I can envision a wild animal committing these deeds, but not Florian! and Pförtner remained silent, because he knew what the Deputy was talking about, the police came to see him at the time of the first investigation to confirm the Deputy's report, he knew who they were looking for, apart from the fact that he considered Florian to be an idiot, he had no other particular impressions of him, but as far as he was concerned, he could be a murderer, he didn't know him well as he hardly ever saw him, so why would he doubt the words of the police? and so he was silent, at the very most nodding from time to time when the Deputy brought up this topic in the great nights of Kana, but the porter did not state his own opinion, he let the Deputy talk it out of himself, and that was all, for his own part he would be tranquil once the whole thing was over, he was rooting for the police to finally nab this criminal and close this affair, he always liked any conflict to be settled quickly, because he loved peace, he loved tranquility, for everything to be undisturbed, for every day to be like the one before, and so he was not too shaken when the news came that it was over, the case was closed, the police were withdrawing, and those beautiful, quiet, tranquil evenings could now return, as in that regard most Kana residents shared Pförtner's view— especially now when MDR-Thuringia had begun broadcasting the so-called daily case numbers: the most important thing was order, balanced, peaceful, tranquil, the undisturbed and timeless uniformity of the days, if this was obtained, then nothing could disturb life, that is, nothing except for these new developments on the health front, because the residents of Kana were more afraid of that than any catastrophe, most important was for everything on the health front to be in order, they stressed, as they listened to the caseload numbers broadcast daily on MDR-Thuringia, so that this was usually the first question: when they asked someone *wie geht es dir*, what they really wanted to know was how the interlocutor was doing on the health front; they didn't inquire *wie geht es Ihnen* or *wie geht es dir?* out of habit, this was not a mere greeting as in so many other countries, but here, in Thuringia, and perhaps in the entire Federal Republic, it was a way of finding out how a person was doing on the health front, inquiries which were not actually intended as a way of asking about the other's health, but which instead were intended to divert the conversation onto the topic of health itself, because in reality the questioner was only and exclusively interested in his own state of health, quite often the answer to the question went right over his head, and the questioner could hardly wait to start talking about how things were for him, how he had this or that, or if the other person began to talk about how things weren't going well for himself on the health front, then the questioner would reply that everything was fine with him or that nothing at all was fine with him, and without even waiting—because compared to his own situation, it didn't matter how the other person's health was—the questioner launched into a detailed discussion of his own state of health, so accordingly: peace and health, more precisely health and peace; in Kana, and perhaps in the entire Federal Republic, this formed the basis of all exchange of views concerning existence, and everything else was left to the children, the youths, or the—generally speaking—naive, those who did not recognize what was essential, to the fanatics forcefully striving toward some so-called grand goal, all the while forgetting that forcefully striving for some grand goal was to no avail if things weren't in order on the health front, as, for example, what happened to Ringer and Feldmann and the Deputy and Jessica, who fell victim to a series of rapidly unfolding tragic events, of course, each case was somewhat different, that is to say very different, for Ringer's wife found him one day in the nicely repainted summer kitchen, where, because of his depression, he had hanged himself, Herr Feldmann and the Deputy were both felled by sudden brain hemorrhages, and Jessica ended up a young victim of unjust fate, because in the prime of her life she perished in an automobile accident as she was driving back with her husband from Dresden from the premier of an Imre Kálmán operetta, so it could be seen that there were great differences between all these cases, and yet these instances of death occurring in such close proximity to each other seemed to point toward some something in life, as if some kind of organizing principle or frightening interrelation were responsible for the respective times of their deaths, although it wasn't, it was just that they all happened to die on subsequent days, the three funeral parlors were pleased because they had already been greatly vexed by the fact that apart from the two Brazilians, as they called them—who'd been buried by the Boss himself, meaning that he hadn't hired the local funeral homes, but entrusted the coffins and the other arrangements to his own people—the deceased, in recent times, had all been taken out of Kana and laid to rest elsewhere, but now, in the case of these four, the relatives had to order a coffin or an urn from them, which of course did not mean that the fortunes of the Hartung or Beyer or Aschenbach funeral parlors suddenly rose greatly in the world, no, you couldn't say that, but it seemed things would be picking up, because "troubles never come singly," as the local saying went, and therefore the three funeral directors hoped for and counted on an augmentation in the overall number of deceased, a number to be determined, of course, by its own natural frequency, although for the time being they were still preoccupied with waiting to find out which one of them would get the order, would the grieving families turn to Hartung or Beyer or Aschenbach, and unfortunately, they all went to Hartung, it was noted in fury at the premises of both Beyer and Aschenbach, the relatives of all four went to Hartung, but why?! to put matters frankly, no one at Beyer or Aschenbach perceived the relatives' decision, if they could express it this way, as *true to life*, because why Hartung, why exactly him, how did the dead get any better treatment at his place than with us?! they didn't understand, and they kept on not understanding until they met up on the day of Ringer's funeral, he was the first to be buried, and they realized that Hartung had most likely employed unethical means and that his maneuvering for the sake of unmerited economic advantage was directly criminal, because it could not have occurred otherwise, and Beyer and Aschenbach were only all the more convinced of this when they found out the next day that both Feldmann and the Deputy had already been buried by Hartung, and on the third day Jessica Volkenant was buried by them as well, where was the justice here?! the four deceased had been buried with unusual haste, despite that, in the case of Ringer, there had been some cavils on the part of the authorities, because depression or no depression, someone had taken his life by his own hand, and the police had to carry out an investigation, but after the widow, in her greatest sorrow, but also with maximum decisiveness, demanded a hasty cremation, the Erfurt head of investigations made an exception for her, moreover taking into account that he had been called by the Staatsschutz and was asked to meet the widow's demands, and to issue the papers for the authorization of the funeral without delay, so that Ringer was cremated only a couple of days after his death, and after this Jessica did not have to wait very long, she was the second one, if we look at the sequence of these funerals, and Jessica had to thank, for her second place in this list, the fact that her husband could simply not accept her death, as not a hair on his head had been touched in the accident, although he was in the car with her, driving, but when he came to himself after the drastic collision and got out of the car, he began, in panic, rushing around, because Jessica wasn't next to him in the passenger seat, the car door was ripped away on that side: Jessica should have been there, next to him, and she wasn't, and Herr Volkenant couldn't find her anywhere, he ran in front, he ran in back, he tore at his hair like someone about to go mad, but there was no Jessica and no and no, Jessica had vanished, and when the police arrived and found her in a ditch next to the highway, a good fifteen meters behind the spot where the collision had occurred, and they told him that they had found her and that he had to identify the body, Herr Volkenant could not identify her, and he said it wasn't her, because the corpse was completely mangled, there was nothing left of the face, indeed it was difficult to see anything of Jessica in this ravaged tangle of flesh and bones, and Herr Volkenant could not see her, he merely wept and he asked: *what shall I do now?! what shall I do now?!* and of course the police officers partially understood and partially didn't understand, and they put Herr Volkenant, still weeping, into one of the ambulances that had shown up, they took him to a medical clinic in Jena, and although he was dosed there with various kinds of tranquilizers, none of them had any effect, they only made him fall asleep, when he woke up, the doctors saw they had made no progress, because Herr Volkenant looked around and began to weep again, and repeated: *what shall I do now?! what shall I do now?!* and so they let him go, they didn't know what to do with him, because they had brought him out of his shock, but they didn't know what to do with his weeping, there was no medicine for that, he just wept and wept, the neighbors couldn't fall asleep because of the sound, because the Volkenants' apartment, above the post office, was separated on both sides from the neighbors by thin walls lacking sound insulation, everything was audible, so the neighbors told whomever they could that something had to be done with this Volkenant, because they had no nights or days, but especially the nights were difficult, because he never stopped crying, and this was not a state they could bear, the neighbors said in the Rathaus, then at the police station, then to Anita Ehrlich, the psychologist, who had recently, and justifiably, grown very popular, but everyone just shrugged their shoulders, there was nothing they could do, there was no cure for weeping and it was not regulated by any kind of law, so that the unhappy situation was finally resolved by Herr Hartung himself when he brought out Jessica and she became the second one to be buried, and this proved to be expedient, because after the funeral, Herr Volkenant, just as explosively as he had begun weeping after the collision, fell silent, he just stopped and grew mute, well, at least it's quiet now, the neighbors living on either side of him breathed a sigh of relief, and from that point on there was a great silence in the post office too, for a long time the residents of Kana thought twice about paying their bills at the post office or sending off that package of home-baked pastries to the children, because this silence from Herr Volkenant was just as hard to bear as his weeping after Jessica's death; he only spoke one more time, when one morning at dawn, he was sorting the letters to be delivered by the letter carrier, and a letter turned up in his hand and he was visibly shaken when he saw the name of the sender and addressee: the envelope was addressed to Herr Herscht, but with no precise address, only the town and the postal code; the sender was Angela Merkel, with a postbox listed as the return address, Herr Volkenant stared at it for a while, then he turned over the envelope, he turned it over again, and he only muttered to himself: what am I supposed to do with this now?! in the end, he put the letter into a bast-fiber box bearing the label "undeliverable," and this was the last sentence that ever left his mouth, no one ever heard his voice again, the letter carrier, of course, spread the news far and wide, so that there was something to talk about in the town, namely, the days had once again become lively, moreover the weather was getting better and better, it was mid-May, with above-freezing temperatures at dawn and far higher temperatures than usual in daytime, the trees burst into leaf, the petunias planted on Bahnhofstraße and around Sankt Margarethenkirche bloomed beautifully, everything around the Herbstcafé and the Rosengarten and the banks of the Saale and on the mountains was covered with green, everything became green, nature took back everything it had lost hold of last autumn, as the mayor expressed it in a public announcement in which he summed up these May days, and he also announced that the intolerable succession of events had reached their end, and in that spirit, the police officers were pulled out of the town, which itself was obvious, because a few days before this announcement was posted, the residents of Kana were seeing ever fewer police officers on duty, until finally the last one disappeared, altogether taking about three or four days, and this, as well as the general tone of the announcement, might have reassured the residents of Kana that they had nothing to fear now—only Karin was on her guard, and if she came into Kana every night, before the break of day she was already back in the pension near

Altenberg where she didn't have too much cause for concern, altogether she'd had to hide out only once before returning to the house, this was after the authorities, clearly with the help of a search dog, had dug up the bodies, they searched the building, and the cops sealed up the locks here as well, but that was all, sealed locks posed no problem, moreover, they meant much more security, for who would suspect a murderer of hiding out here, for she was spending the days in here, and at night she was out in the town, while Florian did exactly the same but in reverse, spending his days in the town, hoping his presence would lure Karin out, and during the nights retreating to the mountains, but nothing, Karin was not showing herself, namely, due to a strange twist of fate, they kept missing each other, until that point when one of them caught up with the other, or the other caught up with the first one, it would have been hard to do justice to this chain of events, just as Frau Ringer waited in vain for justice, because she hoped that after Ringer's complete collapse and death, her own life too would draw to a close, but this didn't happen, instead something completely unexpected did, because of course the whole thing began with dread, because she had lived in dread of what might happen, of Ringer actually doing this, she had never really believed it would happen, and yet when it did happen, she felt a strange strength surging in her soul, everyone—and especially the relatives from Zwickau, who wished the widow to hell— thought that she would be the one to collapse now, but no, she triumphed over the temptations of the abyss into which she almost plunged on those first two days, because to see her beloved spouse as he hung from a horrific beam, his tongue dangling out the side of his mouth, there were many who would have become completely debilitated, immediately choosing to follow their beloved, but for some unknown reason, her life had been saved, and this wasn't due to Frau Feldmann, no, although she had to admit that without her everything would have been much more difficult, but instead a kind of defiance arose in her: she would not give up, she would remain alive, not only would she remain alive, but she would seek that which might guide her to the meaning of existence, so that when she was released from the clinic in Jena, where her treatment had lasted only two days, and she came home, immediately after the funeral, she threw herself into bringing the library back to life; undeservedly, it had not only been neglected for a long time, its doors hadn't even opened in more than a year; the shelves, books, walls, windowsills, the picture frames on the wall and the pictures themselves, the ceiling, all extended a disheartening sight, everything covered in dust, and the entire library was much too dark, this had never bothered her before, indeed, she hadn't really noticed it, but now it bothered her a great deal, she began badgering the mayor for funds, because the windows had to be enlarged, which also meant the installation of new windows, and new bookshelves were needed as well, new books, new ceiling lighting and new rugs, curtains, new catalog cabinets, and in general, these funds were needed, and the mayor, of the Die Linke party—it was right before elections—gave her the funds, and the work of renovating the library began, and Frau Ringer was something like a Joan of Arc who had conquered the pyre and was now building a kingdom, and yes, Frau Ringer wanted to turn the library into a kingdom, a home, as she described it to the parents and the schools whom she encouraged to send their children to the library without worrying about this new virus, because it was well worth it, new books on new shelves, she explained, and as much light as a child unconditionally needs, she promised a small play corner, she promised cool temperatures in the summer and warmth in the winter, and she made all of this happen, moreover, she even organized so-called poetic excursions, successfully, to Dohlenstein, where every participant read aloud a splendid verse from the inimitable lifework of the great poet Heinrich Heine at certain lookout points selected in advance, while the children enjoyed the magnificent views; the parents competed for their children to be taken into one of the library circles organized by Frau Ringer, because now there were four of them, and at first, she did not want to increase their number, but, well, the way these parents were besieging her made her more accommodating, and this was only the story of Frau Ringer, because it also happened afterward that although a *certain* Herr Beyer got onto the town Council—a Nazi with a necktie, as Frau Hopf put it—the mayor from Die Linke was still reelected, because the residents of Kana needed a mayor who wouldn't cave in to all the fearmongering around the pandemic, namely they needed a mayor who would do nothing but simply let the days pass by in unvaried tranquility, two full-time policemen were assigned to the town and they also got two police cars, earlier the property of the city of Jena, in other words everything was turning out as best as could possibly be, and people quickly forgot: soon nobody was talking about what had been going on here for years, the old Nazis were gone from the building at Burgstraße 19, and the building was finally purchased by the left-wing government and renovations began, Frau Hopf could hardly believe her eyes, nor could her husband, he too had seriously begun to hope, just like the others, because after a while it occurred to them that inasmuch as the tourists no longer seemed to be avoiding the town and Thuringia because of the many new Nazis turning up here—certain local governments, including that of Kana, had bowed their head to a higher political will and taken in about ten or twenty refugees—namely, people weren't scared off from vacationing in the area, so the Hopfs could take on two employees and reopen the Garni, but not the restaurant, Frau Hopf shook her head, she no longer had the mood or the strength for that, there was no one to help, let's not even mention Florian, because he still turns up now and then, said Frau Hopf, and that was the first time she'd even pronounced his name ever since she realized who Florian really was, because after the unbelievable events she was so frightened that she tried not to even think about him, because before, he had been on their premises, he had carried crates in for them and everything when they had deliveries, and he would sit right here, she pointed at the kitchen beneath the ground-floor stairs, right here, in our house, next to the table, and he ate scrambled eggs, and he drank cola or soda with syrup, my god, how lucky I am that this giant King Kong didn't beat me to death just like that, for nothing, let's not talk about it, and this was immediately after people had realized who Florian really was, and the residents of Kana had to confront who had been living among them for years as if he were some newborn lamb, and after that, his name never again crossed Frau Hopf's lips, really never once, moreover, if she came across the name Florian in *Barbara*, she immediately turned the page, because I can't even bear to see his name, I simply can't believe it, Frau Feldmann said to her, when, coming home from the funeral, she stopped in quickly for a cup of tea to ask what they should do about buying the coffee when everything around them had changed so much, no, I simply can't bring myself to believe it, and I think I'll never be able to, well, that's how it is, my dear, replied Frau Hopf, and I hope that you don't mind the comparison, but in my view, behind every lamb there may be a wolf that comes creeping out, and then that lamb has to be destroyed, and Frau Feldmann did not contradict her, she could only nod in agreement looking at the essence of the matter, as she thought Frau Hopf was right, and she was grateful for every explanation, because she herself had felt deeply in shock and she really didn't know how to comprehend the whole thing, just as no one really did, especially, of course, those who had known Florian much better than Frau Hopf and Frau Feldmann, as, for example, Frau Ringer: not only did she keep on saying that she didn't believe it, but in fact she really didn't believe it, and at first she made a phone call to Eisenberg, because she hadn't heard anything from Herr Köhler ever since he'd moved away, as she thought he must know something about what happened to Florian, but a woman answered the phone who told her that Herr Köhler had been moved to an institution two months previously, where only a week and a half ago he had passed into eternal sleep, the funeral, of course, had been arranged by Dr. Tietz and his wife, picking out the most beautiful coffin with a golden trim at the Hartung funeral home, and a grave site beneath a wonderful oak tree, because Hartung had come to their aid, and so many people came, the date and the address of the cemetery had been announced in the local press just in time, not only that, it was announced on MDR-Thuringia, and there were so many mourners thronging at the cemetery gates that the custodians appointed grave-diggers as guards, and they kept order: stop pushing now, people, they said, you'll all be able to get in, just line up nicely, and so on, so that you could hardly see the coffin in front of the morgue, the eulogy given by the pastor had to be amplified, so that if most people couldn't see the coffin, at least they could hear about what a distinguished person Adrian Köhler had been, how much gratitude every resident of Kana felt toward him, and how, with his weather reports and his pedagogic activities, he had inscribed himself for all time into the distinguished pages of the town chronicles, and the speeches that were given as the coffin was lowered into the grave were even more distressing, after the principal of the high school and the former students of Adrian Köhler stood by the grave and they described what a wondrous person they had lost, and at the end a stranger spoke, someone who looked like some kind of scientist, no one knew where he was from, from which city, moreover he never even betrayed his name, as if it somehow would have been inappropriate to introduce himself while standing at the grave, but it became clear from his words that he was a scientist: he praised the enormous service that Adrian Köhler had performed at the altar of science, for he had proved the necessity of involving new fields in cosmological and quantum physics theory (especially Fortran research) that were developing with near dizzying velocity, for which

German society, and in particular the residents of Kana, owed him unconditional recognition, Frau Ringer, sobbing, tossed one white rose onto the coffin in the grave and buried her face in her handkerchief, and, weeping as well, Frau Burgmüller tossed a handful of earth onto the coffin together with her neighbor, like two sobbing widows, they stepped forward, arm in arm, and then they hardly departed from the grave, so that they had to be gently nudged away, and the residents of Kana just came and came and they threw fistfuls of earth onto the coffin, the gravediggers, with only a bit of exaggeration, had hardly any work to do when at last they set to their work and they began filling in the grave and heaping the earth above it, and the crowd began to disperse, and one half hour later there was no one left in the cemetery, as if with this, the life of Adrian Köhler had come to an end, although it hadn't, because Frau Ringer, already at the funeral, had been thinking intently about what she could do so that the name of the deceased would continue to live on, but before that, she called one of Ringer's friends, a lawyer from Erfurt, to see if he would take up Florian's case, but the lawyer sat down with her and he explained that if he was found, Florian's culpability seemed so airtight that he could think of no possible viable defense, he would get a life sentence no matter what; then Frau Ringer called a different lawyer whom she didn't know but who seemed adequate, and she asked him over the phone if he would take on the case if Florian took responsibility for the murders, and the lawyer took on the case, he requested the file, but then he withdrew, look, he said to her on the phone, when he called Frau Ringer, I can understand your affection for this young man, but if this is such an open-and-shut case, then a lawyer with a conscience such as myself won't be able to mitigate the sentence, a public defender will be good enough, this is most practical and the economic solution, so that Frau Ringer was left on her own, because she was entirely certain that the Florian whom she had known and the Florian who had murdered *was one and the same person*, Florian had not changed, everything that he had done ensued with lethal precision from who he was and who he had remained, so that she kept on trying, but in vain, there was no trial, because there could be no trial; Hoffmann turned up at the local police station, but he was panting so hard that they had to sit him down in a small waiting room so he could tell them that he had been in Jena and he was coming here with new information, because he had seen Florian again, because Florian was living on Ölwiesenweg, and no, he hadn't been on the lookout for him, he would never do anything like that, that wasn't his way, he said, but he just happened to be looking out the window, and he saw a shaggy figure, limping strongly, heading toward the sports fields, and as Hoffmann was possessed with an extraordinary memory for faces, he immediately recognized that this figure was none other than Florian Herscht, the wanted serial killer, of course he waited until this monster had gone a respectable distance, but then he immediately set out, and now here he was, reporting that he, Freddi Hoffmann, had found the wanted man, and he didn't want to press them, but he wanted to know the exact amount of the reward for this information, although he didn't find out, as the two local police officers ignored his question, they jumped into their patrol cars, and by the time they had informed Jena headquarters—and everyone else who needed to be informed—they were already turning onto the road leading to the Sports Center, so that within a few minutes they were combing the area behind the goalposts, unlocked service weapons in hand, the Jena police showed up after about a quarter of an hour, then the Erfurt cops arrived, and who even knew how many units and from where, and they decided they would take care of this before beginning to comply with the new directives concerning the new virus which seemed to be spreading through Sachsen and all of Thuringia at a frightening pace, they would handle this first, conclude it, wrap it up, close this case in a hurry, the main thing, the two local police established, was to get the area of operations fully under their control so that no one could get out of here alive, the entire area was fenced off under the orders of an Erfurt police lieutenant, of course no one could know exactly where they'd find him, where that center of enclosure might be, where they would clamp down on the perpetrator, but the circle was tightening and they tightened it further, there was no way he could slip out of their hands, each individual unit was convinced, because the circle was tight, and if the report had been correct, the hunted man had no chance of breaking out of this tight circle, but they could not have anticipated that the question of breaking out was irrelevant, as Florian Herscht was putting up no resistance whatsoever, namely, Karin had finally caught sight of him, or Florian had seen her, it was impossible to determine which, in any event, both sought immediate cover, Karin was heading home when she glimpsed Florian in the industrial district, on Im Camisch, in front of the Ibismed building, or Florian noticed her, but it didn't matter now, and so much happened in the flash of an eye, Karin turned left in front of the Ibismed office building entrance and jumped for cover, she tried to slow her breathing while she tossed her pistol from her left to her right hand, and with her right hand she pulled out a knife from her trousers' side pocket, pointing the barrel of the pistol upward, and in doing so she released the safety catch, light as a feather, so no sound was heard; she held the knife, the blade facing up, close to the ground, preparing to stab upward, she waited with her back against the wall, certain she'd notice even the slightest movement, but she heard nothing, she thought that Florian was probably doing the same, waiting on the other side of the small part of the building, but that isn't what happened, because she would never know how what did happen could have happened, altogether she only sensed, in the suddenly muted twilight, that she couldn't breathe normally anymore, and that her hands couldn't move although she was still holding the pistol upward and the knife close to the ground but she couldn't direct them, and this was the last thing that her mind grasped because the next moment was not hers: she never even heard the cracking sound, the horrific cracking sound of her own neck as it broke—the head drooping forward and then falling backward—only Florian heard it, and he could have seen it too if he had looked back, but he didn't; he had only looked forward as he crept closer and closer to Karin, his movements noiseless, and he moved so quickly, with a velocity that never could have been expected from anyone, because while Karin was getting her weapons ready, he had been circling the office building from the back, and he approached from a direction that Karin could not have suspected in such a short amount of time, and he did this so silently, that not even this sound without noise arising from his movements could reach her ears, in the last few meters he advanced closely against the wall, and he grabbed Karin's neck blind, squeezed it until he heard the cracking sound, until he was positive she would never move again, then he left her to slide to the ground like an empty sack, but he was not expecting the head, flipped back, to belong to a body which would twitch one more time as it hit the ground, making the pistol fire, although he could not have been quick enough for this, he heard the shot but moved too late, the bullet flying out reached his thigh, he looked down to see if it had exited his leg, but there wasn't enough light, so he felt along the wall behind himself to find the bullet hole, but he didn't find it, meaning the bullet hadn't emerged from his thigh, but he had to get lost now because the shot was loud, making the mountains above Kana echo for some seconds, and even though there was a full moon in the sky, it didn't show its strength because of the street lighting, so he ran beneath this full moon, his right leg limping, holding his hand over the wound and squeezing it as tightly as he could, and he ran and he ran all along Im Camisch until he reached the center of the town, while *Tilge, Höchster, meine Sünden* was playing softly in his head, suddenly it occurred to him: why was he running? there was no reason for him to run anymore, then he slowed down, and like that, dragging his right leg behind him, he walked across the deserted town; at the Bachstraße intersection he had a clear view of Jenaische Straße; he perceived no movement, so he headed in that direction, and he reached Sankt Margarethenkirche, behind which he could limp down the stairs; he was hearing *Tilge, Höchster, meine Sünden* somewhat more loudly now, and his wound was bleeding profusely, he stopped for a moment to try to stanch the wound more tightly with something, but then he reconsidered as he heard a voice, a voice filtering out through the opened church door, and it quickly became clear, as he edged along the church wall and came closer to the opened door, that the pastor was speaking within, clearly just at that moment a service was being held, namely if he stayed there anyone could come out and see him, because although there were no streetlights here, the moon was emitting its strong light, but so what, it occurred to him again, let whoever wanted to come out of that church, because it didn't matter anymore, and it was as if there inside, the opinion was the same, nobody seemed to want to exit the church, in any event, he started walking down the stairs behind the church, then through the narrow underpass beneath the rail tracks to the Rosengarten, he turned left to the sports fields, *Tilge, Höchster, meine Sünden* was playing so loudly in his head and he didn't even know why he felt so dizzy, was it because of the blood he was losing, or the strength of the victorious, tragic melody, and despite the strong moonlight he couldn't see very well, so he began hurrying, and he passed the soccer and handball goalposts, and quickly reached the vicinity of his former favorite place to sit and think, that was where he was headed right now, even in this dizzy and weakened state, as he approached the two benches beneath the chestnut trees on the banks of the Saale, he seemed to perceive two dark blotches in front of one bench at a distance from him, the shorter bench, exactly that spot that used to be his place, two dark blotches, so he slowed down, and as he really could hardly see anything, he almost came to a complete stop so as not to walk into a trap, then he took one step forward with his left leg, pulling his right leg along, completely noiselessly, all the while concentrating all his strength, convincing himself that there was nothing there, maybe just a shadow, but no, it wasn't the dizziness playing with him or the loss of blood or the Bach psalm raging in his head, because it wasn't a shadow, but there was really something there, not only that, there were two somethings in front of that farther bench, he was close enough now to determine that two wolves were sitting in front of the farther bench, two wolves, more precisely, one of them was sitting, the other one was lying down, he came to a dead halt, but because he was too dizzy and he knew that he had to sit down immediately, otherwise he would collapse, with his last strength, he tensed his muscles so as to be able to ward off the two animals should they attack him, then he took a cautious step toward the nearer bench, but neither one even moved, then he took another step, and from this distance it was already obvious that the two animals clearly had no interest in him being there, he held his breath, he approached, but the wolves didn't move, then the one that was closer to him, the sitting one, slowly, very slowly, turned its head toward him, but not snarling, it merely bared its gums slightly, just enough to show its teeth a bit, but then it closed its mouth again, and turned its head back, as if Florian were merely one more among them and there was nothing to fear, and Florian then realized that it only seemed that the wolves were looking at the waters of the Saale, because as his strength gave out, and he very slowly sank down onto the unoccupied bench next to them, he realized that the two wolves were also at the end of their strength, and that instead of eyes, there were only holes oozing with pus—then the psalm suddenly stopped playing in Florian's head, the pain and the dizziness made him close his eyes, and then he understood that in reality the wolves were not looking at anything but listening, just as he too was listening from this point on, and from this point on all three of them would be listening blindly and forever to the peaceful, tinkling, sweet gurgling of the water a few steps away from them in the merciless night descending heavily upon the land.

The author would like to thank

Gábor Etesi

András Tábori

Rüdiger Hänsch, director of the Erfurt Ermittlungsdienst

Clemens Meyer

Vincent

Ottó Klinger and his coworkers